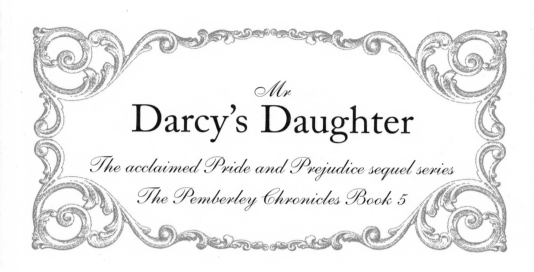

Mr
Darcy's Daughter

The acclaimed Pride and Prejudice sequel series
The Pemberley Chronicles Book 5

Rebecca A⸻

SOURCEBOOKS LANDMARK™
AN IMPRINT OF SOURCEBOOKS, INC.®
NAPERVILLE, ILLINOIS

By the Same Author

The Pemberley Chronicles
The Women of Pemberley
Netherfield Park Revisited
The Ladies of Longbourn
My Cousin Caroline
Postscript from Pemberley
Recollections of Rosings
A Woman of Influence
The Legacy of Pemberley

Published by Sourcebooks Landmark, an imprint of Sourcebooks, Inc.
P.O. Box 4410, Naperville, Illinois 60567-4410
(630) 961-3900
FAX: (630) 961-2168
www.sourcebooks.com

Originally printed and bound in Australia by SNAP Printing, Sydney, NSW, 2000.

Reprinted 2001, 2003, and 2004.

Library of Congress Cataloging-in-Publication Data

Collins, Rebecca Ann.
  Mr. Darcy's daughter / Rebecca Ann Collins.
    p. cm. — (The Pemberley chronicles ; bk. 5)
  ISBN-13: 978-1-4022-1220-8
  ISBN-10: 1-4022-1220-8
  1. England—Social life and customs—19th century—Fiction. I. Austen, Jane,
1775–1817. Pride and prejudice. II. Title.
  PR9619.4.C65M7 2008
  823'.92—dc22
                            2008030187

Printed and bound in the United States of America
VP 10 9 8 7 6 5 4 3 2 1

Dedicated with affection and deep appreciation

to

Miss Jane Austen

On the occasion of the 225th anniversary of her birth.

December 16, 2000

Foreword

IN *THE PEMBERLEY CHRONICLES*, her first novel, Rebecca Ann Collins borrowed the characters created by Jane Austen in *Pride and Prejudice* and chronicled their changing lives in what was a complex and dynamic period of history, nineteenth century England.

Extending the families and their social circle in *The Women of Pemberley*, *Netherfield Park Revisited*, and *The Ladies of Longbourn*, Ms Collins has recreated the world of the Pemberley families in a way that has captured the imagination of many readers of the original Austen novel.

Her gift for telling an interesting story while creating credible, consistent characters is remarkable. Happily, there are no strange and inexplicable distortions of character to outrage Jane Austen's fans and, throughout the series, the author remains faithful to the manners and values espoused by Miss Austen herself. While Ms Collins makes no attempt to imitate Jane Austen's literary style, she maintains a sense of decorum in language and manner that is both pleasing and appropriate.

The Pemberley novels of Rebecca Ann Collins are characterised by the author's assiduous attention to detail. While the characters evolve within their environment, their horizons expand to take in the political, medical, and social context of the time—in Parliament, commerce, and community service. Careful research adds both depth and authenticity to their stories.

Many readers of Ms Collins's books will already know Cassandra Darcy, the daughter of Elizabeth Bennet and Fitzwilliam Darcy. She is a very Austenian young woman, charming and sensible, with a mind of her own. *Mr Darcy's Daughter*, the fifth book in the Pemberley series, is her story and it is one that even Jane Austen might have enjoyed.

Appropriately written by one whose love of Jane Austen's work is her chief inspiration, its publication coincides with the 225th anniversary of Miss Austen's birth: December 16, 2000.

Averil Rose
United Kingdom
December 2000

An Introduction...

MOST WRITERS DEVELOP A special fondness for one or more of their characters. Miss Austen claimed her favourite was Elizabeth Bennet, and several generations of readers have agreed with her choice.

Cassandra Darcy is mine.

Mr Darcy's Daughter is the story of her life as a woman of deep conviction and passionate feelings, challenged not only by a series of unforeseen and difficult circumstances, but, as well, by her love and loyalty to her family.

In Cassy are combined qualities of her mother and father, both of whom embody many of Jane Austen's own values. To care passionately, demonstrating both principle and compassion, while maintaining in her personal conduct the degree of decorum and sense of proportion that marks a woman of education and good sense, was not always easy. Yet, it was what Miss Austen demanded of her women.

If they could also paint, sing, and play the pianoforte, while conducting an intelligent conversation spiced with some gentle wit and humour, why that was very close to perfection.

Cassy Darcy lays no claim to such perfection.

But, like many women of her time, she is a strong influence upon her husband and children, expected to support her family and friends in the crises that confront them. Cassy accepts her role, for the most part, without question. It comes as naturally to her as the love she feels for her family.

The support and love of a good husband is her greatest asset, but it doesn't always protect her from the selfishness or the stupidity of others.

While her selfless love is rewarded with her family's gratitude and affection, she pays a high personal price. When she realises this, it is occasionally too late to change what has occurred. Cassy's struggle to balance the demands placed upon her, while nurturing the warmth of her own intimate relationships, makes for me a love story as honest and poignant as that of her young daughter Lizzie, seriously in love for the first time. Perhaps, even more so.

Many readers of the Pemberley series have asked to know more about Cassandra Darcy, not because she is a paragon of virtue, but because she is like a lot of other women, even though she is Mr Darcy's daughter.

I hope they will enjoy reading her story, as much as I loved telling it.

An *aide-mémoire*, in the form of a list of the main characters and their relationships to one another, is provided in the Appendix.

RAC / 2000

CASSANDRA GARDINER WAS NOT generally given to attacks of anxiety.

Being of a calm disposition, with sufficient good sense and understanding to withstand the appeal of paranoia, she usually had little reason to be troubled or apprehensive. Married happily to Doctor Richard Gardiner, a physician whose knowledge and skill were widely recognised, her life was generally well ordered and satisfying. Her husband and children gave her such affection and pleasure as many women would have envied, and even after five lively children, she was a remarkably vivacious and handsome woman. Moreover, her health was good, her education and understanding excellent; by most standards she would have been judged a very fortunate woman indeed.

Yet, on this mild evening in the Spring of 1864, Cassy was unable to shake off a persistent, inexplicable feeling of unease. It had surfaced as she had returned home from a meeting with her sisters-in-law Caroline Fitzwilliam and Emily Courtney. The women had met to make plans for a campaign to collect funds to equip two new classrooms at the parish school at Kympton, on her father Mr Darcy's estate, Pemberley.

Mr Darcy had recently informed her that the buildings were ready for the new term. They needed only to be suitably furnished and Cassy, together with

Caroline and Emily, had decided to form a committee to raise the funds required. Cassandra had thought to invite Rebecca Tate, the influential wife of Mr Anthony Tate and mother of Josie, who was married to Cassy's brother Julian, and everyone agreed there was no more active and energetic member of the community than Mrs Tate.

While Cassy led a somewhat quiet social life, Mrs Tate, by virtue of her husband's business contacts and her own charitable work, moved in a far wider circle of society. Cassandra was sure she was a good choice, and the others had concurred, noting that Becky Tate would be an asset to their committee.

"If Becky cannot raise the funds from her business friends, no one can," Caroline had said, as they arranged to meet for tea at the Fitzwilliams' farm at Matlock to discuss campaign plans.

But despite her stated enthusiasm for their project, Mrs Tate had failed to appear that afternoon, nor had she sent any apology or explanation for her absence. Cassandra had been rather irritated; it was not very polite or responsible, she thought, trying hard to conceal her aggravation from the others, especially when it was their first meeting.

Disturbingly, it was also very uncharacteristic of Becky Tate, whose reliability was a byword in their community.

Furthermore, Cassy had been counting on Mrs Tate to represent her daughter at the meeting. Julian and Josie, who lived in Cambridge, rarely found time to attend any of these occasions in Derbyshire.

Cassy's parents had long since ceded to the younger generation the organisation of such activities. There was the annual Harvest Fair, the Music Festival, and the Pemberley Children's Choir, which gave concerts around the district. All had been initiated by Elizabeth and had grown so prodigiously in size and popularity, they were now run by professional managers. Cassandra represented her parents on almost all the boards and committees and felt it was her duty to keep her brother Julian informed, even though he showed scant interest in them.

Indeed, to everyone's astonishment, neither Julian nor his wife had attended the wedding of his cousin Frank Grantley to Caroline's daughter Amy at Pemberley just a week or so ago. An express had brought their apologies—Josie was ill—but Cassandra knew her parents had been very disappointed and, though their aunt Mrs Grantley, mother of the groom, had said little, it was easy to see she was both surprised and grieved by their absence.

"I suppose, they must be exceedingly busy at this time," Georgiana Grantley had mused, softly adding, "and Derbyshire is rather a long way from Cambridge, is it not?"

But Cassy had not been fooled. Her gentle aunt was clearly hurt by Julian's non-appearance.

As they had sat waiting that afternoon in the parlour for Mrs Tate to arrive, Caroline had pointedly reminded Cassy that her brother and his wife had not participated in any of the events at Pemberley since they had returned to Cambridge at the end of Summer.

"They do seem quite disinterested, Cassy, content to leave it all to you," she had remarked, adding pointedly, but without any trace of malice, for it was not in Caroline's nature to be deliberately hurtful, "Sometimes, I do wonder whether Julian wants to be Master of Pemberley at all."

Though the remark affected her, Cassandra had laughed and shrugged off the implication, replying casually that she and her parents understood the very great importance of Julian's scientific work at Cambridge.

"He is working very hard on an important scientific study to do with the prevention of certain tropical diseases. His work is highly regarded by his fellow scientists," she had said and continued, "In any event, the matter of becoming the Master of Pemberley can only be speculative at this time. As you well know, Papa is in the best of health and likely to remain so for the foreseeable future."

She had spoken quickly, her voice sounding more defensive than she had intended it to be. The remark had been lightly made, but as soon as she had said it, she could have bitten off her tongue, for Cassandra knew that Caroline and Emily's father, Mr Gardiner, was gravely ill and not expected to live out the year.

Caroline's usually bright countenance was instantly shadowed by an expression of deep sadness, and tears filled Emily's eyes. Cassy apologised at once, sorry for the grief she had caused, however unwittingly, yet there was little she could do or say to comfort her cousins. They both knew the truth only too well. Richard had made quite certain of that.

Thereafter, they had sat in silence, until Emily declared it was time to go home. "Quite obviously, Becky Tate is not coming, there is no point waiting any longer. Besides," she said, "I have some parish work to do, and Mr Courtney will worry if I am not home before dark."

The mild evening was drawing in as Cassy reached her home. On alighting from the carriage and entering the house, she was greeted by James, her youngest son, who was but four years old. "Where's Papa?" he demanded, reaching up to embrace his mother, as she divested herself of her hat and wrap. Cassandra was surprised to learn that her husband was not home already.

Dr Gardiner, whose enviable reputation had the sometimes unfortunate consequence of keeping him working late at the hospital, always called in at his parents' home near Lambton, at the end of each day. Aware of his father's critical condition and his mother's consequent distress, he never failed to visit them, no matter how busy his day had been. Often, his eldest son Edward, only recently down from medical school in Edinburgh, would accompany him.

The Gardiners were always glad to see them, and Mr Gardiner had quipped that two doctors must be better than one. Not even his debilitating condition could dull Mr Gardiner's sense of humour. Throughout his ordeal, he had remained for the most part uncomplaining and cheerful.

A quiet, serious young man, his grandson Edward had a strong social conscience, which made it almost inevitable that he would soon follow in his father's footsteps. Unlike his younger brother Darcy, whose interest in business and politics had steered him in the direction of London and Westminster, Edward rarely concerned himself with anything outside the world of medicine, unless it was music, which appeared to be his only other interest. A keen listener and a proficient practitioner on the pianoforte himself, he would travel many miles to attend a good performance.

Their mother, who loved them both dearly, wanted nothing more for her sons than that they should lead happy and useful lives as their father had done for all the years of their remarkably felicitous marriage.

To this end, she had given them all her love and devoted most of her energy and time to her family. She had been rewarded with their unconditional affection and a good deal of satisfaction.

In this last year, however, the shadow of Mr Gardiner's illness, as he lay weakened by bouts of heart disease, had fallen over their lives. Though Richard did not speak of it often or at length, lest it should distress her and the younger children, particularly James, who was his grandfather's favourite, Cassy knew well that her husband felt deeply about his father's illness and was troubled by his inability to do more to ease his discomfort.

Richard Gardiner was involved in medical research and had consulted many colleagues in the hope of finding some treatment that would alleviate Mr Gardiner's condition, but without much success. Time and again, his wife had detected his mood of sadness and tried to comfort him. Always, he was grateful for her love and concern, yet there was an inevitability about the fate that awaited his father, which made him feel helpless and frustrated.

❧

As the sun dipped behind the crags and peaks to the Northwest, setting ablaze the gorse on the hill slopes, while pitching into darkness the river gorges and valleys below, Cassy, whose disquiet had increased considerably over the past half hour, picked up her wrap and, pulling it around her shoulders, walked down the drive, which led to the road that curled away towards Lambton. The wind coming down from the peaks was cold and sent an involuntary shiver through her body.

Richard had never been this late before.

Seeing her mother leave the house, her elder daughter Lizzie, who had been practising at the pianoforte in the parlour, stopped playing abruptly and went out to join her. They were close and Lizzie had sensed her mother's unease. When she caught up with her, she asked, "What is it, Mama? What's been troubling you? Has there been some bad news, about Grandfather, I mean? Have you heard something?"

Cassy, glad of her company, replied quickly, "No my dear, not at all; I was only wondering why Papa and Edward are so late tonight. They should have been home an hour or more ago."

Lizzie knew her father always called at his parents' home and was sure it must be bad news about Mr Gardiner that was delaying him. Taking her mother's arm, she said quietly, "Could it be that Grandfather's condition has worsened suddenly?" and hearing her sigh, she went on.

"Mama, you know we have been warned to expect it at any time. Papa has tried to prepare us for it; even my dear grandmother knows it will not be long now," she said, her voice both gentle and amazingly mature for her age.

Cassy marvelled at her daughter's composure and wished she could have said something sensible. But she was devoted to her father-in-law and all she could say was, "I know, my love, but it does not make it any easier to bear, does it?"

As her feelings appeared to get the better of her and she took out her handkerchief, Lizzie reached for her hand.

At that very moment, they heard the sounds of the carriage, even before it came into view around the deep bend in the road from Lambton.

"They're here!" cried Lizzie cheerfully, as the vehicle turned into the drive and Edward leaned out to greet them.

Cassy smiled and dried her tears, as Lizzie quickened her steps to reach the door as they alighted. She went directly to her brother, who kissed his mother and went indoors. Lizzie followed him, eager for news, as he entered the parlour, where tea awaited them.

Richard, meanwhile, his face grave, his voice serious, put an arm around his wife and took her upstairs, stopping only to accept a welcoming hug from his youngest son. The boy, hearing his voice, had raced out of the nursery, defying his nurse's pleas, to greet his father. Having disengaged himself from the child's embrace, with a promise that he would visit the nursery later, Dr Gardiner returned to his wife.

After her first flush of relief at seeing them safely home, reassured there had been no sudden deterioration in Mr Gardiner's condition, Cassy was beginning to worry again. She was bewildered by the gravity of her husband's countenance. What, she wondered, could have caused such disquiet, if it was not his father's health?

Richard did not keep her long in suspense. Once in their private apartments, he shut the door and, having sat her down, took from his pocket a letter. It was short, not quite filling a page, and it was from her brother Julian.

"Cassy, my love," said Richard, by way of explanation, "this letter was delivered to me by express at the hospital this afternoon. As you see, it is from your brother."

He held it out to her. Cassy, already apprehensive of the news it may contain, took the letter. It was written in the untidy scrawl that Julian used, claiming he had never found the time to practice formal copperplate, but it was even less legible than usual, clearly penned in great haste. He wrote:

My dear Richard,

Please accept my apologies for the inconvenience I know this letter will cause you and my dear sister, but my situation is truly desperate.

I believe that you alone can convince my dear wife Josie of the need to seek some form of treatment for the ailment that has afflicted her for several months.

I have tried, without success, on many occasions, to persuade, plead, and cajole her into seeing one of the physicians here in Cambridge (and there are one or two who come highly recommended), but she has refused to do so. She says she is not unwell and has no need of their services.

Richard, I could wish with all my heart that this were true, but the evidence is clear enough, though she will not acknowledge it. Josie is clearly not herself and anyone who knows her will say so, without the aid of any medical experience or qualification.

She is out of sorts, dispirited, and has become very weak and thin, due mainly to a complete lack of interest in food. She, who always had a healthy appetite, has now to be persuaded to eat as much as a child's portion at meals. Between times, she will take nothing more nourishing than weak tea or a glass of barley water.

I know she has a great deal of respect for you, Richard, and will take your advice more seriously than she does mine. I truly fear for her life, if nothing can be done, and swiftly, to arrest the decline in her health and, even more urgently, her spirits.

Which is the reason I write, even though I know how busy you are and how anxious for your father's health you must be, to beg you to come to Cambridge, as soon as you are able.

It is no exaggeration to say that you may be able to save my dear Josie's life.

Yours etc,

Julian Darcy.

There was no mistaking the urgency, almost the panic, in Julian's words. A man of sound scientific discipline, he was not given to gross overstatement. Plainly, he was grieved by his inability to do anything useful to help his ailing wife. Her own recalcitrance, her refusal to take any treatment, indeed to even see a physician, was obviously causing him much distress and his letter to his brother-in-law was a last resort, a desperate plea for help.

Cassandra was pale when she finished reading the letter and handed it back to her husband.

"Poor Julian, what a dreadful letter! What must he have suffered, and no doubt continues to suffer, to have been driven to write such a letter? We must go, of course, but how shall it be done? With your father's grave condition…"

Her husband, who had been standing in front of the fire, sat down beside her and took her hand in his, "My father's condition, though grave, is, at the moment, stable. I have suggested that Edward stay with him at Lambton, until we return from Cambridge. He is competent and able to administer such medication as is required and deal with any emergency," he said.

"Edward? Are you sure?" Cassy was uncertain; their son was well qualified to be sure, but he had had little clinical experience.

Richard was more confident. "My darling, I am quite certain, else I would not have suggested it. Besides, I have asked Edward and he has agreed. He will follow my instructions exactly and, in an emergency, send immediately for Dr Forrester. I have also explained the situation to my mother, and she knows we must go to Josie and Julian. They need our help."

He stood up, keeping hold of her hands, which were cold with anxiety, and drew her into his arms to comfort her.

"I have already despatched a message to Julian by telegraph, so all there is left to do is to make the necessary arrangements for our journey," he said, holding her close, understanding her concern, and trying to reassure her.

Her anxiety somewhat eased, Cassandra asked quietly, "Should Lizzie go with us? She has always got on very well with Josie. It may help."

Her husband was cautious. "I would rather she did not, until I have ascertained what it is that afflicts Josie. If, as I believe, it is a non-contagious condition, a temporary malaise brought on more by her forlorn spirit than an infectious bacterium, it would be safe for Lizzie to visit her, perhaps later in the month," he explained patiently.

"It may help cheer her up. However, until we are certain there is no danger of infection, I do not think Lizzie should go."

Cassy agreed at once. It had not occurred to her that her daughter may be exposed to infection by visiting Josie. Reminded of the possibility, she was content to be ruled by her husband on the matter. Lizzie would remain at home. Cassy was glad her younger daughter Laura Ann was away for a few weeks, visiting her cousin Sophie in Leicestershire.

Preparations were hurriedly and methodically made and, on the morrow, which turned out to be a cold, blustery sort of day, of the kind one had learned to expect in Spring, they set out for Cambridge. But first, they were to go to Pemberley to acquaint Mr and Mrs Darcy with the reason for their journey.

~⋅❦⋅~

Arriving at Pemberley, they found the Darcys and Bingleys discussing the calamitous affair of the Sutton children, who had been abducted by their own father. Mrs Sutton, though unknown personally to the Gardiners, was a friend of Anne-Marie Bingley. They knew that she had recently moved to Hertfordshire and taught music at the School for Young Ladies at Longbourn, which was run by Charlotte Collins and Anna Bingley, wife of their cousin Jonathan.

They now learned that Mrs Sutton's estranged husband had followed his wife to Hertfordshire and kidnapped her daughters. Neither Cassy nor Richard knew very much of the detail, but it was clearly a serious matter, and Mr Darcy had just despatched a letter to Jonathan Bingley containing vital information received about the whereabouts of the children.

When, in the midst of all this excitement, Cassandra broke the news of Julian's letter, Elizabeth could barely contain her distress. She had already confided in her sister Jane her immense disappointment over Julian's apparent lack of interest in the activities and traditions of Pemberley. The latest news about Josie made matters much worse!

She made Cassy promise to write and inform her of Josie's condition. "If there is anything your father or I can do to help, you know we will not hesitate…" she pleaded.

It was clear to Elizabeth that it would be of no use to offer to accompany them. Despite her best efforts, and it was generally acknowledged that she had tried very hard, Elizabeth and her daughter-in-law had never been intimate. Indeed, they never exchanged confidences at all. It was a matter of great regret to her that, unlike Richard Gardiner, whose regard and affection for her and Mr Darcy had always been a source of great happiness to them, their son's wife had never appeared to be entirely comfortable at Pemberley.

"Josie always seems as though she is only visiting and about to leave at any moment," she had once said to Cassy.

Trying to reassure her mother, Cassy had responded by saying that Josie was still young and somewhat in awe of the grandeur of Pemberley.

"I doubt she has considered seriously the fact that one day, and we pray it will be in the very distant future, she will be the Mistress of Pemberley," Cassy had explained.

Once again, Elizabeth had said, "If only they would settle here and make Pemberley their home, there would be so much to occupy her, so much to learn," but her daughter had wisely advised that this was probably not the appropriate moment to suggest such a move, sensible though it may seem.

Cassy knew also the extent of her father's disappointment that Julian did not appear committed to the estate, content to leave much of the work and all of the decisions to Mr Darcy and his manager. It was, she knew, a source of great sadness to him for he loved Pemberley and had hoped his son would feel the same. For a few years it had looked as if he would, but since moving to Cambridge and becoming absorbed in his research, Julian seemed to have lost interest in Pemberley. Besides, he was rapidly gaining a reputation in Europe and winning praise from his colleagues at Cambridge for his work—and clearly that came first.

Cassy was not unaware also that Josie, whose dearest wish was to have her work published in London or Cambridge, had been bitterly disappointed when her manuscript was rejected by several publishers. Her frustration at being so unappreciated was clearly taking its toll upon her young mind.

Cassandra felt deeply for her mother and father and shared their regret, but she was equally understanding of her unhappy sister-in-law and brother. It was easy, she knew, to be censorious but far more difficult to comprehend, and her husband, wise and compassionate, agreed.

"We cannot know the root of their problems, Cassy. Frequently, medical conditions are a reflection of mental and emotional debilitation, and one is hard put to diagnose the ailment without all the facts, especially if the patient is unlikely to be candid about his or her situation," he had said, as they had set out that morning.

Cassy knew he was right and when her aunt Jane Bingley, whose blissful marriage seemed to be based entirely upon domestic felicity and good fortune, suggested that perhaps Julian and Josie should have another child, Cassy was quite firm in her assertion that it would not resolve their problems.

"Josie is finding it difficult to cope with young Anthony; he is a lively child, bright and eager to learn, and she has her hands full keeping up with him. I doubt that another child will help in the circumstances."

Begging her mother and aunt not to speak too openly of these matters, lest the servants' gossip be relayed to the Tates at Matlock and cause offence, and urging them to remember that Richard, as a medical practitioner, treated all such information in strict confidence, Cassy rose, embraced her mother and aunt, and said her good-byes.

Her father and husband had come into the room and, from Mr Darcy's countenance, it was plain that Richard had told him something of Julian's predicament. Darcy looked grave and concerned as he bade them farewell and watched them drive away. In the warmth of his parting from her, Cassy felt the depth of his concern, yet he said little—unwilling, no doubt, to heighten her mother's already considerable fears.

Standing beside her husband, Elizabeth could scarcely hold back her tears. Conscious of her distress, he tried to console her, without success. Elizabeth, having suffered the loss of one son in a dreadful riding accident, was wondering what new tribulation awaited her with Julian.

Dinner at Pemberley was a solemn meal and no one, not even Bingley, asked for music, cards, or any other light diversion afterwards. The continuing rain added to the general lack of enthusiasm. Darcy decided to read by the fire and, while Jane and Elizabeth talked in whispers about the troubling news Cassy had brought, Bingley, who knew nothing of it, fell fast asleep. Everyone had been anxious for news of the kidnapped Sutton children and talked of the plight of their hapless mother. Jane could not imagine the anguish of the poor woman and prayed her children may soon be restored to her, but no one spoke openly of Julian and Josie.

When they retired, earlier than usual, to their rooms, Elizabeth's disquiet was obvious to her husband. As they had been speaking at dinner of the Sutton children, he, believing she was still concerned about them, revealed that he had taken some action on that score.

"I have despatched a letter to Jonathan with sufficient information received from my man Hobbs to enable them, with the help of the police, to discover the children and restore them to their mother. There is no need to worry any more," he said, but when Elizabeth, who had been gazing out of the window at the rain, turned to face him, he was astonished to see tears in her eyes.

"Why, Lizzie, my dear," he began, but she interrupted him, "Darcy, it is *not* for Mrs Sutton's children that I fear, though God knows they need our prayers; it is for Julian. Have you not understood that Josie is seriously ill? Poor Julian must have been desperate to have written as he has done to Richard, begging him to come at once."

Darcy indicated that he had heard that Josie was unwell and had assumed that since Richard was the best physician they knew, Julian had requested his attendance.

Believing that her husband knew very little of the substance of the problem, for no doubt Richard Gardiner had been discreet, Elizabeth sat beside him on the bed and told him everything Cassy had revealed.

"Neither Richard nor Cassy has any knowledge of her ailment. Richard has decided to go at once, despite the fact that our Uncle Gardiner is gravely ill, because Julian has declared in his letter that Josie will see no other physician. He says she has been ill for several weeks," she explained.

At first, Darcy was silent. He had heard something of the matter from his son-in-law, sufficient to concern him, but this was far more serious than he had thought. He had no wish to panic his wife; he felt deeply for her and their son.

Elizabeth believed he was probably shocked by her revelations and, breaking the silence, she asked gently, "What do you think could be the matter with Josie?"

Darcy sighed and shook his head.

"I am not a physician, my dear, and I would not pretend to understand the afflictions a young woman may suffer, but since you ask, I would hazard a guess that loneliness and deep disappointment would be the main causes of her malaise. There is little to involve her at Cambridge. All Julian's friends are probably scientists like himself, and while their work is unarguably valuable and important, it is unlikely to interest Josie. They do tend to talk incessantly of arcane subjects and little else. She has never mentioned any friends, and Anthony is too little to be much company for her; she is probably bored as well as lonely."

"But she has her own interests; she writes…" his wife interposed.

"Indeed she does, but then, she has failed to interest anyone in her manuscript. Cassy tells me Josie had hopes of having it accepted by one of the publishing houses in London but to no avail. She must be very disappointed," he explained, and there was genuine compassion in his voice.

Elizabeth could hear it; Darcy had once commented favourably on Josie's work and had collected and preserved in the library at Pemberley some of her pieces published in the *Matlock Review,* which was part of her father's publishing empire. But Josie had wanted to be accepted by the metropolitan publishers, sadly without success.

"But surely," said Elizabeth, "would such a disappointment be sufficient to send her into a decline? Cassy says she is weakened in both body and spirit; is this possible?"

Darcy was thoughtful. "I gathered from Richard that she has been so for some time and refuses to see a physician. He feels her condition may well be rooted in the mind. But to answer your question, Lizzie, is it not possible to comprehend how one who is passionately committed to a cause or an ambition, no less than one who is deeply in love, may, if repeatedly thwarted and denied her dearest wish, find less and less to live for?"

Elizabeth was outraged by this suggestion. "But Darcy, Josie has Anthony and Julian to live for!" she protested.

"Indeed she does, my love," he countered, "but Anthony is a child, and Julian is so immersed in his work, which takes him from home frequently and keeps him working late, even when he is there. He has few interests outside his work and is not very communicative, at the best of times. Can you not understand that, for Josie, it must be a rather lonely existence, even a depressing one?"

Seeing her bewilderment, for Elizabeth, since her marriage, had wanted no greater excitement than that which her life with him and their family at Pemberley provided, he put his arms around her to comfort her.

Even though unconvinced by his argument, she appreciated, as always, his kindness and the reassuring warmth of his love. Darcy, she realised, had come a very long way since those early days in Hertfordshire, when she had deemed him to be reserved, insensitive, and a proud man who cared little for the feelings of others.

How wrong she had been. Since their marriage, she had come to esteem and value his sense of honour, depend upon his good judgment, and, indeed, to enjoy and cherish the depth of his love for her. She knew, too, that he was concerned for all those for whom he was responsible, be they family, friends, or servants.

That he loved her and their children dearly, she had never doubted.

While she still permitted herself the privilege of teasing him occasionally, on the grounds that a wife may, with her husband, take certain liberties denied to others, she had to admit that his character had risen so high in her estimation that any minor shortcomings had been totally eclipsed.

In their daughter, Elizabeth saw many of the same qualities that distinguished her father. Cassy Darcy, for that was how many of her friends and childhood playmates spoke of her, even though she had been married for many years to Dr Gardiner, was as outgoing and open as her father had been reserved and shy as a young man. Yet, like him, she cared passionately about the people and places she loved and placed their welfare above all things. Blessed with Elizabeth's charm as well as the intelligence of her father, generous and kind with it, Cassy was indeed her father's daughter.

A worthy child of Pemberley, she was the firm favourite of all those men and women who lived and worked on the estate. They had watched her grow up, survive the tragic death of her brother William, fall in love and marry the distinguished Dr Gardiner, and raise a fine young family.

To them, she was the best and, indeed, many would have wished to see her become the next Mistress of Pemberley.

END OF PROLOGUE

MR DARCY'S DAUGHTER

Part One

THE INCLEMENT WEATHER INTO which the Gardiners drove as they left the boundaries of Pemberley did nothing to improve Cassandra's apprehensive mood.

Travelling South through Leicestershire, they had hoped to reach Northhampton before nightfall, but the driving rain rendered that prospect more hazardous and less likely with every mile.

Forced to break journey at the small town of Market Harborough, they took rooms at the local hostelry, only to find Rebecca Tate and her maid Nelly ensconced next door. They had met at the top of the stairs, going down to dinner, and soon discovered that Julian Darcy had also written to his mother-in-law, though not, it appeared, in the same desperate terms that he had used in his letter to Richard Gardiner.

Rebecca apologised to Cassy for her non-attendance at their meeting on the previous afternoon, confessing that Julian's note had driven all else from her mind, leaving her time only to make hurried preparations for their journey to Cambridge.

"With Mr Tate already in London, I decided that Nelly and I would go to Cambridge on our own," she declared, adding, "I felt I could not wait one more day, when there may have been something I could do to help. Oh, my poor Josie, I cannot imagine what has afflicted her. Why Cassy, you must remember what a bright, happy girl she used to be when she lived at home in Matlock. It must be the house—I am sure of it. It's cold and badly ventilated, quite unhealthy, especially in Winter. I said when they moved in, it was most unsuitable," she declared.

Both Richard and Cassy held their peace, not wishing to alarm her by revealing what they already knew. It was becoming clear to them that Julian had not been as candid with his mother-in-law as he had been with them. Cassy knew her husband would reveal nothing, nor would she.

At dinner, Richard enquired politely as to how Mrs Tate and her maid had travelled to Market Harborough from Matlock. It transpired that they were using one of the Tates' smaller vehicles. Mr Tate, they were told, had taken the carriage to London. Cassy was immensely relieved. It dispensed with the obligation for Richard to offer them seats in his carriage for the rest of the journey, which he would surely have done had they been travelling by coach. As it happened, they were well accommodated and, before retiring to their respective rooms, they agreed to leave for Cambridge after an early breakfast.

When they set out on the following morning, Cassy confessed to her husband, "I doubt if I could have concealed for much longer what we know of Josie's condition, if Becky Tate had been travelling with us to Cambridge."

He agreed. "It would certainly have been difficult to pretend that we knew no more than she does," he said.

The streets were wet as they drove into Cambridge.

The air was cold, and a sharp wind whipped the branches of the trees in the park and penetrated the carriage. Cassandra drew her wrap close around her, and yet she was cold and uncomfortable. The rain, though not as hard as before, was falling steadily as they approached the modest house that Julian and Josie rented in a quiet close not far from his college. It was not an unattractive dwelling, from an architectural point of view, but the garden appeared neglected, with sprouting bulbs and weeds competing for attention, and the house, with its blinds closed, seemed dark and unwelcoming. Once indoors, the aspect improved a little. Mrs Tate was at pains to explain how she had, on a previous visit, attempted to brighten up the parlour with new drapes and a few items of modern furniture, banishing an old horsehair sofa and two worn armchairs to the attic.

Julian met them in the hall, into which they were admitted by an anxious-looking young maidservant. While Mrs Tate insisted upon going upstairs to her daughter immediately, Richard and Cassy were ushered into the large but rather untidy parlour to the right of the hallway, where tea was to be taken.

Despite the best efforts of Mrs Tate, there was no disguising the general drabness of the room. Dark wood frames and striped wallpaper did little to help, while piles of books and journals lying on tables and strewn on the floor beside the chairs added clutter to a cheerless environment.

Only the fire burned brightly, keeping them warm, while the rain continued outside. How on earth, Cassy wondered, was anyone to recover from depression in surroundings such as these?

Writing later to her mother, she said:

> *Mama, everything is in such a state of disarray; it would drive me insane to live here. I cannot believe that Josie has been so ill as not to notice the disorderly condition of the house and the neglected garden. As for my poor brother, how anyone who has spent most of his life at Pemberley could possibly endure such wretched surroundings, not from poverty or privation, but by choice, I cannot imagine. Yet Julian does not appear to notice. His study, if it could be called that, so untidy and disorganised does it seem, is his chief retreat, when he is not with Josie or at work in his beloved laboratory.*

By the time Mrs Tate came downstairs, tea had been served and the fire stoked up to a good blaze. Julian had insisted that they partake of tea and toasted muffins while he went upstairs to his wife. Once he had left the room, Cassandra turned expectantly to Mrs Tate, who was clearly eager to talk. "How is Josie?" she asked and Mrs Tate, speaking in a kind of stage whisper, loud enough for anyone to hear who cared to listen, said, "Very weak and pale, very weak, indeed, poor dear. It seems she has had little or no nourishment for days."

She sounded exceedingly anxious and puzzled. Becky Tate was the same age as Cassy, but despite her many talents, seemed much less able to cope with the situation that confronted them.

"Has Josie been refusing to take food as well as medication?" asked Richard, his brow furrowed by a frown. Mrs Tate nodded.

"It certainly seems so, Dr Gardiner; not that Josie would say anything, but I slipped out and asked her maid, when she removed the tea tray, if her mistress had not been eating well and she said, 'No, not at all well.' Indeed, it would appear she eats less than a child would at meals and then only to please her husband, who begs her to take some nourishment. In between times, she drinks only weak tea or barley water and, very occasionally, takes a small piece of fruit," she explained, while wearing a very bewildered expression.

Rebecca Tate was usually a sensible, practical sort of person, yet it was difficult for her to understand what had happened to her once bright and lively daughter.

Cassy noticed that Richard was shaking his head, and she could tell from his solemn countenance that he was worried, too.

"Refusing medication is bad enough—declining food is much more serious. It means that her body would be enfeebled by sheer lack of nourishment, and thereby, less able to cope with whatever it is that afflicts her," he said, unable to conceal his concern.

Shortly afterwards, Julian returned to say he had spoken with Josie and she was willing to see Richard now. Cassy thought it sounded as if she was granting him a privilege, which was strange! They went upstairs, all but Cassy who remained alone in the parlour, casting an eye upon the clutter that surrounded her.

Presently, the maid came to clear away the tea things and Cassy recognised her. It was Susan, one of the maids from the Tates' household, who had been Josie's personal maid and had moved with her to Pemberley after her marriage to Julian, and later to Cambridge.

Clearly delighted to see Cassandra, the girl curtseyed briefly, put the tray back on the table, wiped her hands on her apron, and became quite talkative.

"Miss Cassy—beg pardon, ma'am, I mean Mrs Gardiner—I am so very happy to see you, ma'am. Looking so well, too, if I may say so. Is your family well, ma'am, Miss Lizzie and Master Edward?" she asked, eager for information. Equally pleased to see her and remembering the poor girl must be homesick, so far from her family in Derbyshire, Cassy responded kindly, assuring the girl that her family was in excellent health, all but her dear father-in-law Mr Gardiner.

"Oh ma'am, I am sorry to hear that. It must be very hard for poor Mrs Gardiner, looking after the master alone," she said, and Cassy reassured her that Mr Gardiner was very well cared for and her aunt had many helpers.

"Both his daughters, Mrs Courtney and Mrs Fitzwilliam, are there often and Dr Gardiner and my son Mr Edward, who is now a physician himself, attend upon him every day. Indeed, Mr Edward is with his grandfather at this very moment, staying at Lambton until our return."

Susan expressed her relief. "Ah, that surely is a blessing, ma'am," she said and added in a woebegone sort of voice, "I wish I could say the same of my Miss Josie. She will see no doctors and take no medicine at all."

Alerted by her words, Cassy asked quickly, "Susan, do you mean Miss Josie—I mean Mrs Darcy—refuses to take any medication for her condition? Has not a doctor seen her at all?"

Susan's eyes widened, reflecting her alarm.

"No, ma'am, she will not see anyone, nor will she take any proper medicine. It is only with much coaxing that I can get her to take a spoonful of honey for her chest or some chamomile tea for her headaches, when they are really bad. She has had nothing more in weeks, ma'am. It really is a sad thing to see her wasting away."

Cassy was appalled. "And what about her food?" she asked. The maid rolled her eyes skywards and shook her head.

"That, too, ma'am. She will eat like a bird, and then only when the master pleads with her to do so. Poor Mr Julian, he is so worried about her, he forgets his hat or his scarf and has to rush back for them, else he will leave his tea until it is cold and gulp it down before rushing out the door. It's a wonder he can still work, ma'am."

Cassy agreed, though she said nothing to the girl, as she rose and walked about the room. It seemed things were a good deal worse than they had suspected. Hearing footsteps descending the stairs, Susan picked up the tea tray and left the room, leaving Cassy gazing out of the bay window that looked out on a forlorn old rosebush, so overgrown it had hardly any blooms. Yet, she recalled, the last time they had been here, it had been covered in roses and when she had opened the window, their sweet scent had filled the room.

Her brother entered the parlour and Cassy, turning to greet him, could see he was miserable. Several years her junior, Julian looked depressed and vulnerable as he stood there, his tousled hair and rumpled shirt, as much as his anxious expression, evidence of his anguish. Cassy went to him and took his hands in hers, trying to offer some reassurance, looking for the right words to assuage his pain. She was sure, she said, that Richard would be able to help Josie; after all, he had been their family doctor since she was a little girl.

"If only she would take some medicine and a little nourishment, I am sure she will begin to feel better," he said and then added helplessly, "but Cassy, she will take neither, no matter what I say!"

Cassy felt tears sting her eyes; she had always felt responsible for her young brother, especially because he had been born when everyone was still grieving for their beloved William. They had all treasured Julian, yet he did not appear to have grown into the role he was expected to play. There was a great deal to learn about running an estate, but Julian had shown little interest in it. Even as a boy, he had no talent for practical matters and relied upon their mother herself or the servants for advice on everything.

His sister knew, only too well, that the young man who would one day succeed her father as Master of Pemberley would need to be stronger and more determined than Julian was now.

Beset with domestic problems, he seemed even weaker and less likely than before to take up with confidence the onerous responsibilities of Pemberley, where he would influence the lives of many men, women, and children, who would depend upon his strength and judgment for their livelihoods and security.

Standing in the middle of that drab room, he looked so forlorn that she was moved to say, "Please try not to worry too much, Julian dear. Richard will do his very best. I know Josie trusts him and, when he has persuaded her to take some medication and good food, I have no doubt we will see her condition improve."

Julian did not appear convinced. "Oh Cassy, I do hope you are right. There have been times, awful frightening moments, when I have felt that she does not wish to recover at all."

His voice was so filled with despair that Cassy was shocked.

"Hush, Julian, you must never say that. Why on earth would your wife, who has everything to live for, feel so? She has you, her family, and young Anthony," but he interrupted her.

"Plainly, my dear sister, we are not enough to make her completely happy. Her life, she claims, is empty of purpose; she points out that I have a burning desire to find scientific ways of preventing diseases that kill people, but cannot understand her longing to have her work published. Cassy, I have offered to have it published at my expense, but she will not have it; she says that would not do: it would be no different to having it printed in her father's papers, and she must have it accepted by one of the reputable publishing houses. As you know, this has not occurred and she is bitterly disappointed."

Even as she listened, Cassandra could not help wondering whether this was really the entire story behind Josie's malaise.

"Julian, are you quite sure that is the only reason for her unhappiness? Is there no other cause?" she asked.

There was a long pause during which Cassy studied her brother's countenance as he struggled to find words to express what he was going to say; at last, with a huge effort, he spoke.

"Cassy, I wish I could truthfully say it was, but I cannot. I have tried to pretend otherwise, but I fear I must face the truth. I think, Cassy, my dear Josie no longer loves me."

He sounded so disconsolate, looked so melancholy, she was cut to the heart, just looking at him.

"Julian!" she cried, "What nonsense is this? Whatever makes you say such a thing? Josie has been ill and depressed, but to believe she does not love you, or has no desire to recover, what evidence have you of this outrageous claim?"

Before he could respond, if indeed he was going to make any response at all, Mrs Tate and Richard were heard coming downstairs and no further discussion of the subject was possible.

As they entered the room, talking together, Julian excused himself, claiming there were some papers he had to read before dinner, and went to his study, where he remained for the rest of the afternoon.

A short while later, Cassandra went up to Josie's room. She was very shocked to find Josie so pale and thin, as if after a long and debilitating illness. She was sitting up in bed, a knitted shawl around her thin shoulders, her hair, which had once been much admired for its colour and lustre, twisted into a tight plait. Cassandra could hardly recognise the lively young Josie Tate, who had married her brother a mere five years ago.

"Cassy," her voice was small and thin when she spoke, "it is very kind of you to come all this way to see me, and Richard, too. It is very good of him to come. Mama has told me how very ill Mr Gardiner is; I am so sorry to be so much trouble to you all."

Cassandra sat on the bed beside her and stroked her hand. It was frail and small like a child's. "Josie, my dear, you are not causing us any trouble, especially not if you promise to do as Richard advises and take some proper medication and some good, nourishing food. We shall soon have you fit and well again," she said, trying hard to sound cheerful.

Yet Josie, though she nodded and smiled a pale sort of half-smile, said nothing to show that she intended to be amenable. She let Cassy sit with her and hold her hand, but made no promises. Indeed, when Cassy left the room, she could not help feeling even more disturbed than when she had entered it, for she had elicited no positive response at all.

Cassandra's distress was particularly poignant, for it was to her that Julian had turned, having discovered almost by chance that he was in love with Josie Tate. She recalled his anxiety about meeting her father, the formidable Mr Anthony Tate, who had subsequently turned out to be a most reasonable man. He had also been concerned that Josie was not as yet nineteen and very much in awe of Mr and Mrs Darcy and the grandeur of Pemberley, of which he would, one day, be master.

Cassy recalled the occasion of her brother's twenty-first birthday celebrations and the ball at Pemberley, where there had been present several young women, some prettier and possibly more eligible than Josie; but Julian had preferred the lively and intelligent Miss Tate, with whom he could talk of travel and read poetry. Then it had seemed so simple; two young people in love—they had been so happy together. It was heartrending to see them now, Julian so dispirited and Josie so sad and withdrawn, she seemed almost not to be there at all.

Cassy had felt a good deal of sympathy for the pair. They had both been very young and, unlike her husband, Richard, who had been a great favourite with both her parents long before their engagement, Josie Tate had been a relative outsider at Pemberley. Indeed, in spite of the best endeavours of Mr and Mrs Darcy to draw her into their circle, Cassy had felt that Josie and, occasionally, even Julian had appeared as though they never felt quite at home there.

How else, she wondered, could one account for their preference for the rather dreary environment in which they chose to live, while their gracious apartments at Pemberley lay vacant for most of the year?

Though pressed by both Julian and Mrs Tate to stay to dinner, the Gardiners left and made their way to a hotel in the town, where Richard had stayed previously and was warmly welcomed. There, with some degree of privacy, they were able to talk over dinner.

Cassy was eager to discover her husband's opinion. At first, Richard was unusually silent and thoughtful and his wife was concerned lest he refused to discuss it at all. But by the time they had finished the main course, he began to relax and she realised that he had been silent because he was deeply concerned for his young brother-in-law and his wife. After a glass or two of wine and some excellent cheese, his mood was further lightened and he confessed that he had never before seen a case like it.

"Not in all these years have I had a patient quite like Josie. Young, intelligent, well educated, with a good husband and a beautiful son, it is the sort of situation most women would envy, yet she is sunk in a slough of despair, from which she appears not to want to be released. Each time I question her about her physical symptoms, she denies that she is unwell, yet she is so pale and listless, she seems a shadow of her former self.

"When I mention food, she pulls a face, as if it were something unpleasant and abhorrent to her. She will take neither medication nor nourishment. So what, my dear Cassy, am I to make of it? How shall I ever restore her body to health, and even more perplexing, by what means shall I free her mind from this dreadful despair?" He sounded unusually pessimistic.

Listening to him, Cassy found herself in a quandary. Should she tell him of her brother's rather irrational musings that Josie might not wish to be restored to health at all? While she did not wish to betray her brother's state of mind, on reflection she decided that if Richard was to treat Josie with any chance of success, he needed to know the truth.

When, with some degree of trepidation, she did tell him, he did not appear surprised. Indeed, he said, he had almost reached the same conclusion himself.

"It is difficult not to conclude that she is deliberately pursuing a grievous and most painful course, either to punish herself for some perceived guilt or to punish someone else—presumably her husband or her mother—I cannot, at the moment, tell which it is," he said, and Cassy was quite confused.

"But why?" she cried. "What guilt could she possibly have to bear? As for the other possibility, why should she wish to punish the very people who love her?" and Richard had to hush her, for her voice had risen with exasperation as she spoke.

"Hush, dearest, it is not right that we should discuss this matter here; let us wait until we are upstairs," he said, and only when they had retired to their room, did they resume the conversation.

"Is it possible that poor Josie believes we do not care for her?" Cassy asked, still uncomprehending.

"It is possible," said Richard, "that Josie believes that the rest of her family, all of us, myself included, do not understand her. She may wish for praise, attention, whatever it is she feels she is not receiving, and this perverse, self-inflicted illness is her way of telling us all about it."

"But, Richard, Julian loves her dearly. He has told me so, only today," she protested.

He smiled. "Of course he does, but has he told her so? Does he, in all he says and does, demonstrate that love? I think not, my dear, for it is clear he is engrossed, for most of the time, in his work."

They talked late into the night before retiring to bed. The situation so depressed Cassy, she lay sleepless until the early hours of the morning. Only when Richard revealed that he had decided to seek the counsel of an eminent colleague on the morrow, did she finally fall asleep.

The following morning, Richard Gardiner set out to call on a distinguished scholar and physician at one of the colleges. Cassy, having finished breakfast, wrote to her mother as she had promised, recounting their journey and her impressions on arrival at her brother's house.

After some brief comments, she addressed the reason for their visit:

I wish I had better news for you, dear Mama, but I have not.

I cannot believe that Josie has deteriorated to this extent in so short a time. Indeed, to look at her, you would be hard put to recognise the lively young girl who was married to Julian five years ago, or the healthy young woman who used to run up and down the stairs at Pemberley or pursue little Anthony all over the lawns.

She is a mere shadow of the girl we knew and my poor brother is so unhappy, I cannot begin to tell you how sad he is. He talks despairingly of her not wishing to recover and seems to feel he is responsible.

Yet, Richard says he can find no physical sign of disease in her.

He is gone this morning to consult another physician, who is, I believe, an eminent scholar here at Cambridge, and Richard hopes he will have some advice for him. I pray he will and that Richard may succeed in helping both Josie and poor Julian, else I do not know what is to become of them.

I do not mean to alarm you and Papa, but I am so very fearful that
things here are going very wrong and I do not know what we can do to help.

There is but one piece of good news—Mrs Tate is here, too, with her
maid, Nelly, and no doubt will help relieve the burden upon Julian a little.
I shall not delay this further, as I wish to catch the post.

I shall write again as soon as there is any news to hand.

Your loving daughter,

Cassy.

On his return some hours later, Richard sought out his wife, who, having despatched her letters to the post, had returned upstairs to their room. He found her disconsolate and sad, unable, she said, to erase from her mind the melancholy picture of Josie, wan and thin, and Julian, unhappy, despairing, convinced his wife no longer loved him. She had not revealed this piece of information to her husband earlier, reluctant to add to his burden of concern.

But now, unable to hold back, she told him, and when she did, he was most disturbed. This was something he had not expected of Julian, who was generally a logical and reasonable man, not given to irrational declarations.

"Are you quite sure, my love? Did Julian say in so many words?"

"'I fear, Cassy, that my dear Josie no longer loves me,'" she completed the sentence for him, quoting her brother's words.

Richard Gardiner, whose life had been filled with the affection of his parents, the love of his wife and children, and the esteem of friends and colleagues, could barely conceive of the wretched situation in which his unhappy brother-in-law apparently found himself.

"Poor Julian, struggling to cope with his work, which is both important and demanding, a wife sick with melancholy, and the belief that she no longer loves him. It is surely unendurable," he said softly, his voice betraying his distress. "Can you imagine, Cassy, how bereft he must feel?"

Cassy went to him at once and put her arms around him; neither could imagine such a situation in their own lives.

"I can, indeed, but what can we do to help him?" she asked, weeping.

Feeling a growing sense of helplessness, they clung together, saddened, aching, seeking solace from each other, as they faced the daunting prospect of trying to resolve problems whose causes lay hidden from them, finding their only comfort in the love they shared. Yet their own deep passion only compounded their concern about the state of Julian and Josie's lives.

Cassy, no less than her husband, was confounded by the situation that confronted her brother and his wife. Growing up at Pemberley, where the strength of her parents' love had sustained their family in the midst of tragedy, she had married Richard Gardiner, whose own parents had enjoyed a long and contented marriage. Consequently, she had scarcely any personal knowledge of the bitterness and grief that she had encountered with Julian and Josie.

Her own experience of marriage had taken her from eager young love to a deeply satisfying, mature, and passionate relationship with her husband and children. It permeated every aspect of her life and sharpened all her sensibilities; so much so, that strangers meeting them for the first time would become aware of the warmth and strength of their affection for one another.

To both Richard and Cassy, their marriage was a deep well of contentment. To put such a source of happiness in jeopardy, for any reason whatsoever, would have been utterly unthinkable. Sensing her anguish and understanding her need for reassurance, Richard was loving and consoling.

Later, he revealed that he had had a long and enlightening discussion with a colleague, a man for whom he had immense professional respect. This physician had healed many men after the terror and shock of war and was an acknowledged authority on the causes and treatment of acute trauma.

Where once priests and exorcists had held sway, scientific ideas were being applied to ease the curse of melancholia. Richard claimed he had learned much from their discussion and planned to talk to both Julian and his wife.

"Perhaps, if they can be convinced of the need to speak of their fears and anxieties to each other or to my colleague, who understands their situation, there may be a chance for some healing. At the moment, they are each locked in a prison of their own making, into which one will not permit the other entry," he explained.

❧

Back at Pemberley, meanwhile, Elizabeth and Darcy had waited impatiently for news from Cambridge. When it came, in the form of Cassandra's letter, it brought little relief. Elizabeth, having read it twice over, could not make it out at all.

"What can be the matter?" she asked her husband, who, having reread their daughter's words, was at a loss to explain the circumstances, not having been privy to their problems.

His wife persisted, "Darcy, what has happened to poor Julian and Josie? They were so happy here last year—I had hoped they would return for the Summer."

Darcy tried to find a comforting explanation but could not. He too was baffled. His earlier simple prognosis, that Josie was probably bored, was being rapidly eroded by the realisation that she was possibly more seriously ill than any of them had imagined.

"My dear, I think we shall all have to wait until Richard and Cassy return to discover the real cause of the problem. Cassy would not have enough of the detail to give us any real understanding, but Richard would know, and I am sure he will explain it to us," he said.

Even as he spoke, he could see that Elizabeth was unconvinced; trying to reassure her, he was gentle and persuasive, understanding her grief. Losing her beloved William had been a dreadful blow and, though Julian could never replace him, he had brought some light and pleasure back into her life. Now, Julian was miserable and Lizzie suffered with him.

"There has to be some reason, Lizzie; if Richard can find no physical cause for Josie's affliction, there is bound to be another explanation. When he discovers it, he will also find the solution. Meanwhile, dearest, please do not upset yourself unduly or you will also become unwell," he said, anxious for her, using whatever means he could to alleviate her distress. Her happiness had been his concern throughout their long marriage.

Elizabeth smiled and took his hand; it was only a small gesture, but it meant she had accepted the comfort he offered and was glad of the relief. As on many previous occasions, his strength and devotion helped her cope with what might otherwise have been an unbearable burden of pain.

When Richard and Cassandra Gardiner returned to Julian's house the following afternoon, they found, to their astonishment, Mrs Tate and Josie sitting in the parlour in front of the fire. Their maid, Susan, beaming all over her face, had just brought in tea and scones, and while Josie was not exactly eating with relish, she was at least attempting to consume some part of what was on her plate.

A cheerful Mrs Tate informed them that Julian was expected at any moment, and they were to be joined at dinner by a visitor from London.

"A Mr Barrett, who is in Cambridge on business, called this morning and though Julian was unable to see him, being about to leave for his college, he has been asked to dine with us tonight," she explained, adding the information that she had not met him herself, but Julian and Josie knew Mr Barrett well.

"I myself would like very much to meet Mr Barrett, being in the business of writing, too, as you know," Mrs Tate said, prompting Cassy to ask if Mr Barrett was a writer.

At this, Josie, who had put down her plate, responded, surprising Cassy.

"No, but he does know a great many writers, being himself involved in the book trade. He stocks all the best volumes," she said.

It was the first time she had spoken, and both Richard and Cassy were astonished at the firmness and clarity of her voice, which only a day or two ago had sounded so weak and thin.

After the initial surprise, however, Cassy declared that she was delighted to see that Josie was feeling sufficiently well to venture downstairs again. Richard went further, pointing out that she was already looking much better, with more colour in her cheeks, and expressing his confidence that Josie would soon be on her way to recovery. Both of them congratulated Mrs Tate, giving her credit for having effected such a transformation in her daughter in so short a time.

Later, when Cassy left the room to go upstairs, she met Susan on the landing, carrying a gown, which she had pressed. The girl was so excited she could hardly contain herself, eager to tell Cassy of her mistress's recovery. "It's Miss Josie's gown for tonight, ma'am; it's ever so long since she got dressed up, I am to do her hair up too, ma'am."

Cassy took the opportunity to ask if Josie had begun to take her medication again, and if Mrs Tate had persuaded her to do so. She was taken aback quite when Susan said emphatically, "Oh no, ma'am, it's not Mrs Tate; it's all on account of Mr Barrett." Then seeing the look of consternation on Cassy's face as she said "Mr Barrett," Susan added quickly, "The gentleman that's coming to dinner, ma'am. It's all his doing."

"Whatever do you mean, Susan?" asked Cassy, thinking the girl was babbling, as some silly young women are wont to do, but Susan insisted, "Indeed ma'am, when he was here last year, he was very taken with Miss Josie's writings, you know, ma'am, her poetry and such."

Cassy was unaware that her young sister-in-law wrote poetry, but let that pass, as she persevered, keen to learn more about the involvement of Mr Barrett.

"Was he?" Cassy was interested.

"Yes, ma'am, he sat with her and read some out loud, in the parlour; oh, it was lovely, ma'am. He has such a fine voice. Miss Josie was ever so pleased, because he said it was so good, it should be put in a book. Miss Josie could not stop talking about it for days and days, ma'am."

"And what happened after that?" Cassy asked, for it was plain the maid had more to tell and Cassy was keen to hear it.

"Nothing, ma'am," said Susan, pulling a face. "Mr Barrett had to return to London and we heard no more of it. Miss Josie wrote him a letter to his office in London, I know she did, because I took it to the post, but I never heard if he replied, ma'am. But this morning, when he called on the master and was invited to return to dine tonight, the mistress was so pleased, she was up out of bed within an hour and wanted her clothes pressed and her hair washed and curled; she is coming down to dinner for the first time in weeks, ma'am." Susan was plainly excited by the prospect.

Cassy shook her head, still puzzled by the apparent speed with which Josie's recovery had been effected. Mrs Tate's maid, Nelly, appeared on the stairs and Susan's conversation seemed to dry up suddenly.

When Cassy returned to the parlour, Rebecca invited them to dinner.

"I am sure Julian will want you to stay," she said, smiling, and to her husband's surprise, Cassy accepted with some alacrity. She was very keen to meet Mr Barrett, whose appearance had caused so much activity and interest in the household.

Julian Darcy arrived home earlier than usual. So happy was he to find his wife downstairs taking tea, he rushed out again immediately, returning with a bunch of Spring flowers, which he presented to her. Mrs Tate, beaming with pleasure, summoned Susan to fetch a vase and arrange the flowers, which were then given pride of place on the centre table, which had been cleared of all its clutter.

Julian looked ecstatic, but Cassy could not help noticing that her brother's joy was not exactly matched by the response of his wife. Josie, she noted, had smiled and thanked her husband softly, but with no more enthusiasm or warmth than she would any stranger who may have brought her flowers.

Cassandra was beginning to wonder whether the malaise afflicting Josie and Julian was rather more deep-seated than any of them had believed. She said nothing to her husband though, not even when they went away to dress for dinner, and he expressed some surprise that she had so eagerly accepted the invitation to dine.

"I would not have thought you would want to return there tonight," he said, but she smiled and replied that she had been so very glad to see Josie downstairs and Julian was obviously so happy, it had seemed appropriate to join them and celebrate the occasion.

Richard nodded and said no more.

"You do not mind, do you, dearest?" she asked, and he said no, he did not. "For my part," he claimed, "it should afford me an opportunity to observe my patient without intruding upon her. It is possible that she has realised that it is in her power to change her situation. I sincerely hope that it is the beginning of her recovery."

Josie was already downstairs when they arrived at the Darcys' house. Dressed in a most becoming gown of a peach-toned silk, which lent colour to her pale cheeks, with her pretty hair brushed and looped up into a very attractive style, the hostess looked remarkably well. Few would have believed she had been an invalid for weeks.

When Cassy commented upon her changed appearance, Josie smiled and said it was all her Mama's work and Susan's. Cassy could well believe it. When Mrs Tate appeared, she looked so pleased with her daughter, she could not stop talking about how well she looked.

As for the maid Susan, she was so excited, she could barely attend to her duties and once or twice Cassy caught her exchanging a knowing glance with her mistress, as if they shared a secret.

When their visitor arrived, he was ushered in and introduced to Richard and Cassandra by Julian as "our friend, Mr Barrett" and to Mrs Tate, who was effusively pleased to meet him.

Mr Barrett was neither handsome nor very tall, nor was he particularly elegant in dress and manners, affecting the somewhat informal attire that was fashionable with writers and the like. Indeed, he seemed a very ordinary sort of gentleman, until he spoke. Cassy noticed then that his voice, which was quiet and well modulated, had a most genteel accent and a warm, intimate quality. It was what some people called "a cultured voice." Very suitable for reading poetry, Cassy thought. When they were introduced, he had bowed to her and Mrs Tate, then kissed Josie's hand as she sat on the sofa in front of the fire, presenting her with a little book bound in green leather. He said something to her quietly, as he handed it over, which made her smile. Cassy did not hear his words; clearly she was not meant to, nor was anyone other than Josie, who managed a very acceptable smile and said, "Thank you very much indeed, Mr Barrett."

Julian and Josie had both greeted him cordially and welcomed him to their home and Mr Barrett was determined to please them all.

At dinner, although she ate very little, Josie sat at table, listened carefully, spoke quietly, and even managed to ask their guest a question or two, which he answered with great attention and courtesy. Mr Barrett, who sat between her and her mother, maintained a conversation with both mother and daughter throughout the meal, turning frequently from one to the other, as if to ascertain if they had been satisfied with his remarks. Richard said later that you could see the man was in business, so well did he apply himself to the business of making a good impression upon the people he met.

Richard concentrated his attention upon Julian, with whom he spent most of the evening, while Cassy observed the rest of the party.

Once they moved back into the parlour—for the house had no real drawing room—tea and coffee were served and Josie, assisted by her mother, managed very well, Cassy thought. Later, Mrs Tate excused herself and went upstairs, but Josie appeared not to tire at all.

It was late when Mr Barrett took his leave, and Josie almost immediately decided that she was tired and would like to retire. Susan was sent for to assist her. An attentive husband shepherded her to the stairs before returning to his guests.

Taking the opportunity of being alone with him, Richard spoke gently, "Now, Julian, Josie appears to have made an excellent start; it is you who must make her feel that it is worth going on and making a complete recovery. There must be no sliding back. You must do all you can," he advised, and extracting a promise that Julian would keep them informed of her progress, they returned to their lodgings for the night. Their earlier feelings of frustration had been replaced by relief and a fair degree of bewilderment, as well, for they could find little to account for Josie's rapid recovery.

Two days later, finding no sign of any retardation in Josie's progress and on hearing only good news from her mother and husband, Cassy and Richard left for home, leaving Mrs Tate to continue the good work and watch over her daughter and her rather chaotic household.

When they saw Josie and Julian for the last time before their departure, Cassy promised to send young Lizzie to them in the Summer, and while Josie did not seem very enthusiastic, both she and Julian declared they would look forward to her visit.

"It will do us all good to have a bright young person around," said Julian. Josie agreed and sent her love to Lizzie and the rest of their family.

Returning to Pemberley, bringing what they deemed to be a satisfactory report of Josie's condition, they were to discover that there was already plenty of good news around. The Sutton children had been found and restored to their mother; their violent father was now safely in the hands of the constabulary.

"Thanks mainly to the prompt action of Mr Elliott, the new Member of Parliament. He seems to be a most resourceful man," Mr Darcy told them.

They were pleased to be able to relate that Josie's condition seemed to have improved quite markedly in the past few days, confirming the belief of both Richard and Mr Darcy that it had been a malaise brought on by disposition rather than disease. Cassy still had some reservations, of which she chose not to speak to her parents, but hoped to put to her husband when an opportunity arose. Now, she decided, was not the right time; there were far too many things happening.

Her mother had even more interesting news.

"The same Mr Elliott who rescued the Sutton children is now engaged to Anne-Marie and they are to be married before Christmas!" she announced. "We have had letters from Jonathan and Anne-Marie."

All this had taken place in the space of a week! Richard was astonished and his wife absolutely delighted. She had been well aware of the romance between Anne-Marie and Mr Elliott, Cassy said, and was exceedingly pleased with the news.

Ever since she had learned the truth about Anne-Marie's desolate marriage to Mr Bradshaw, Cassy had prayed that her cousin would, one day, find happiness. She fervently hoped that this marriage would be the answer to that prayer.

Of Mr Colin Elliott, they had had excellent reports from their cousin Emma Wilson and her husband James, who sat in the Parliament with him. More recently, Colonel Fitzwilliam and Caroline had spoken in glowing terms of his courage and determination to leave the Tory Party and join the Reformists.

Earlier, they had met at Pemberley, when both Mr Elliott and Anne-Marie had been visiting Derbyshire, separately but at the same time. Seeing them together, Cassy and her mother had been convinced that he at the very least was very much in love, while she was probably on the verge of it, even if she did not appear to be aware of it at the time.

The news of their engagement was, for Cassy, the very best news of all. So pleased was she, and so much did she have to say about it to her family, it helped push the problems of Julian and Josie into the background for a while.

⁓❦⁓

As if that were not sufficient, Summer brought a further distraction, with the return from London of their younger son Darcy. He came bearing plenty of news, as he always did. There had been much excitement in April and May, with the visit of Mr Garibaldi from Italy bringing his supporters into the streets, followed by the clear and unequivocal declaration by Mr Gladstone of his support for the Reform Bill, giving working men the vote.

"Everyone says Mr Gladstone will soon be Prime Minister," Darcy declared, as he joined his parents for breakfast.

"Your uncle Fitzwilliam may have a different view," said his father, reminding them that Colonel Fitzwilliam remained a staunch admirer of Palmerston. Young Darcy was sceptical. "Palmerston's finished; he has little support even among the Whigs, and Gladstone is the favourite of the Liberals. No one doubts that he will soon be Prime Minister," he said, with the confidence of the young that will brook no contradiction.

His parents smiled, aware that things were rarely that simple.

Darcy Gardiner's interest in politics was, as yet, somewhat peripheral. He enjoyed listening to the big speeches in the Parliament and seemed to revel in the cut and thrust of debate. But, like many other young men of his age, he was unsure if he wanted to endure the tedium of Parliamentary membership and all that it involved. It was something he expected to have to decide sometime in the distant future.

His uncle, Jonathan Bingley, once a distinguished Member of the Commons, had urged him to take it seriously, because, as he had said, "The Parliament needs young, active men, and the people deserve better representatives than men who have few enlightened views and hardly any vision at all, voting only to preserve their privileges." Jonathan Bingley was an ardent Reformist.

Young Darcy had been very impressed with his uncle's words and had promised to give it serious thought. He was, however, at twenty-four, still unsettled about his future ambitions; attracted to both business and politics, but too young to have much experience of either, he appeared reluctant to commit himself to any cause. The declaration at breakfast had been the first time his parents had heard him speak so emphatically on the subject.

Recently, Darcy Gardiner had spent a good deal of time in the company of a gentleman lately arrived from America. Of Irish descent, his parents had emigrated to the United States at the time of the potato famine in the 1840s and made good there. He had been sent to school in England, had spent some time travelling in Europe, and had inherited a substantial fortune from an uncle who had moved to Canada, where he had died without an heir.

Mr Michael Carr had fascinated young Darcy with his width of experience, his wide range of interests, and the two had become firm friends. He was, he had revealed, looking to purchase a suitable property in England, preferably in the Midlands. Darcy, who knew nothing of land values and real estate, had suggested that he talk to his grandfather Mr Gardiner, who, he had said, "was prodigiously good at business and knows everything there is to know about property in the district." He had added, however, that it was a pity his grandfather was ill, else he was sure he would have assisted him in every way.

Having related all this to his parents at breakfast, Darcy announced casually that he had invited Mr Carr to stay. What was more, he would be arriving that afternoon. This announcement caused some mild consternation, as his mother suggested that she might have liked a little more notice; but in the end Cassy was, as usual, prepared to welcome him. Any friend of her son's was sure to be treated as one of the family and room would always be found to accommodate him.

It was no different with Mr Carr, who was due to arrive on the coach from Derby that afternoon. Darcy took the curricle to meet him, while the rest of the household rushed to prepare a room for their guest, and Cook had to be advised about an appropriate menu for dinner.

"He is American and may be fairly fastidious," said Cassy, but young Lizzie reassured them. "Darcy says he's Irish first and will eat anything at all," she said, which was well and good, except Cook thought it meant he had a very good appetite, so she had better make double the quantity of everything!

The coach from Derby was late, delayed by a sick passenger who had to be set down at Ripley. When young Darcy and his friend reached the Gardiners' house, it was after six o'clock and the ladies had already gone upstairs to rest before dressing for dinner. Only Dr Gardiner was downstairs in his study, having just returned from Lambton, where he had gone, as usual, to attend on his father.

When Mr Carr was introduced to him, Richard was immediately struck by his resemblance to a portrait in the long gallery at Pemberley. However, not wishing to embarrass their guest, he said nothing, greeting him cordially. As they shook hands, Mr Carr thanked him most sincerely for his generosity in accommodating him at such short notice. "I'd have stayed at the local inn, rather than inconvenience you, sir," he said apologetically, "but Darcy insisted it was all right." Richard endorsed his son's words and welcomed their visitor, reassuring him he had not inconvenienced anyone at all.

"My eldest son Edward is staying temporarily with my parents at Lambton, so we have plenty of room," he said.

Mr Carr immediately asked after Mr Gardiner's health, saying Darcy had intimated that his grandfather was gravely ill.

"I do hope his condition is not serious, sir," he said, to which Richard replied that it was no more serious than it had been yesterday, but could worsen, without warning, at any time.

"Which is why Edward, who is himself a physician, stays with him," he explained as they went upstairs.

Darcy was eager for his parents to approve of his new friend. He had found Michael Carr a more stimulating and interesting companion than many of the rich young men in the city and had hoped, by inviting him to Derbyshire, to persuade him to settle in the county.

Richard found Cassy completing her toilette, when he joined her in their apartments. He stood behind her as she sat at her dressing table, pinning up her hair.

"Mr Carr appears to be a very personable young man," he said and seeing her start, added, "Don't worry, my dear, everything has been attended to. He's been shown to his room and his bags have been taken upstairs. He seems quite comfortable."

"How does he look? Is he handsome and tall? Does he speak like an American?" she asked, smiling.

"Hmm. Tall, yes, not really handsome, but very striking, a memorable face, I would say, and remarkably like one I have seen on a portrait that hangs in your father's collection at Pemberley."

Cassy was intrigued. Meeting his eyes in the mirror, she asked, "Which portrait? Not one of the ancient ancestors?"

Her husband laughed. "With all that armour, I doubt I would have noticed a resemblance if there had been one. No, it's not one of them. I cannot recall exactly, but you will probably know it as soon as you see him." Cassy was intrigued and questioned him further, but he could tell her little more.

They dressed and went down to dinner and, when the gentlemen joined them, Darcy Gardiner introduced his friend Mr Michael Carr to his mother and sisters, whom he greeted with great courtesy.

It was Laura Ann who whispered to her sister, "Lizzie, Mr Carr looks very like the picture of the gentleman in a green coat, which hangs next to the pretty lady with a big hat, in the gallery at Pemberley, does he not?"

When Lizzie reported this to her mother, while the gentlemen were getting their drinks, Cassy remembered it well.

The pretty woman in the big hat was the wife of her father's uncle, James Fitzwilliam, who had lived all his life in Ireland; but Cassy had no idea who the man in the green coat was, nor what his picture was doing in her father's collection. They had never paid much attention to him, but she promised her daughters she would ask her father at the first opportunity. She did caution them both, however, not to stare at their guest on account of this. "It is very rude and we do not want him to think we are uncouth country bumpkins, do we, my dears?" she had said, as she went to join the others.

Mr Carr proved to be a very pleasant and entertaining guest, and they spent a lively evening being regaled with tales of Ireland, America, and France, where he had lately visited. They heard of his plans to purchase a property in England and his hopes to settle in the country. He could certainly tell a good story, and he could sing, as he amply demonstrated when they repaired to the drawing room after dinner, entertaining them with a couple of lyrics, proving he had an excellent voice as well as a good sense of humour.

When at last they retired to their rooms, Cassy admitted to her husband that Mr Carr was indeed a most agreeable young man.

"I do hope he finds a suitable property in the area," she said. "He would make an excellent neighbour, I am sure."

Richard had to agree and then, just moments before turning out the light, he said, "Of course, there is Will Camden's place, with the farm and horse stud…"

Cassy sat up in bed, wide awake. "Of course there is. Will is keen to sell; he and his wife are all excited about emigrating to New South Wales."

"I cannot think why; it's the other side of the world and Will has never farmed sheep," said Richard, sleepily, no longer interested.

"But it does mean the property is available, Richard," she persisted, adding reasonably, "Perhaps, my dear, you ought to tell Mr Carr."

Richard promised to draw his attention to it on the morrow, smiling to himself at the sudden eagerness of his wife to assist Mr Carr to acquire a property in the area.

"This keenness of yours for our guest to purchase this property would not be linked in any way to the fact that he is an eligible young bachelor, and our little Lizzie will soon be eighteen, would it, my love?" he asked quietly, only to provoke an indignant protest from his wife.

"Richard, how could you suggest such a thing? Our Lizzie is only a child; I would not dream of it. But, you must agree, Mr Carr is a very presentable young man. He is Darcy's friend and has a small fortune to invest in a suitable estate, so why should he not purchase it from Will Camden? We know it to be an excellent property; surely there is no reason why they may not both be happy with the transaction?"

"Oh, no reason at all, my dear, none at all. I shall certainly let him know it's on the market," her husband replied, chuckling as he put out the light, wondering aloud as he did so whether Mr Carr would have any idea at all of the plans that were afoot for his future happiness.

Cassy had hoped, when they were in bed, to quiz her husband about his impressions of Mr Barrett and the remarkable recovery his visit had effected upon Josie's spirits. But, what with the excitement of Mr Carr's arrival and now the expectation that there was a property he could like well enough, Josie had gone right out of her head. So pleased was she with the prospect of the sale of the Camden property, she fell quickly and peacefully asleep.

❦

The following morning dawned with mist and light rain, but soon cleared to a brilliant day of blue skies and sunshine.

Richard had risen early, as always, and ridden out across the dales. Returning from his ride, he came upon Mr Carr taking a solitary walk along the banks of the Wye, which formed one boundary of their property. Seeing his guest, Richard pulled up, dismounted, and continued the rest of the journey on foot.

"This is a most attractive place you have here, Dr Gardiner," said Mr Carr. "I have been admiring the changing prospect that greets the eye at almost every turn in the road."

Richard acknowledged his praise, modestly informing him that it had been a wedding gift to them from his parents.

"It is both pretty and convenient, situated halfway between Bakewell and the dales of Matlock. If it were not for their generosity, I should not have been able to afford the place, being only recently qualified at the time. My wife and I were very grateful; we have been exceedingly happy here," he explained, and there was no doubting the enthusiasm in his voice.

"I can well believe it. It is a remarkably beautiful place," said Carr, adding, "I would pay anything for such a property."

Richard laughed. "Well, I am sorry to disappoint you, Mr Carr, but it is not for sale."

His guest, fearing he had offended his host, apologised immediately.

"Oh sir, I do apologise. I did not mean to suggest that I would offer you money for your home..." He was quite red with embarrassment and Richard swiftly reassured him that no offence had been taken.

He seemed genuinely relieved and then, to his surprise, Dr Gardiner said, "My son tells me you are looking to purchase a property in Derbyshire. Is this correct?"

"Yes indeed, sir, I most certainly am, but I know little of buying and selling property, especially in England. I just know I love the countryside in these parts and, since my grandmother was originally from around here, before she married my grandfather and returned to Ireland with him, I would very much like to buy in the area."

"Would a small mixed farm interest you? One with a horse stud?" Richard asked, casually. Mr Carr's eyes lit up. "A farm with a horse stud! Is there such a property here? And is it on the market?" he asked excitedly.

Richard nodded. "There is—at Rushmore, over towards Lambton, and not far from my parents' property. The owner, Will Camden, is looking for a suitable buyer; he and his family are emigrating to Australia to start a farm in New South Wales. They have had several offers for the stud; it's an excellent investment, but Will refuses to break up the property.

"He will only sell it together with the home farm because of his concern for his tenants. He does not wish to leave them at the mercy of some land-grabbing developer, who will turn them out and enclose their farms or subdivide and sell the land from under them. This has meant that he has not yet been able to close a sale. Now, if you are genuinely interested, I could introduce you. I must warn you, however, since he is soon to leave the country, he will insist on a cash settlement."

Mr Carr looked ready to dance, so pleased was he with this news.

"I would appreciate that very much, sir, and there would be no problem about a cash settlement; my intention is to use the money left to me by my uncle. It is in my bank already. When do you think I might see the property?"

Richard smiled at his enthusiasm. He was very American, he thought, impulsive, enthusiastic, throwing caution to the winds...

"Well, I usually visit my parents every afternoon. If you and Darcy would meet me at the inn at Lambton, I could take you to meet Will Camden. It is a very short distance from the inn. I shall have to send a message to advise him of your interest, of course. If he is agreeable, you could inspect the property, and if you are still keen, you could meet later to negotiate terms," he explained.

They had almost reached the end of the long drive to the house when Darcy Gardiner and his two sisters came out to meet them; they were obviously keen to show Mr Carr around the grounds. Richard, leaving his guest in their care, handed his horse to the groom and went upstairs to change.

Cassy had seen them arrive together; she was eager for information. Yet she knew from the smile on his face that her husband would tease her before he would reveal anything. Which he did. She plied him with questions about Mr Carr's interest in the Rushmore property, but he revealed little. When he was dressed and ready to go to breakfast, he stopped in front of her and put his arms around her. She was rather flustered, not at all like her usual amenable self.

"Please, Richard, do stop teasing. I am not matchmaking, I promise; our Lizzie is far too young and anyway, girls are not as eager to rush into marriage these days."

He kissed her then and said, "Of course, my dear; I am sorry. I did not mean to provoke you, but I know how much you want to help our guest secure a good property in Derbyshire and I thought you would like to know that, this afternoon, I am to introduce him to Will Camden."

Cassy almost exploded at having been kept in the dark this long and it took all his loving charm to calm her down.

"Hush, dearest; they may be back, and we would not want him to think we are a noisy, quarrelling family, would we?" he argued.

This was the last straw and Dr Gardiner was only saved from dire retribution by Laura Ann, who put her head round the door and begged them to come down to breakfast, because she was very hungry.

Her father escaped, taking his daughter with him, while Cassy followed, still flushed with impatience. She was unwilling to admit, even to herself, that Mr Carr had seemed to her like the first truly eligible gentleman they had seen in these parts in quite a while, and though she had no desire to be making a match for Lizzie, she thought her daughter deserved to see a little more of him. It would do her good to be aware of eligible young men, she thought.

If things turned out well and he did purchase the Rushmore property, they would all have an opportunity to get to know Mr Carr a little better. She made a little resolution to mention the matter to her mother when they met. Elizabeth was sure to have some useful ideas about the situation and would not tease her like her husband did.

After breakfast, Richard made his peace with his loving wife and left for the hospital, promising to tell her everything when he returned that evening.

"You will know it all, my love, I promise," he vowed. Appeased by his pledge, she forgave him for vexing her that morning and let him go, but not before she had urged him to recommend Mr Carr to Will Camden as a prospective buyer.

A lighthearted riposte was on the tip of his tongue, but seeing her face and knowing how much love there was between them, he had not the heart to say another aggravating word. Even as he turned to wave to them before driving away, he saw Darcy standing with his mother at the top of the steps, while Mr Carr and the two girls had set out for a walk around the park, which they had promised their guest at breakfast.

Richard could not help smiling; he had glanced at his wife across the table when they were arranging it between them and, to his surprise, she appeared not to be listening. Doubtless, she was untroubled by it; yet twenty-four hours ago Mr Carr, apart from being Darcy's friend, had been a complete stranger.

As they drove on towards Matlock, Richard recalled the hilarious tales his mother used to tell of Mrs Bennet's relentless efforts at matchmaking for her five daughters, when they lived at Longbourn.

It had been her sole preoccupation, except for the dire condition of her nerves, for several years, during which time every eligible man who visited the district had been viewed and pursued as a possible marriage prospect for one of her girls.

Both Mr Darcy and Mr Bingley had been objects of her interest, until the former fell out of favour, temporarily, to be replaced by an officer in the regiment of the militia that was encamped nearby. He, alas, had turned out to be a bounder who had eloped with her youngest daughter, Lydia, whom he had to be bribed into marrying!

However, Mrs Gardiner had admitted that Mrs Bennet had been proved right about Bingley and Jane, who had fallen in love almost at first sight, while Elizabeth's romance with Mr Darcy had developed in spite of her mother's efforts. It was such a pity, Richard thought, that his dear wife Cassy had never known her infamous grandmother. It might have made for some interesting conversations.

❦

Around four o'clock in the afternoon, Dr Gardiner drove to the inn at Lambton to wait for Mr Carr and Darcy. He had already sent a message to Will Camden that he was bringing along a friend of Darcy's who had expressed an interest in the Rushmore property and had received an enthusiastic response. The Camdens, who were committed to emigrating to New South Wales, were keen to sell.

The landlord at the inn was well known to the Gardiners; the family had lived in the area for many years, and by his marriage to the daughter of the Master of Pemberley, Richard Gardiner had consolidated his position as a local. In addition, his reputation as a skilled and thoughtful physician had secured him a special place in the community. All of which probably contributed to the very cordial welcome he received when he arrived at the inn that afternoon.

The same did not apply to the two rather raffishly dressed young men, who sauntered in shortly afterwards and ordered food and drink.

Richard, who had retired to an alcove from which he could see an approaching vehicle, overheard them questioning the landlord. They had arrived in the area last night from Birmingham and taken rooms at the inn, with a view to inspecting a couple of properties in the district, they said. The mention of property alerted Richard, who listened while pretending to read his newspaper.

It seemed, they were interested in an old run-down place outside Cromford and had also driven out to Rushmore Farm to look at the Camden horse stud. Both men were enthusiastic about the stud, with its collection of fine horses, but neither was keen on the farm that went with it.

"It is only a small place, no more than a hundred acres, with no prospect of expansion or development, unless one were to get rid of the tenants, who seem to have been there forever," said one, and the landlord agreed that the families had lived and worked the farm at Rushmore for many generations.

"You'll not get them out easily," he warned.

The other man was more optimistic. "I'd enclose the place and turn them out. The law lets you do it; it would be the only way to make the property profitable," he declared, adding that he would want to keep the trout stream as part of his portion.

"Apart from the stud, it's the only part of the property I would want to keep. The house is old and needs knocking down."

Richard realised that these men were the type of buyers Will Camden had already rejected, but time was running out and soon he would be forced to accept one of their offers, however reluctantly. It would be an absolute tragedy if Rushmore Farm and Stud were to fall into the hands of men like these or others of their ilk. The two men were still in the dining room when Darcy and Michael Carr arrived in the curricle. One of the men rose and went to the window to look at the new arrivals and then walked over to the landlord to ask if he knew who they were. Meanwhile, Richard had gone out to caution Darcy and Mr Carr that they had better be discreet in the presence of the competition. They decided not to go in and, as they prepared to drive to Rushmore Farm, he told them what he had heard.

Mr Carr looked very concerned, but Darcy seemed untroubled. "I do not believe that Mr Camden will sell to these type of men," he said confidently. His father was more circumspect.

"He may not have an alternative—time is short and he will need to sell fairly soon," he said, and they set off up the road. Mr Carr joined Richard in the carriage, while Darcy followed in the curricle.

Michael Carr was concerned; he had spent most of the morning talking to the Gardiners' steward, he said, and he had heard nothing but good reports of the Rushmore stud and the farm.

"Your man thinks it's an excellent property; he believes Mr Camden is foolish to sell," he said, and Richard laughed. "Thomas grew up on the Camden farm; it was his childhood home. Little wonder he doesn't like to see it up for sale," he explained and added thoughtfully, "Many of the folk who live and work around here have ties with the Camden Estates as they do with Pemberley. Some were born there, and the prosperity of their villages depends upon the good management of those two estates. They may be fearful that another round of enclosures and indiscriminate development will destroy their livelihood."

Mr Carr was impressed by the level of concern shown by both Dr Gardiner and his son; clearly the Gardiners had the interests of their community at heart, he thought. When he spoke, he hoped to reassure them of his own motives.

"I have certainly no interest in enclosing or subdividing any property I purchase. My intention is not to make a profit, but to purchase a place where I can enjoy the kind of life I wish to lead. My business interests in transport and trade are in New York and London; here, I would want mainly to enjoy the countryside and all it offers.

"Now, if the horse stud is as good as Thomas says it is, that would surely be an added attraction and a valuable investment, but my chief aim is the acquisition of a pleasing and convenient country residence."

"But what about the farm?" asked Richard. "Those men at the inn were right about the farm—it is not large enough to allow the use of mechanised farming methods. There is little scope for expansion unless you intend to fell the woods, and there are long-term tenants."

He did not wish to raise Mr Carr's expectations too high.

"If the stud is good value and the house is solid enough, I do not think the size of the farm would present a problem," said Carr. He fell silent as the horses strained a little to take them over the last rise in the road before it ran out in a wide sweeping meadow, cradled in a deep bend in the river and overlooked by an arc of rugged hills, rising high above the property. It was both picturesque and secure, allowing only one way in, with the foothills of the Peak District forming one natural boundary and the River Wye another. They stopped and climbed out to survey the prospect.

Both Darcy and Richard could sense that Carr was impressed. He said nothing, but while his silence implied that he was at a loss for words, his countenance proclaimed that he was well pleased with what he saw.

The land was both fair and productive, the fields well tended, the riverbanks thick with flowers. The house, an old but solid early Georgian building, stood on rising land backed by its own woods, and beyond the orchard lay the paddocks and stables of the Rushmore stud.

Will Camden had ridden down to meet them at the farm gate. When Richard introduced them, it was easy to see that the two men were keen to assess one another, but as Mr Carr held out his hand and said, "Mr Camden, I am astonished that any man who has spent his life in this place would be willing to part with it," it was clear that Will Camden was already won over.

An hour and a half later, after they had walked over much of the grounds and inspected the stud and the house, it was clear Mr Carr's intentions were fixed. He could find nothing to say that was not good and nowhere to look which he did not admire. So determined was he to secure the place that he insisted they talk business immediately rather than wait to meet another day. Richard left Darcy with them, as they negotiated their way through the transaction, and made for home.

When Cassy met him at the foot of the stairs, he embraced her fondly and said, "Well, my dear, you have your wish and Mr Carr has his property, I think," and seeing the look of astonishment upon her face as she stood before him, a hand to her open mouth, her eyes wide like a child's, he added, "Unless something goes very wrong with the negotiations, it seems that Will Camden has a buyer for Rushmore Farm and Stud."

"But so soon? Did he not want to see any other properties?" she asked, almost disbelieving it had all happened so quickly.

"Not after he saw the property, walked around the house, inspected the stud, and patted the horses. He claimed it was just what he wanted, and if I am not mistaken, he will pay an excellent price for it, too. So, my darling, you were quite right; it is a happy transaction that satisfies everyone, and I think I deserve a reward for my part in it," he said as he took her upstairs, presumably to make good his claim.

❧

Meanwhile, Lizzie and Laura Ann had gone down to the village with Laura's governess, Miss Fenton, and on their way back were happily overtaken by Darcy and Mr Carr in the curricle. Miss Fenton had broken the heel of her shoe and was walking awkwardly and, because there was no room for all of them in the vehicle, Mr Carr gallantly leapt out and helped her in. He then lifted little Laura in, too, claiming they were both small enough to fit into his place and, as they drove on, offered his arm to Lizzie. She took it gratefully, for the road had been steep and she was tired from supporting Miss Fenton.

When they reached the house, they found that everyone had disappeared upstairs. Mr Carr went into the parlour and Lizzie, doing her duty as hostess, asked if he would like some tea.

"I would indeed," he replied and as she went to order it, he stoked up the fire. By the time she returned with the maid bringing tea and muffins, he had got a good blaze going. Lizzie dispensed the tea and toasted muffins unselfconsciously, totally at ease in her own home. Mr Carr was so completely satisfied with his day's work, he seemed to want little more than to relax in silence, while Lizzie sat watching the pictures in the fire. So they remained until the servants came in to light the lamps.

"Good heavens, it's almost dinnertime," Lizzie exclaimed and, jumping to her feet, excused herself and ran upstairs, leaving Mr Carr amidst the remains of a very pleasant afternoon tea, conscious only of feeling completely contented. He had no recollection of feeling this way ever before.

At dinner, to which everyone including the host and hostess was late, for some unaccountable reason, it was revealed, by young Darcy first and then confirmed by Mr Carr, that Will Camden and he had agreed upon a price and they were to have their lawyers meet to draw up the documents.

"If there are no legal problems affecting the sale, there should be no further delay," said Mr Carr.

Darcy chuckled. "I don't think I have ever heard of a deal done as speedily as this one. Mr Camden must be pleased."

His friend smiled. "There was no reason to delay; I was so certain it was what I wanted and Camden was happy with my offer, so I had to secure it as quickly as I could. As I said, if there are no legal obstacles to the sale, I can see no reason to wait any longer."

"And do you intend to live on the property, Mr Carr?" asked Cassy.

Carr was thoughtful, but answered unequivocally, "I certainly hope to spend some time there, quite a lot of time, in fact, since I have no other residence in England. But I do have business interests in London and Europe, which would probably take me away for a few days at a time, several times a year. Once the property is mine, I hope I may ask your advice, Dr Gardiner, on the appointment of a suitable manager. Mr Camden's steward has retired and he has not appointed anyone in his place—a sensible move since he was selling, but it does leave me with an important position to fill and I have no local knowledge at all."

Richard looked a little concerned.

"I am not the best person to advise you, Mr Carr; I rely entirely on Thomas to make appointments here. I would suggest that you consult Will Camden's uncle, Sir Thomas Camden, or better still, my father-in-law, Mr Darcy. They are the owners of the largest estates in the district and will give you sound advice on such matters."

Mr Carr was grateful for the suggestion but wondered how he might meet these two distinguished gentlemen.

"They will both be attending the first cricket match of the season next Saturday; it's a big occasion for the community—Darcy will take you along, I'm sure. Will you not, my dear?" asked Cassy.

"Of course," her son replied with great alacrity. "Everyone goes to the cricket; it's an excuse for a picnic, if the weather is kind."

"Do you play, Mr Carr?" Cassy asked, pointing out that the district teams were always looking for new talent.

"Sadly no, Mrs Gardiner. It is one aspect of my English schooling which I never quite mastered. The best I could do at school was mind the scoreboard," he confessed ruefully.

"That's good; you can help with keeping scores then," said Lizzie, and by now Mr Carr was beginning to look a little uneasy.

Next Saturday was almost a week away—he had not intended, he said, to impose on them for a further week. Perhaps he could move to the inn; he was sure he could get rooms there, he suggested.

But he was immediately discouraged from doing any such thing.

First Darcy, then Richard, and lastly Cassy assured him that there was no need at all; he was most welcome to stay.

"Besides," said Richard, "you will probably want to revisit Rushmore Farm with your attorney and make a journey to the Council at Matlock before the purchase is finally settled."

All these logical arguments, as well as the attraction of a cricket match and picnic in such congenial company, very quickly convinced Mr Carr that he should stay on.

❧

Inevitably, the matter of the portrait at Pemberley came up for discussion between Cassy and her daughters, and she was determined that she would speak with her mother before next Saturday.

She meant to discover, if possible, the identity of the young man in the green coat and how his portrait came to be in the Pemberley collection. While she could not recall the portrait in great detail, both Laura and Lizzie had supported her husband's contention that its subject bore a strong resemblance to their guest. Cassy was keen, if this were true, to uncover the connection between them.

To this end, she arranged for her husband to take her to Pemberley on the following day, being Sunday, while their son Darcy and Mr Carr made plans with Thomas for a day's fishing further up the river. Lizzie and Laura, always happy to see their grandparents, went with their parents to Pemberley.

Mr and Mrs Darcy were delighted, on returning from church, to find the Gardiners' carriage at the entrance and their visitors waiting for them in the saloon. Mrs Grantham, the housekeeper, had already produced tea, cakes, and fruit, which the girls were addressing with some enthusiasm.

Mr Darcy, who on first seeing the vehicle had feared that there was bad news from Lambton, was overjoyed when Richard informed him that his father was quite comfortable and indeed there was good news from Rushmore Farm.

"I believe Will Camden has finally got a genuine buyer," he said and Mr Darcy, ever anxious that the wrong people should not get their hands on the Camdens' farm, asked quickly, "It is not one of those dreadful buccaneers from Birmingham, is it?"

"Not at all, sir," said Richard, preparing to tell all as they walked out onto the terrace, leaving the ladies together to finish their tea.

Hardly waiting for the tea things to be removed, Cassy urged her mother to accompany her upstairs to the long gallery. Elizabeth was intrigued, and as her daughter told her of the arrival of young Darcy's friend Mr Michael Carr and his interest in Rushmore Farm, she agreed that such an intelligent and clearly eligible person should certainly be encouraged to remain as long as possible in the neighbourhood.

"It is an excellent thing for the girls to meet eligible young men, even if nothing comes of it. It is important for their self-esteem that they know how to deal with them. Your father has always said that Anne-Marie Bingley would never have accepted that dreadful bore, Mr Bradshaw, in the first place, had she been introduced to a few more interesting young men, instead of being wholly absorbed in her work with the wounded soldiers at the hospital. Now your little Lizzie is of an age when young men will take some notice of her and she of them, presumably, and the more acceptable young fellows she meets, the more easily will she make the right choice, when the time comes," said Elizabeth.

Cassy agreed absolutely with her mother. "That is exactly my contention, Mama. Richard thinks I am matchmaking, but this is not true."

Elizabeth was sympathetic and understanding. "Of course it isn't. I know that, but I'm afraid, my dear, men will think that. I remember, very clearly, each time we accepted an invitation to a ball, Papa assumed that at least one of us would come back engaged. We were merely appraising the prospects, so to speak; at least I was. Your dear Aunt Jane and Mr Bingley fell headlong in love at their very first meeting and neither would look at another person, thereafter. I do not believe young Lizzie will be in that sort of danger."

Cassy assured her mother that this was not the case at all. Lizzie, she said, was as yet totally disinterested in the prospect of matrimony. Indeed she only went to balls and parties to please her friends, who begged her to come, and occasionally to partner her brothers.

Cassandra was eager to steer the conversation and her mother in the direction of the gallery, determined to discover the identity of the man in the green coat, but sadly, when they got there, her mother was no help at all. "Dearest, I have no idea who he is, some sort of stable boy, I would say from his clothes, but as to his name... your Papa might know. See, it was done by the same artist who painted this portrait of his aunt, Mrs Fitzwilliam." She pointed to the much larger picture of a very handsome woman in a large feather-trimmed hat.

Cassy went in search of her father and, finding him in the saloon with her husband, asked, "Papa, would you come up to the gallery with me? There is a picture which interests me greatly, and Mama says you would know the subject."

Richard chuckled. "This is the mysterious subject that is causing all this interest, sir."

Mr Darcy looked surprised. Cassy had not shown much interest in the portraits before, but he could never refuse his daughter anything.

Laura Ann and Lizzie had also joined them and the entire party went upstairs and proceeded to the gallery, where Elizabeth waited in front of the two portraits.

"Now, which is it? And why has it caught your attention?" asked Mr Darcy.

"It's the young gentleman in a green coat, Grandpa," said Laura Ann, skipping to his side.

"Is that who it is?" Mr Darcy seemed astonished, having expected to be asked about one of the more esoteric paintings in his collection.

When everyone answered in the affirmative and Laura Ann added, "He looks exactly like Darcy's friend, Mr Carr," her grandfather said, in a very matter-of-fact voice, "Does he? Well, my dears, I am not entirely surprised, because that was Robert Carr, my Uncle James Fitzwilliam's stable boy."

As a cry of comprehension went up from one and all, he went on, "There is quite a story to that picture. It was all before my time, but I had it from Mrs Reynolds, who was told it by my mother, when they returned from my uncle's funeral in Ireland."

As everyone gathered around to hear the tale, Mr Darcy continued. "My aunt, the lady in the elaborate hat, was Moira Fitzwilliam, and she was a fine horsewoman. She used to get young Robert, who was very good with horses, we are told, to ride with her around the estate. It was all quite innocent, but she was very much younger than my uncle, and though the lad was only fifteen, her husband became jealous of him.

"When she had his portrait painted by the same artist who had been commissioned to do hers, he was absolutely furious and dismissed the boy and his father, who worked on the farm as well. Lord knows why, he was only a boy, but that's jealousy for you. Makes even the sanest men irrational and stupid."

"And how did these portraits come to be in your collection, Papa?" Cassy asked, now that she had seen and accounted for the resemblance between the portrait and their guest.

Mr Darcy explained, "When my uncle died, my mother, who was his cousin, went to Ireland to attend the funeral, accompanied by my father. When the will was read, they discovered that she had been left the collection of family portraits. Not all of them were particularly good or interesting, so they gave them away to other members of the family, keeping just a few, these two among them. It is possible my mother liked them more than my father did. I had quite forgotten about the stable boy until Cassy enquired today."

"I'm surprised Mr Fitzwilliam kept the one of the lad, if he was so angry about it," said Elizabeth.

"I believe it was found in his wife's private apartments; she had died of pneumonia, some years before he did," Mr Darcy explained.

"She must have been quite fond of the boy," Richard mused, and Mr Darcy pointed out that the Fitzwilliams had no sons.

"Could Robert Carr have been Mr Michael Carr's father?" young Lizzie asked, and Mr Darcy replied that it was far more likely that Robert Carr may have been the grandfather of their guest, if he was under thirty years of age.

Cassy believed the gentleman could not be more than thirty and Laura Ann, who appeared very well informed, declared that he was a few years older than their brother Darcy; he had told her so, she claimed.

"It must mean he is a grandson of Robert Carr; that would certainly account for the remarkable resemblance," said Richard, but then cautioned his wife and daughters against making any mention of this matter to their guest.

"You must not embarrass him by questioning him about his parentage," he warned.

"But how will we ever find out?" cried Laura Ann. Her grandmother smiled. "Leave it to me, my dears, I am sure we can find a way. But your Papa is quite right. It would be very unseemly to question Mr Carr about his grandfather—after all, we have no idea what may have happened after the family left the Fitzwilliams' estate."

"Oh yes, we do," said young Laura Ann again. "My brother said Mr Carr's family were forced to leave Ireland and go to America, where they worked exceedingly hard and made lots of money."

"Well then, it looks as if all's well that ends well, but I still do not think you should ask questions about his parents; that would be very rude and insensitive," said Elizabeth, and the girls promised not to bring the matter up, unless Mr Carr spoke of it himself.

By this time, Mr Darcy, tiring of the conversation, urged them to leave the gallery, which was rather cold, and Elizabeth invited them to stay to lunch. Everyone knew what a feast Sunday lunch was at Pemberley and no one was averse to accepting her invitation.

During the meal and afterwards, the talk was mainly of Mr Carr and his possible purchase of the Rushmore Farm and Stud. Elizabeth was curious to learn more about the gentleman and questioned Richard and Cassy closely about their son's friend. But Mr Darcy seemed quite sanguine about his move into the neighbourhood.

"I will admit, Richard, I have been very concerned, ever since we learned of Will Camden's intention to sell up. Over the last few years we have seen several places taken over by men from Manchester and Birmingham, with no real interest in the area and no understanding of the people here. Many of these properties have been subdivided and sold to profiteering blackguards who have done nothing at all for the community. Men and women who have lived and worked these lands for generations are being displaced by developers and rogues."

He sounded furious and Richard hastened to reassure his father-in-law that Mr Carr had given both Camden and himself an assurance that he had no intention of ever subdividing the land.

"He assures me that he wants only to enjoy what the county has to offer. He is not investing in a commercial venture," said Richard.

Lizzie, who had been listening to her grandfather, spoke up softly at this point, "I think Papa is right. Mr Carr says he would like very much to settle here, because he feels at home in these parts. His grandmother was born here, he said."

"Really?" said Elizabeth, interested again, "Did he say where?"

"Rowsley, I think," said Lizzie, trying to recall what she had heard him say, as they sat eating toasted muffins in front of the fire.

Cassy was very alert again. "That must be the girl who married Robert Carr, the stable boy. Oh, I wish I knew more of his story."

"Well, you are all going to have to be very patient and very polite and say nothing—until we can ask Mr Carr to Pemberley and let him see the portrait," said her mother, with a conspiratorial smile that had even Mr Darcy laughing at her.

"I think you can depend upon your mother, Cassy," he said, as they rose to leave the table. "She will not rest until the mystery of the stable boy has been fully resolved."

Preparations for the cricket match and the picnic seemed to take up most of everyone's time during the next few days. It was also the day of the Kympton Parish Church Fair and that kept Cassandra and her sister-in-law, Emily Courtney, who was married to the Rector, very busy indeed.

The weather, which could occasionally turn nasty at this time of year, seemed to be perfect, and much effort was being put into organising everything so it would all be just right.

Lizzie and Laura had decided that Mr Carr, since he could not play, would be the scorer. He, therefore, had to be initiated into all the complexities of scoring a game of cricket, of which he remembered very little. "Oh, don't worry too much; the umpire will make the right signals and we will tell you what you are to write down on the score sheets," said Lizzie.

"But you must not get it wrong," warned her sister, "or there will be a dreadful fuss, should one team lose by a couple of runs as a result of a scoring error!"

"This sounds more terrifying than the stock market! Darcy, your sisters have me petrified; do you really think I can do this?" he asked.

Young Darcy, who was captain of one of the teams, tried to reassure him. "There's nothing to it. Just do as they say; they know all about it." The girls laughed, but Mr Carr was feeling as nervous as ever.

Dr Gardiner was even less sympathetic. "You will be perfectly fine if you just watch the umpire and follow his signals," he said, and poor Mr Carr seemed even more confused.

This was beginning to sound more like hard work than play, he thought, but Cassandra was very kind and promised to help him if things became too difficult. "It is not as bad it sounds," she said. "There's usually lots of time between wickets falling unless there's a rout! I shall see you aren't left to cope alone. I shall find someone to help you."

"That is very good of you, Mrs Gardiner. I feel more confident now," he said, and they laughed as they watched the servants bringing in the baskets that were being unloaded from a cart in the yard. They were all to be packed with food for the match.

Mr Carr was astounded—it looked as if they were preparing to feed a regiment, he said, and Cassandra laughed and assured him that the food would all be gone very soon.

"Everyone works up an excellent appetite at the cricket, you'll see," she said, predicting that the young men in the teams would probably eat most of it. "They do get very hungry after a game," she warned.

Mr Carr could well believe it. Meanwhile, Darcy had set out for the cricket ground, where the teams were to meet before the match. It was his first year as captain of the village team and he was very keen they should win. His mother, wishing him luck at the door, watched him go with a lump in her throat. Though she never would admit it, he was her favourite and she prayed he would do well. Cassy was devoted to her children and paid the price. Love like this was so intense, it hurt.

The day had turned out crisp, mild, and bright, perfect for cricket. After an early but hearty breakfast, the family scurried to be dressed in time for the carriages, which were due to leave in an hour.

Michael Carr, who stood watching all the bustle, wondered at the effort the English would put into organising a friendly game of cricket. He had never seen anything like it.

When they reached the spot, a picturesque meadow adjacent to the Kympton churchyard, there was already a small crowd of spectators sitting around in the shade of the ancient trees, which ringed the ground. Some members of the teams, Darcy among them, were practising their skills on the green. Lizzie and Laura took charge of the scoreboard, which had been mounted on an easel, and proceeded to instruct Mr Carr in the intricate business of keeping cricket scores while attempting to enjoy the game.

Meanwhile, Cassy and her helpers were busy organising the refreshments. To all intents and purposes, their attentions appeared to be concentrated upon the picnic rather than the match. Some of the spectators had already begun to open up their hampers and baskets. The match had not even started; when Mr Carr pointed this out, Lizzie laughed, "Oh Mr Carr, you really do not know very much about cricket, do you? No match would be a success unless the spectators went home with lots of food and ale inside them. That's part of the tradition in the country." Mr Carr nodded, realising that he had much to learn if he was going to become part of this fascinating community.

On the stroke of ten, the game began, with the umpires coming out onto the field and the visiting players following, led by their captain. A hearty cheer went up; the home team was going to bat first.

From then on, Mr Carr had not a moment's rest; as each ball was bowled and either stroked back to the bowler or hit into the field for runs, his young assistants would either cheer or jeer and then urge him to record the score, which he duly did upon a score sheet.

Tim, a young apprentice assigned by Cassy to help them, would then race off to inscribe the score with white chalk on the scoreboard, to the applause of at least half the spectators.

The players, young men and old, ran, bowled, flung themselves on the grass to save a run, or leapt to catch a ball in the air to end a batsman's life at the crease, all performing seemingly impossible feats, while for the most part standing around the field in what might be mistaken for relaxed and lack-adaisical postures. Some even appeared to be asleep. This was a mere façade, for they would suddenly jerk into life and race after a ball or leap in the air to take a catch. As they did so, the "umpires" would turn around, face the spectators, and make strange, stiff gestures, which Mr Carr would not have comprehended at all, but Lizzie and Laura swiftly interpreted the signs and converted them into numbers of runs, fours, sixes, and so on, which he then wrote down on the score sheet.

Every so often, the umpire's signal meant that someone was "out" and there would be cheers or groans from all around the ground. One never knew whether the groans would be louder than the cheers, or whether some anonymous voice would call out encouragement or abuse as the wicket fell or the runs were taken.

As the day wore on, these voices became increasingly vociferous.

When the "innings" came to an end, with the last of the home-team batsmen given out on a catch behind the wicket, the girls cheered loyally as Darcy Gardiner, who had carried his bat through the entire innings, walked off the field undefeated, to tremendous applause.

Mr Carr noticed that Darcy's mother was cheering even louder than the others as he came in and disappeared into the tent that served as a dressing room for the players.

"Time for lunch," Laura Ann announced, packing up the score sheets and other impedimenta on the table. It was explained to Mr Carr that lunch was always taken between the innings, when the first team batting was "out," which in fact meant they were in and not out on the field at all, because they had lost all their wickets.

"Unless of course, they have declared," said Lizzie.

"Declared? Declared what?" he asked.

His question brought gales of giggles and it was left to young Tim to explain that occasionally a team, which had made a large number of runs, would declare their innings closed before every wicket had fallen. Despite the fact that his head was spinning with all the esoteric information he had tried to remember through the morning, Michael Carr could not deny that he was enjoying himself.

At lunchtime, Dr and Mrs Gardiner came to take him across to the very elegant tent on the other side of the ground, which housed the parties from Pemberley and Camden Hall.

"You must meet my parents," said Cassandra, and as they entered the tent, Richard made the introductions to the very tall and distinguished Mr Darcy, his lovely, amiable wife Elizabeth, and their guest, Sir Thomas Camden.

Mr Carr could see immediately to whom Cassandra Gardiner owed her looks. Striking, though not conventionally pretty, she was quite the most charming woman he had met in many years. Both her parents still retained their handsome features, softened by the years, no doubt, but remarkable nonetheless.

Michael Carr had expected to be treated with some reserve and courtesy by the Darcys, but he was overwhelmed by their genial hospitality, as they congratulated him both on his scoring of the match and his purchase of Rushmore

Farm, in that order. Quite obviously, his success at one counted almost as much as his accomplishment of the other. Mr Carr could not help but be amused as he explained that the young Misses Gardiner had done most of the hard work. He did not have to say anything more; people just nodded and shook his hand, saying, "Well done, excellent! Can't do a thing without a good scorer..."

Elizabeth Darcy caught him smiling after Sir Thomas had congratulated him heartily on his scoring, while acknowledging his purchase of the Rushmore property with a mere nod and a gruff, "Very glad to hear it."

"Mr Carr, are not your American friends as keen on their sport as we in England are?" she asked, with a barely concealed jest in her voice. He realised she was teasing and said, "Indeed, Mrs Darcy, they are, but never to the extent of enthusiasm I have seen here today at a little village cricket match!"

Elizabeth had to assure him that she had taken quite a long time to become accustomed to it herself.

"My brother-in-law, Mr Bingley, still coaches his team at Ashford Park; unhappily he is not able to join us, having suffered an injury to his knee at their last outing! I am grateful Mr Darcy is only the patron of our team—if he were as involved, we would hardly see him at home," she said, with a light laugh, as their grandson, Darcy Gardiner, arrived to the applause of his admirers. He was quite clearly the hero of the day. Sir Thomas and Mr Darcy were both lavish in their praise of his excellent innings and urged him on to win when the opposing team went in to bat.

Darcy promised he would do his best. "I can hardly wait, sir; I think we have their measure," he said, pretending to bowl an orange he had picked up from the table, before rushing away to join his team, their advice ringing in his ears.

Mr Carr commented on Darcy's popularity and Elizabeth asked, "Have you known my grandson long, Mr Carr?"

"Long enough to recognise him for one of the finest young men of my acquaintance, Mrs Darcy," he replied, adding, "We met in London at the home of a mutual friend some eighteen months ago. I was only briefly in England on business, but we got on so well together, I sought him out when I returned last year and we have been good friends ever since. He is an exceptionally intelligent young man, and charming with it; since I have been in Derbyshire meeting his family, I can see where he gets it."

Elizabeth looked quickly across at him and it was not just the way he said

"Der-by-shire"; she hoped he was not flattering her with good reports of her family. Seeing his expression and judging from the sincerity of his voice, she decided he was not.

It was almost time for the teams to go out on the field again, when a loud clap of thunder exploded across the grounds and Elizabeth, startled, covered her ears with her hands. Several people went outside to take a look at the sky, which was a brilliant blue with hardly a cloud in sight.

Laura Ann came to get Mr Carr. "Do hurry; we have to start keeping scores again," she urged. Yet, even as the players took the field and the batsmen took their places, there was a further rumble in the distance. This time the entire crowd groaned as one, seeing, far away over the peaks, a Summer storm brewing.

With the wind from the West, it was only a matter of time before the storm would be upon them. A few more overs were bowled, a wicket or two fell, and then the scudding clouds were over the ground; minutes later the rain came, falling, as it often did in Summer, not gently but in sheets.

The spectators all ran for cover, but Lizzie and Laura insisted that the score sheets be collected and protected from the rain first.

"You cannot lose the score sheets; it's important for the records," said Laura, and Lizzie agreed, making sure everything was packed up before they ran indoors.

Mr Carr was wet and not a little put out. He had to hide his relief, while everyone around him was expressing their disappointment, especially young Darcy, who was confident they could have had the visitors out before tea.

The rain persisted for over an hour and, even when it ceased, the light was too poor to allow a resumption of play. What was worse, there were still heavy clouds above the hills, threatening to fall down upon them at any moment. With no hope of continuing, the match, sadly, was declared to be a draw and the crowds, disconsolate and damp, began to wend their way home. They'd had a good day, but were disappointed not to see a result.

It was as they were packing up that Mrs Darcy sent word to her daughter, inviting everyone in their party back to Pemberley for tea. Cassy was delighted. She knew immediately that her mother had a plan in mind. Within minutes, she had spread the word, and soon they were packing themselves into their carriages for the short journey to Pemberley.

Mr Carr was at first not sure he should go. He was wet and weary of cricket talk. Besides, he had not been invited specifically, he said to Mrs Gardiner, and he needed to change his coat, which was quite damp.

"Oh, what nonsense is this, Mr Carr? Of course you are invited. You are with our party, are you not? What is more, you have been working so hard to keep scores, we cannot let you go home alone and sit by yourself in front of the fire. Of course you must come to Pemberley. As for your coat, I agree it is damp and we must have you out of it or you may catch cold, but it is quicker to drive to Pemberley than to return to Matlock. Come now, Richard will take you and you can have one of my father's coats until yours is dry."

She was so persuasive and would not take no for an answer, it seemed churlish to refuse. When little Laura Ann added her weight ("Do you not want to see Pemberley, Mr Carr?" she asked. "It is beautiful."), he could no longer argue and went without further ado to join his host who was waiting to convey him in his vehicle.

❦

Mr Carr's first glimpse of Pemberley was overwhelming. The rain had passed and the afternoon sun was falling upon the stonework and glass as they drove into the park. Richard Gardiner, who was by now so familiar with the place, he knew every part of it, fell silent, allowing his guest to take in the particular beauty of the house and surrounding grounds.

As they crossed the stone bridge and drove towards the house, Mr Carr said in a voice that betrayed his astonishment, "This is superb—a most magnificent estate, Dr Gardiner."

When they alighted, entered the hall, and were then shown into the splendid saloon, which looked out over the park, he continued, "I have seen many richer and more opulent mansions in America, and older, more historic houses in France, but this surpasses them all.

"It is grand without presumption, noble in its proportions, yet not in the least ostentatious. Mr and Mrs Darcy are truly blessed to have such a home."

Richard could not but agree and, while the servants were busy fetching a coat for Mr Carr to wear until his own was dried and pressed, he prescribed some hot sweet tea and whisky to ward off a cold. When Mr and Mrs Darcy and the rest of the family arrived, both men were enjoying the comfort of an excellent blaze.

"I can see they have been looking after you, Mr Carr," said Elizabeth as the gentlemen rose. "No, do sit down and enjoy your tea while I change my shoes. I cannot afford to catch cold; it would ruin the Summer for me."

The gentlemen were left on their own until the younger members of the family arrived and then it was all cricket talk, as the misfortune of the rain-drenched match was discussed again. Mr Carr was beginning to wonder if they talked of anything else, when Mrs Darcy returned and, taking pity on him, said, "Mr Carr, I am sure you have heard quite enough of the cricket for one day, probably for the whole Summer; would you like to come with me and see something of the house?"

He leapt up to join her. "Oh, indeed I would, Mrs Darcy; I have heard much about Pemberley from young Darcy, but nothing prepared me for this. I have been truly astonished by its elegance and beauty. I would love to see more."

Once again, Elizabeth, wary of flattery, looked sharply across at her companion and, again, she was sure there was only sincerity, despite the extravagance of his words.

Perhaps, she decided, Americans were more lavish with praise. She had heard they were, but not having known any of them before, she could not judge. Mr Carr was probably just being enthusiastic, she thought.

As they went upstairs, Elizabeth saw Cassandra cross the hall and called to her to join them. Understanding her mother's meaning, Cassy followed them up the stairs. Approaching the gallery, Elizabeth took them past the portraits of Darcys of generations long gone, until they approached that part of the room where the recent family portraits were hung. There, on the wall, beside the portrait of Mrs Fitzwilliam and the smaller picture of the young man in a green coat, was a singularly lovely cameo-style portrait of Lizzie Gardiner. It had been started last year, when Lizzie had stayed with her grandparents while her parents travelled overseas, and had only recently been framed and hung. It had a delicacy that was very appealing indeed.

Cassy, seeing the finished work for the first time, was amazed at her mother's clever scheme of drawing attention to all three pictures grouped together on the wall. She said nothing, waiting for some response from Mr Carr, but for once he seemed to have been struck dumb, not, as it happened, by the charming portrait of Lizzie, but by the picture of the young man in a green coat, which hung beside it.

Looking at the picture, with Mr Carr standing in front of it, the resemblance was quite uncanny. Cassy had no doubt of the connection between the two men.

When he did speak, having recovered his voice, Mr Carr immediately acknowledged that the portrait of young Miss Gardiner was beautiful and did the young lady justice, but soon afterwards, he had turned to Elizabeth with the question she had been expecting. "Mrs Darcy, may I ask if you know who the young man in this picture might be?"

As Cassandra stepped back and held her breath, her mother said, in a voice so casual as to be astonishing, "I know very little of these family portraits, Mr Carr; you will understand that many of them were acquired before I came to Pemberley. Both these portraits were brought to Pemberley from Ireland by Mr Darcy's parents. It is thought the lad used to work on the Fitzwilliams' estate and I have heard Mr Darcy say he was one Robert Carr."

The words were hardly out of her mouth, when he, almost bursting with impatience, cried, "Robert Carr! Why Mrs Darcy, then this young man must be my grandfather! Is anything more known about him? When was this portrait painted?" he asked, eager for more information.

Even as Cassy watched, her mother explained with great sensitivity the connection between the portrait of young Robert Carr the stable boy and that of Mrs Moira Fitzwilliam. "This was all very long ago, of course, when Mr Darcy was a boy, but Mrs Reynolds knew it all and related some of it to Mr Darcy," she explained and so, very gradually, was the mystery of the boy in a green coat revealed to Mr Carr.

He was truly astounded by his fortuitous—as he thought—discovery. Understandably, for he had heard one side of the story from his own parents, but there had been no suggestion whatsoever of a link with the distinguished Darcy family of Derbyshire.

"I have always wanted to discover the story of my grandfather's flight from Ireland," he confessed. "I knew only that he had married a young woman from the village of Rowsley in Derbyshire, while he was working as a groom for a family in Derby and she was the children's governess. I believed I would have to travel to Ireland to uncover the rest. I cannot tell you how delighted I am, Mrs Darcy, and how very grateful to you for having given me this opportunity. I must thank you very much indeed."

Now it was Elizabeth who was beginning to feel uneasy, for all his gratitude was based upon a belief that she had not contrived this entire episode. Cassy was watching her mother with some anxiety, wondering what she would do, when Mr Carr had a very particular request: "Mrs Darcy, I wonder if may have your permission to have a copy made for my father? It would give him and my mother so much pleasure to see it. Unfortunately, there is not a single likeness of my grandfather in the family, save for a small pencil sketch done by an itinerant artist. A copy of this painting would be a wonderful gift. Would you permit it?" he asked, and Cassy could see how keen he was for her answer.

Elizabeth said she would need to ask her husband, but she was confident he would have no objection. Mr Carr was overjoyed.

As they went downstairs together, those gathered in the saloon, oblivious of what had happened in the gallery, were enjoying the excellent afternoon tea that Mrs Grantham had provided. They greeted Mr Carr and proceeded to congratulate him all over again on his fine performance as a scorer or his acquisition of Rushmore Farm or both. It was plain he had made his mark in the community on both counts.

Cassy went directly to tell her husband of Mr Carr's response to the portrait of the young man in the green coat, while Elizabeth took Mr Darcy aside to pass on Mr Carr's request. As she did so, she revealed to him the rest of Michael Carr's story. Mr Darcy smiled. "So it is as I said: he is the grandson of Robert Carr the stable boy," he said.

"Indeed, so it seems, and he is exceedingly pleased to have discovered the portrait here, for it seems the family has no likeness of his grandfather at all, save for a pencil sketch. You would not mind if he had it copied, would you dearest?" Elizabeth asked, confident of his reply.

Mr Darcy had no objection at all. "Of course not," he replied. "It is a pretty piece of work, but not one of any great value—he can have as many copies made as he likes."

Pleased, Elizabeth told their guest of her husband's consent and earned his undying gratitude. "I cannot thank you enough, Mrs Darcy. I shall proceed to Derby at the earliest opportunity and engage a suitable artist for the work," he said.

Mr Carr was plainly delighted and could scarcely wait to get back to Matlock with the Gardiners, before revealing his "discovery" to the entire family. He had no suspicions at all of the elaborate scheme that had been hatched to bring him and his ancestor's portrait together.

❦

Much later, when all their visitors had left and they were alone in their private sitting room, Elizabeth asked her husband a question she had been turning over in her mind all evening. "Do you not mind, my dear, that Mr Carr has decided to purchase the Rushmore property?"

Darcy, who had been contemplating the fire and a particularly enjoyable afternoon, seemed surprised by her question.

"Mind? Why should I mind, Lizzie?" he replied. "I have never had any interest in the place, though I confess, I was concerned that it may go to some crass developer from Birmingham. I have made it plain to Will Camden that I would rather not have one of them as a neighbour."

"You do not mind, then, that Mr Carr, who is the grandson of your Uncle Fitzwilliam's stable boy, will buy a valuable property in the neighbourhood?" she asked, seeming to press him further. Mr Darcy appeared affronted and hurt by this suggestion.

"Lizzie, how could you ask such a question? Surely, you cannot be serious? Mr Carr appears to be a young man of substance and good sense. Why would his grandfather's occupation have any bearing on his suitability to own and manage Rushmore? Indeed, might one not argue that an interest in horses appears to run in the family and that may well be a good thing, if he is to make a success of the stud?"

He was clearly outraged, as he went on.

"Besides, I believe my uncle treated young Robert Carr very badly. As Mrs Reynolds told it, the lad was totally innocent and yet, because my uncle was a jealous old man with a pretty young wife, he dismissed the boy and his father at a time when work was hard to get, condemning the family to a life of privation and possible penury. I am glad to learn that he came through it well and the family has made good in America. Now, if his grandson has returned to live in England and wishes to purchase Will Camden's farm, for what I am informed by Sir Thomas is a very fair price, why should I mind?"

Elizabeth smiled and went to sit beside him on the sofa. "I did not think you would, my dear; it is a sort of poetic justice, is it not?" she asked, taking his hand in hers.

"It certainly is and I am glad of it," he said and then, turning to her, asked, "Were you really testing me, Lizzie?" Realising from her expression that she was only playing a game, his reproof came swiftly, "I thought you knew me better than to ask such a question."

She laughed and reassured him that indeed she did. Elizabeth remembered how very far her husband had come over the years of their marriage from the haughty, reserved man she had met at the dance in the assembly hall at Meryton. *That* Mr Darcy, who had found it intolerable to dance with a lady below his station in life, unless she were exceptionally beautiful, would scarcely have acknowledged the existence of a stable boy, much less approve of a man whose grandfather had been one. She could not tell if her husband shared her memories; she thought not, for they had long put all those painful days behind them.

But Elizabeth was proud of the man he had become and, by asking the question as she had done, she had sought only to reiterate all those qualities she loved and admired in him. So sound was their understanding of one another, so close their intimacy, that it did not take long for her to convince him that she had never seriously believed him capable of such prejudice, nor for her to be forgiven for having wounded his feelings with her provocative question.

Meanwhile, Cassy, having told Richard the story of Mr Carr and the portrait of his grandfather, wondered how her husband would respond to the news. In fact, he responded hardly at all, merely acknowledging that Mr Carr must have been very gratified and, indeed, so must she and the girls, for now the mystery of his resemblance to the portrait had been resolved.

Cassy put his lack of interest down to weariness; it had been a tiring day. She could not, however, help contemplating the possibility that her husband's response might be different, were Mr Carr to become, at some future date, a suitor for their daughter's hand.

But, she told herself sensibly, he was not and it did not signify.

꩜

As the Summer waned into Autumn, the days were crowded with parties, village fairs, and well dressings, with walks and picnics in the dales.

There was some talk of business failures and recession, but there was prosperity, too. The countryside seemed salubrious and bountiful, especially to

Mr Carr, who had stayed on in Derbyshire, moving to live at Rushmore Farm following the departure for New South Wales of Will Camden and his family.

Michael Carr was eager to become acquainted with his staff, his tenants, and the people of the neighbourhood in which he proposed to make his new home. To this end, he assiduously attended the county shows and meetings of the council and, though a Roman Catholic, even made an appearance at the Kympton Church Harvest Thanksgiving Service. The Rector, Reverend Courtney, welcomed him and the congregation showed their pleasure when many stopped to greet him afterwards.

At the local inn, he soon made a friend of the landlord and learned that a couple of men from Cromford were still in the area, looking at properties, and had been especially disappointed at losing the Rushmore stud to him. "You'd be wise to watch out for them, sir," the innkeeper had warned. "They're a rough lot and seem like sore losers, too."

Mr Carr was so pleased with life at the moment, it was unlikely that such a mild caution would worry him. He made no mention of it to anyone. He had seen the two men around the district, but took little notice of their presence.

In the Autumn, too, Darcy Gardiner went up to London to hear Mr Colin Elliott, who was engaged to their cousin Anne-Marie Bingley, make his final speech as a member of the Tory Party. It was to be a momentous occasion and Darcy was determined to be there. With him went young Lizzie, who, after spending a week in London with her brother, was to proceed to Cambridge to make good the promise made by her mother to her aunt and uncle.

Brother and sister had both promised faithfully to write to their mother, but Cassy knew better than to count on her son for good letters. When he did write, they were always short, scrappy little pieces, in which he merely gave her bits of London news, which she already knew.

This time, however, he reported faithfully on Mr Elliott's speech and the party given by Mr and Mrs James Wilson to celebrate the occasion of James Wilson's twentieth year in the Parliament. Although it was not a very satisfactory account, being brief and somewhat disjointed, it was better than nothing, Cassy thought with a sigh, as she opened up the second letter that had arrived that day.

This was from Lizzie and was, as usual, well written and full of news, all that a good letter should be. Cassy sat down to enjoy it.

Lizzie wrote:

Dearest Mama and Papa,

It is hard to believe that it is almost three weeks since I left you to come to London and a fortnight since my last letter. I had hoped to write again before leaving London, but Darcy was always wanting to go somewhere and, when I was at home, someone would call to see him and want to leave a message for him. He seems to be very popular, and there was very little time to spare for myself and even less time to write.

While we were in London, we were both asked to a party at our Uncle Wilson's place in Grosvenor Street to celebrate his twentieth year in the Commons. My brother had already been to the Parliament that afternoon. It was a grand affair with an entire chamber ensemble playing all evening and dozens of very distinguished and important people present.

Anne-Marie was there with her husband-to-be Mr Elliott, who is very handsome indeed, though quiet and serious looking. Anna Bingley assured us he was not at all dull, though, and Darcy said his speech to the Commons was excellent. Everyone there seemed to agree. When he came into the room with Anne-Marie on his arm, there was applause. I thought it was to congratulate the engaged couple, who looked very handsome together, but Darcy said, "Don't be so silly, Lizzie, it's because Mr Elliott has just resigned from the Tory Party." It seems he is to support Mr Gladstone in the Parliament. Is that good? My Uncle Wilson seemed to think it was. He appeared very elated about it and congratulated Mr Elliott on his decision. Anne-Marie looked very beautiful, as always.

We left for Cambridge at the end of the week. What a change it is from London! Life here is very quiet and sober, quieter still in the home of my Uncle Julian Darcy. He, when he is at home, spends almost all his time in his study, except when he joins us at meals or goes upstairs to bed at night.

Cassandra sighed, "Poor Julian, still working too hard…" and read on.

Aunt Josie is quiet, too, but in a different way. She writes and reads and writes some more and reads again. Some afternoons she has visitors, like the Misses Wallace-Groom. Dora and Hetty visit often (they must be Dorothy and Henrietta, I suppose, but no one calls them that) and they read poetry and talk about it together for hours. A gentleman named Barrett comes, too, and reads with them. Occasionally, they read for him and he listens and comments upon their poems, and they are all very pleased with themselves.

Poor little Anthony finds all this very boring and I am usually sent to walk with him in the park or play in the nursery, which I would much rather do, for I find their poetry very dull indeed.

When we take tea together, I help Susan bring in the tea and cakes, and the Misses Wallace-Groom tell me all about their adventures during the last London Season. Aunt Josie is not very interested, but she does like them because they like her poetry. I heard her tell Mr Barrett one day, while we were waiting for them to arrive, that they are both 'very discerning young women.' I had to look it up and found it means 'discriminating or refined in taste' and I have to say I could see no sign of it in either of them. Their dress is very modish, but they care nothing for literature or music and neither can play a single instrument or sing.

What is more, I fear they are not altogether sincere, because when Aunt Josie is busy reading her poetry, I have noticed Miss Hetty Wallace-Groom trying to flirt with Mr Barrett. (Hetty is pretty and plump and laughs a lot, while Dora is thin and serious.)

Despite all this, I am sure, Mama, that you will be pleased to hear that Aunt Josie is more active and cheerful and, though she does not speak very much of matters other than her poetry and little Anthony, she does at least come downstairs every day and takes her evening meal with the rest of us.

According to her maid, Susan, she is much improved since last Spring. Susan is, I think, her only real friend and confidante. She is so very loyal, Mama, I think she would do anything for Aunt Josie.

The letter concluded affectionately, as always, with love to all her family and was followed by a postscript…

Tomorrow, we are to go out to a reading of a play by a friend of Mr Barrett, Andrew Jones. While I am not really looking forward to it, Aunt

Josie is very excited indeed. Mr Jones is the son of a publisher and very important, she says. I don't know him at all.

Susan is here to take this to the post, so I must close, with more love... etc.

Cassandra read the letter through twice before putting it away.

It was just like all Lizzie's letters, vivid, with plenty of detail and opinions. Cassy could visualise clearly the grand party at the Wilsons' town house in Grosvenor Street and the contrast with the quiet little house in Cambridge where her brother lived. She could picture the scene, with Josie reading poetry in the parlour, and wondered what the Misses Wallace-Groom were really like. Clearly Lizzie did not like them.

Josie was an intelligent young woman; Cassy could not understand her friendship with such girls as Lizzie had described. They seemed shallow, with small, uncultivated minds. Why, she wondered, would they court Josie's friendship? As for Mr Barrett, she recalled the maid Susan's tale of his promise to publish Josie's book. Could that be the reason behind her cheerfulness? Cassy wondered. She hoped in her heart, for her brother's sake, that this was the case.

A week later, a note from Anna Bingley, her cousin Jonathan's wife, brought more hope. An invitation had arrived for Anne-Marie's wedding in December to Mr Colin Elliott. In a note enclosed with it, Anna had written to say that Julian and Josie had been invited, too, and had accepted.

Anna wrote:

They are to arrive the day before the wedding day and stay with us at Netherfield Park for a few days. We are all looking forward to seeing them again.

Cassy was so pleased, she could not wait for her husband to return, so keen was she to take the good news to her parents. If Julian and Josie had accepted the invitation to the wedding, it must mean that Josie had recovered her health and her spirits. Taken together with Lizzie's letter, this was an excellent sign and Cassy knew her mother would be especially happy to hear it. She sent for the small carriage and drove over to Pemberley.

Elizabeth was overjoyed. Mother and daughter celebrated their good news together, speculating about the possibility that Josie was feeling much better because her work was at least being appreciated by her friends. They knew very little about the Misses Wallace-Groom, but of Mr Barrett they had heard more.

"And, who knows, my dear, she may even have an offer from a publisher. Did you not say this Mr Barrett was in the book trade?"

"Indeed, Mama, we had that from Josie herself and now Lizzie says his friend Mr Jones is a publisher. I do hope you are right. Julian will be delighted," said Cassy, unwilling to spoil the moment with any niggling doubts about the credibility of their scheme. It was sufficient for her that Julian and Josie were to be at Anne-Marie's wedding.

They had both been looking out for Mr Darcy, who had walked down to the stables to take a look at a colt he had purchased for his grandson.

"Your father is very enthusiastic about this colt; he thinks he will do well for young James in a year or two," said Elizabeth.

Cassy went over to the window where her mother sat and looking out, said, "There he is, Mama, over by the lake; he's coming this way."

She was eager to give her father the good news, too.

"There's a man with him. Who is it, Cassy? I have not got my glasses with me, so I cannot make him out," said her mother.

"Why, I believe it is Mr Carr and he seems to have arrived in Richard's curricle. I wonder what brings him here..." she mused, then recalling suddenly that her husband Richard had taken the curricle that morning, Cassy exclaimed, "Oh, my God!" left her mother, and raced down the stairs, crossed the hall in a few seconds, and ran down the wide steps of Pemberley House to meet Mr Carr and her father as they approached.

She could think only of her husband and what might have happened to him. One look at their faces told her that something serious had occurred. As Mr Darcy came towards her, she cried out, "Papa, what is it? What has happened? Is it Richard? Has there been an accident? Tell me, please..."

Her father put his arms around her and she could sense the sorrow in his voice, as he said, quietly, "It is Mr Gardiner, my dear. Richard has been called to Lambton urgently; he has sent Mr Carr for you. You must go at once; your mother and I will follow very soon."

Cassy did not know whether it was sorrow or relief, but she could not control the sobs that shook her as she stood holding fast to her father.

Elizabeth, who had followed her out and heard his words, was standing at the entrance with tears running down her cheeks.

Her dear Uncle Gardiner was gone.

Mr Darcy went to comfort her, while Cassy collected her basket and shawl and returned to find Mr Carr waiting for her beside the curricle. He helped her into her seat, placed a rug around her knees, and took the vehicle around the drive and out onto the road to travel the few miles to the Gardiners' place at Lambton.

Mr Carr did not speak and Cassy was glad of his silence. There was nothing she could say, no way she could explain. The bad news that the family had dreaded, yet known was inevitable, had come at last.

When they reached Oakleigh, the Gardiners' property, Mr Carr helped Cassy alight. She thanked him and went directly indoors to the room where she knew the family would be gathered. She found them—Mrs Gardiner, Caroline, and Emily—in tears, trying to comfort one another. She embraced them all, sharing their loss.

Richard, who had been summoned by his son Edward, had only just reached his father's bedside as he passed peacefully into unconsciousness. Seeing Cassy arrive, he came to her and gathered her into a tight embrace as she wept. He knew how dearly she had been loved by his father and with what devotion that affection had been returned. Cassy had been as dear to Mr Gardiner as his own two daughters.

He recalled his father's words on the day of their wedding: "You are a very fortunate young man, Richard," he had said. "I know of no other young woman in the world to whom you could have been wed with greater certainty of happiness."

The years had proved him right.

His younger brother Robert and his wife Rose were away in London with their children. Mrs Gardiner, her face still taut with the strain of many anxious days and nights, came to ask if Richard could arrange to send them an urgent message by electric telegraph.

"There are others, too, who must be informed—Emma and James and Jonathan, of course," she said and he assured her it would all be done, urging her to rest, lest her own health should be affected.

Recalling that Mr Carr, not wishing to intrude upon the family's grief, was waiting in the parlour, Cassy said, "Richard, could we not ask for Mr Carr's help?" and as they went out to find him, Mrs Gardiner called to them, "You must inform Julian, Richard; your father was very fond of Julian."

By the time Mr and Mrs Darcy arrived, Richard and Mr Carr were busy compiling lists and composing suitable messages to be despatched to the family and many friends of Mr Gardiner. Meanwhile, Cassy sought to comfort her sister-in-law Caroline, who was so grief-stricken, she had to be taken upstairs to bed.

Hearing the carriage from Pemberley arrive, Cassy came downstairs to receive her parents. Mr Darcy looked so profoundly sad and Elizabeth could not restrain her grief, as they embraced their daughter again before seeking out Mrs Gardiner. The Gardiners held a very special place in their hearts. Having been instrumental in bringing the couple together all those years ago, they had remained loving and intimate friends.

As well, Mr Gardiner, by inviting Mr Darcy to become a partner in his lucrative trading company, had opened up an entirely new world of business and commerce for the young gentleman from Derbyshire, whose interests and experience had hitherto been constrained by his exclusive and rather restricted circle of acquaintances.

Darcy had been very grateful. For him and Elizabeth, this was going to be a very harrowing funeral. It was probably the realisation of this fact that prompted Cassy to offer to help with the arrangements at Pemberley.

Mr Gardiner had asked that he be laid to rest in the churchyard there and Cassy knew preparations would have to be made for the relatives and friends who would attend, as well as those who would be accommodated at Pemberley. She knew, too, that in the absence of her brother Julian, her parents would need and welcome her help.

"Oh, if only Lizzie were here," she said with a sigh, as they returned that night to Matlock. "Emily and Caroline are both so desolate, I have not the heart to ask for their help."

Richard assured her that he would always be there if she needed him and urged her to seek the help of the Granthams, husband and wife, who were manager and housekeeper at Pemberley and had been with the Darcys for many years.

"They will know exactly what is required and carry out all the work with their usual efficiency, I am sure," he said and Cassy said she was confident they would.

"Besides," said her husband, "it will be best, my love, if you were not to be seen taking over what should by rights be Julian's role." Cassy agreed; she had no desire to do so, but with her brother away in Cambridge, it was the least she could do for her parents.

"I am sure Julian will understand," she said, to which Richard replied, "I am quite certain *he* will, but will everyone else?"

They both realised that gossip in the neighbourhood was best avoided.

Cassandra worked hard but with great discretion over the next few days. Her only consolation was that keeping busy stopped her from weeping and, of course, there was the hope that her brother and possibly Josie would soon arrive, bringing her daughter Lizzie with them.

Sadly, it was a hope that faded as the day of the funeral dawned.

No one had arrived from Cambridge, nor had any word been received, until the very last moment, when a telegraphed message was delivered apologising for Julian's late arrival and his wife's inability to attend.

It meant Lizzie Gardiner was late, too.

Even as the funeral service began in the church at Pemberley, there was no sign of Julian and, when the lesson assigned to him had to be read, it was Mr Darcy who stepped up to read it. Cassandra knew how deeply disappointed and hurt her parents would be, their personal loss exacerbated by the absence of their son.

As the service was ending, Julian arrived with Lizzie, who slipped into a pew beside her sister Laura Ann, while Julian entered unnoticed and stood at the back of the church. Only Lizzie knew he was there, until it was over and they came out into the churchyard and saw him standing outside.

It was Cassy who, as the mourners and friends began to leave, took her father's arm and moved him away from the graveside, while Jonathan Bingley hastened to support his aunt and help her into the carriage that waited to take them to Pemberley.

Later, Julian apologised to his family and especially to Mrs Gardiner; his work, he claimed, had delayed him and caused them to miss the coach. As for Josie, she was still not strong enough to make long journeys and had been advised to stay home, he said. Indeed, he was compelled to return to Cambridge immediately following the funeral and would not even be staying the night at Pemberley.

Mrs Gardiner nodded and concealed her feelings behind her widow's veil, but Cassy could not. Her tears made it plain, if her words did not, that she was bitterly disappointed with her brother's conduct.

"How could he? How could he be so unfeeling, so inconsiderate of others? Oh, Richard, I am so angry," she cried, her voice rising in exasperation. But he would not be drawn into recriminations.

Grief, he said, was hard enough to bear without the added burden of anger. "Hush, my dear, this is not worthy of you," he said. "Julian has his own problems to cope with. Let us not contaminate our sorrow with anger and bitterness; it will only heighten the pain and prove far more difficult to heal."

As on many previous occasions, his wise counsel and love sustained her, letting her grieve without rancour and find strength enough to support her parents.

Cassy recalled vividly the days after her brother William had been killed, when her parents, in the depths of their terrible grief, had all but forgotten her own. It had been to Richard she had gone for help. Richard, to whom she had become engaged on that fateful day, had held her and comforted her, loved and consoled her until she found peace within her heart, in the midst of a veritable maelstrom of emotions.

Then, too, there had been anger and great bitterness. Unable to reach her parents, she had felt alone and afraid. She had been much younger then and had turned to him because he was older and mature. Now she relied upon him, confident that he could help her bear any pain, knowing his strength would enhance her own.

꘎

Relatives and friends returning to Pemberley after the funeral were surprised to find Cassandra receiving them and making arrangements for their stay. Her strength and loyalty were commendable, they all agreed, as they watched her move quietly, confer with the staff, organise meals, quieten fretful children, comfort grieving relatives, and handle with no fuss at all the myriad of things that the occasion demanded. Her gentle manner concealed a methodical and efficient mind that had always stood her in good stead.

Elizabeth and her sister Jane had retired upstairs with Mrs Gardiner and Caroline, until all but the closest relatives had departed. Jonathan and Anna Bingley were staying on at Pemberley, but Mrs Gardiner and her daughters wished to return to Lambton and left accompanied by Edward and Darcy.

It had been a most difficult day, with grief compounded by resentment. Having helped their parents through the evening, Richard and Cassandra left for home, close to exhaustion. Their sons, having returned from Lambton, had dined and waited up for them, but young Lizzie was fast asleep on the sofa. Having travelled through the previous night with Julian, she was weary.

When their parents returned, the brothers were giving vent to their own vexation at some of the day's events. Darcy was most censorious, unable to believe that his Uncle Julian had actually been late to the funeral on account of his work.

"It is quite incredible that he should make such an excuse. It is far more likely that Aunt Josie was the cause. Ask Lizzie; she has told us already that they were late for the coach because Aunt Josie was arguing with him. I think it is absolutely abominable behaviour on his part."

Edward, who had carried the heavy responsibility of watching over Mr Gardiner in the last difficult days as his life ebbed away, was no less critical, but characteristically unwilling to apportion blame.

"Darcy, it is of no use at all to blame Aunt Josie; after all, if our uncle had wished to leave the house in time, he could have done so. He is using Aunt Josie as an excuse for his own inability to do his duty. It is his own indecisive nature that is at fault. He vacillates and will not take action when he needs to."

Darcy was about to contest this thesis, when their father, who had just awakened Lizzie and sent her upstairs to bed, intervened to bring an end to the argument.

"What good does it do now?" he asked. "Your grandfather loved Julian dearly; he admired his dedication to scientific study and his desire for independence. Unfortunately, Julian appears to have neither the wit nor the sensibility to understand the value of such feelings.

"Doubtless he has his own troubles. Josie is not yet recovered from her illness and Julian is reluctant to do or say anything that might worsen her condition. He has other problems, too, which are largely self-inflicted; he insists upon working all hours, gets very little sleep or fresh air, and takes insufficient nourishment. The pallor of his skin is evidence of this. I pity him; it must be a wretched life," he said and made to leave the room.

At the door, he turned to his sons and thanked them for their help through the period of their grandfather's illness, especially Edward, for his close attention to Mr Gardiner during the past few weeks.

"I cannot thank you enough for all you have done and I know your grand-mother feels the same," and then he stopped and added, "Your Mama has borne an almost unbearable burden for many months now; not merely has she done a great deal of work, but she has carried a weight of hurt and anguish, compounded by the strange behaviour of her brother and his wife, of which we have just spoken. I know you will not wish to encumber her with any further sorrow by debating the guilt or otherwise of Julian Darcy's conduct in this house."

Both young men rose and nodded gravely, accepting without question the wisdom and good sense of their father's words.

Upstairs, Richard found Cassy, who had gone directly to their room. Like a hurt child, who longs for the comfort of its familiar bed, she had crept, fully dressed, under the covers, lying there still wide awake and tearful. There was no mistaking the source of her anguish, yet Richard was wary of aggravating her grief by trying to speak of it. Cassy was sore and needed soothing.

Gently, he helped her take down her hair and get out of her mourning gown. He put away her clothes, fetched her nightgown, and drew the bedclothes up around her. She thanked him and, when he cradled her in his arms, letting the weariness overwhelm her, she fell asleep at last.

END OF PART ONE

MR DARCY'S DAUGHTER

Part Two

THE FAMILIES WERE TO meet again, at Netherfield Park, for the wedding of Jonathan Bingley's daughter Anne-Marie and Mr Colin Elliott, MP, in December of that year. It was to be, by their own choice, a quiet occasion. Neither the bride-to-be nor her groom had wished for any fuss, and following the death of Mr Gardiner, their families were happy to comply. Preparations were afoot, however, for a modest celebration, with the village church being refurbished and the choir under the direction of the Rector, Mr Griffin, practising with great dedication for the occasion.

It was on returning from one of these sessions, during which she had been called upon to assist at the church organ, that Anna Bingley found her husband reading a long and informative letter from his mother, Mrs Jane Bingley of Ashford Park. It brought news that created some considerable interest, if not exactly a controversy, among members of the family at Netherfield.

After the usual familial greetings and enquiries, Mrs Bingley wrote:

...and my dear Jonathan and Anna, I am told by my dear sister Lizzie that the news was quite a shock to several people present, including Mr Robert Gardiner and his wife Rose. It had been supposed, I expect, that when Mr Gardiner passed on, his younger son Robert would take over the

running of the Commercial Trading Company and the share of the business held by his father.

Everyone, except Mr Darcy, who was his closest confidant, believed this to be the case. Indeed, I know that my Aunt Gardiner did and so apparently did Robert and Rose. In fact, it might be said that the family had assumed that control of the company would pass to Robert.

Unhappily for Robert, however, it now appears that Mr Gardiner had decided quite some time ago, for the will had not been recently altered, that Caroline, his eldest child, not Robert, would manage the business and inherit his shares in the enterprise, with a life interest to his wife, of course.

Mr Darcy seems to have been the only person, apart from his solicitor, in whom our uncle confided and he kept his counsel very well. Not even your Aunt Lizzie was aware of the arrangement.

Jonathan did not appear unduly perturbed by the news and Anna, who knew little of the business affairs of the Gardiners, asked if he were not surprised.

"No, my dear, I am not," he replied. "Mr Gardiner was one of the best businessmen I have ever known and it is not surprising that he should be wary of handing control of his business to Robert. He is a fine gentleman, to be sure, but is easygoing and too willing to let others tell him what to do. Had my uncle left the business in his hands, it is more than likely that his wife Rose or his father-in-law James Fitzwilliam would have had the running of it."

He handed his mother's letter to Anna and, as she continued reading, more was revealed:

Your Aunt Lizzie tells me that, at the reading of the will, when the announcement was made, Caroline gasped and turned rather pale—clearly, she had not expected it—while her husband Colonel Fitzwilliam looked quite astonished.

Lizzie says Robert did not flinch, but his wife looked very cross and shortly afterwards left the room, claiming she needed some fresh air! I think that she had rather taken it all for granted and was somewhat disgruntled at the turn of events. I do hope she does not hold it against Caroline, for that would be a shame. Caroline is such a sweet girl and means no harm to anyone.

When your father was told, he seemed quite at ease with the idea, saying that Caroline was a very clever young woman and he could not see what the fuss was about. I am inclined to agree with your father, but we shall have to wait and see what Mr Darcy has to say.

Jane Bingley concluded with a paragraph devoted to advice on his daughter's wedding, her best regards to Anna, and a most loving salutation to her young grandsons, Nicholas and Simon.

When Anna had read the letter through, she asked her husband if it was possible that Mr Gardiner had perhaps realised that Robert and Rose preferred living in London for most of the year, where they had both made many new friends. "I know Rose finds life in Derbyshire dull; she has said so quite openly," she said.

Jonathan thought this was possible but he was cautious in making a judgment. "Mr Darcy would know the real reason," he said, "but he would never break a confidence and disclose it. My own opinion is that Mr Gardiner has long preferred Caroline to take charge of the business and her mother's shares in it. She is intelligent and hard working, even if she is a hopeless romantic at times; she has always had a good head for business and does understand commerce better than most of us. We should not forget, she was also his favourite daughter."

"Do you believe Mr Darcy knew of his intention?" Anna asked.

"I do and, if he did, he must have approved of it, because he owns a share of the business together with my father. Had he not believed that Caroline was capable of managing it successfully, he would have advised Mr Gardiner against it."

"I suppose Robert must feel hard done by," said Anna.

"I cannot imagine why," her husband replied. "There is no suggestion in Mother's letter that he has lost any part of his own inheritance; if one were to look at it from another perspective, Robert, who has never shown a great deal of interest in the company, has been spared a good deal of the hard work, but will continue to receive an income from it."

Anna laughed and told him that was an answer worthy of a politician, adding, "If you are right, then there is no reason for Rose Gardiner to feel any resentment towards Caroline, is there?"

"No indeed, there is not, for she and Robert are free to live where they choose and pursue whatever interests they may wish," her husband replied. "Be that as it may, Anna, my dear, I am quite sure Mr Gardiner had very sound reasons for his decision."

"Which we may never discover," said Anna, as she collected her things and made to leave the room, but her husband had the last word.

"My dear, I am quite certain that it will not be beyond the wit of my mother and Aunt Lizzie to discover them. I will wager any amount you care to name that before too long, we shall all know Mr Gardiner's reasons."

❧

Back at Pemberley, in a conversation over dinner, Mr and Mrs Darcy and their guests were involved in a similar discussion. Having been privy to Mr Gardiner's decision and, indeed, having been asked to witness the changes to his will a year or more ago, Mr Darcy was convinced of the rightness of the course he had adopted.

Mr Gardiner had long felt that Robert, despite his professed desire to participate in the family business, would not be the most appropriate of his four children to take over the responsibility of managing the company. Indeed, he had recently confided in Mr Darcy that he had for some time harboured serious doubts about the man Robert had appointed to run the Manchester office, which handled most of their shipping. Mr Gardiner had been made aware of some discrepancies in the accounts and urged his son to look more closely at his work, yet Robert, after what Mr Gardiner thought was a fairly cursory examination of the books, had assured him there was no cause for concern and everything was in order.

Mr Darcy had also seen a letter to Caroline from her father, handed to her by the lawyer Mr Jennings after the reading of the will, which detailed, among other matters, his continuing anxiety about the conduct of Mr Stokes, the manager of the Manchester office. Urging Caroline to pay close attention to his work, it contained also some sound advice:

> If you need to consult anyone, you may find that you can trust the judgment of Mr Darcy or your brother Richard. Ask their advice if you wish, but should you prefer to rely upon your own, my dear Caroline, I am happy to trust yours.

Your husband should be a good source of advice; Colonel Fitzwilliam has proved himself to be adept and careful in matters of business and I am convinced that together you will do well in this important endeavour.

Remember, my dear, that your mother's continuing comfort and peace of mind, your own fortune, and the income that will flow to your brothers and sister, as well as my valued partners Mr Darcy and Mr Bingley, are now all in your care. I know you will not let them down.

Caroline, on reading the letter, had felt proud at being chosen by her father for the onerous task, yet daunted by the responsibility he had placed in her hands. She had put the letter away, revealing its contents only to Mr Darcy and later to Richard and Cassandra.

Besides the good advice and some affectionate words of farewell, Mr Gardiner had added a postscript, which Cassy found interesting.

In it he urged Caroline to beware of those who may advise the sale of parts of the business to outsiders:

Remember, dear Caroline, it is with you I leave the most valuable part of my life's work. Apart from the property at Oakleigh, which I purchased for your mother, the company is my entire fortune. Bound up in it is the prosperity and happiness of several people, including my family and those faithful employees who have worked for us for many years. Now it is in your hands.

When Cassandra had accompanied her husband to the reading of his father's will, she, like most other members of the family, had not expected any surprises. Mr Gardiner was, above all, a stable, steady businessman, with no tendency towards eccentricity or aberration.

The first few bequests to each of his grandchildren and to faithful staff and servants were only to be expected. He was well known for his generosity. Cassy was delighted when her sons and daughters received substantial endowments, but rather more than surprised when she figured separately in his will, receiving a very generous bequest. Her share holding was almost doubled, as were those of Richard, Emily, and Robert.

When, however, Mr Jennings proceeded to read the words that gave Caroline control of the rest of her father's shares and the management of the company, with a codicil that prevented her from selling any of it without the consent of her mother and her brother Richard, Cassy had been astonished. Her hand had crept surreptitiously into her husband's as she had wondered what had prompted Mr Gardiner to follow such a course. She saw, too, the shocked face of her brother-in-law Robert and his wife's flushed countenance as she left the room a few minutes later.

It was plain they were both shocked and Rose was very angry.

Looking at Mrs Gardiner, sitting between her two daughters, Cassy could tell from her face that her mother-in-law had been as ignorant of her husband's intentions as the rest of them. Only Mr Darcy had seemed unsurprised. Indeed, as it appeared later, when the documents were laid upon the table by Mr Jennings for all to read, her father had witnessed Mr Gardiner's signature at the end of the paragraph, which contained the detailed instruction to Caroline.

Cassy *was* surprised.

When they met again at Pemberley for dinner, Mr Bingley and Jane were there, too. Inevitably, the conversation revolved around Mr Gardiner's decision to place Caroline in charge of the business.

"Do you suppose, Papa, that Mr Gardiner thought Caroline was better able to manage the business than Robert?" Cassy asked, quietly.

Mr Darcy answered her gently but firmly, leaving no one in any doubt of his opinion on the matter.

"I am quite sure he did, my dear, and with good reason. Robert has for some years worked at his duties but, despite his best efforts, it was clear to his father that his heart was not in it. Robert, sadly, has neither the natural ability for commerce that his father had, nor did he attempt to acquire the skills that are necessary to manage such an enterprise in the modern commercial world."

"Oh come, sir, is that not being unfair to Robert?" asked Richard.

But Mr Darcy was unrepentant.

"Is it really, Richard? I know you do not wish to criticise your brother, and it is generous of you to defend him, but I think we would all agree that neither you nor I nor Bingley here, would feel able to step into your father's shoes, would we not?"

Richard nodded, and so did Bingley; there was general agreement on that score.

"Well then, how do you suppose Robert, who has less experience than either Bingley or myself, who, since his marriage, has spent more time in

London and Paris than in Manchester or Derbyshire, and never once attempted to improve his qualifications for the position, how do you suppose he would cope with the situation?"

Cassy understood her father's argument, but wished to ask another question. "And what do you believe convinced Mr Gardiner that Caroline could do better?" she asked, and her father smiled and relaxed, as he explained, "Now there, I can give you a precise answer, because she had already proved it."

And as those around the table looked puzzled, he continued.

"Not many people are aware of this; I was, but my lips were sealed. Now it can be told, if only to assure you that no injustice has been done. Some time ago, Mr Gardiner was advised by his doctors and, I think, by you, Richard, to reduce his hours of work and the amount of travelling he did. Consequently, he had Caroline over to Oakleigh regularly to help him with his correspondence and check his books. Occasionally, he sent her to Manchester with Colonel Fitzwilliam, on his behalf. She apparently showed a remarkable aptitude for the work and was eager to learn.

"A year or so ago, she uncovered some discrepancies in the statements of accounts from the Manchester office and brought them to Mr Gardiner's attention. Although Robert was advised of this by his father, he claimed to have found nothing wrong with the books kept by Mr Stokes.

"Meanwhile, a similar problem was discovered in the accounts from London and Mr Gardiner despatched Caroline, together with myself and Robert, to London. There, we contacted the lawyers and the accountants and, after a proper investigation, the clerk in charge of the books was prosecuted and some of the monies recovered, entirely due to Caroline's patient and meticulous work. Robert had had no idea what was going on.

"Mr Gardiner was most impressed with Caroline's work as he was disappointed in Robert's lack of application, and I am prepared to believe that he made up his mind on the matter of his will soon afterwards."

"Did he not ask Robert how he had missed the errors and give him the chance to explain?" asked Elizabeth.

"No, my dear," Mr Darcy replied. "I believe he did not wish to humiliate his son; besides, by the time the courts had dealt with the case, Robert and Rose had already left for Paris. It was at the time of the great art exhibition at the Louvre."

Mr Darcy smiled and went on. "Mr Gardiner was not only a good businessman; he was also a kind father. But, while he wished to spare his son's feelings, he was not prepared to risk the entire business by leaving it in indifferent hands."

Clearly, Mr Darcy had been consulted by Mr Gardiner, and it was apparent to all present that he had approved of the decision as a sensible and prudent one.

Shortly afterwards, the ladies rose and left the room and, by the time the gentlemen rejoined them, the subjects of their conversations had changed. The ladies were engaged in discussing Anne-Marie's wedding and speculating about everything from the bridal clothes to the refurbishment of Longbourn. Elizabeth had heard of it in a letter from Charlotte Collins and indeed had invited her to spend some time at Pemberley while the work was in progress, "if the workmen made too much noise."

The gentlemen had somewhat graver matters to speak of. Richard reported that Mr Carr had made mention of two men who had accosted him at the inn one evening and offered to buy the Rushmore stud.

"They had claimed to represent an interested party from London, to whom money was no object; he could name his price. When he turned them down, indicating that he had no intention of selling, they left, but he had the distinct impression they were unlikely to take no for an answer," said Richard, and Mr Darcy looked very concerned indeed.

It was agreed that Mr Carr should be advised to steer clear of them.

Darcy recalled a very nasty experience he'd had several years ago with a similar group of land speculators from London.

"They're a bad lot. I would warn Carr to be very watchful, especially as he lives alone up at the farm. He should be vigilant. These men cannot be trusted," he warned. Richard agreed to convey his advice to Mr Carr, who was expected to return from Derby on the morrow.

"He has a very good man in Jack Boyden," he said, and Mr Darcy agreed.

"Indeed he has. I believe Mr Grantham recommended him to Carr; he was apprenticed at Pemberley for several years before leaving to work in Derby. If Carr needed a sound man to manage the stud, he has certainly found one. However, it is essential that Carr keeps his hand in and does not behave like an absentee landlord. I have found that when the landowner lives on his property and takes an interest in the running of it, his stewards and managers do likewise."

At this, Mr Bingley spoke up to support Darcy.

"You are absolutely right, Darcy. Why, only last year, a property at Ashbourne came on the market after the owner was declared bankrupt, having spent his time in London, knowing nothing of the fraudulent practices of his agent. He had been ruined."

Pondering this salutary lesson, they repaired to the drawing room, where coffee was served and Mr Bingley begged for some music.

Cassandra was willing to oblige and the rest of the evening passed lightly by. There was no further discussion of Mr Gardiner's will; the prospect of Anne-Marie's wedding seemed a more attractive topic, one on which there was unanimous agreement.

Cassandra's account of her father's opinions on the subject of Mr Gardiner's will reached Jonathan and Anna Bingley at Netherfield Park by a circuitous path, through a letter from Jonathan's sister Emma Wilson. So astonished had Emma been at the revelations in a letter she had received from Cassy that she had enclosed it within her own and despatched it to her brother forthwith.

In the accompanying note Emma wrote:

If Mr Darcy and Mr Gardiner are right, as Cassy reports, then Caroline Fitzwilliam will be one of the most remarkable women I know. There are not many women who control a successful trading company. With her charm and good looks and her husband's political influence, Caroline will be very powerful indeed, Mr Wilson believes. I enclose Cassy's letter for your perusal...

Reading Cassandra's letter to his sister, Jonathan could only agree.

Passing it to his wife, he said, with the certainty of one who does not expect to be contradicted, "And I have no doubt at all that she will be exceedingly successful, too."

Having read both letters, Anna had to concur with her husband. Everything she knew about Caroline Fitzwilliam confirmed his belief that Mr Gardiner had made a prudent, if unusual decision.

Anne-Marie's wedding day drew near and the families from Derbyshire, Leicester, and Kent prepared for their journeys to Netherfield. Despite the recent death of Mr Gardiner, several of them travelled to Hertfordshire for the occasion. Mrs Gardiner, naturally, did not join them, while her son Robert and his wife Rose had already left to spend the Winter in Europe with friends.

The rest of the family were looking forward to seeing Jonathan Bingley's eldest daughter happily wed at last. They were all aware, though some did not know the detail of the circumstances, that her first marriage to the Reverend Bradshaw had been far from happy and that she had suffered without complaint until his sudden death some two years ago. They wanted to wish her and Mr Elliott happiness and good fortune.

Mr and Mrs Darcy had another reason for anticipating the occasion with some pleasure. They expected to see their son Julian and his wife at the wedding. Reports had reached them that Josie was much recovered from her earlier illness and had given them hope that they would see the two of them together for the first time in many months.

Imagine their disappointment then, when on the evening before the wedding, while the families were taking tea in the parlour, a hired vehicle drew up at the entrance to Netherfield House and Julian Darcy alighted alone. He had travelled post from Cambridge.

Josie, he explained apologetically, was as yet not well enough to travel the distance from Cambridge to Hertfordshire in Winter. No amount of questioning could elicit from him any further information about her health or situation.

Elizabeth was tearful when she told her sister Jane the unhappy news.

"It seems such a long time since we saw her, Jane. I am beginning to wonder whether there is something more to this reluctance on her part to meet with us. Is it possible that we, or even I, may have offended her, albeit unwittingly, so she will not meet with me?"

Jane could not imagine how such a thing may have occurred. While she was aware that Josie Tate was not her sister's first choice as a bride for her son (she had openly admitted to a preference for Amy Fitzwilliam), Jane knew that once Julian's wishes were known to them, both Elizabeth and Mr Darcy had welcomed Josie to Pemberley.

"Lizzie, that is nonsense and you know it," she said. "Nothing that you or Mr Darcy have done could have caused such offence. If it had, however unwittingly, we would have heard of it, one way or another. Either Rebecca or Mr Tate would surely have given us some indication. I cannot believe it, Lizzie. There has to be another reason." Jane was quite adamant that her sister was not to blame. After a few moments' silence, she asked, "Do you think, Lizzie, that there could be some trouble between them? Julian and Josie, I mean? I remember well that when Jonathan was having problems with Amelia-Jane, she would not accept any of my invitations to Ashford Park. Could it be that Julian and Josie are experiencing similar difficulties?"

"I cannot think why," said her sister. "Amelia-Jane was an immature young girl, with little to recommend her save her looks, while Josie is an intelligent and accomplished young woman. She and Julian share so many interests, I cannot believe there could be similar problems between them."

Jane tried again. "Perhaps if you were to ask Cassy if young Lizzie noticed anything untoward, when she was staying with them," she suggested, and Elizabeth agreed that was a good idea.

"I shall try to get her alone after the wedding and ask her myself," she said with determination, hoping that young Lizzie Gardiner might throw some light on what was fast becoming a vexing mystery.

The wedding was exactly as the bride and groom had wished it to be: a quiet, happy celebration for their families. There were tears and smiles, music, dancing, plenty of food and wine, and Lizzie Gardiner was so busy enjoying herself that Elizabeth found no opportunity to get her popular granddaughter alone.

She did, however, succeed in questioning Cassandra, who had expressed her own disappointment to her mother at the non-arrival of her sister-in-law, thus giving her an ideal opening.

But before Elizabeth could ask the question, Cassy mentioned that Julian had asked her, during the wedding breakfast, if Lizzie may be permitted to return with him to Cambridge.

"He thinks she is very good for Josie, being young and cheerful, and would like her to spend the time until Christmas with them."

"And have you agreed?" asked her mother.

Cassy shook her head.

"I cannot, because Lizzie is committed to help Emily with the parish Nativity play on Christmas Eve. She will not let her down; they have been working on it for weeks. I have told Julian I will consider sending her to them in the New Year," she replied and then suddenly asked, "Mama, do you really think all is well between them? I am very afraid. I sense my brother is not happy, yet he will say nothing. It is not just that Josie is unwell; he seems unduly anxious and uncertain, I cannot believe it is simply a matter of her health."

Elizabeth saw her opportunity and took it. "Did Lizzie not notice anything unusual when she stayed with them?" she asked.

Cassy shrugged her shoulders. "Not unless you consider Julian being closeted in his study for hours on end, while she reads poetry with her friends unusual."

Elizabeth frowned. "Who are these friends?"

"Not anyone we know, although I have met a Mr Barrett, who is in the book trade. There are two young women, Misses Wallace-something-or-other, not very intelligent by Lizzie's measure, and Mr Barrett's friend, a publisher named Andrew Jones," said Cassy.

"And are they all Julian's friends, too?" Elizabeth enquired.

"I do not think so," Cassy replied. "Lizzie gave me the impression that Julian was usually at his laboratory when they arrived to read poetry and take coffee, while she was often sent away to play with Anthony."

Elizabeth looked surprised and was about to ask another question, but they were interrupted by some applause for the bride and groom, who had been persuaded to join in the dancing. As other guests joined them, they could no longer continue their conversation. Cassy was claimed by her husband, who wanted to dance, and went away leaving her mother seriously concerned. Her conversation with Cassy had served only to increase her apprehensions, which now bordered upon alarm.

That night, as they retired to their room, Elizabeth was eager to tell her husband what she had learned from their daughter. When Jane had hinted that marital troubles may lie at the heart of Julian and Josie's problems, Elizabeth had been unwilling to credit it. She had felt she knew them well enough to set aside such concerns.

Her son was a serious and honest young man and Josie had given every indication of being the kind of intelligent young woman who would suit him well. That they had loved each other, she had never doubted.

Yet now, since Cassy had told her of the groups of friends who frequented the house, men and women who were not also friends of Julian, attending poetry readings and taking tea and coffee while Julian was away at work, Elizabeth had begun to have niggling doubts in her mind. While she was reluctant to encumber her husband with what might turn out to be a false alarm, nevertheless, she felt the need to confide in him as she had always done, if only to have him laugh at her fears and dismiss them out of hand.

Mr Darcy had hidden his disappointment at Josie's absence well. During the wedding party he had pleased his hosts with his good humour and a brief speech complimenting the happy pair, which was exceedingly well received. Indeed, as they retired upstairs, he was feeling reasonably content, if a little weary, after a long day. Elizabeth was loathe to spoil the moment, yet as she told him what she had heard, she knew he was not going to dismiss it as far-fetched and silly, as she had hoped he would.

He remained grave and silent as she spoke, and when she asked, "Darcy, is there nothing we can do to help them?" he seemed to her, for the first time in their life together, uncertain of how to answer.

When he did speak, he was very solemn. "Lizzie, my dear, if this is true, I am deeply concerned, for it does seem as though Julian has a graver problem on his hands than any of us imagined. A young woman of Josie's character and intelligence will not indulge in this type of behaviour, unless there is something seriously wrong with her marriage."

Elizabeth was astounded. "Are you suggesting that Julian is to blame? Do you not see that it is Josie who is making a fool of him, and of herself, by entertaining these gentlemen, if that is who they are, in her home, when her husband is at work?"

Darcy took her hands in his. "Hush, my dear, I am not suggesting that anyone is to blame. I am only pointing out the fact that an amiable and intelligent woman would not, if she is happy and content, feel the need to do as you have described. Now, there may be a perfectly reasonable explanation. Perhaps, little Lizzie does not know it, but Julian may have been quite happy for these poetry readings to be conducted in his absence. No one has suggested otherwise, certainly not Julian. Yet, I must admit, he does not seem as cheerful as a man who has been invited to address a convocation of scientists in Paris is entitled to be."

"Address a convocation in Paris? When?" Elizabeth asked excitedly.

"In the Spring, I believe. He told me of it and asked if we would have Anthony and Josie over to stay at Pemberley while he went away. I said, of course we would, with pleasure. But I did not know then what you have told me."

Darcy sounded depressed, but his wife was more cheerful now. What her husband had just revealed had put quite a different complexion upon her view of the situation.

"Well then, it cannot be so bad after all; perhaps we are reading too much into these meetings. They may well be harmless and genuine poetry readings. If Josie is planning to come to us in Spring, it must mean they are quite happy together. Do you not think so?" she asked, longing to be told her fears were groundless.

Her husband would have liked to oblige, but her earlier words had sown a seed of doubt in his own mind. While he was unwilling to believe that Josie was deceiving her husband or indulging in some clandestine liaison, he did feel the need to make some enquiries, to ascertain if matters were as they should be, for there was no doubt in Mr Darcy's mind that something was amiss.

"I would not want to intrude myself into their situation, Lizzie, but perhaps Richard may be willing, as their physician, to talk to Julian. If there is a problem, he is far more likely to confide in Richard," he said and, seeing her anxious countenance, tried to reassure her.

"I shall speak with Richard tomorrow morning at breakfast. There, you can rest assured; if there is a problem, he will discover it and do whatever needs to be done."

It was not much consolation, but with the lateness of the hour, there was no more anyone could do.

⊰⊱

Elizabeth did not sleep well and was awake with the first streaks of dawn light in the sky, looking out on the familiar grounds of Netherfield Park, recalling her first visit here, and wondering at the manner in which their lives had changed over the years. Mr Darcy dressed and went downstairs early, hoping to speak with his son-in-law before too many of the family were about. He found Richard in the dining room, reading the newspaper, and discovered to his surprise that Julian had already breakfasted and left.

Richard conveyed his apologies. "He was eager to get the coach which goes from Meryton to Hertford, where he will change to the post. He asked me to convey his love and regards and says he hopes to see you at Christmas."

Richard could not fail to notice the look of exasperation that crossed his father-in-law's face at this news. "Were you hoping to see him, sir? Was it about something in particular?" he asked.

"Indeed, I was; but it was my hope, also, to ask you to counsel him, as his doctor as well as his brother-in-law," Mr Darcy said and proceeded to tell Richard of the anxieties that had assailed both him and Elizabeth about Julian's marriage.

Richard Gardiner listened, his countenance darkening as he heard the details of Mr Darcy's concerns. He had heard none of this. Perhaps, Lizzie had urged her mother not to speak of it to anyone. Cassy must have had a very good reason, he thought, for keeping it from him; they had few secrets from one another.

Understanding the gravity of Mr Darcy's concerns, he promised to consider carefully what might be done, without offending either Julian or his wife by appearing to pry into their lives. As their doctor, he knew he had a responsibility towards them but was wary of intruding.

"I shall do my best, sir, to discover if there is or is not a serious problem. I have seen no evidence of it myself, but I shall try to ascertain the truth. I am reluctant to interfere in their lives, but if Julian will confide in me, I shall be happy to listen and offer what advice I can.

"I do have an opportunity to visit him in Cambridge in the New Year, before he goes to Europe for the convention; if I do not succeed in seeing him privately at Christmas, I shall speak with him then."

It was the best he could do and while both Darcy and Elizabeth were appreciative of his promised efforts, they feared he might be too late.

Somewhat better was the news that Julian had said he would see his parents at Christmas. For Elizabeth, it was at least something to look forward to with pleasure.

❧

Christmas at Pemberley was always a big family occasion.

As the staff made preparations for the season, airing rooms and making up beds for the guests who were expected to stay, and planning menus for the festive meals, Elizabeth, with Cassandra's help, made arrangements for the seasonal entertainment.

In recent years, a new tradition, inspired by the German antecedents of the late Prince Consort, had been adopted. To the delight of the children, a great tree, usually one of the dark spruces from the woods above the house, was brought in and placed in a large container in the centre of the saloon. It was then the joyous task of the family to dress the graceful tree with ornaments, candles, glass baubles, and garlands of holly and ivy, transforming it into a magical Christmas tree.

There was a sense of quiet excitement around the house; everyone knew Master Julian and his family were expected and something special was being planned. There was no mistaking the pleasure with which the master and mistress looked forward to the occasion.

There was much to be done. The choir of children from the estate had to be taken through their paces, practising their Christmas program and, while Cassy did her best, they missed Kitty and her husband Dr Jenkins. They had moved to Wales less than a year ago, where Dr Jenkins had been offered a larger, more needy parish in one of the new coal mining communities, where he was also closer to his own widowed mother.

For Elizabeth, it was the first Christmas without her younger sister at hand to help and she missed her far more than she had expected she would. Though a new young rector had taken over at the Pemberley church, he did not have the same talent for music and certainly not the fine Welsh tenor that Dr Jenkins had brought to the choir.

For all that, Elizabeth could not hide her eagerness, anticipating the arrival of Julian and Josie with little Anthony. It had been several months since she had seen her grandson and almost a year since Josie had visited Pemberley.

Seeing her mother's elation as the day approached for their arrival, Cassy prayed she would not be disappointed yet again.

If the weather turned bitter, as it so often did in the Midlands, might not Julian arrive alone as before or, worse, not come at all? She shuddered at the thought. But the weather gods were kind and, apart from a dusting of light snow, it looked to be a fine, crisp season.

When, on Christmas Eve, an unfamiliar vehicle was seen driving down into the park and crossing the bridge, Elizabeth's maid rushed to summon her mistress. By the time she had been found and alerted to their arrival, the carriage was at the door and Julian, having alighted, was helping his wife out. Behind came her maid Susan and young Anthony.

Elizabeth's anxious, loving eyes could find nothing at all amiss with the seemingly perfect little family that stood in the hall before being ushered into the saloon, there to be welcomed with hugs and kisses and greeted with all sorts of festive acclamations.

Soon Mr Darcy, hearing the happy commotion downstairs, joined them as they were plied with food and drink, while Anthony, who had always been a favourite with his grandfather, kept them all entertained.

He was a playful, pretty child and, except for a tendency towards thinness, he looked very well and earned his parents many compliments for his behaviour, which was exemplary.

"Josie refuses to spoil him, though I think Susan would, if she could," said Julian and everyone was full of praise for both mother and son.

Later after they had had their fill of refreshments, they were shown upstairs to their rooms. Jenny Grantham, the housekeeper, had arranged for them to have the suite of rooms that had been Julian's, but Elizabeth offered them a choice of any other suite they might prefer.

"We are not expecting a large number of guests to stay this year—Aunt Jane and Mr Bingley, your cousin Sophie and her family, and Aunt Gardiner, who has promised to come if the weather holds.

"The Grantleys have gone to Kent this year, so if you prefer it, you can have the suite that is usually theirs. It is larger and overlooks the park," she suggested, but Josie smiled, "No indeed, Mrs Darcy, these rooms are perfect. I recall you showed them to me when they were refurbished for Julian," she said.

Elizabeth smiled, recalling the day she had first shown her future daughter-in-law around Pemberley. It seemed a very long time ago, yet it was but a few years. She was pleased that Josie had remembered.

When they met again before dinner that night, she thought Josie looked very well in a fashionable new gown with her hair swept up into an elegant style that was favoured by the society ladies of London.

She did not look at all pale or sickly, as she had looked in Cambridge earlier that year; rather she appeared bright and cheerful throughout the party for the children of the estate and, when it was time to go in to dinner, she accompanied her husband into the room and made a point of sitting beside her mother-in-law.

Elizabeth was very touched and quite determined to forget any reservations she'd had about Josie. There could be no truth in any of them, she decided. Josie certainly did not appear unhappy.

Sadly, the same could not be said of Julian, whose anxious expression, which had haunted his mother since their meeting at Netherfield earlier in the season, seemed only to have intensified.

To be fair, he did his best to participate in everything, from singing carols with the children to charades, which Elizabeth knew he hated, but she remained unconvinced.

On Christmas Day, the family went to church and gathered afterwards at Pemberley House, exchanging gifts and indulging in all those customary pursuits that seem to have a special meaning at Christmastime. The children's choir, which Elizabeth had started when she first came to Pemberley as a bride, sang sweetly, enhancing the atmosphere of tranquility, and the Christmas tree drew the children like a beacon.

There was good news, too, from Jane and Bingley who arrived bearing a letter with warm greetings to the rest of the family from Jonathan and Anna Bingley at Netherfield. In his letter, Jonathan had revealed that his eldest son Charles, a physician, who had spent some years working in London among the poor in some of the worst slums of the city, was moving back to Hertfordshire.

"It means," Jane explained, "that their search for a good physician for Anne-Marie's hospital at Bell's Field is over. Jonathan says, when Charles told her of his decision, Anne-Marie was so excited, she sat down that very night, even though she and Mr Elliott were on their honeymoon, and wrote her father a letter to break the good news!"

This piece of information brought a mixed response.

Mr Bingley could not speak highly enough of his granddaughter's dedication. "Anne-Marie's devotion to her cause, be it the wounded soldiers or the care of ailing children, will always take precedence over anything else."

Josie, who had been silent throughout this conversation, spoke up for the first time, and her words surprised them all. "Is there not some danger in such a life? Is it not likely that a woman may put all else before her own satisfaction and thereby forego her chance of happiness altogether?" she asked.

Although she had spoken very quietly, the unambiguous import of her words carried to everyone around the dinner table. Yet, it was a while before someone responded.

Mr Bingley, surprised at being picked up on his words, was silent, seeming to concentrate upon his dinner, but his wife Jane said, "But Josie, it is the kind of work in which Anne-Marie has always found great satisfaction. It is her life. She was never happier than when she was tending the wounded at Harwood Park. She felt she was doing something really worthwhile."

Josie agreed but added, "Indeed, Mrs Bingley, and so she was, until she let herself be persuaded that she may do even more worthwhile work by marrying the Reverend Bradshaw. Now, surely no one denies *that* was a disastrous decision."

There was a gasp from Jane, who looked down immediately, clearly hurt by her words.

"Josie, please," Cassy interrupted, scarcely able to help herself.

There was absolute silence around the table; it was as if someone had flung a bucket of icy water over the gathered company. Both Jane and Mrs Gardiner looked stunned and censorious, Darcy's expression was one of impenetrable gloom, while Elizabeth, for once, could find no words to fill the yawning gap of time as the minutes ticked by. Poor Julian looked absolutely wretched.

Jenny Grantham must have known something was amiss, for she chose that very moment to send in the flaming Christmas pudding and break the cold silence. While no one said anything very significant, at least they could all eat, and the plump, fragrant Christmas pudding, in all its glory, brought the usual admiring exclamations and compliments to the cook.

Unhappily, it did nothing to improve Julian's mood of depression and, by the time the ladies withdrew to the drawing room, he had excused himself and retired to his room. As those downstairs heard the door slam shut, Elizabeth and Cassy exchanged glances, while Josie moved away to study a familiar work of art with a new level of intensity.

~❧~

On the morrow, being Boxing Day, Cassandra arrived after breakfast to join her parents when they handed out the traditional Christmas boxes to the household staff and farm workers. To her surprise, her brother was there, too. Clearly, Mr and Mrs Darcy were pleased.

Some former servants were too frail or sick to attend the festivities at the house, and Cassy had agreed to take their boxes to them, together with hampers of festive fare prepared by Mrs Grantham. She sought out Julian and invited him to accompany her. Josie, she was told, was still asleep, tired after her long journey and the previous day's celebrations, but Julian was happy to oblige.

As brother and sister set out together around the estate, he seemed to recover some of his spirits. They talked lightly and cheerfully of times past and the people they had known. When they visited the house of Mrs Thompson, who had been their nurse for many years, now crippled with rheumatism, she was so pleased to see them that tears flowed down her cheeks. Julian was visibly moved.

As they left the cottage and he helped his sister into the carriage, he said, in a voice that left her in no doubt of his mood, "Ah, Cassy, if only one could bring back those carefree childhood days. I shall never forget the kindness of Mrs Thompson and her niece Nellie, who used to play with me endlessly; if only my son could have someone to love and indulge him as they did."

Astonished not only by his words, but by the depth of feeling in his voice, Cassy slowed the carriage down and asked, "Julian, what do you mean? Is there something you have not told any of us? Why do you speak so sadly of Anthony? Is he not loved and cared for?"

Her voice was low and troubled and her brother knew he had to speak now. His words, at first, were slow and halting, but then they broke free of the restraint he had placed upon himself for well over a year and tumbled out, as he could no longer hold them back. He spoke quietly but with an intensity that surprised and disturbed Cassy, who listened, scarcely able to believe what she heard.

"Cassy, you will probably never understand my situation, you who are so serenely happy and content in your marriage with Richard. But I must tell someone; I can no longer keep this to myself. My wife Josie no longer loves me and has made it quite plain that she stays with me only because of our son. I am no longer necessary to her happiness; indeed, one might even say I was inimical to it."

Seeing his sister's shocked expression, he put a hand upon hers to comfort her. "You must not look so startled, Cassy; remember, I did try to warn you when you visited us." He reminded her of the occasion in the parlour of their house in Cambridge, when she had scolded him for his pessimism.

"As for Anthony, he does not receive as much of his mother's love and care as he did before. He is a good, well-behaved child, and I must give her credit for that; but now, it is Susan, her maid, who has almost sole care of him. Josie is kept busy with her writers' circle and her poetry readings; they take up a great deal of her time."

His words were quite matter of fact, as though he had long accepted the status quo and could see no way to change it.

Cassandra could not continue to listen without asking, "My dear brother, are you telling me that Josie neglects her child? This surely cannot be true; I know she loves Anthony dearly."

He shook his head and said, "I cannot use that word, Cassy. I am sure Josie would not believe for one moment that she neglects him; she ensures that he has everything he needs. But the affection and care that he gets comes mainly from Susan, to whom he is closer than to either of his parents."

Cassy said she had noticed how attached the child was to the young maid but had assumed there was nothing unusual in it.

"Children do become very fond of those who care for them," she said.

"Except that you and I know that, much as we loved Mrs Thompson or Nellie, it was Mama who came first, always."

Cassy had to agree. Her brother was right, yet she was confused by his words and wished she could get clearer answers to her questions.

They were approaching the point in the road where they had to turn off towards Pemberley House, and he begged her not to speak a word of this to their parents.

"Because it would cause them so much pain and I could not bear to be the source of it," he said.

"But, Julian," Cassy persisted, "what is behind this strange behaviour? There must be a reason why Josie acts this way, surely?"

He would say nothing more. She tried but did not succeed in getting him to give her an answer; nor would he make any criticism of Josie. All he would say was that his wife seemed to have grown tired and impatient with his research work which, since it was all about invisible creatures who could only be seen under a microscope, held no interest for her at all.

"She says she is now hopeful of getting an anthology of her work published in London and, of course, that takes precedence over all else in her life. It will be the culmination of all her hopes, the fulfillment of a childhood dream, which she has never abandoned," he said.

As Cassy, by now too shocked and distressed to speak, concentrated upon getting the vehicle over the bridge, he pleaded, "Promise me, Cassy, that you will not let Josie discover that I have spoken with you on this matter."

His sister listened, incredulous, as he went on, "She must not feel any change in your attitude towards her, nor must she be in any way isolated, or she will know I have broken my silence and she will not forgive me. I will lose her and my son. Please, will you give me your word, Cassy? Will you keep my secret?"

Cassandra could not refuse; so insistent was he, she had to promise, adding that she would send young Lizzie to them in the New Year.

He looked genuinely pleased. "God bless you, Cassy, you are the kindest sister a fellow could hope for. Lizzie will do us all a deal of good; Anthony adores her," he said, smiling in spite of himself. In that fleeting moment, she caught a rare glimpse of the young brother she had helped raise all those years ago when, with William gone, she had wondered if there would ever be another Darcy to become the Master of Pemberley and young Julian had seemed the answer to all her prayers.

⁓

When they reached the house, they discovered that Mr and Mrs Tate, Josie's parents, had called and, having taken refreshments with the family, they had left taking Josie, Anthony, and the maid Susan with them.

When Cassy expressed some surprise, Elizabeth explained cheerfully, "It is only for a day; they will be back tomorrow afternoon. Meanwhile, we shall have you all to ourselves, Julian, and you must tell us about this convention you are to address in Paris. That must be a great honour."

Cassy noticed that her brother Julian did not look very cheerful at all. It was as though he was not convinced that his wife and son would be back on the morrow. He did, however, cheer up considerably when, a short while later, his nephews Edward and Darcy Gardiner arrived and were invited to stay to dinner.

They had much to talk about. Edward, though the quieter of the two, was most interested in Julian's research, being himself a physician, while Darcy could always be relied upon to entertain a party with a fund of lively political anecdotes and a talent for parody that was guaranteed to amuse.

"You must come with us to Rushmore Farm tomorrow, Julian. You will like my friend Michael Carr, the new owner; he has some astonishing tales of life in America," he said. Julian who had not known that the farm had been sold, so out of touch was he with matters concerning the county, was eager to hear more and, as the afternoon wore on, his spirits seemed to improve quite markedly. As Cassy said afterwards to her sons, she had not seen him engage in such animated conversation with anyone else.

After the Gardiners had left, Julian grew more thoughtful; outside the weather changed and snow began to fall. It snowed all night and great drifts covered the grounds. When the following day dawned almost reluctantly, since there was no sun to speak of, any hopes he may have had of driving out to Matlock and Rushmore Farm were dashed, as news came that the road between Pemberley and Matlock was blocked by snow and two carriages had already been stranded on the bridge.

Another day passed with no message from Josie or the Tates, and Julian's concern was more obvious, especially since he was due to return to his college in Cambridge by the New Year. His parents, now alone with their unhappy son, sensed and understood his anxiety but could do little to reassure him.

~❦~

On New Year's Eve, when they heard that the road had been finally cleared of snow and other debris and made safe for vehicles, Mr Darcy sent his manager to the Tates' place in Matlock with a note requesting that Josie and Anthony return to Pemberley, and inviting the Tates to dinner with the family.

Julian was already packed and ready to leave on the morrow, but was persuaded by his mother to stay and travel to Cambridge a day later.

"You can all travel down with Richard. Cassy tells me he is leaving for London on the day after tomorrow; please stay, Julian, it will make your Papa and me very happy," she had pleaded, and Julian had stayed.

Perhaps the prospect of enjoying the company of his brother-in-law on the journey had influenced his decision, for Julian had admired and loved Richard since childhood. If there was one man he would have liked to emulate in all his ways, it was Dr Gardiner. He had never doubted that his sister had made the best marriage possible.

The party from Matlock arrived and, from the outset, it was clear to both Cassy and her mother that relations between Julian and Josie were badly strained. Indeed, apart from a cursory greeting, they barely spoke to one another. In an obviously calculated gesture at dinner, Josie placed herself between Mr Darcy and her mother.

Mrs Tate made up for any lack of conversation on the part of her daughter, though, telling everyone that she was delighted that Josie was now writing some poetry.

"She is far more likely to have it published than if she had persisted with those solemn pieces about the ills of society. Everybody knows about the poor and the suffering and all the evil things that go on in the world, but no one wants to read about them. It is too depressing. Do you not agree, Mr Darcy?" she asked, with the disingenuous aplomb of one who has had her work published in her husband's journals for many years, with no requirement to justify their relevance to anyone.

Cassy almost winced and noticed that her brother was gazing into his wine glass with a level of concentration he usually reserved for the microscopic bacteria in his laboratory. She looked quickly at Josie, who seemed pleased with her mother's approbation, and then at Mr Darcy, who in his customary way, took some time to respond.

"You are quite right, Mrs Tate; poetry is certainly more popular than serious prose, but if everyone wrote only poetry, who would draw attention to the grave problems that afflict our world and where might we seek answers to them? I have nothing against good poetry and take much pleasure in it, but I also recall that Josie wrote a number of excellent pieces for the *Review* and wrote exceedingly well. I have some of her work in a folio in the library, and it would be a great pity if she were to give up serious writing altogether."

Josie's father nodded his agreement. He had hoped to persuade his daughter to write regularly for the *Review*, with little success.

"But if no one will publish it, what good will it do?" asked Josie, and her father-in-law's voice was gentle when he replied, "Many writers have faced rejection at first, my dear; you are young enough to persevere and have patience. If your work is good and well written, as I am sure it is, you will not remain unpublished for long."

Josie bit her lip and looked down at her plate; patience had never been her strong suit. Julian said nothing, but his eyes met Cassy's across the table and the sadness in them was unmistakable.

When they parted later, there was time only to whisper some encouragement and hope he would take heart. But Cassy was now quite certain that her brother's marriage was in deep trouble.

When Richard Gardiner called for them a day later, the family and staff at Pemberley had gathered to bid them farewell and Godspeed. As the time came for them to leave, few could hold back the tears, especially not Elizabeth, for all her uncertainties had returned.

~

That afternoon, the weather worsened as the snow returned and fell steadily for two days and nights, stranding travellers and isolating families in their homes all over the county. The news from Hertfordshire, when it came in a letter from Anna, delayed in the mail, was even worse.

There had been a catastrophic accident on the railway bridge at Sidley's Creek, not two miles from Longbourn. Anne-Marie and her husband Colin Elliott, just back from Europe, together with Dr Charles Bingley and groups of volunteers from the surrounding farms and villages, had spent days and nights working first at the crash site and later at the new Children's Hospital, which had been hastily opened to take in the wounded. Many had died, mostly women and children, day trippers from the Midlands on an excursion to London, but the efforts of Charles Bingley and Anne-Marie and their helpers were being hailed in the local press, as the travellers realised that they owed their lives to the work of a few dedicated men and women.

Anna had sent vivid accounts of the carnage at Sidley's Creek and of the heroic efforts of Dr Bingley and Mr and Mrs Elliott in what were appalling conditions.

She concluded:

We are all so proud of them, especially Anne-Marie and Charles, but indeed credit is due to all the ordinary folk, who came from miles around to help save the lives of these unfortunate travellers. Without their efforts, many more lives would have been lost.

Elizabeth passed the letter to her husband. Darcy, depressed as he was by the tales of death and destruction, set about collecting the reports together and sent them to Josie, with a note which drew her attention to the work of Anne-Marie and her brother Dr Charles Bingley.

"Sometimes," he wrote, "dedication to a cause, like virtue, is its own reward and yet, at other times, it can be worth so much more."

It was not unkindly meant; simply an endorsement of the words of his friend Bingley and his wife Jane, whose praise for their granddaughter's unselfish dedication to a cause, had brought a dissenting comment from Josie. He let Elizabeth see his note before sending it away to the post.

"Is it likely that Josie will pay any attention?" she asked, without much enthusiasm. Her husband smiled, and said, "Perhaps not now, because she is too absorbed in her own discontent; but she is an intelligent young woman and will realise one day that there is more to happiness than self-indulgence. It is not an easy lesson to master, but we must all learn it."

This was no sanctimonious sermon; Elizabeth knew that her husband spoke from experience. It was a lesson they had both learned well.

※

With Richard away, Cassy was miserable and annoyed at herself for being so. Her distress was, she felt, self-inflicted, caused chiefly by the need to keep the confidence placed in her hands by her brother. It denied her the benefit of confiding in her husband and of giving some comfort to her mother, who she knew was wracked with anxiety for her son and his family. Her promise to respect Julian's confidence was causing her a great deal of anguish.

Never in all her years of marriage to Richard had she kept any of her fears or misgivings from him, not for any significant time at any rate. Apart from her dependence upon his good sense and judgment, to deceive him, however innocently, was anathema to her. Yet, this time, she had argued, there was no alternative. Julian had insisted, begged even, that no one must know.

Cassy wished with all her heart that Richard would return and give her some indication whether her brother had confided in him, too. She suffered, not knowing that her husband was himself charged with a mission by his father-in-law, who was keen to discover how deeply troubled Julian's marriage was.

When he did return, however, he gave no sign of having learnt any more than he had known of the matter before he had left. He talked of the journey, which had been reasonable, since they had just escaped the hazardous weather, and of London, where he had met and conferred very satisfactorily with his father's lawyer on matters regarding his mother's property. Cassy could not discover what, if anything, had transpired between him and Julian. It was exceedingly frustrating and made her own situation considerably more difficult.

~*~

With the warmer weather, the buds on the trees began to swell and burst, as Spring returned, albeit tentatively, to the dales. Mr Carr, who had been away in London on business for some weeks, returned to Rushmore Farm and, on a fine Spring morning, as Lizzie was preparing for her journey to Cambridge, he called on the Gardiners to invite them to spend a day and dine with him at Rushmore Farm.

He had expended much money and even more time repairing and refurbishing the house and restoring the gardens that had long been neglected. It had been not only a labour of love, for he had become very attached to the farm, but a chance to demonstrate to his friends how hard he had worked and to return their very generous hospitality.

The Gardiners, all but Edward, who had joined a busy practice in Derby in the New Year, were delighted to accept, especially Cassy and her daughters, who had not been to the farm in several years. The Camdens, since their decision to emigrate, had spent little time on entertaining their neighbours.

Laura Ann recalled that she had visited the farm, when she was very little. "I remember that it looked like an enormous barn," she said, and Lizzie, not wishing to offend Mr Carr, turned to him and said quickly, "I am sure my sister's memory must be faulty, Mr Carr, for I cannot believe you would have purchased a place that looked like a barn!"

Mr Carr laughed heartily and assured them that if it was a barn, then he had made sure it was a pretty comfortable one, and he hoped some of the work he had done through the Winter had rendered the old place a little more handsome and a good deal more presentable than just any old barn.

Then turning to little Laura Ann, he added, "And I can promise you, Miss Laura, there are no mice in my barn, though there is a very large owl, who lives in the old oak tree, returning every night to exactly the same branch."

While this piece of information provoked a question from Laura to her mother about owls and mice, young Darcy, meanwhile, having visited his friend through the Winter, while he had worked on his property, was moved to protest.

"You are much too modest my friend; Rushmore Farm is a fine, solid old place, albeit one that had been neglected a while, but you have done wonders with it. Mama, you will not believe what a transformation he has effected; he has polished the woodwork and burnished the brass, why he has even had new plumbing and gas lamps installed."

"Oh, have you?" said Lizzie, sounding a little disappointed, as Cassy congratulated him upon his wisdom in improving the property. "Modern plumbing I *do* agree with, but I think candlelight is much prettier than gaslight. It seems too yellow and changes the colours of things, does it not, Mama?" Lizzie asked.

Cassy agreed that she had a preference for the softer glow of candlelight in the living rooms, and Mr Carr promised immediately that they would have only candles and no gas lamps in the parlour and dining room at the farm, if that was what the ladies desired.

"I do agree that the glow of candles creates a more romantic ambience," he said and added, "The French are partial to it also, probably for the same reason."

"It hides the flaws on ladies' faces," said Lizzie, quite artlessly, bringing a most gallant response from Mr Carr about the total lack of such a requirement in her case, that made her blush and sink into silence. When he left, having extracted a firm promise that they would all meet at Rushmore Farm on Saturday, it was quite clear that Lizzie had been rather more impressed with their visitor, whom she was seeing again after several months, than she had been before. Perhaps he had improved upon closer acquaintance.

That night, having agonised all week, Cassy could no longer bear her isolation from her husband. She told him all she knew of her brother's predicament, pleading with him not to betray her to Julian when they met. "I think he finally confided in me because he could no longer hold within his own heart the pain and shame he feels," she said. "I have wanted to speak of it to you, Richard, to ask your opinion, but I could not, because he made me promise I would tell no one," she explained, and Richard promised no one would know.

Then, to her surprise, he told her of the mission he had been given by Mr Darcy. "He wishes me to try, as their physician, to discover how grave the situation is between them. Your Mama, having heard Lizzie's account of the visits of Mr Barrett and others for poetry readings while Julian was away at work, has been troubled and your Papa wishes to discover the truth," he explained.

"And do you believe they will?" she asked.

Richard shrugged his shoulders. "I should think that, after observing Julian and Josie during their visit to Pemberley at Christmas, they will be in no doubt that there is a very grave problem, but it is unlikely that they will understand, unless Julian tells them, how deeply entrenched it is."

"What will you do, Richard?"

He looked uncertain. "I have to admit, my love, that I am at a loss as to what I should do. I have no wish to intrude; neither Julian nor Josie will welcome it. Were I to say anything before he mentions it, Julian will know that you have spoken to me of his troubles."

Cassy sat up in bed, her eyes wide with worry. She was genuinely afraid that if nothing were done, great harm may come to her brother and his family. She could not see either Julian or Josie finding a way out of the confused and unhappy tangle in which they were trapped. They seemed to have neither the will nor the strength to attempt it.

A thought occurred to her. "Richard, if you could take him to your club or to dinner, away from the house and Josie, somewhere he was free to speak openly, I am certain he will confide in you. I know he spoke to me when we were alone on Boxing Day, because he had to tell someone; it was too much to bottle up within him. Do you not think so, my dear? Please, will you try? He is so miserable, Richard, it is beyond belief!" she cried and he took her in his arms, comforting her, knowing how deeply she felt her brother's pain.

Her tears flowed then, not only for Julian, but for her parents. "They have suffered so much; when William died, I thought Mama would never recover. After Julian was born, there were some years of happiness and hope, and now this! It is not fair," she said and wept, as he held her as he had often done in the past.

Richard knew that Cassy's wounds, like those of her parents, would never be completely healed. Beloved by everyone who knew him, bright, talented, yet unassuming, William Darcy had lost his young, promising life in a stupid accident that had devastated them all. It was the type of tragedy from which a family found it difficult to recover. The Darcys were no exception.

That it had happened on the day when Richard and Cassy had become engaged, cruelly cutting short their blissful celebration, had added a sharp poignancy to their love. Indeed, it had been the first test of it, as Cassy, unable to reach her grieving parents, had turned to him for comfort and strength to sustain her through the dreadful days and months that had followed.

After the first shock of her brother's death, one of Cassy's worst fears had been that the lack of a male heir to her father's estate may mean that she would have to inherit Pemberley. It was the very last thing she wanted.

With the birth a few years later of Julian, that fear at least had passed and Cassy had taught her young brother everything he needed to know to be the next Master of Pemberley.

But now, with Julian's life falling apart, it seemed she was going to be at the centre of it once more. Her parents would expect it of her and so would the community. It was a prospect that unsettled and alarmed her. Richard did his best to reassure her, promising to speak with her brother when he took Lizzie to stay with them.

Grateful for his strength, love, and consistent kindness, she let him persuade her that all was not lost.

"Look at it this way, my love, if Josie has not left her husband because of the boy, it is clear she loves the child and may well stay with him—and while she stays, there is hope they may be reconciled," he said, and though he sounded rather less confident this time, Cassy wanted to believe it was true. It was the only comfort she had.

They had a particularly fine Spring day for their visit to Rushmore Farm. Mr Carr rode down to meet them and accompany the party along the road to Lambton and thence to Rushmore Farm. Mr Carr and Darcy Gardiner, on horseback, rode ahead of them as Richard, Cassy, their two daughters, and young James followed in the open carriage.

The sun was warm, and there was the merest whisper of a breeze as they made their way towards the river and across the bridge. With the trees in bloom and the meadows flushed green and gold with new growth, the countryside looked as pretty as a painting. Laura Ann exclaimed at the carpet of wild flowers under the trees.

When they came over the crest of a small hill and had their first glimpse of the house, its windows gleaming as they caught the morning sun, Lizzie was overwhelmed by the change in the old place. She could only remember Will Camden's place as a rambling old house with dark timbers and dull grey walls. Now, as the house welcomed them with its polished shutters and white painted walls, the transformation was remarkable. Richard and Cassy were most favourably impressed. The old Georgian house was back to looking its best.

"This is very impressive, Mr Carr," said Richard, and Mr Carr was clearly gratified. "It is no mansion, sir, I grant you, but I think it is handsome enough," he said modestly.

As they went indoors, Cassy echoed her husband's words. "I must congratulate you on the fine work you have done throughout, Mr Carr. I see you have still to complete the refurbishment of the rooms," she said and was immediately asked if she would advise on colours and fabrics for drapes and blinds. Work had been completed on only two of the larger rooms and one bedroom upstairs, he confessed; the guest rooms and other living areas remained to be done.

"I have need of more advice before I undertake any changes," he explained, as they entered a large room with an enormous fireplace and bay windows that provided a very pretty view across the water meadows to the river beyond.

"And what have you in mind for this room?" asked Cassy and, before he could reply, Lizzie, who was following them, spoke her thoughts aloud.

"This is such a fine room, with so much light and space; it could be a place where an entire family could spend time in whatever interests and pursuits took their fancy. One might read or sew, another could play the pianoforte or join in a game of cards and still not get in each other's way; indeed, it is an ideal recreation room," she said and Laura, who had been listening, asked, "But Mr Carr does not have a family, Lizzie, what use would it be to him?"

"Hush, Laura," said Cassy, and Mr Carr made some lighthearted remark about the possibility of a family using the room in the future, but poor Lizzie was so disconcerted, she could not say another word. Moving to the windows she gazed out at the view, while she heard her sister ask, "Do you hope to have a family, Mr Carr?" at which the gentleman, who laughed too readily to be comfortable, Lizzie thought, rambled on saying something that sounded like "Is that not the hope of every man, Miss Laura?"

Lizzie prayed that Laura would ask no more questions and, to her great relief, her brother Darcy came in and demanded to be taken to see the new foals in the stables and that, mercifully, was the end of it.

Everyone trooped down to the meadow, where the horses were either tethered or allowed to canter freely around the paddock, while in the stables were the mares with their foals. The enthusiasm with which these endearing creatures were greeted and the excitement of being allowed to stroke them and hand feed them ensured that the awkwardness of the previous few minutes was soon forgotten.

By the time they returned to the house for refreshments, which had been laid out on trestle tables covered with crisp white tablecloths under the ancient oak tree, the day was considerably warmer and everyone was cheerful. Mr Carr, playing host, was ready to put them all at ease, plying them with food and recounting stories of his sojourn in America.

Later, they went indoors and, after dinner, which was a simple rather than sumptuous meal, they withdrew to the parlour, where stood a pianoforte, a beautiful old instrument, only recently delivered.

Lizzie and her sister were persuaded to play and sing for them. Lizzie was an accomplished performer, with many years of dedicated study, while Laura sang with a youthful enthusiasm that usually made up for any lack of style.

After their short recital, Mr Carr joined them, revealing his own very acceptable talent, as he played and sang, gathering the rest of the company around and encouraging them to join in. Richard and Cassy had not sung together for years, yet with some gentle persuasion, found themselves involved in this most pleasing entertainment, which left them feeling very nostalgic indeed.

To an observer, it would have appeared to be a happy, almost carefree occasion, but both Cassandra and her husband carried a heavy burden of anxiety and, to them, this was but a delightful interlude.

Returning home that night, there was much praise for Mr Carr; his hospitality and manners were pronounced perfect and, of course, all the remarkable work he had accomplished at Rushmore Farm deserved their highest accolades. Dr Gardiner commented upon the improvement to the value of the property;

young Darcy thought the stud would be much better managed by the new steward, Mr Boyden; and Cassy claimed she had been most impressed with the tasteful refurbishment of the rooms downstairs.

"It has been done with simplicity and restraint, without compromising the character of the old building. He would certainly have Papa's approval and, as you know, that is not lightly given."

Her husband agreed and, because Lizzie had been quiet and said nothing at all, he asked, "And what did you like best, Lizzie?"

When her daughter took a while to answer, Cassy wondered whether she was being inordinately coy. She had noted that their host had complimented her upon her performance at the pianoforte; he had gone over to the instrument and taken out some sheet music, which he had invited Lizzie to try, but Cassy had overheard Lizzie refuse politely, claiming she needed to practice before she could perform a new composition. Whereupon, Mr Carr had given her the music and urged her to take it with her to practice at home, assuring her it was only a trifling little French melody, but a pretty one. Cassy heard him say he was quite sure she would master it easily.

She had not heard him say, as he escorted them to their carriage, when they were leaving, "Miss Gardiner, I hope I will have the pleasure before too long of hearing you sing 'Les Petites Oiseaux,'" and on hearing her answer that she would do her best to master it, he had added, "I shall certainly look forward to it."

As it happened, when Lizzie answered, "I think, Mama, I liked the garden best; it's so natural and wild looking," her mother smiled indulgently and said, "That is because Mr Carr has not had the time to tame it yet. Will Camden's mother designed the gardens around Rushmore Farm, but neither Will nor his wife ever took much interest in them. No doubt Mr Carr, when he has completed work on the house, will turn his attention to the rather unruly grounds that surround it."

Lizzie said nothing, but in her heart, she hoped Mr Carr would do nothing of the sort. She wished he would leave it just as he had found it. The untamed woodlands that seemed almost about to encroach upon the farm and the tranquil water meadows were home to a myriad of wild creatures. They had a special beauty that appealed to her sensibility.

"Oh dear," she thought, hearing her mother's words, "I do hope Mr Carr will not go out one day and have it all chopped down and get some expensive landscape designer from London to put in a lot of pools and shrubs and silly statues in its place. That would be just dreadful!"

They were to leave for Cambridge on the Monday following, but one of the horses was sick and needed attention, causing the journey to be postponed by a day or two. Fortuitously, it seemed, Mr Carr who was also travelling on that day, but only to Derby, called in to wish them a safe journey. When invited to take tea with them before proceeding on his way, he accepted with some alacrity.

Cassandra, being busy with arrangements for her husband's departure, greeted him, asked that tea be served in the morning room, and left him with Lizzie and her brother, while she went upstairs. Richard was making some notes for Edward about a patient who might have need of medication in his absence and, as she watched him, it was all Cassy could do to hold back her tears. She knew in her heart that his journey, undertaken chiefly to please her parents, was unlikely to result in anything more than the confirmation of the depressing news she had already received from her brother.

Earlier, she had counselled her daughter, urging her to write and keep her mother informed of any developments taking place in her uncle's household. She did not have much hope that circumstances would change for the better; she could only pray they would not get much worse.

Meanwhile, downstairs, Mr Carr, having taken tea, was preparing to leave; Lizzie had just told him how much she had liked the grounds around Rushmore Farm.

"When you return from Cambridge in the Summer, Miss Gardiner, I shall have done a good deal more work on the grounds. I hope you will like them even more, then," he said.

At these words, Lizzie, quite genuinely alarmed that he was about to "tame the unruly woodlands" as her mother had predicted he would, pleaded, "Please Mr Carr, I do hope you do not intend to cut down the woods and drain the water meadows for pasture."

Mr Carr seemed astounded. "Cut down the woods? Why Miss Gardiner, whatever made you think I could do such a thing? The woods around Rushmore Farm are, for me, the most beautiful part of the property; they are full of grand old trees. I would never dream of it, I assure you," he said earnestly. "As for draining the water meadows, you must not forget I am an Irishman, Miss Gardiner. I love the water meadows. I would no more drain them than chop down the splendid old oak that stands at the front of the house."

Lizzie's bright smile signalled her complete approval, and Mr Carr looked decidedly pleased with her response.

"Clearly you think as I do, Miss Gardiner," he said, and she agreed, "Oh yes indeed, I think they are the loveliest part of Rushmore Farm, Mr Carr; you have done much to improve the house, but without the woods and the meadows and all the wonderful creatures that live in them, it would be just an ordinary farm. The woods and meadows make all the difference. I am delighted that you intend to leave them just as they are."

Clearly happy to have her approval, he said, "I most certainly do. I can assure you that when you return from Cambridge, the special beauty of the place will not have been changed. When I spoke just now of work I intended to do, I was thinking of the paddocks and stables for the horses. They need restoring."

Lizzie's eyes shone with pleasure, but there was no time for more conversation for Dr Gardiner and Cassy were coming downstairs.

Lizzie gave him her hand as they parted and, at the very moment when he raised it to his lips, Cassy entered the room.

Young Darcy, standing at the door, had inadvertently obscured them from his mother's view, which was just as well, for Cassy Gardiner had far too many things to worry about, without beginning to be concerned about the possibility of her daughter, who was not yet nineteen, being courted by the Irish-American grandson of a stable boy.

As it happened, Mr Carr said his farewells quickly, thanked the Gardiners, and left, taking young Darcy with him. They had business in Derby, to do with the horse stud, Darcy said. Both Cassy and her husband had noted the easy friendship that existed between their son and Mr Carr. Richard was particularly pleased. "Mr Carr seems a mature and sensible man; I hope his example will encourage Darcy to settle into a suitable career," he said, as the two men drove away.

Lizzie embraced her mother before her father assisted her into the carriage. Cassy smiled for them, but watched them go with a heavy heart. The disturbing echo of Josie's words at Pemberley, about the sad fate of women who sacrificed their personal happiness in the service of others, and the memory of her brother's despondent countenance as he met her eyes could not be easily dispelled.

Through the Spring of 1865 and into the Summer, Michael Carr continued to work hard at the farm, building up and developing the property he felt he had so advantageously and fortuitously acquired. Ever since he had come into his uncle's money, he had longed for a place of his own. Not so as to win the favour of those members of society who valued a man by the extent of his property, but because he longed to feel a part of a community, however small.

Never having lived in Ireland, he had little more than ties of sentiment to the old country; as for America, where he had spent his early childhood and some of his later years, he felt no more at home there than he would in Brazil or Canada, where many men had gone in search of fortune and power.

In France, it had been different; he had enjoyed the life and loved the country, with its ancient heritage and rich culture, but he was always at a disadvantage. However proficient he became at the language, France was not his home. He had made many friends, but remained always the outsider. Only in England, where he had been at school for many years, had he felt some sense of belonging. Since he had returned recently and become friends with young Darcy Gardiner and met his family, his entire world had changed.

With the acquisition of his own little piece of England, in a part of the country that had once been home to his grandparents, he had at last begun to feel the tug of a homeland upon his heart.

He worked hard at improving the place and hoped to have it ready when Summer returned. Perhaps, he asked young Darcy, they might even play a game of cricket here. Darcy wasn't certain; he would have to ask his team, he said, but he was sure something could be arranged.

"What about a country dance, after the customary cricket match at Kympton?" he suggested. Darcy was certain *that* would be very well received. "Because," he explained, "apart from the annual Harvest Festival and the ball at Pemberley, to which not everyone is invited, there are few places the younger folk of the village can attend for a dance. Not everyone wants to go into Derby to the assembly rooms. I am sure if you have a dance at Rushmore Farm, you will be enormously popular with all the families in the district."

Mr Carr thought he liked the sound of that. It would be a very good way to get to know all his neighbours, landholders and tenants alike.

"Perhaps, we could have fireworks?" he suggested, and Darcy thought that was a very good scheme, indeed.

It would all require a great deal of work, of course, but Mr Carr was confident it could be done and Darcy promised to help.

Unhappily for Mr Carr, however, they were overtaken soon afterwards by events in London, where the political situation was gaining in heat and rhetoric what it was losing in logic and clarity. At breakfast, some days later, reading from a letter he had received from Mr Colin Elliott, MP, Darcy Gardiner announced, "Lord Palmerston, having won a vote of confidence in the Commons, by the skin of his teeth, is now, at the age of eighty, intending to fight another election, on no issue at all, except that of his own popularity. The man's a megalomaniac!"

Before the day was out, Darcy, whose fascination with politics had been stoked to a blaze by the news, was preparing to set off for Westminster with the intention of "being in at the death" and involving himself in Mr Elliott's campaign for re-election.

That, unfortunately, left Mr Carr on his own, with no one to turn to for advice, since with the onset of Spring, Cassy Gardiner was deeply involved in the affairs of her father's estate, Pemberley.

Already there had been disputes between old tenants and newcomers, which needed settling, and the allocation of grazing rights on the Common, which was made available to all, was coming up again as a potentially contentious issue. Mr Darcy's steward had appealed for Cassy's help in resolving the matter. She had her hands full.

Returning from Cambridge, her husband had brought no news, except that both Julian and Josie had welcomed Lizzie with what appeared to be genuine pleasure. "No doubt, they will enjoy having Lizzie to sit between them at table each night," he said. "I must confess I found the quite palpable atmosphere of coldness very difficult indeed."

"Poor little Lizzie, I do hope she is not going to be miserable," said Cassy, almost wishing she had not kept her promise to send them her daughter for company. Richard was certain that Lizzie, being intelligent and sensible, would find sufficient things to occupy her. "Anthony was clearly delighted to see her," he said, and Cassy was reminded once more of Julian's sad tale about the boy.

Meanwhile, as if to mock her own discontent, letters from Kent and Hertfordshire brought good news aplenty. Her cousins, Emma and James Wilson, were at the centre of a resurgent campaign to press for electoral reform. Emma wrote:

With the possibility of Mr Gladstone being elected with sufficient support to lead the Liberal and Reformist MPs in the new Parliament (for they have quite given up on Lord Palmerston), there is a very real prospect that what we have all hoped for may come to pass at last.

James says he is embarrassed that England is being so tardy about giving ordinary men the vote. (As for the women, no one is prepared to speculate when that might even be regarded as a debatable proposition!)

Your Darcy is here and being exceedingly helpful. He has so much energy and keeps everyone entertained with his imitations of Lord Palmerston.

Emma was clearly enjoying the prospect.

Cassy, who had never been able to summon up enough enthusiasm to become involved in politics herself, could not help but admire her cousin's devotion to her husband's cause of reform.

Not long afterwards, from Netherfield came even more good news, as the Bingleys, Jonathan and Anna, celebrated the return of Jonathan's son Charles to Hertfordshire. Not only did they express their pleasure at his decision to work at the new Children's Hospital, but the letter brought also the very special news that Jonathan's daughter Anne-Marie was expecting her first child at Christmas. Having no children from her first marriage, Anne-Marie had longed for a child.

Anna wrote of their happiness:

Especially because dear Anne-Marie has suffered so much in the past, one almost has to pray that this time it will turn out all right. She and Mr Elliott are delighted, of course, but just at this moment seem to be concentrating more upon the election which looms in July than the baby due in December.

Everyone seemed to have their share of good news, thought Cassy, even Mr Bowles, Jonathan's steward, who had been a lonely widower for twenty years, was married again. Her mother had heard from Mrs Charlotte Collins that Mr Bowles and his wife Harriet, who had been Charlotte's faithful companion for many years, were now in charge of managing the household at Longbourn. No doubt, *they* would be very happy, too!

To Cassandra, all this bliss was beginning to sound tedious. Why, she wondered, was her family so beset with woe?

Her own keen anguish sprang from her brother's desperate situation, which was so compounded by trouble that, as a consequence, her own life and that of her family had been unavoidably affected as well. She was also well aware of the depressing effect all this had had upon her parents.

Two days later, the arrival of a letter from Lizzie brought some relief. She was well and in good spirits. She had visited Julian's college and seen the great library that was the heart of its treasures, as well the laboratory where he did most of his work. Strangely, she said, Aunt Josie had never seen it.

"My uncle says she has never asked to visit, although he would have liked to have shown her its amazing secrets," she wrote.

Lizzie wrote also of a soirée and supper party—which she and Josie had attended in the company of the two Misses Wallace-Groom—at which they had met both Mr Barrett and his friend the publisher, Mr Andrew Jones. According to Lizzie, anybody who aspired to be anything in the literary world had been present, and Mr Dickens had been expected to do a reading from his latest book but had not turned up.

The reason given by our hosts was that the great man was sick with bron-chitis, but Mama, you will not be surprised to learn that the gossips had it he was in France with his mistress, Miss Nelly Ternan!

wrote Lizzie. Cassy was rather shocked but read on.

You will also be happy to hear, Mama, that my dear brother Darcy arrived quite unexpectedly last week and wanted me to accompany him to a ball at a private house in Regent Street. I was at first reluctant to go, because I had not brought anything suitable to wear for such an occasion, but Aunt Josie lent me one of her gowns, a beautiful confection of cream silk and lace with a large rose on the shoulder. I finally went and my brother declared that I looked "very acceptable," which I suppose from him is a compliment.

To my surprise, I discovered, when we arrived at the house, that Mr Carr was to be one of our party. Darcy claimed his friend was in London for a few days on business and had been coaxed into joining us. Mr Carr admitted later that he had been very reluctant, since he scarcely knew anyone at all, except Darcy, but he was very glad he had allowed himself to be persuaded. If I were to tell the truth, dear Mama, so was I, for Mr Carr and my brother were the only men present with whom one could have a sensible conversation.

Most of the ladies were rather silly and very overdressed, while a lot of the young gentlemen were foppish and had nothing to say, only town talk. When we danced, they would ask, patronisingly, "And where have you come from, Miss Gardiner?" as if one were a mouse.

And when I replied, "From Derbyshire," they would roll their eyes and some would say, "And where, my dear young lady, is that?" as if they had never heard of it. Others pretended to believe it was in Scotland!

After a while, I grew tired of this stupidity and would answer, "From Cambridge," which made them sit up and take a bit more notice, at least. But oh, Mama, they were all so dull, I was very glad of Mr Carr's company, though being American, he did not know many of the new dances at all. Darcy and I have promised to teach him in time for the Pemberley Ball.

He was full of news about the work he has been doing at the farm. It seems he expects to have it all finished in time for the Midsummer Festival. There is none of that here. Oh I do long to be home again.

Cassy was glad to know that Lizzie, in spite of her complaint of boredom, seemed to be enjoying herself.

There was, however, no more news of Julian or Josie, except for one line at the end, which must have been added as an afterthought.

Mama, I almost forgot, it seems Mr Andrew Jones has promised Mr Barrett that he would "consider very favourably" a proposal to publish

Aunt Josie's anthology of poems. Aunt Josie is very excited; she and Mr Barrett have been celebrating all day.

…and with that cryptic line, followed by her usual affectionate salutation, the letter ended, to her mother's utter consternation.

"Josie and Mr Barrett were celebrating? Celebrating what?"

Cassy, left in terrible suspense, wondered about the implications of Lizzie's words for her brother and his wife.

What was Julian doing? she asked herself. She was in two minds about writing to her daughter at once, demanding more information, but was afraid the letter may fall into Josie's hands and she, believing she was being spied upon, could possibly turn against Lizzie.

Cassy was wild to know what was going on. If only her sister-in-law Caroline were here, she thought, she could confide in her; but Caroline and her son David were gone to Manchester on business. Cassy was feeling very frustrated indeed.

She had just sat down to write to her daughter anyway, to ask for more information, when the doorbell rang. An express had been delivered; it was from Julian. Her brother wrote briefly, informing her that he was on his way to Matlock and was bringing Lizzie and little Anthony with him.

Cassandra had no idea what this meant, nor did she understand why Lizzie was returning with no warning. Could she have been taken ill? Cassy wondered, more worried now than ever.

Having spent the afternoon in an agony of uncertainty, in which a dozen different possibilities, each worse than the other, occurred to her, she heard her husband's carriage arrive and ran downstairs. He greeted her and, as they went upstairs together, he could sense that she was impatient to tell him something.

When they were in their apartments, she handed him both letters— Lizzie's written several days ago and Julian's much more recent express. Richard read each one slowly and, as he finished reading Julian's hastily scribbled note, his expression, which had been rather serious when he arrived, became very grave indeed. He did not speak for several minutes as she waited anxiously for his response.

When he spoke, his voice was quiet and very calm, as though he had deliberately composed himself to break the news to her as gently as possible. "I think, my love, you must prepare yourself for a shock. I, too, have received an express from Julian, delivered to the hospital this afternoon. It would appear both letters were despatched together.

"He does not say very much more than he does in yours, but it is quite clear to me that Josie is no longer with him. He says he is bringing Anthony to us, because there is no longer anyone to care for the boy, and as for Lizzie, he states that it would not be seemly for her to stay on at his house alone. Now, I can only deduce from those words that his wife has left the house. If that is the case, I entirely agree that Lizzie cannot remain there alone."

Cassandra could not believe what she was hearing, yet she could not contest a word of it. Logic and reason, good sense even, no longer seemed to apply to what was rapidly becoming a nightmare. Nothing had prepared her for this possibility.

Despite the kindness of her husband, as he tried to alleviate her distress, the shock was just too much for her. Tears coursed down her cheeks, and she hid her face in her pillow, as she tried to absorb the implications of what she had just heard. It was an appalling prospect, one she had not expected to confront in her life ever. That such a thing should befall a member of her family, indeed her own dear brother, was unthinkable. There was little Richard could do or say to comfort her. She was apprehensive and confused. A bewildering afternoon was followed by an evening of anxiety, during which no question could be answered, and a sleepless night.

Julian Darcy arrived in the late afternoon of the following day, having travelled from Cambridge in a hired vehicle, stopping only for refreshment and to change horses on the way. When he alighted and carried his sleeping son into the house, Cassy could see her brother was suffering both shock and exhaustion.

His eyes were red with lack of sleep and she was stunned by the desolation of his entire demeanour; he appeared to move as if in a trance, said nothing, and made no attempt to explain anything.

Only young Lizzie seemed to have her wits about her. She took the sleeping child from his arms and carried him upstairs to her room, where she laid him in her bed, removed his jacket and boots, loosened his inner clothing, and let him sleep. But even Lizzie had nothing to say that could in some way enhance her mother's comprehension of the situation they faced.

Dr Gardiner had returned early from the hospital to await his brother-in-law's arrival. When he saw Julian, he went to him at once and took his hand. Julian nodded, embraced his sister, and walking directly into the sitting room, he almost collapsed into an armchair by the fire. Richard hastened to get him a drink and Cassy sent for refreshments, but Julian did not say a word. When at last he did speak, his words came quietly and very quickly, as though he was ashamed of what he was saying and wished to get it over with.

"Cassy, Richard, what can I say? I am sorry, deeply sorry to cause you all this trouble. I would have given anything to spare you and my parents this pain. But there was nothing I could do." He paused and said simply, "Josie is gone away to London with Mr Barrett."

There was an audible gasp; Cassy was incredulous.

"What?"

"Yes, and she left this note." He took from his pocket a scrap of blue notepaper, adding, "He has promised to publish her poetry and perhaps also a collection of articles and essays, she says. She claims she is going, not because she loves him, but because she needs her freedom. She says she can no longer write and work as she wants to under my roof." His voice was flat and cold, like that of someone reporting the death of a stranger, a person for whom they felt nothing at all.

In the awful silence that followed, Cassy could neither speak nor weep.

She sat before him, feeling cold and ill, as she heard her husband ask, "And have you made any attempt to find her or speak with her?" as he poured out another drink, which Julian swallowed hurriedly, before replying, "No, I have not, Richard; there is nothing I can say, nothing I have not said before, which will make her change her mind.

"Josie told me a long time ago that she no longer loved me; she felt I was putting my own work before her and that I had not taken her work seriously. It was not enough to say that I loved her and Anthony dearly, which I did, better than my life; she wanted something more, which, clearly she had decided I could not give her."

"What was it, did she say?" Richard asked.

"Not in so many words," Julian replied, "but it was clear she was unhappy and discontented. Perhaps she wanted more praise for her work or more accommodation of her literary friends. I never objected to them coming to the house, but if I had work to do, I would, after some time, withdraw to my study. Josie was offended. She thought I did not value them, because their work was not scientific, like mine was.

"This was not true. I never was rude or arrogant with them; I am not an arrogant person. It is simply the case that I had little in common with them, people like Barrett and Jones and the Wallace-Groom women; I had little to say to them and they certainly found even less to say to me," he explained sadly. "But I must confess, I did not think she would leave. I always hoped she would stay, for Anthony's sake, at least. Clearly, I was mistaken. I suppose Barrett's promise to publish her book must have tipped the scales against us."

He sounded so resigned, so totally abandoned, that Cassy cried out, "But my dear Julian, did you not try to stop her, plead with her?"

He shook his head. "I had no chance, Cassy; she was gone when I returned home from the college, taking Susan, her maid, with her and most of her clothes and jewellery. Earlier in the week, she had dismissed the nurse, Mrs Hunt, while Lizzie and Anthony were out walking in the park. Josie claimed Mrs Hunt had been gossiping with the servants; except for the cook and Mr Bates, there were just Lizzie, Anthony, myself, and the maid left."

Seeing his sister's shocked expression, he added, "I did not know what to do, Cassy; it was your Lizzie who suggested that we bring Anthony here. She said she could care for him until we found a suitable nurse. I did not know what else I could have done."

Richard and Cassy spoke, almost as one, to assure him he had done the right thing. Lizzie's suggestion had been a sensible and practical one, they said; Anthony would be safe and cared for by all of them and he would have James for company, too. Their youngest son was almost the same age as Anthony. The relief on Julian's face was plain to see. Cassy had tears in her eyes but struggled to hold them back, lest they should exacerbate her brother's grief.

Shortly afterwards, Lizzie came downstairs to say that Anthony was still fast asleep; she had asked the chambermaid to prepare the spare room for Julian and have an extra bed made up in her own room for the child.

"Once he settles down here, he can share James's room, can he not, Mama?" she asked, and Cassy agreed, amazed at the calmness with which Lizzie had made all the arrangements.

Richard had noticed that Julian was quite exhausted and decided it was best to show him to his room, while Lizzie put her arms around her mother and suggested that she, too, should rest a while before dinner.

"Mama, you need have no concerns at all about Anthony," she said as they went upstairs. "I am well able to care for him and he is not at all a difficult child. Indeed I have had the care of him for most of this month, since Aunt Josie has had little time for him and Susan has been kept busy with her mistress's errands. Anthony, who is a very bright little fellow, became my companion and friend."

Cassy looked at her daughter, searching her face, seeing her in a whole new light.

"Tell me, Lizzie, how long have you known this was going to happen?" she asked.

Lizzie's voice was matter of fact, deliberately undramatic. "I have suspected it for quite some time, Mama, but I have only known for certain this week. Do you recall the party of which I wrote, the one we attended with Hetty and Dora Wallace-Groom and there met Mr Barrett and Mr Jones?"

Cassy nodded, recalling the letter clearly.

"Well, I suspected then that something was afoot, but I was unsure whether it was Mr Barrett or Mr Jones. I think Aunt Josie believes that Mr Barrett is in love with her."

"And is he?" asked her mother.

"I think not, Mama. I have seen him flirting with Hetty Wallace-Groom when Aunt Josie is not present; but I think she believes that he loves her and will help get her book published by his friend Mr Jones, who is a partner in a publishing firm in London. I am convinced that is the only reason why she has encouraged him and finally gone to him. I cannot believe she loves him; I have certainly seen no sign of it, yet she lets him think she does."

Cassy's face was grave. "Lizzie, my dear, if you knew what was going on, why did you not write me something of what was happening?" she asked, but Lizzie shook her head and, suddenly, her eyes filled with tears.

"What good would it have done, Mama? Neither you nor Papa could have stopped her. She had Susan pack her trunk with her best clothes and jewellery almost a week before she left. I saw the trunk in Susan's room and questioned her, but she made some excuse about Josie wanting to be rid of some old, unfashionable garments.

"Which means Susan knew it all?" Cassy was outraged.

"Yes and, as I have told you, she will do anything for Aunt Josie, so devoted is she to her. But, even Susan does not entirely approve of Mr Barrett. She doesn't trust him, nor Mr Jones, and I do not blame her," said Lizzie.

Another, even more dreadful possibility had occurred to Cassy. "Lizzie, is it possible Josie may be duped by both these men?" she asked.

Lizzie could not be sure; she did not know them well enough, she said, to make such a judgment. It was possible that Barrett was fond of Josie and would help her publish her book, but she could not be sure. Of Andrew Jones she knew little, she said, and what she knew she did not like. It was clear to her mother that Lizzie had little respect for either man.

Cassy felt her heart sink, as she contemplated the situation. There was no hope or comfort to be found anywhere. Each new question that was answered appeared to bring even more uncertainty. There was only one absolute certainty: her parents would have to be told the truth; there could be no question of dissembling, for surely the news would soon be known in London.

"Oh, Lizzie, this is such a wretched situation; the shock will kill poor Mama," she said, her face betraying the extent of her anxiety.

"As for Papa, I do not know how he will bear it. He has always spoken up for Josie; even when Mama and Aunt Jane were very critical of her for not taking an interest in Pemberley, Papa defended her, pointing out that she was very young and ambitious and entitled to be so."

Lizzie knew exactly what her mother meant. She had heard her grandfather praise Josie's work and she, too, wondered how her grandparents, who had already lost one son, would cope with the disastrous fate of the other. For surely, what was a terrible personal loss for Julian Darcy must also be a catastrophe for Pemberley, when the man who was to be its next master was suddenly deserted by his wife.

Her mother insisted upon hearing all the particulars, asking several questions, not all of which Lizzie could answer.

"You must tell me everything, Lizzie. I need to know it all if I am to answer the questions that will surely come from Mama, not to mention Rebecca Tate. Now, *she* must have had a dreadful shock. I wonder, could she have had any apprehension of Josie's intentions?"

Lizzie was of the belief that neither Mrs Tate nor her husband would have had any inkling of what Josie intended doing.

"They could not have had any misgivings, because I know that Mr Tate is acquainted with Mr Jones's firm; they do business together and indeed Andrew Jones has been invited to stay at the Tates' place in London on occasions. I have heard them speak of it. I have no doubt he would have introduced Mr Barrett to the family; they are very close," said Lizzie.

"Is Barrett well regarded?" asked Cassy, curious to discover the background of this stranger who had caused such sudden turmoil in their family.

Lizzie gave a wry smile. "I hardly know how to answer that, Mama. If you believe Hetty Wallace-Groom, he is a paragon among men, but Mrs Hunt, the nurse, had a very different opinion. She had worked for a family in London with whom he was once intimate. She could tell stories of his ability to charm and deceive and quite a few tales of reckless conduct, leading to a great falling-out between them. Indeed, she told Susan of it, in an attempt to alert her mistress, but all she got for her trouble was instant dismissal for gossiping," she explained.

"Oh dear," said Cassy, "and what of Mr Jones: is he a better man than his friend?"

"I rather doubt it, Mama, if you mean is he a gentleman? I suppose in the society sense of the word, yes, he is; but he is not to be trusted. In his appearance, he is attractive in a languid style, as one might expect a poet or musician to look, but to my mind, he is far worse than Barrett, for he has an appearance of innocence, which is far from the reality. I would not credit a word he says."

Cassandra was astonished at how self-composed her daughter was, in the midst of this confusion; she, who a year ago had seemed too young to go away to stay with her uncle and aunt in Cambridge, had apparently learned to make shrewd judgments about the people she had met there. Cassy doubted that she would have been so capable or indeed so sanguine herself at that age.

"Poor Julian," she said, "to have his wife embroiled in such dubious company; how it must hurt him," and Lizzie agreed.

"It was sad to see how he accepted, without protest, everything that was happening in his own house. I think he loved her and was afraid to cross her in any way, for fear of losing her," she said.

"And then he lost her anyway," said her mother, and the sadness in her voice was immeasurable.

It was agreed between them that they would speak of it to no one at the moment, especially not before the servants, for then it was bound to become common currency in the village and would soon be conveyed to Pemberley. "I know that concealment is not possible for long, but we must try, at least until Julian and my parents have met and found a way to comprehend and deal with it together," said Cassy, determined that the village gossips would not get any satisfaction from her.

At dinner, there were only the four of them, for Edward was dining in Derby. No one mentioned Josie at table and, afterwards, Julian thanked them all, asked to be excused, and went upstairs to bed. On the morrow, after he had rested, Cassandra would take her brother to Pemberley to break the unhappy news to their parents.

Her own account of their meeting, given in a letter to Jonathan and Anna Bingley, who remained her close confidantes, made no secret of her feelings. She placed most of the blame at the feet of her sister-in-law.

Dearest Jonathan and Anna,

It is almost impossible for me to write of this terrible, terrible thing that has happened, without weeping. Yet I know I must hold back my tears and suppress my outrage, for the pain this has inflicted upon my dear parents is well nigh unbearable and I have no wish to add one single grain to their burden.

Having given some of the salient facts, without revealing all of the strange details of Josie's behaviour, she continued...

Please, dear Anna and Jonathan, spare a thought in your prayers for my Mama, who after the death of our dear William, has spent years hoping that Julian will grow up to take Papa's place one day, only to have this happen.

She has lived for Papa and her family; can you not understand how she must feel? As for Papa, who has always defended Josie, even when Mama and I have been rather impatient of her lack of interest in Pemberley, he must now feel betrayed.

I cannot describe how distraught they were, Mama especially, when Julian told them she had gone with this Mr Barrett, whoever he may be, to London and showed them the cold little note she had left.

She writes of her desire for freedom to pursue her work; never have I seen my dear father look so shocked. He hardly said a word for fully five minutes, as he stood with her note in his hand, gazing out of the window.

When he did speak, he asked Julian if he had ever read his wife's work or talked to her about it. When Julian confessed that he had often been too busy, Papa simply shook his head and said very quietly, "Perhaps, if you had tried, Julian, it may have helped. Now, I suppose it is too late and we may never know."

I can see that he does not lay the blame at her door alone. Mama does, though; she said it was a wicked thing to abandon your child and husband and run off to another man, only because you want him to publish your books. It was a fool's errand, she said.

Dearest Anna, I may sound harsh, but I have to agree with Mama on this matter. Josie has said, in her note to my brother, that she does not love Mr Barrett, and my Lizzie, who spent most of Spring with them, confirms that she saw no sign of affection either. Now, no matter how much it meant to me, I could not have left my husband and children for such an ambition. Do you not agree that such an action betrays our own worth as well as those we love? Furthermore, even from a purely practical point of view, what guarantee of success or happiness is there in such an enterprise?

I feel poor Josie will be forever haunted by her actions, and whatever fame or satisfaction she gains will also be tainted by them.

My poor brother, meanwhile, must return to his college, where it is likely everyone will by now be aware of his wretched predicament, and complete his work before he leaves for France. Whether he will return to work in Cambridge, I cannot say.

Anthony, meanwhile, will remain with us and probably study with James's tutor next year. The poor child seems quite baffled by what has happened.

My dear Jonathan, I know how much affection Mama and Papa have for you and I would plead, if it were at all possible, that you visit them when you can find the time. It would greatly improve their spirits.

Richard and I also look forward to seeing you and Anna again, when you can drag yourselves away from the peaceful haven that is Netherfield.

Forgive me if I sound as if our lives have been one long slough of despond. This is not true for we have had very many happy years, until this one!

Were it not for Richard and my dear children, I should have been miserable indeed. My Lizzie has been a comfort and a most agreeable companion. A year ago she was a child; today she is a wise young woman, for whose understanding and company I am most grateful.

The letter ended with the fondest of salutations.

Jonathan Bingley sighed. "It seems, my love, I was wrong in thinking that Cassy and Richard were blessed with complete happiness. Like a sunlit garden, there appeared to be nothing that could darken their lives; sadly, it would seem that is no longer true," he said as he handed Cassy's letter to his wife.

Following the return of Julian Darcy to Cambridge, Cassandra, aware of the need to assist her father, became even more deeply involved in the affairs of Pemberley, while Lizzie undertook the organisation of young Anthony's life.

The little boy, strangely, did not seem to miss either of his parents very much and though sometimes, in his sleep or at play, he would call out for one of them, Lizzie discovered that if the call were swiftly and affectionately answered by her or her mother, he appeared to be satisfied. Plainly, the child had no deep bond with either parent.

He was a pleasing, affectionate little fellow and was no trouble to teach, so eager was he to learn and keep up with his cousin James, while Lizzie, having developed a special relationship with him in London, enjoyed his confidence.

Until arrangements could be made in the New Year to engage a tutor for both boys, Lizzie had taken over the task of teaching them. Often, when the weather was fine, she would take them out for a nature walk, up the road, through the village, and into the woods or meadows, an experience they all thoroughly enjoyed.

It was on one of these days that Lizzie saw a familiar figure come out of the tobacconist's shop in the main street. The man, on seeing them, stopped and tipped his hat. In that instant, she recognised him: it was Mr Andrew Jones. The two boys had stopped to look in the window of a shop that sold toy soldiers and, though she would have liked to have got them away sooner, Lizzie could not persuade them to leave. Seeing her waiting for the children, Mr Jones crossed the street and quite deliberately walked towards them. Lizzie was both annoyed and confused. She had no desire to speak with him; indeed, in the circumstances, a friend of Mr Barrett was the very last person she wanted to meet. She had by now taken both her charges by the hand, so that when he came up to her, all she could do to acknowledge his greeting was to nod and say good day, while he stood before her, smiling broadly.

After this most perfunctory exchange, she urged the boys to hurry lest they be late for tea. Andrew Jones tried to keep up with them, but Lizzie, who knew the village well, had the advantage over him and, claiming they had someone to see in the village, she plunged first down one narrow street and then another, until they came upon the lane that ran all the way down to the river and across the footbridge.

Despite the unsuitability of her shoes for tramping across fields, she pressed on, encouraged by the obvious pleasure of the boys who were enjoying this unusual adventure, jumping puddles and scrambling over stiles, until they were within sight of home. There, she stopped to catch her breath and clean the mud off her shoes. Her face was flushed with the exercise and she was cross at herself for being so upset at meeting Mr Jones.

Even as she went upstairs to her room, having surrendered her two muddy pupils to the housekeeper for bathing and changing, Lizzie wondered what could have brought Jones into the district. Surely, she thought, he must know that the families of both Julian and Josie lived in the area and, as a friend of Barrett's, he would not be welcome among them. She marvelled at his arrogance in believing that she would acknowledge him and be seen walking with him in the village. It was a preposterous notion. Lizzie could still feel her anger rising as she thought about it and wished with all her heart that she had had the presence of mind and the wit to say something that would have put him in his place.

When she had indulged herself with a long, hot, lavender-scented bath, put on fresh clothes and shoes, and brushed out her hair, she began to feel a little calmer. It was still not quite tea time, but the maid had brought her some anyway, which she took with her into the sitting room. She hoped to practice for a while at the pianoforte and, having selected some music, had been seated at the instrument only a little while, when she heard the sound of a carriage coming up the drive.

Believing it to be her mother, who had been at Pemberley all day, attending to the concerns of Mr Darcy's tenants, Lizzie continued playing. Moments later, the maid opened the door of the room to admit Mr Carr. Lizzie sprang up from her seat as he came towards her. He looked rather awkward and uneasy, she thought and wondered what could be amiss, when taking her hand, he said, "Miss Gardiner, forgive me if I have intruded upon you, but I have only just heard the sad news about your uncle, Mr Julian Darcy...I am so very sorry."

Lizzie's cheeks flamed with embarrassment. How could he have discovered it? Who could have told him? she wondered.

"Mr Carr, thank you for your concern; indeed it is a very unhappy situation for my uncle and the rest of his family, but may I ask how you learned of his misfortune? Was it from my brother Darcy?" she asked, bewildered that the news had reached him so swiftly.

"No indeed, it was only by the merest accident," he explained. "I went into the inn at Matlock around midday and there met a fellow who was interested, so the landlord told me, in buying a pair of horses. When I was introduced to him, I recalled that we had met before, in London at a club where I had been with a mutual friend."

Even more confused, Lizzie asked, "And did *he* tell you of my uncle's troubles? Who is this man?"

"Indeed he did," Carr replied. "He claimed he knew Mr Julian Darcy and his wife well; he is from London, a Mr Jones, Andrew Jones."

"Mr Jones!" The name sprang from her lips like a gunshot, before she could stop it. Her outrage was plain, even to Mr Carr.

"Do you know him?" he asked, and she was quick to deny it. "I would not say I knew him at all. We have met once or twice at my uncle's house."

Mr Carr nodded and, clearly unaware of any problem, went on, "Well, he is staying in the area before proceeding to spend some time shooting with friends in Cromford, he said. He wishes to acquire a pair of horses and was interested in mine. I'm afraid I had to disappoint him; I am not selling any horses, though I told him he was welcome to visit the stud and take a look at them, if he had a mind to do so," he explained, while Lizzie could scarcely contain her anger.

At this point, Mr Carr, alerted by the sharpness of Lizzie's voice as well as the frown on her face, added, "It was when he heard that I had come to purchase the property through the good offices of your father and brother that he, aware of the family connection, told me of your Uncle Julian's unhappy situation."

"I was completely ignorant of the circumstances, but he seemed very well informed. When he appeared to want to tell me more about Mrs Darcy and his friend Barrett, of whom I had no knowledge at all, I confess I felt uneasy and made an excuse to get away."

Lizzie could well believe it. He looked most awkward and unhappy but, determined to be helpful, he said his piece. "Miss Gardiner, if this is true, I am very sorry. I came directly to offer any assistance that you or your parents may need at this time. If there is anything at all that I can do to help, please do not hesitate to ask."

There was no doubting the sincerity of his offer and the quite genuine concern in his voice. The gravity of his countenance was evidence that he had been shocked by the news.

Lizzie, who had at first felt vexed and uncomfortable at this intrusion into their lives, soon realised that Mr Carr was not to blame; it had been the insufferable Mr Jones who had been so eager to gossip about Josie and Mr Barrett. Mr Carr had come only to offer sympathy and help, if it was needed, and was surely to be commended, not blamed.

This time, she spoke more gently and with greater appreciation.

"Thank you, Mr Carr; I am sorry to have to say there is some truth in what you have heard. Josie, Mrs Darcy, has left my uncle's house, though with what motive, we are not as yet certain. I will convey your sentiments to my parents, and I am sure they will appreciate your concern," she said, "especially Mama, who is at Pemberley today helping my grandfather, Mr Darcy, with the management of his estate, undertaking many of the tasks that should have been the responsibility of my Uncle Julian."

Mr Carr nodded, appearing to understand the difficulties they faced, and once again offered his help. "I can only say again that if there is anything at all I can do, I should be most happy...you must feel free to call on me..."

However, when Lizzie, beginning now to feel kinder towards him, offered him some tea, he politely declined, sensitive perhaps to the feelings of the family and not wishing to intrude upon them any longer.

"I must be back at the farm, Miss Gardiner, but I shall call again if I may. Please convey my regards to your parents. I take it your brother Darcy is still in London?" Lizzie nodded as they went out into the hall. They were almost at the door when Cassandra arrived, alighting from the carriage and coming quickly up the steps into the house.

On seeing Mr Carr in the hall, she greeted him cordially and, having assured him he was definitely not intruding, invited him to return to the sitting room and take tea with her. "I have something very particular to ask of you," she said, and Mr Carr was happy to oblige. This was exactly what he had hoped to do.

"Lizzie, darling, would you ask Alice to fetch a large pot of tea? I shall probably need two cups at least and I am sure Mr Carr will join us, will you not?" said Cassy, turning to him, and this time he did not decline.

As Lizzie went to order more tea, she wondered how Mr Carr and her mother would negotiate the perilous waters of her uncle's situation, but she need not have worried. When she returned, with Alice bearing tea and cake, she found them deep in discussion not of Julian Darcy's marital problems, but the vexatious claims of some leaseholders who, having recently come into the district, were demanding access to the Commons, land which had been for generations the preserve of the people in the two villages that lay within the boundaries of the estates of Pemberley and Camden Park.

"You see, Mr Carr, my father and Sir Thomas Camden chose not to enclose the Commons and deprive the people of their rights. Now, these men, who have themselves evicted many poor tenant farmers from their lands, want the same rights. My father will not hear of it, and I believe Sir Thomas agrees with him. I need to discover whether their claims have any legal force. I do not wish to alert these men by calling in my father's attorney, but if you were to make some discreet enquiries…"

Mr Carr was happy to be of use and, even before she had finished her question, he had offered to see his attorney and obtain an opinion for her. Cassy was very pleased.

"Thank you very much indeed, Mr Carr," she said, as Lizzie poured out the tea. "It would not have been so aggravating if they had a genuine interest in the improvement of the land, but most of them are merely seeking to make a profit by harassing perfectly decent people and pushing them off their small holdings. My father is very angry about it; he has already accommodated two families who have been evicted by these men, families that have farmed here for generations. It is an abominable practice."

Mr Carr agreed and, as they took tea together, Lizzie looked on with some amusement. This businesslike side of her mother she did not often see. No doubt she was getting accustomed to dealing with such matters at Pemberley, Lizzie thought, with a wry smile.

A little later, she was surprised to hear her mother say, "Mr Carr, there is another little matter you can help us with," and as he turned to her, Cassy continued, "Your housekeeper, Mrs Allan, has a sister, Mrs Baines, who used to work for my mother at Pemberley. She has two daughters. Mary the elder girl is married, but Margaret, who cannot be more than eighteen, is still at home, or so my mother believes.

"If this is the case, I should like to offer her some regular work here, assisting my housekeeper and helping with the two boys, James and my brother's son Anthony, who will be staying with us. I wonder if I may trouble you to convey a message to Mrs Allan and through her to Mrs Baines? If she is agreeable, I should like to see her and Margaret in the next day or so."

As Lizzie watched, somewhat bemused, Mr Carr appeared not at all put out by her mother's request and promised to convey the message to his housekeeper that very evening. Indeed, he appeared now much more at ease than when he had first arrived, clearly happy to be of service. Having finished his tea, he left, but not before he had been invited to dine with them on the Sunday following, an invitation he accepted with obvious pleasure.

When he had gone, Cassandra put down her empty cup and declared that Mr Carr was such a kind, obliging young man.

"He puts me in mind of dear Mr Gardiner; he was very similar, always happy to help anyone who asked, ever ready to put himself out for a friend. He was such a wonderful man," she mused sadly.

Lizzie smiled and agreed that Mr Carr was indeed kind and obliging, but was it fair, she asked, to make use of him to run errands for them? She had been amused by the casual manner in which her mother had asked him to take a message to his housekeeper. This was certainly not the sort of thing Mrs Darcy or her sister Mrs Jane Bingley would have done.

But Cassy expressed astonishment at her question.

"Run errands? Lizzie, I am surprised at you! Whatever do you mean by run errands? Why, Mr Carr, having heard of the awful business of your Uncle Julian and Aunt Josie, had very kindly offered to help, 'in any way,' he said. 'Please do not hesitate to ask,' he said. So, having taken him into our confidence as a neighbour and a friend of your brother's, a gentleman of whom your Papa approves, I asked for his help in a couple of small but important matters, which I could not attend to myself. As you saw, Mr Carr agreed gladly. Said he was most happy to oblige. There is surely nothing wrong in that? Is there?"

Lizzie, faced with this completely logical, if somewhat unusual argument, gave in. "No, Mama, of course not. It is only that I feel we should not treat Mr Carr any differently to the way we would treat our other friends and neighbours," she said, and Cassy replied, "Do you mean, would I ask Sir Thomas Camden to give a message to his housekeeper? Oh Lizzie, that would be silly, because I do not believe Sir Thomas ever speaks to his housekeeper, unless it were to complain of some inadequacy; that is his way. Mr Carr is different; he is younger, for one thing, of a different generation, and remember, Lizzie, he is an American. They do not stand on ceremony as we do."

And seeing her daughter's smile widen considerably, she said, "Come now, Lizzie, you cannot tell me that he wasn't happy to be asked to help?"

Realising that she had no chance of winning this debate, Lizzie surrendered, and mother and daughter went upstairs together to rest before dressing for dinner.

Lying in her bed, Lizzie could see from her window the branches of the old elm, moving restlessly against the blue of the late-afternoon sky arching overhead. Lizzie loved the elm, like an old friend. She, with her brother Darcy, had often climbed into its sturdy arms to look at the world beyond their own domestic environment. You could see all the way across the river and into the village beyond, and if you were brave enough to climb higher, Darcy used to tell her, you could see into the next county, with the smoke rising from the kilns of the potteries. Lizzie had never climbed high enough, afraid that she would be caught by their nurse, who would surely disapprove of young girls clambering around in trees. There was also the ever-present fear that she may fall and break a leg.

But, Lizzie did recall an occasion, some years ago, when Josie Tate, who was the same age as Darcy, had climbed so high into the tree, she had been terrified, unable to get back down again, and had to be rescued by the gardener using a ladder and rope.

There had been a great fuss about that. Lizzie smiled as she recalled her mother's stern words to Darcy for leading Josie astray.

They had all been great friends then; that was, of course, before their Uncle Julian had fallen in love with her and things had changed considerably for Josie Tate.

~❦~

By the time Mr Carr returned to dine with them on Sunday, several things had taken place. Darcy Gardiner had returned, coming away from the election campaign to spend a week at home, and he had brought bad news. The story of Julian and Josie had "got around London," he said, and several people were speaking quite disparagingly of Josie.

"The women see her as a wicked, selfish creature, who has deserted her husband and child, while the men think she is a stupid woman who has been gulled into leaving a decent man for a charlatan. No one has a good word for Barrett, except Miss Hetty Wallace-Groom, who claims that Aunt Josie seduced him away from her!"

Darcy was scathing. "It would be laughable, if it were not so tragic, especially for poor Uncle Julian, who is portrayed as a decent but weak man, a bookworm who allowed another man to steal his wife from under his nose, without a word of protest!"

Neither Lizzie nor her mother, to whom he revealed these appalling tales, was surprised. It was the sort of gossip one expected to hear in London. They begged him, however, not to let his grandparents hear of it.

"It would break their hearts," said Cassy. "As for Julian, he will soon be out of it for some time, when he goes to Paris. It will do him good to be among men who are his equal in intelligence and education."

Another matter, closer to home, had been settled, too. Cassandra had engaged young Margaret Baines, who had arrived accompanied by her mother, who had agreed to the terms proposed for her employment.

Mrs Baines, herself a widow, lived alone and asked if her daughter could return home at night, after work. Margaret, she had said, was her only companion, and Cassandra had made no objection.

Since the majority of her work would concern the care of the two little boys, it was quite possible, she said, to let the girl return home each night, unless there was some exceptional circumstance. She could also have Sundays off to spend with her mother. It was an arrangement that pleased every one of the parties.

Cassy was happy with her choice. Margaret Baines was a good-humoured, pleasant girl with a bright smile and a lustrous head of auburn hair that belied her gentle and compliant manner. She would be good for the children, Cassy thought, and arranged for her to start work at the house the following week. Mrs Baines was delighted, too. She had served Mrs Darcy at Pemberley and thought it fitting that her daughter should be chosen to work for Miss Cassandra.

It was also the week when Edward announced that he was courting the daughter of the senior partner in his medical practice and told his mother he would like his parents to meet Miss Angela Anderson, who had graciously consented to be his wife.

Cassandra agreed, even though she had had very little notice of her son's inclination to marry the lady. Indeed, except for a dinner party at which both families had been present, Cassy hardly knew Miss Anderson at all. Edward had kept his interest very quiet indeed.

Naturally, she asked some questions and then wrote a note inviting Miss Anderson and her younger sister Catherine to lunch with the family on Sunday. Edward would take it to her on the following day; he was sure she would accept, he said.

Cassy was pleased. Here, at last, was something wholesome and happy to occupy them. Miss Anderson would soon become the subject of speculation and study—from her looks and clothes to her nature, her taste in books and music, and, of course, the size of her fortune. Of the latter, they confidently predicted it would be quite reasonable. Her father was a senior physician and surgeon and had a very large and lucrative practice in Derby, catering primarily to the needs of the wives and children of rich bankers and businessmen. That Edward had courted and won her with such discretion, waiting until he was sure both of her feelings and his own, was truly typical of his unassuming and careful nature, said his mother.

"Edward is not the sort to rush headlong into a marriage," she said, adding with a sigh, "but then, neither was Julian!"

When Cassy told her husband the news, he seemed pleased, especially since he knew the lady's father in a professional capacity.

"He is a very distinguished physician of high repute," he told Cassy, and added that he had also met Miss Anderson when she had accompanied her father to a meeting of the medical fraternity to honour Miss Florence Nightingale. "She is by no means a bashful or unlearned young woman," said Richard, recalling that she had shown a good deal of interest in Miss Nightingale's ideas on hospital hygiene and the prevention of disease.

"She is their eldest daughter and is much loved by her parents; Edward is a fortunate fellow to have gained their consent," he added, causing his wife to protest with vigour that her Edward was himself very clever, with a good future ahead of him and was such a fine young man that he should be considered a good match for any young lady in the county.

Her husband, amused at the strength of her loyalty and her spirited defence of their son, agreed, but not before he had teased her a little longer, rousing even more passionate claims on Edward's behalf.

Cassy's unyielding fidelity to her family, whether it was her parents, her in-laws, or her husband and children, was absolute. She would do or say anything to defend them against anyone. It was an endearing trait that had always amused her husband.

Miss Anderson accepted the invitation for herself and her sister Catherine and so did the Rector, Mr Gray, and his wife.

There was, therefore, quite a large party assembled for dinner on the Sunday, which had started without much promise but turned out very fair indeed. Edward and his lady, who, it was generally agreed, was quite amiable and pretty, but not really beautiful, were to sit beside Cassy, with the Rector and Mrs Gray, while Lizzie found herself seated between her father and Mr Carr, with her brother Darcy and Laura Ann opposite her.

They were all united on the excellence of the meal and sent many compliments to the cook, but there soon appeared to be a distinct divergence in the content and tenor of the conversation at the two ends of the dining table. While Edward, his mother, Miss Anderson, and her sister Catherine chatted quietly and soberly with the Rector and Mrs Gray about subjects that raised not a very high level of excitement, at the other end of the table, Darcy, Lizzie, and Mr Carr entertained themselves and Dr Gardiner with lighthearted prognostications and hilarious speculation about the possible outcome of the election and how disconcerted the Queen would be if Palmerston, rather than Lord Derby, won the day. Darcy Gardiner's impersonations of the royal personage and Lord Palmerston had them greatly amused.

Mr Carr confessed that he had a problem of understanding, too. Having spent most of his life in two republics, he claimed he could not comprehend the role of the Queen in English politics. The Queen, whom he described as "a rather glum-looking lady in black" (which remark he was immediately forced by young Laura Ann to "withdraw or be tried forthwith for treason"), had no real constitutional power, he said, yet all the politicians seemed to be vying for her approval!

"I confess, I find this to be strange in the extreme," he remarked.

"But, no stranger, surely," said Lizzie, "than the role of a President who must send an American army to subdue other Americans who demand freedom for themselves, but refuse to free their slaves?"

This adroit riposte brought instant and willing capitulation from Mr Carr. "Touché, Miss Gardiner, I have no answer to that conundrum."

"I can see you are going to need a few lessons in English history, Mr Carr," said Richard, and Darcy declared that Lizzie would be the best person to teach him, since she was a great student of history herself.

This brought on a further lively discussion, which continued through dessert, until it was time for the ladies to withdraw to the drawing room.

While there had been a good deal of conversation on a range of subjects through the evening, there was an unspoken conspiracy of silence on the one topic that was uppermost in the minds of many in the family, for no one had mentioned either Julian or Josie at all.

Lizzie felt for her mother, knowing how concerned she was for her brother; yet now, they were all behaving as if he did not exist. No one spoke of him anymore, yet he had done nothing wrong except to be guilty of too great a concentration upon his work.

Perhaps, thought Lizzie, this constituted neglect of his wife and had helped destroy her love for him. Lizzie had not worked out, in her own mind, how deeply either party was to blame for the debacle that followed, but she was absolutely certain of the culpability of Mr Barrett and his friend Mr Jones.

When the gentlemen returned to the drawing room, the pianoforte was opened and the ladies and gentlemen were invited to entertain the party.

While Miss Anderson modestly declined, her young sister obliged with a spirited rendition of a march by Schubert that would have had anyone who was feeling drowsy instantly wide awake. The generous applause she received encouraged her to give them another, less vigorous piece, after which Lizzie was urged to take her place at the instrument.

Lizzie was a confident and talented pianist, for she'd had many years of study with her cousin William Courtney, who was now a very distinguished practitioner. She played one or two fine compositions that had everyone demanding more and then, to the very great delight of at least one member of the party, she played and sang "Les Petites Oiseaux."

Before leaving, Mr Carr thanked his hosts most sincerely and made a point of telling their daughter how much he had enjoyed her singing. Lizzie smiled, acknowledging his praise, and when he expressed the hope that he would hear her sing again, said, without affectation, "Of course, Mr Carr, and thank you for the song."

Michael Carr had observed Miss Gardiner as she talked, played, sang, and then helped her mother with the tea, all it had seemed to him, in a most charming manner. He could not recall another young lady whose every quality and action had been so pleasing to him.

And she was exceedingly pretty, too.

❧

The Summer of 1865 was memorable for many reasons.

Darcy Gardiner had returned to Westminster and then proceeded to Hertfordshire, where Mr Colin Elliott was engaged in an exhilarating election campaign to hold off a Tory opponent, one who claimed that civilisation itself would be at risk if the Reformists had their way and Mr Gladstone were to form a government. It was a campaign that had worked often, but on this occasion appeared not to be credible.

In July, to their chagrin, the Tories faced defeat again and, to the immense delight of Colin Elliott, James Wilson, and his other supporters, it seemed that their campaign for reform was back on the agenda. Lord Russell had given Mr Gladstone a cast-iron promise, and even the return of Palmerston as leader could not dull their jubilation. He was eighty after all and would soon have to retire. In fact, three months later, Palmerston was dead and Lord Russell took over leadership of the party.

Returning triumphant from London, Darcy Gardiner was immediately dragooned by his sisters into helping with preparations for the country dance, which he had persuaded his friend Mr Carr to give at Rushmore Farm. There was much to be done and very little time left in which to get it done. His help, they said, was absolutely vital to the success of the occasion.

Cassandra had been too busy with her father's estate to offer much more than encouragement to Mr Carr in organising his first important social function at Rushmore Farm, but both Lizzie and Laura Ann had been active in assisting with plans and suggestions, as well as practical help, during the days leading up to the dance. It was fortunate for them that little Anthony and James had both taken so quickly and happily to their new companion, Margaret Baines, who was proving invaluable, so releasing them to assist Mr Carr.

At the farm, many things had to be organised precisely.

Unlike at Pemberley, there was no ballroom, which meant the indoor spaces had to be cleared and made ready for dancing, while a great marquee was erected on the lawn for the diners and drinkers, who were expected to far outnumber the dancers.

Workmen had to be found to erect a stage for the musicians and a host of men and women were engaged to cook and serve the food, which had to be plentiful. Mr Carr was determined that he would not be seen as some skinflint who let his guests go home hungry.

Looking at the lists he had prepared, Lizzie declared there was certainly no danger of that, rather there might well be many cases of indigestion caused by over-indulgence, she warned.

On returning home one afternoon, after spending the morning at Rushmore Farm, supervising the arrangements for the musicians, Lizzie found waiting for her a letter from her Aunt Emma Wilson in reply to one she had written on a matter that had disturbed her greatly.

The appearance in the neighbourhood of Mr Andrew Jones had caused her much disquiet, prompting her to write to her aunt, complaining of his brazen and insensitive attempt to approach her in the village and asking whether, if he did so again, she should speak her mind:

> *I should so like to convey my feelings of utter revulsion at his conduct and that of his friend, for I am convinced he was involved in assisting Mr Barrett to induce Aunt Josie to leave her home and family. Perhaps, if I do so, he may be persuaded not to pester me at least, if not to leave the district entirely.*

Emma Wilson had been a source of comfort and counsel before, and Lizzie found it easier to confide in her, rather than raise the matter with her mother, who had more than enough to worry about. Emma's sage advice, arriving as it did a few days before the dance, was exactly what her niece needed. She wrote:

Regarding the matter of the odious Mr Andrew Jones, 'twere best, my darling Lizzie, when all things are considered, including your own welfare and my peace of mind, to leave the wretched man to his own devices. Unhappily, there is no law against the kind of heinous behaviour of which they are guilty.

Do not, I beg you, become embroiled in any conversation or disputation with him, which he, for his own wicked purposes, may falsely report or deliberately misconstrue, in order to denigrate you. It is enough that he and his friend have damaged one young woman in our family already; I would urge you, my dear niece, to ignore him altogether.

In replying to her aunt, whose advice she had sought, Lizzie seemed unsure of her feelings:

Dearest Aunt, while I must thank you for your very timely and wise advice, I am already preparing for you another query, equally vexing.

First, let me say that I entirely agree that there is nothing to be gained by pursuing the matter of my Uncle Julian's marriage and Aunt Josie's conduct with Mr Jones. But surely, dear Aunt, there must be some way in which the right persons must bear the opprobrium for what happened?

Our family, it seems to me, appears ready to forget it ever happened. Little Anthony is settled with us, Uncle Julian is gone to France, and that is an end of it, as far as they are concerned.

What is to happen to poor Aunt Josie? Is she to go on living with Mr Barrett indefinitely? Is there no way in which those, who by manipulation and deceit inveigled her into this destructive adventure, which has forever tainted the lives of her husband and son, not to mention all her other family connections, is there no means by which they may be brought to book?

While I leave you with this puzzle, let me say that, contrary to what may seem to be the case, I am not eager to begin some vengeful crusade against Mr Jones, even though I find his very presence in this area disgusting in the extreme. So you, dear Aunt, need have no fear that I will act impetuously and confront him; I am too timid for such an undertaking. But, I do live in hope that he and his friend will get their just deserts and pray that, God willing, I may live to see it.

Meanwhile, I have much more cheerful news for you; see, I am not all gloom and despair. There are many good and decent people and pleasant things may yet happen to take our minds away from the likes of Barrett and Jones.

The day after tomorrow is the day of the dance, given by Mr Carr at Rushmore Farm, and we are all attending. It promises to be an enormous affair, with everyone for miles around being invited. Mr Carr's American upbringing, which makes him astonishingly generous and hospitable, appears to have extinguished totally the traits of his more parsimonious Irish ancestors.

But I do not wish to appear critical, for indeed, I am not. He is a very kind, great-hearted man and my brother Darcy, who counts him as a dear friend, will die for him, if need be.

There is one more thing and I do wish you could have been here to witness it: Darcy and I are to open the dancing!

Now is that not something to celebrate?

The letter was left unfinished for the moment...

When Emma Wilson received it some days later, it had been concluded after the dance at Rushmore Farm.

"I certainly wish I could have been there," she said, and added to herself, "I would also like very much to know a little more about this Mr Michael Carr. What manner of man is he?"

Her husband heard her question, put down his paper, and said, "Do you mean the young American who has purchased the Camden stud? Darcy Gardiner seems to know him pretty well," he said, and Emma shook her head, for she doubted if applying to young Darcy would get her very much more information than she had received from her niece already. To judge by the letter, neither Darcy Gardiner nor his sister was entirely impartial, when it came to Mr Carr.

It was a fact amply demonstrated at the dance, where Mr Carr, grateful for all they had done to ensure the success of the occasion, had made a brief speech to his guests, thanking them for their attendance and expressing his appreciation of the help he had received, especially from the Gardiner family. They were, he told the assembled company, his honoured guests tonight.

Invitations had gone out to all the families—gentry, middle class, and those from the farms and villages on either side of his property. Most people had accepted, whether out of appreciation or curiosity, it was hard to say. There was, therefore, a great crowd of people gathered at the farm and, with food and drink in such generous quantities, there was plenty for everyone to do. There were fireworks and country dancing on the lawn for everyone to enjoy.

Guests who wanted mainly to eat and drink had no complaints, while those who wished to dance or watch others dance found themselves accommodated in a large, tastefully appointed room, with a small but well-practised orchestra providing appropriate music. When Darcy Gardiner and his sister, who even he admitted was looking very lovely that evening, opened the dancing, the onlookers were so enchanted, they applauded and Cassy, her parents, and her Aunt Jane were justly proud of the young pair.

Later, Mr Carr, who had danced the sedate first quadrille with a young lady from the neighbourhood, sought out Lizzie and led her to the centre of the floor. Lizzie and her brother had been teaching him the intricacies of some of the new European dances for some weeks now, and she was about to discover the success or otherwise of their efforts.

After they had successfully negotiated one simple popular dance, the orchestra paused and struck up the opening bars of a Viennese waltz. Mr Carr turned to Lizzie and said softly, "Miss Gardiner, you are about to witness my first serious attempt at the waltz. I trust you are adequately prepared for the consequences."

Lizzie laughed, aware that they were one of only three couples on the floor and the cynosure of all eyes. "For shame, Mr Carr, after all the practice you have had, I expect you to waltz perfectly well tonight or you will have to explain how it is that a man who can perform that silly barn dance they call a polka cannot master something as graceful as a waltz," she said, hoping to tease him into responding.

He smiled but said nothing. However, when they began to dance, her eyes widened in surprise, for he was leading her smoothly in the most perfect waltz.

As they went round the floor, she declared, "You are a fraud, Mr Carr; this is too good to be the result of a few weeks' practice. Either you are a practiced dancer and were simply teasing us or you have had other lessons."

He promised faithfully that he'd had no other teachers than her brother and herself.

"In which case," she said, "you must be the best student of dance in the country. Truly, this is good, very good."

He smiled again and remained modestly silent as they danced, and Lizzie decided she would simply enjoy the experience. When the music ended, he led her to her seat and thanked her with a deep bow. He was elated at her words, however lightly spoken, and as if to underline them, there was applause for the couple from those observing them around the room.

In the days that followed, many members of the family would speculate about the night of the dance at Rushmore Farm and wonder at the consequences that flowed from it. The party from Pemberley had been very impressed with the success of the occasion. Recalling that Mr Carr had thanked the Gardiners at the outset, Elizabeth and Jane put it down to the talent of the Gardiners, who were always good at that sort of thing. Mr Darcy expressed his admiration for the splendid organisation and generous hospitality of their host.

Cassy thought her children had excelled themselves, especially Darcy and Lizzie, to whom congratulations must be due, she said, and her husband declared that Mr Carr had proved an excellent host. Young Darcy Gardiner thought he had never seen so many pretty girls in the one room before and wondered where, among the dales, they had all been hiding. While Laura Ann, who had fallen asleep in the carriage on the way home, woke up momentarily to tell them that she had heard the people watching the dancing say that Miss Lizzie Gardiner was the loveliest girl in the room. She then went right back to sleep again.

And Lizzie? Well, Lizzie blushed at the compliment but kept her thoughts mostly to herself, though confessing, when pressed, that she had enjoyed herself more than she had expected to, though she was very tired and was looking forward to bed.

However, when she got home and into bed, she said a little prayer.

"Dear God," she prayed, "please do not let me make a fool of myself, or make a terrible mistake as my Aunt Josie did. Please let me think clearly and do what is right, because, dear God, I do believe that I am in very great danger of falling in love with Mr Carr!"

Having made the confession to herself as well as to the Almighty, she kept turning it around in her mind. Whichever way she considered the proposition, she could not deny its truth.

Unable to sleep, she rose and concluded her letter to her aunt, Emma Wilson.

The dance was a great success. I do not believe there was anyone who did not enjoy themselves. As for Mr Carr, he has won universal praise for his good humour and generous hospitality. It has been, for him, an exceedingly successful introduction to the people in this part of the county. Those who knew him are confirmed in their good opinion of him and those who did not are most pleasantly surprised.

As for me, dear Aunt, before you ask, yes I do like him, I think I like him very much; he is like no other gentleman I have met in my life.

Your loving niece,

Lizzie.

Following the dance, the remaining weeks of waning Summer slipped swiftly by. During most of this time, Cassandra was increasingly occupied with matters pertaining to the Pemberley Estate and, in particular, providing to her father the information he needed to make decisions about the work set out for the following year.

Mr Darcy's steward and manager were frequently surprised at the extent of her knowledge and the depth of her understanding of their work, as well as the ease with which she could deal with their tenants. They were forgetting, no doubt, that as a young girl, Cassy had spent a great deal of time with her father, riding all over the estate, learning all that she needed to know, so she could teach her young brother Julian everything she had acquired, preparing him for the day when he would take over his inheritance.

Meanwhile, young Lizzie, who saw less of her mother than before, found herself alone, with a multitude of thoughts and feelings that had begun to preoccupy her mind. Strangely, almost every one of them seemed to involve Mr Carr. The gentleman had called on the family a day or two after the dance, ostensibly to thank them personally for their contribution to the success of the function and, finding only Lizzie and Laura Ann at home, he had taken tea and, having sat with them for half an hour or so, departed.

Lizzie was grateful that he had made no particular difference in his treatment of herself and her sister. She was anxious to avoid the questions that might follow, if Laura Ann were to become aware of her feelings. And yet, she wondered whether, if he had any particular feelings for her, he might not have indicated it by some discreet sign, a look, a glance, or a word, perhaps taking the opportunity to speak when Laura Ann had gone to order tea. He had not and that set up yet another worrying trend of thought in her mind, which restlessly returned to it over and over again. Was she imagining it all?

Thereafter, they did not hear from him for almost a week, leaving Lizzie in a state of dreadful uncertainty, wondering if he had been looking for some encouragement from her at their last meeting and, not finding it, gone away believing her to be indifferent to him. She had no way of knowing.

❦

As the days passed, with no one to confide in, since even her brother Darcy was once again gone to London, Lizzie was beginning to fret and even her mother had noticed. She appeared to have lost her appetite and seemed restless, which was most unusual.

"Perhaps you need a holiday, my dear. Would you like me to write to Aunt Emma and ask if you may spend a month with them in Kent? I am sure they would love to have you, and the countryside around Standish Park is at its very best at this time of year. I wish I could have had some time to spare; I'd go with you," said her mother.

Alarmed at the prospect of being sent away to Kent, while the object of her interest remained in Derbyshire, much as she loved her Aunt Emma, Lizzie leapt up from her chair and declared that she was perfectly well and did not need a holiday.

"I do not need to go away, Mama; I am not unwell. I think I need some fresh air and exercise; I shall walk down to the village and get some ribbon for Laura's bonnet. I have been putting off doing it, and she will soon begin to doubt that I mean to do it at all," she said and ran upstairs to get her bonnet and cape.

Her mother, who was about to leave for Pemberley with her younger daughter, smiled and said nothing, but decided she would write to Emma

Wilson anyway. Lizzie did look as if she needed a change, she thought, she had worked very hard in the past fortnight and was probably tired. She was certain Emma Wilson would be happy to have her to stay.

Waiting until the carriage taking her mother and sister had turned out of the drive, Lizzie put on her bonnet and left the house, walking briskly down the road to the village, choosing it rather than the path through the woods, in the hope she might meet someone who might be coming up towards the house. If that person turned out to be Mr Carr, it would seem like a happy coincidence, she thought.

Sadly, she met no one of any significance, for the road was deserted, save for a couple of farm labourers and a neighbouring family taking their chickens to market. The children waved to her cheerfully and Lizzie, despite her own rather melancholy mood, waved back.

Once in the village, she spent only a little time at the haberdashery shop, buying the ribbon for Laura's bonnet, before going into one of her favourite haunts, Mrs Hardy's bookstore. Mrs Hardy's daughter Harriet had been at church on Sunday and, after the service was over, she had stopped to mention that they had recently received copies of a new novel by Mrs Gaskell, entitled *Sylvia's Lovers*. Harriet said she expected it would be very popular among the ladies of the district.

At first, Lizzie had not thought she would be sufficiently interested to want to purchase it, but once in the village, she looked for an excuse to linger a while and the bookshop provided the best possible reason.

She went in and Harriet was helping another customer, while Mrs Hardy was nowhere to be seen. While she waited for Harriet to be free, Lizzie browsed among the shelves, idly reading the titles and picking up a copy of the new book.

The door of the shop opened and someone entered. Though she could not see the person, by the sound of boots on the floor and the swish of a cape, she knew it was a man. Lizzie did not turn around at once, even though some instinct told her he was known to her. Believing it to be Mr Carr, she thought, Well, he can surely see me here; if he does not wish to speak with me, I shall not put myself forward to notice him.

At that very moment, Harriet, freed from her duties, addressed her by name and asked if she would like some help. Before Lizzie could answer, the man, who had been standing a few feet away with his back to her, turned abruptly and said, "Miss Gardiner, I see you are as interested in reading books as I am in publishing them."

Startled, since his was the very last voice she had expected or wanted to hear, Lizzie literally jumped. "Mr Jones, I had no idea you were still in the area…" she muttered, trying to say something sensible, without wishing to give him any excuse to believe that she was willing to engage in a conversation. But Jones was not to be easily dissuaded, and having waited for her to make her purchase, without buying anything himself, he followed her out of the shop into the street.

Shaken, Lizzie was at a loss for words. She remembered all the advice her Aunt Emma had given her, and her mind was racing to find a plausible excuse that would let her get away from him without giving offence, for she feared what he might do or say, should she anger him. It soon became abundantly clear to her, from his persistence, that he was determined to walk with her and there was very little she could do to be rid of him, as he strode down the street beside her as though they were friends.

He kept asking her questions, which she answered mechanically, briefly, giving little thought to their substance. When she fell silent for a few minutes, he tried again, asking if he may see what book she had purchased at the bookshop. Once again, Lizzie would have liked to have refused, telling him it was none of his business, but instead, she felt intimidated and meekly handed him the parcel, which he untied and, taking out the book, declared in a loud, jocular voice, "*Sylvia's Lovers*, eh? There's an interesting choice! Now I know that you are not as innocent as you pretend to be, Miss Gardiner.

"When I met you with Josie, I used to think you a regular little bluestocking, but I know different now. But do not worry, your secret is safe with me; I shall not tell on you. I find it very interesting indeed, you should be reading Mrs Gaskell… it is not exactly the type of novel…" and he broke off, because as they reached a street corner, Lizzie had retrieved her book and, leaving him standing, raced across the road, almost running into the path of a vehicle and through a crowd of children, into the saddlery, where a moment ago, she had caught sight of Mr Carr passing through the doorway.

As she had sought desperately for a means of escape from the unwelcome company of Mr Jones, Mr Carr's tall figure and familiar hat had attracted her eye and, without a second thought, she had decided to approach him.

As she rushed in, breathless, her bonnet pushed back by the breeze as she ran, her face flushed with the exertion, Mr Carr turned around and, seeing her thus, spoke with more concern than politeness. "Miss Gardiner! What on earth is the matter, are you not well?" and as he spoke, he signalled to the saddler's apprentice to fetch a chair for the young lady.

Lizzie could not speak at first, and when she tried, her words were quite unintelligible. To avoid other customers intruding upon her, the saddler's wife, a kind woman, presuming she was unwell, asked if the young lady would like to sit in the back room a while and Lizzie, though protesting she was not ill, gratefully accepted her invitation.

Once there, she sat down and was given a cup of hot, sweet tea. It helped alleviate the shock she had suffered and she blurted out her fears to Mr Carr, recounting the incident with Mr Jones and her acute distress at being accosted by him on this as well as a previous occasion.

As he listened, looking concerned and surprised, she said, "I know I should probably have pretended that I was unaffected, but I could not; each time he spoke, I was reminded most forcefully of the way he and his friend Mr Barrett had shamefully deceived my dear Uncle Julian and dishonoured poor Aunt Josie. I could not bear it; clearly he thought he could just address me in the shop or saunter up to me in the street and engage me in casual conversation." Her voice was shaking as she continued, "It was as though he thought I felt no outrage at all at the way they had behaved and would be prepared to encourage his advances."

Lizzie's voice broke and soon she was in tears.

Mr Carr, having proffered a large handkerchief, stepped away for a few moments to let her alone until she had ceased weeping. When, at last, she dried her eyes and blew her nose, he said, gently, "Miss Gardiner, you must let me take you home now; my carriage is at hand, just in the laneway behind the saddlery. We can leave by the back door and no one in the street will see you."

She told him then that she had seen him enter the saddlery and rushed across the road in the hope that he would help her get away from Mr Jones. "It was plain to me, he intended to walk with me all the way home if possible. I could not have borne that. What would Mama have thought, or my grandparents, whose son's life he has helped ruin?"

Mr Carr agreed that such a situation would have been quite intolerable and she had done well to get away from Jones. He then thanked the saddler and his wife, paid them, and promised to return to collect his saddle, before taking Lizzie out into the laneway, where his vehicle waited. Having helped her in and tucked a rug around her knees, he drove off, taking the back roads until he was clear of the village, swinging across the common and back onto the Matlock Road.

It was a longer and rougher route, he said, apologising for the discomfort it might cause her, but at least they were unlikely to meet Mr Jones.

Lizzie smiled, for the first time since she had heard Mr Jones's voice in the shop, and said that the bumps in the road were far preferable to the prospect of meeting Mr Jones again.

Mr Carr encouraged her to smile by assuring her that she was quite safe from such an eventuality. "You need have no fears about this man Jones. I will personally inform him that his approaches to you are not welcome; indeed, I will take your brother Darcy with me to reinforce the message and make certain that he understands that he is to leave you alone. You must have the freedom to walk around the district that is your home, the village you have known since childhood, without fear of being accosted by some stranger you do not wish to meet. I give you my word, Miss Gardiner, that I will see he does not trouble you again."

Lizzie's relief was so great, she could not hold back the tears that welled up in her eyes; he stopped the vehicle and provided yet another clean handkerchief, waiting a while until she was calm before driving on.

Despite her tears, Lizzie was not unduly embarrassed, for he had been solicitous and sensible of her feelings and, it seemed to her, he was kindness and consideration itself. When at last they reached the house, he helped her out, took her indoors, and stayed with her until he could be assured that she was quite composed.

Before he left her, she thanked him and gave him her hand, which he held for a while in both of his before lifting it to his lips.

"Now remember, Lizzie," he said, "you have no need to fear, but if you are at all concerned, do not go alone into the village for the next week or so, until we are certain Mr Jones has left the district."

And with that he went, leaving her smiling, despite her fears, for she was conscious of the fact that he had spoken her name and called her Lizzie for the first time in their acquaintance. Going upstairs to her room, she closed the door and lay on her bed. She felt exhausted, drained of energy, yet surprisingly elated.

The sense of helplessness she had suffered in the company of Jones had frightened her, but the joyous relief she had felt, finding Mr Carr in the shop, had been such a wonderful feeling as she had never known before. Her emotions had swung so swiftly from one extreme to the other, she had felt breathless for some minutes, unable to explain why she was in such a state. Yet, he had been so patient and kind. Lying in bed, Lizzie relived the experience and thought deeply about her feelings. Was it possible, she wondered, that these new sensations were the beginnings of love? Or could they be merely some temporary excitement? She wished she could tell the difference.

With no one in whom she could confide, Lizzie was reluctant to admit, even to herself, that she was in love with Michael Carr. Between them, there had been none of the covert flirtation she had witnessed between other lovers. Mr Carr was clearly not the type of man who would indulge in such a jejune pastime and, while Lizzie saw no harm in the gentle teasing in which she sometimes indulged, she despised the blatant coquetry of women like Hetty Wallace-Groom.

The thought of Hetty and Mr Barrett brought to mind her Aunt Josie and she blushed, recalling that Mr Carr knew all about the grief and shame associated with her aunt's recent conduct. She could only hope that he would not associate her with anything similar. She thrust the thought aside. It would be unthinkable.

The longer Lizzie considered it, the more certain she became that hers was a genuine affection. The realisation of her feelings for Mr Carr had taken her by surprise at first, but as she contemplated them, she felt increasingly more comfortable with them. As for his feelings towards her, his conduct had always been exemplary—courteous, concerned and, more recently, tending towards fondness. Today, she had detected a degree of tenderness, to which she, being vulnerable, had responded without reserve. She had felt safe with him, trusted him, and was coming gradually to believe she loved him.

Even as she relived the day, with its terror and joy, Lizzie could feel the deepening warmth of their association. She was being drawn into something new, she was not entirely certain what, but it was more pleasurable than anything she had known before. She felt no apprehension, but wished desperately that she had someone to confide in. If only, she thought again and again, if only she had someone she could talk to, someone who knew what love felt like!

Unhappily for young Lizzie Gardiner, at a time in her life when she most needed a confidante, one who could help her understand the turbulence of her feelings, she had none.

❧

The cold fingers of the North wind had already begun to reach down and strip the leaves from the trees; those that had already turned gold and russet in early Autumn were crumpled and strewn around, as the year moved closer to Winter. In the fields a good harvest had been gathered in; it had been a fruitful season and, following the thanksgiving at the church, the young people in the parish had planned a picnic to Dovedale.

But, a cold spell had come without warning, spoiling their plans, and a disappointed party of young folk was about to return home when they met Mr Carr returning on horseback from Matlock. Stopping to greet them and hearing of their aborted plans, he invited them up to Rushmore Farm, which promised more shelter and warmth than their original destination.

The delighted picnickers, including Darcy Gardiner, his two sisters, their cousins from Kympton—Jessica and Jude Courtney, and a few other young men and ladies from the parish, packed up their baskets, climbed into their vehicles, and followed their benefactor up the road to the farm.

With a great log fire ablaze, ample food, and good company, the day was spent in the pleasantest possible ways that a party of young people might devise. Jessica Courtney, the Rector's daughter, who had come along as a chaperone, had brought her book and curled up on the sofa by the window to read.

The room in which they were accommodated was the very room, which many months ago, Lizzie had described as the perfect recreation room for a family. Since then, it had been refurbished and appointed to look exactly as she had imagined.

Reminding her of the earlier occasion, Mr Carr asked, "What is your opinion of the room now, Miss Gardiner? Do you approve?"

Lizzie was enthusiastic in her reply. "Indeed, I do, Mr Carr; it has been perfectly done. I cannot have imagined it better."

"I have you to thank for it. Without your most original suggestion, it may have become a billiard room or a place where the gentlemen met to drink and boast of their success after a shoot; instead we have this charming room, one that a family and its friends may all enjoy. It is now my favourite room in the house and I owe it all to you," he said graciously, and she replied with suitable modesty, "It's kind of you to say so, but I think you have done exceedingly well; the soft hues and pleasing tones of the drapes and carpets are quite perfect."

Despite the lowering clouds, the threatened storm did not eventuate and, by early afternoon, the wind eased and the sun came out, enabling them to leave the house and walk out to enjoy the beauty of the woods and meadows, which surrounded the farm. Those who had never visited the property followed Darcy Gardiner, whose familiarity with his friend's estate made him the ideal guide.

Lizzie, who had not met Mr Carr alone since the day in the village when he had saved her from being pestered by Jones, found herself walking with him, as they made their way along a path that cut across the woodlands towards the stream that flowed through the property.

As the path grew more steep, he took her hand, as if it were the most natural thing to do, and let her lean on him when they had to climb down towards the water, as she used her right hand to pick up her skirts.

They had reached a point where the stream made a shallow pool among the rocks, which one might cross by means of stepping stones. Lizzie, who was accustomed to admiring the grandeur of the grounds at Pemberley, was completely enchanted by the natural simplicity of the woodlands here and wanted very much to get across the pool, so she could do as the others had done and follow the stream to its confluence with the River Wye on the borders of the property.

She was about to place her foot on the first of the stepping stones, when Mr Carr held her back, and standing astride the rock pool, lifted her over the water and stood her down on dry land. "There you are," he said. "At least, you will not have wet feet."

Lizzie, very conscious of his closeness when he had picked her up, said lightly, as he set her down, "Thank you and I shall have you to thank when I do not catch cold."

"Indeed, we cannot have that," he said, adding, "Come, we must hurry or we shall miss the others," and reaching for her hand again, he helped her along the rocky path.

Lizzie's face was flushed and she did not look up at him as they walked, but she made no effort to take her hand away from his. They had walked on for quite a while, before they heard the rest of the party returning. They had already climbed to the crest of the hill descending to the river; their excited voices were heard describing the view of the valley below.

Lizzie looked up at her companion and he seemed to understand the unspoken message in her eyes, as he patted her hand reassuringly and let it go, just seconds before Darcy, Laura, Rachel, and the rest emerged, crashing through the undergrowth and snapping the ferns underfoot.

Lizzie cried out, "Oh, look out! You must not crush the undergrowth so, or you will kill all the little creatures that live in it."

The others stopped in their tracks and everyone went suddenly silent.

For Lizzie, the magic was suddenly gone. It was time to return and they tramped back to the farm and gathered up their things, preparing to leave. The daylight was almost gone, too.

But, Lizzie could not forget how she had felt, at that moment in the woods. It seemed to her that Mr Carr remembered it also, for when he helped her into the carriage, his hand grasped hers firmly and stayed so for a moment or two after she was seated, while they said their good-byes. Darcy was driving and did not see them, and little Laura Ann was too tired after her walk in the woods to notice anything at all.

When Mr Carr asked, "And may I call on you at home on Sunday, Lizzie?" her eyes shone and she smiled as she said, "Yes, yes of course, Mr Carr."

The Gardiners had scarcely reached their house when the storm that had been threatening all afternoon broke across the dales. The rain poured down relentlessly for an hour or more.

"That must be the last of the Summer storms, returning in Autumn," said Cassy as they sat taking tea in the sitting room. Looking out at the rain as it lashed the trees and spilt the last of their leaves across the lawn, Cassy suddenly cried out, "Good God! Who could that be in this weather? I could have sworn I saw a woman run across the lawn and back towards the kitchen."

Darcy and Lizzie, who'd been curled up on the rug in front of the fire, toasting muffins, got up and went to the windows; they could see no one. "You must have imagined it, Mama," said her son, while Lizzie thought it may have been the broken bough of a tree, being dragged across by the wind.

They had just returned to their places by the fire when Mrs Bates, the housekeeper, entered the room. She seemed troubled and wary. "Beg your pardon, ma'am, but there is here a young person, says her name is Susan; she is asking to see Miss Elizabeth, ma'am."

"Susan? Did you say Susan? Why that must be Aunt Josie's maid!" Lizzie was up and out of the room in seconds.

"Where is she?" she asked.

"I've made her sit by the fire, Miss Elizabeth; she was soaked through, the poor creature. It seems she has walked here from Lambton," Mrs Bates replied.

"Oh, my God," Lizzie exclaimed, as she rushed into the kitchen followed closely by her mother, who was puzzled as to what this might mean. Sure enough, sitting by the fire, wet and bedraggled, looking absolutely miserable, was Susan, Josie's faithful maid.

"Mama, it *is* Susan. My God, she is shaking with cold; hurry, get some towels and dry clothes, else she will catch pneumonia," Lizzie cried, and Cassy sent the maids racing upstairs to do her bidding.

The girl's hands were blue with cold and she was shivering even though she sat close to the fire. She kept trying to tell them something, but Cassy insisted it could wait until she was dry and warm, with a large mug of hot, sweet tea in her hands.

Some half an hour later, they took Susan upstairs to Lizzie's room, where sitting in front of the fire, she related an extraordinary tale that both Cassy and her daughter heard as though it concerned some fictitious character in a melo-dramatic romance, so incredible did it seem.

Susan gave a terrible, bitter account of foolish, misplaced trust and cruel betrayal. Josie, she told them, was in dire need of help. She had tried, during the first few weeks after she left her home, to discover how and when Mr Barrett intended to have her book of poems published. He had led her to believe it had all been arranged with his friend Mr Jones, but then he had made several excuses—his friend had gone overseas to Italy on business, was attending a family wedding, had become involved in some important business in Scotland, and so on.

Lizzie, knowing exactly where Jones had been for most of the Summer, bit her lip to keep from interrupting.

As each month passed, Josie had become more impatient and Barrett had grown less and less considerate of her feelings, Susan said.

"Poor Mrs Darcy, ma'am, she wanted so much to hope that he would do as he had promised. She hoped he would keep his word about the book; she tried to keep her spirits up, but sadly, ma'am, he never said nothing to her about it. And if she would ask him, he'd get angry and shout at her, telling her not to bother him."

Cassandra looked at her daughter and saw the compassion in her troubled face as Susan continued, "Then, when most of the money she had brought with her was over, she was too proud to ask him for any, so she sent me out to pawn or sell her pieces of jewellery and her trinkets. She will never have the means to redeem them; they're gone forever, ma'am, all her lovely things Mr Julian had given her, all but her wedding ring, are gone and all of my little savings, too."

"And where is she now, Susan? Is she still with Barrett?" asked Cassandra.

Susan shook her head vigorously. "Oh no, ma'am, we left the house one day while he had gone down to Richmond to a friend's wedding. Miss Josie was keen to leave. I had found us a couple of rooms in a boardinghouse on the other side of town," she said.

"Is that where she is?" asked Cassy.

"Yes, ma'am, but Miss Josie is very sick, ma'am. It's her chest; you should hear her wheezing—it's something terrible. Please, ma'am, she needs a doctor," said the girl, and Cassy asked, "Did she send you?"

"No, ma'am, she did not want me to come; she was ashamed and sorry, but I knew she would die if I did not try to get her some medication, at least. I had to come; I knew Miss Lizzie would not refuse to help her. Please, ma'am, will you help?" she pleaded, and there were tears running down her tired, woebegone face.

Stunned, Cassandra stood mute, but Lizzie said, "Of course we will help. She needs a doctor and Papa could probably recommend one in London. You were quite right to come, Susan. Mama, how soon can we go to her?" she asked and Cassy, realising that time was very short, said, "Well, we shall have to wait for your father, but I daresay we can make preparations, get our things together, and be ready for an early start tomorrow. Susan, you will come with us and take us to this boardinghouse?"

Susan nodded eagerly. "Yes, ma'am, but Miss Josie is very poorly and needs some good food. She has not eaten a decent piece of meat or fish in weeks. She has no appetite; I did ask the woman who runs the house to look after her and see she eats her meals, but she is very busy, ma'am, and has no time to spare."

Cassy sent for the cook immediately to ask that some simple, wholesome food be prepared and packed to be taken on the morrow to London.

"She will need nourishment as well as medication, if she is to recover," she said and later she would pack a basket of fresh fruit, cheese, and honey from the larder for the ill-nourished patient, hoping they would not all be in vain. If Josie was as ill as Susan had made out, Cassy was very afraid for her, especially if the Winter was a harsh one this year.

∼❧∼

When Richard Gardiner arrived home, the whole sorry tale was retold by his wife and daughter, as he sat, shocked and appalled, before the fire, wondering how a young woman of intelligence and sound upbringing could have been so totally bereft of judgment as to let herself be so badly deceived.

"I cannot believe it. How could Josie have been so naïve, so wanting in understanding? I know she was always reputed to be self-willed, much like her father Mr Tate, but she was also intelligent and sensible. I saw no signs of irre-sponsible or impetuous behaviour in her, when she lived here in Matlock, nor after her marriage to Julian, when they were at Pemberley. That she could allow herself to be taken in and betrayed in this way is incredible. Mr and Mrs Darcy will be very shocked."

"And Mr Tate will probably want to have Barrett horsewhipped as well, Papa, but it is poor Josie who needs our help now, for unless something is done to help her, she will probably die," cried Lizzie, urgently.

Lizzie's entreaties startled him and Richard decided that he would go himself, rather than send them with a letter to a physician in London. Besides, this was a family matter and he felt responsible.

A decision had also to be made as to whether the Darcys and the Tates should be told, and it was generally agreed between them that nothing should be said until they had seen Josie and ascertained her true condition.

"Her father has refused to have anything to do with her; even when Mrs Tate begged him to go to London and try to recover her, he would not budge," said Cassy, and her husband recalled Mr Tate's rage. "He loved her dearly; he was so devastated and has felt bereft since she left her home and family, it would do no good to tell him anything until we have her safely lodged in some respectable place," Richard said.

⟡

As they prepared to leave on the following morning, being Sunday, there was one thing more that Lizzie had to resolve. Mr Carr had asked if he might call on her on Sunday and she had agreed. Now, she was concerned that he would arrive and, finding her gone to London with no explanation, he may draw the wrong conclusion.

He will surely believe that I have changed my mind and have gone away to avoid him or some such; at the very least, he will think me very rude, she thought.

There was only one thing to be done; she would have to take her brother Darcy into her confidence. She could then ask him to deliver a brief explanatory note to his friend.

It was quite late, when after dinner and some time at the billiard table, Darcy went up to his room. Their parents had already retired to bed, preparing for an early start on the morrow. There was a soft knock on the door and, to his very great surprise, his sister entered.

"Why, Lizzie, what keeps you awake so late?" he asked and she put a finger to her lips and silenced him, indicating she had something to say that was for his ears alone. He listened, as she told him of her dilemma and asked for his help.

Darcy had heard her out without a word, but when she had finished, he was determined to tease her. "Lizzie, you sly little thing, do you mean to tell me that you and Mr Carr have been falling in love behind my back and he is coming here tomorrow to propose to you? I am delighted, of course, but you might have told me; after all I am your brother!" he said in mock indignation, a stance that was somewhat undermined by the fact that he spoke in a whisper.

Lizzie was adamant. "I have said nothing of the sort. I have no idea what he proposes to do or say, but I do know he has asked if he may call on Sunday and I have agreed. Now if I were to go to London, giving no explanation for my absence, will it not seem rude and ill-mannered in the extreme? Surely you do not wish me to treat your good friend so, do you, Darcy?" she asked.

"Absolutely not, nor would I want him to think my little sister ill-mannered. But you have both been very secretive, keeping me in the dark," he complained, then smiling broadly, asked, "So, you wish me to explain? What will you have me say?"

Lizzie took from her pocket a note she had already written and addressed to Mr Carr. As she handed it to her brother, she said with an air of nonchalance, "It is not sealed, you may read it if you wish; there is nothing silly in there, only a simple explanation of the facts. I know he will understand; he is a kind and decent gentleman. But if you should choose, Darcy, you may add some little detail about poor Aunt Josie, so he knows how very urgent the situation was and why we had to go at once.

"I have said we hope to return within a week. Papa will probably need to be back in Matlock even earlier, but whether I am able to leave Josie will depend entirely upon her health and how soon she recovers," she explained and her brother, as always, impressed by his young sister's generous spirit, promised to do exactly as she asked.

"You need have no further anxiety, Lizzie. I shall tell him why you had to go to London and, perhaps, I may add how desolated you were at the prospect of missing him on Sunday, eh?"

Lizzie threw a pillow at his head as she left the room, still a little fearful.

Darcy was right, she was sorry to have to go; she had never wanted so much to stay and longed to know what Mr Carr might have said to her on Sunday, but she knew her duty, too. Her brother could believe what he pleased, but Lizzie was still unsure what the day might have brought.

It was cold and wet when they reached the outskirts of London.

Susan indicated which route they should follow and, as they left the main streets of the city and drove into the rutted lanes and byways, Cassy and her daughter glanced outside and then looked dubiously at one another, apprehensive of what they might find. These far from salubrious surroundings were not the best environment for one who was suffering a respiratory affliction of the kind Susan had described.

"It's her chest, ma'am; it sounds terrible when she coughs, like an old pair of bellows inside her."

Richard was certain Josie was suffering from a common bacterial infection that afflicted several of the poor in Winter. If not arrested and treated in time, it could lead to pneumonia.

"The sooner she can be given good, nourishing food, medication, and fresh air, the better," he said, and the deeper they drove into the fringes of the city, the more worried he looked.

They turned into a narrow but fairly clean street, lined with old, red brick houses, and Susan called to the driver to slow down. Finally, she made him stop before a solid, three-storied house, with a cast-iron gate set in its front wall. It was clearly the abode of a person with rather more substance to protect than the rest of the street.

As they got out of their carriage, half the women and children in the houses opposite came out to look at them. This was neighbourly curiosity in East London, thought Cassy, as she alighted and looked around. She was glad they were all very simply dressed for travelling with no furs or jewellery to excite the interest of onlookers.

A servant came to the gate and, seeing Susan, she unlocked it and let them into the house. They stood in a narrow hallway, from which two doors opened to the left and right of the stairs.

At least, thought Cassy, it is clean, though shabby.

Susan was about to take them to the room Josie occupied, when the mistress of the boardinghouse appeared on the landing and, addressing Susan, said, "I am glad you are back; she has not been well at all and has hardly eaten anything. Are these her relations?"

She was a large woman, with a stern though not unkindly face and a very big voice.

Susan spoke quickly, as if afraid to offend her. "Yes, ma'am, they are come from Derbyshire," she replied, "and this is Dr Gardiner, ma'am."

The woman looked him over and said, still standing halfway up the stairs, "Dr Gardiner? Well, the lady in there is surely in need of your attention, sir, but I hope one of you can pay the rent she owes me, for I've had none for a fortnight."

Richard stepped up to the foot of the stairs and spoke quietly, but with the kind of dignified authority that characterised all his dealings.

"Madam, you need have no fears on that score; you will be paid every penny you are owed, rest assured. However, I am a doctor and the lady in that room is my patient. She is very ill and I must see her without delay. If something unfortunate were to happen to her, while we stood out here quibbling about the rent, it would not look good for you when the police and the coroner came to enquire, would it? So let us attend to her needs first and we will settle your bills thereafter," he said.

The woman, clearly impressed by the firmness of Dr Gardiner's tone as by the possibility of a police enquiry intruding upon her establishment, indicated that they could proceed. Susan opened the door and, as they went in, it was all Lizzie could do not to cry out. Cassandra could not believe her eyes.

On a narrow, iron bed, with a thin mattress barely covered over with a plain linen sheet, lay Josie, propped up against two pillows, a blanket over her knees, and a woolen shawl around her shoulders. She looked pale and ill, so wretched, so utterly forlorn, that no one could say a word, but Susan, who rushed to her side and said in a bright, happy voice, "Miss Josie, they are here, I've fetched Miss Lizzie and Dr Gardiner and Mrs Gardiner. They are all come to help you get well."

Josie took her hand and held it, before turning her head to look at the visitors who seemed to fill the small space in the room. Cassy went to her at once, but Josie was too weak even to smile. On the table beside her bed stood a small bowl of soup—thin, stone cold, and unappetizing; clearly it had been her meagre lunch, of which she had probably taken a few spoons full.

Conscious of the dire condition of his patient, Richard gently moved his wife and daughter aside and, drawing up the only chair in the room, set about examining her. While Cassy stayed with them, Lizzie waited in the adjoining room with Susan, who had been sent to get hot water, soap, and a clean towel for the doctor.

Looking out of the window, all Lizzie could see was a row of terraces with chimney pots sticking up into the sky like so many strange-shaped dwarfs. They sat atop the roofs of grimy, dark brick buildings which had passed their usefulness as homes for the middle class and were now being used to house the families of thousands of rural workers, who were flooding into London, looking for jobs. Anne-Marie had told her once of seeing four and even five poverty-stricken families crowded into one of these boardinghouses, with little sanitation and often no water. At least, she thought, this place was clean, though it was as cold as charity.

Lizzie was not to know then what they learned later; that the boarding mistress was also the madam of another establishment, sited upstairs: one which employed a variety of young women, catering to the demands of "gentlemen" who visited after dark. This was the main source of her income, for which the "boardinghouse" provided a respectable front.

Even without this knowledge, Lizzie was depressed by the atmosphere of the place and hoped they could soon get Josie away.

It was almost half an hour later that her parents emerged from Josie's room. Both looked shaken and dejected.

Richard spoke first. "She must be removed, at once, to a place where she may be bathed and cared for, given proper food and medication, and kept warm and comfortable. Above all, she must have some fresh air; the air in the room is foul, with just one window that is closed to keep out the cold and the smells from the street. It just will not do. If she remains here much longer, she will not last long."

There was no doubting the veracity of his words.

Cassy looked troubled. "But my dear, where shall we take her? She cannot travel far."

"Certainly not, there is only one possible place, Cassy; your father's town house at Portman Square is the only one I can recommend. There is no one staying there at the moment; it is warm and well appointed with all the conveniences, in salubrious surroundings, with easy access to doctors and the hospital, if need be. There are also servants aplenty, who could fetch and carry for you, without poor Susan having to do it all herself. After all, Josie is still Julian's wife and you can take the responsibility to move her there and inform your father. Mr Darcy is a compassionate man; he will have no objection, I will stake my life upon it," he replied.

Cassy realised from his words as well as the gravity of his countenance that she had to act fast and asked Susan to pack.

"Should we not send a message to Uncle Julian, too?" Lizzie asked, anxiously.

"All in good time, my dear," replied her father. "Once we have Josie out of here and settled in at Portman Square, there will be time to inform Julian. I have no doubt at all that he will return at once."

Arrangements were made to pay the outstanding bills, which included rent, charges for food, which Josie had not eaten, and a laundry bill which was laughable, considering the state of the bed linen; but at last, it was done and Josie, wrapped up warmly in a travelling rug, was carried out to the carriage, in which she, with Susan and Lizzie, were driven slowly to the Darcys' town house, while Richard and Cassy went ahead in a hansom cab.

Once at the house, Cassy gave orders for a room to be made ready, selecting one of the warmest and lightest rooms in the place, and when Josie arrived, she was taken there with all care. Susan prepared to bathe and change her ailing mistress and help her into clean nightclothes and a freshly made bed, a luxury she had not known for weeks, while Richard went out to the apothecary to obtain the medication she needed, if she was to have any chance of recovery.

They stayed with her a week, during which time they sent urgent messages to Pemberley, to Mr and Mrs Tate, and to Julian Darcy at an address in France. Initially, Josie seemed to respond to the medication, care, and pleasant surroundings in which she found herself. But in truth, she made little progress, remaining pale and weak, with no appetite for even the most delectable food.

Richard had begun to suspect tuberculosis, deep seated in her lungs, and his suspicions were unhappily confirmed by a colleague at the hospital, whose opinion he sought.

Lizzie and Cassandra were inconsolable on being told the prognosis, unable to accept that everything that had been done to recover her might prove to be in vain. It took all of Richard's understanding and patient explanation to persuade them that it was not for lack of action or care on their part that Josie was deemed to be beyond recovery.

He explained that her affliction probably had far deeper roots, though it may have been exacerbated by the deprivation and misery of the last few months.

Julian Darcy arrived first, very early one morning, having travelled over two days and nights from France. When his brother-in-law explained Josie's condition, he at first refused to believe it, but gradually accepting the inevitable, stayed with her constantly, reading to her, telling her of his work, and assuring her she was going to get well.

When he came downstairs, Cassy could not bear to see the grief in his eyes. Yet when he was with his wife, he would cheer up and persuade her to take her food and medication, as though she was well on the way to recovery. She responded well, too, giving him hope.

Soon afterwards, Mrs Tate and a nurse from Matlock came to join Cassy, who had decided to stay on, while Lizzie and Richard returned home.

The latter had done all he could, leaving his patient now in the care of one of the best physicians at St Thomas's Hospital, who visited daily.

Lizzie went reluctantly, but knew that there was not a great deal more she could do for Josie, now Mrs Tate was here.

Cassy remained because, as Mr Darcy's daughter, she had the authority to give orders and get things done at the house, like no one else could; besides, she felt her brother needed her.

Cassy had written her parents a letter that Elizabeth and Darcy read many times over, trying to glean some hope in the midst of the gloom.

She wrote:

Dearest Mama and Papa,

It is with a heavy heart that I write, though we have been rejoicing at our success in discovering poor Josie and taking her back to Portman Square, from such a place as you would never have dreamed to have found a member of our family. I shall spare you the awful details, for I am sure Richard will tell you more; suffice it to say that she is gravely ill with tuberculosis and, though it breaks my heart to say this, she is not expected to live beyond a few months.

Since we have been here, however, she is much more cheerful and eats a little better. Her faithful maid Susan attends her night and day. Josie never complains. Best news of all is that Julian is here, having travelled for days and nights across from France, and dear Mama, you should have seen her face when he walked into the room. My dear brother has suffered much, but he is a good, kind man and has completely forgiven Josie and will not say a word against her.

Cassy's letter concluded with the hope that she would see them in London, soon. Mr Darcy and Elizabeth decided they would go to London immediately; Elizabeth was determined to go, even though it was almost Winter and she hated London in the Winter cold.

Before setting out, however, Mr Darcy paid a visit to Anthony Tate, to plead with him to accompany them to London.

"I believe you must go, Tate. Julian is there; he has come from France and if he can forgive, so can you. You cannot turn your face from your daughter now; remember she may not have long to live."

Mr Tate was shocked by his words. "How is that? Do they not have the best doctors and the best medicines in London? No one has told me that my daughter will die!" he thundered.

Clearly, Mrs Tate had omitted this fact in her letter to her husband, or he had not read it through. On hearing it from Mr Darcy, he flew into a temper, cursed everybody including the government and the entire medical profession, and told Darcy he would be ready to leave in an hour.

Mr Darcy returned to Pemberley and, even before he spoke, his wife knew he had succeeded, where everyone else had failed to persuade Anthony Tate to see his daughter.

"He will come, my dear, but he is a very angry man. You will need to be patient with him. His disappointment and sorrow are so great, he cannot bear it and can only react with rage, even though he is unable to find the right people to blame and so rails against everybody."

Elizabeth knew how very hurt Mr Darcy had been by Josie's actions and could understand how much greater must be a father's grief.

❧

A week or two later, there was some good news; Cassandra wrote that Josie was in much better spirits after the arrival of her father and the Darcys and was now anxious to see her son. This time, it was entirely up to Lizzie; her brother Darcy was away in Derby and her father was attending a dying patient in Chesterfield, whom he could not leave even for a day.

Mr Carr, who was visiting her at the time, offered to accompany them; indeed, he said, they could travel in his carriage, which would be far faster and more comfortable than the public coach. Having consulted her father and taking both Anthony's nurse and her own maid, Ellen, with them, Lizzie left for London in Mr Carr's carriage, not knowing how the journey would turn out. She had never travelled without a member of her family before and, as for Anthony, she prayed the child would not fall ill or become tired and fractious on the way.

The journey was long and tedious, though the roads were far less crowded and hazardous than before, for more and more heavy goods were being carried on rail. It meant there were fewer over-laden vehicles on the road posing a potent threat to smaller carriages. It was also for the most part uneventful, except when they broke the journey for meals and to rest and water the horses. Staying overnight at Luton, before proceeding to London, they lodged at a local inn, where Mr Carr, conscious of the need for decorum to be observed, asked for two rooms for Lizzie and her maid, the child and his nurse. Having ascertained that they were comfortably and safely lodged, he proceeded a mile up the road to a hostelry, where the horses could be stabled and fed, and there took a room for the night.

Lizzie was not unconscious of the motives behind his actions. It was, for her, an indication of the sincerity of his feelings for her and his determination to protect her from gossip. He had assured her father that he would take very good care of them and he was keeping his word meticulously. Lizzie was certain that, had it not been for the exigencies of the situation, brought about by the arrival of Susan that stormy night and the subsequent discovery of the parlous state of Josie's health, which events had thrown every other plan into confusion, Mr Carr would by now have spoken, giving her some indication of his intentions.

Indeed, when she had returned from London with her father, her brother Darcy had indicated as much. He had, he said, given Mr Carr her note when he arrived on the Sunday and had watched, with some amusement, the disappointment that had swept over his countenance.

"He was most anxious to know if you were in good health and, had you not given me a hint of it, Lizzie, I might have teased him about being so downcast. But, since you had taken me into your confidence, I did not. Instead, I gave him a few more details about Aunt Josie's unhappy situation. He was most sympathetic and asked, as usual, if there was anything he could do to help."

Lizzie had smiled, even as she listened. She could well believe it.

It was typical of Mr Carr that he would offer to help. There was never an emergency in which he would not offer his assistance, readily and without regard to the cost to himself. It was a character trait that had endeared him to her from the very start of their acquaintance. In an era of increasing selfishness, when men were urged to compete for every advantage over one another, a man who would put himself out for others, without seeking some return, was rare indeed.

She recalled how a few days after she had returned home, he had called and was keen to discover how events had transpired in London.

"Is Mrs Darcy recovering well? And has any action been taken against those who so callously took advantage of her?" he had asked, his face dark with anger, after she had told him of the desperate state in which they had found Josie. It was with great sadness that she had told him of their fears, based upon her father's diagnosis and its confirmation by his eminent colleague.

"Sadly, it would seem that my aunt has contracted tuberculosis, Mr Carr, and it is not certain she has either the strength or the will to fight the disease," she had said, adding by way of explanation, "She has wasted away over the last six months; she was never very sturdy, but she is now a mere shadow of herself. One piece of good news, however, is that my Uncle Julian is come from France to be with her."

At this Mr Carr had seemed very moved, especially when Lizzie had added, "and he has hardly left her side, since."

"He must love her very dearly," he'd said, to which Lizzie could only reply, with genuine feeling, "Oh yes indeed, Mr Carr, he certainly does."

One glance at his face had been sufficient to let her see how deeply he was moved and, for the first time, Lizzie believed he was about to say something more but, he did not.

Clearly, it was neither the time nor the appropriate circumstance for a declaration of love, if that was what he had intended; the words that might have been said remained unspoken.

Lizzie had, however, no doubt at all of her own feelings. During the seemingly interminable days and nights, when she had been in London with her mother, attending upon Josie, she'd had plenty of time to think about Mr Carr. The realisation that he, above any other man she knew, possessed the character and disposition that would suit her in a husband had come to her with a clarity she could no longer deny.

Apart from a very early and juvenile infatuation for her handsome cousin Charles Bingley, who had barely noticed her existence, Lizzie had never experienced the youthful excitement of being in love.

Unlike many young girls of her age, she was not overly interested in the pastimes that threw young women into the paths of eligible young men with the potential to become serious suitors. Lizzie disliked and assiduously avoided hunting and shooting parties, did not play cards, and took no pleasure at all in flirting; and while she enjoyed dancing and was very good at it, she was partnered most often by her brothers and their friends with whom she had grown up.

None of them had she been able to take seriously for long enough to fall in love with. She had often marvelled at the capacity of heroines in books to fall in love at first sight with complete strangers, a practice she thought must be quite hazardous, even if they did turn out, in the final chapter, to be the sons of noblemen with large fortunes!

With Mr Carr, however, things had always been different. He was older than most of the young men she knew. Her brother Darcy had said he was almost thirty, which, from the vantage point of nineteen, seemed an age of considerable maturity, presenting for Lizzie a remarkable contrast to the rather skittish young men she met at county functions. There was the fact that he always treated her seriously, talking to her as an equal, listening to her views, and sometimes debating them, without the patronising manner adopted by many of the young men she had met in London. He was handsome and tall, too, she had noticed, of course.

As she considered her feelings, Lizzie had to admit that, if the truth were told, her partiality for him dated from her realisation that, of all the gentlemen she had met, Mr Carr was the only one who made her feel like a young woman rather than a schoolgirl. It was not uncommon for girls with elder brothers to find themselves treated like children still in the schoolroom. All her brother's friends, remembering her in a pinafore and braids, did just that, except Mr Carr.

Although they had never engaged in flirtation, she had no doubt that her feelings were engaged and was beginning to believe that his were, too. When he had kissed her hand, she had felt her heart race and she had known, without a word being spoken, that deeper affections than friendliness were involved on both sides.

She knew in her heart that he was aware of it, too; it was manifest in his manner towards her when they were alone and often, it had seemed, they had been on the verge of admitting it to one another. Yet, at other times, they would sit together and talk of ordinary things, of matters on the farm, the horses he had purchased, or a piece of music they had enjoyed, as though they were old friends, rather than new, as yet unacknowledged, lovers.

On the afternoon that the news came from London of Josie's wish to see her son, they had been discussing the greenhouse he was building at the farm.

"A greenhouse? What would you grow in it?" she had asked, and he'd replied that you could grow almost anything in it, proceeding to tell her of his father who grew tropical fruit and flowers in a greenhouse in America, throughout the year.

Lizzie had been intrigued and wanted to know more, but he had something else to tell her, tactfully, gently, aware of her sensibility.

"Miss Gardiner, I have some good news. I think you will be happy to hear that a certain person, whose presence in this neighbourhood was unwelcome to you, appears to have quit the district."

As Lizzie listened with obvious relief, he continued. "Your brother and I made some enquiries, while you were in London, intending to make it clear to him that his approaches to you were unwelcome and should cease forthwith. But, we were spared the trouble when we learnt he had moved to live in Derby. I understand he is involved in the printing trade. I trust you will not be troubled by him again," he declared and Lizzie, smiling, thanked him for the assurance and asked, "Does that mean it will be safe for me to go into the village or to Matlock?"

"I certainly hope so, Miss Gardiner, but may I suggest that it may be wise at first to take a companion with you—your sister Laura or a maidservant or perhaps a friend."

"A friend?" she had said, laughing a little at the suggestion, but he had been quite serious.

"Indeed, and if you are in need of one and no one is to hand, may I offer myself? I should be very happy to accompany you," he had said, in a most gentlemanly show of gallantry that made her blush.

Lizzie remarked that perhaps an escort might not be necessary, if Mr Jones was really gone from the district, but she thanked him for his kindness, all the same.

That night, in Luton, Lizzie lay awake and turned all these things over in her mind. She wondered when she would know what his feelings were. She wanted to hear him speak of his affection for her. Then, she would know both his mind and her own, for certain.

The following morning, when they resumed their journey, Mr Carr seemed unaccountably quieter and Lizzie was concerned that she, either by omission or commission, had offended him in some way. Acutely conscious of the value of his assistance and fearing she may not have said as much to him, giving him an erroneous impression that she had taken his help for granted, she began to worry. It could not have been a particularly diverting journey for him, she thought, accompanying a young lady with two servants and a five-year-old boy.

Lizzie knew how much she and her family owed to his generosity and kindness. She could not bear to think that he would feel they were not well appreciated and resolved to set things right.

It was mid-morning when they stopped once more, for refreshment and to water the horses at Barnet, not far from London. It was a pleasant spot and little Anthony was keen to exercise his legs.

Unable to suppress her concerns any longer, Lizzie, seeing Mr Carr standing at some distance from the carriage, as they waited for the others to return, seized the opportunity of their being alone to approach him.

"Mr Carr," she said "forgive me for breaking in upon your thoughts, but I have not been able to thank you enough for your kindness, not only in putting your carriage at our disposal, but also accompanying us on this journey. Please let me say how very much we appreciate your generosity. This cannot be a very interesting journey for you, and I fear we may have taken you away from important work on the farm at this time of year…"

But he would not let her continue; plainly moved by her words, he spoke quickly, "My dear Miss Gardiner, Lizzie, there is no need for you to thank me; it was the very least I could do at such a time as this, when you and your family have suffered so much anguish. I do not expect gratitude, my dear, dear Lizzie; you must know by now that nothing would be too much trouble, if I could be of assistance to you? You need only ask. Indeed," and at this point, he looked back at the inn to ascertain whether the rest of their party were in sight, but as they were not, continued, "my only regret, if I have one, is that I have not spoken earlier, before this sad news arrived; but there, I shall say no more, for I have resolved to speak first with your father, before I address you on this matter."

Lizzie could hardly believe what she was hearing.

She had imagined such a moment, thinking that when the time came, if indeed he did wish to propose to her, he would do so formally, probably standing in front of the fireplace in the drawing room of her parents' home. He was such a proper gentleman, she had never dreamed that she would be listening to what was clearly the prelude to a proposal of marriage, even if it was not couched in the customary language used on such occasions, in the courtyard of a coaching inn!

When she felt confident enough to look up at him, he was regarding her with such a look of deep concern and apprehension that she wondered if she had heard aright.

"Mr Carr, do you mean…" she began slowly, trying to think as she spoke how best to respond, but he put a finger upon her lips and said, "Please Lizzie, do not say anything in haste; I would prefer that you wait until we have had time to talk in private and I, having obtained your father's permission, am able to speak openly of my feelings for you."

This time, Lizzie knew she *had* heard right and determined to speak, saying with a degree of confidence that quite surprised him, "Mr Carr, I am almost twenty years of age; you do not need Papa's permission to speak to me about anything. If there is something you wish to say…"

Before she had finished her sentence, his words, released from restraint, tumbled out, as he reached for her hand. "My dearest Lizzie, as if you did not know already, then let me say it, that I love you with all my heart and if you will marry me, I would be the happiest man alive."

Lizzie looked at him and smiled, and it was unlikely that he could not have understood from her smile what her feelings were on hearing his words. The impression of pleasure may well have been confirmed by her words, had not Anthony appeared, at that very moment, running towards them, followed by Ellen and his nurse.

Turning from Lizzie to the boy, Mr Carr stooped, picked him up and, to his delight, swung him high into the air, before placing him safely within the carriage. As he did so, Lizzie's smile widened, as she contemplated his exuberant response and reflected on what his reaction might have been, had she been able to give him a more complete answer.

Once the others were in the carriage, he helped her into the seat beside his own and, as he took her hand to do so, she felt again the warmth and strength she had always found so reassuring.

Throughout the rest of the journey, Lizzie tried not to meet his eyes too often, lest she should betray her feelings to the maid or the nurse, who sat at the opposite window with Anthony between them, and their love would become the subject of gossip, even before they had spoken of it themselves. However, whenever the condition of the road required it and the lurching of the carriage afforded him the opportunity, he would reach out to shield her from any discomfort. That she felt no inclination to withdraw her hand from him on these occasions, letting it lie in his, beneath the folds of her cape, was sufficient answer to his question, for the moment.

Lizzie knew that with Josie gravely ill, there would be no opportunity for Mr Carr to approach her father. Nor was it appropriate, she thought, to trouble her mother at this time, knowing how busy she had been and was likely to remain for a while yet. No, she thought, with a small sigh, it would have to wait until they were all back in Derbyshire. She did wonder, though, how she would keep her tumultuous feelings a secret from everyone until then.

As a consequence, though the warmth of Lizzie's smile and her agreeable manner may have indicated to Mr Carr that the sentiments he had expressed were in no way unwelcome and might well be requited, no opportune moment arose for them to speak of the matter again, save for a hasty farewell before he left London to return to Rushmore Farm. He felt rather like a man who, having received a rare gift, was forbidden to open and enjoy it. The waiting was agonising, but exquisitely so.

On reaching Portman Square, they had been met by Cassandra and Mrs Tate, who gave them the good news. Josie, they said, was stronger and, with Julian and now little Anthony here, they had great hopes of her continuing to improve. Anthony was taken immediately to see his mother, and later Julian came downstairs to confirm the tenderness and poignancy of their reunion.

"It is a far more potent medicine in such cases as these than anything prescribed by a doctor," he said. He then thanked both Lizzie and Mr Carr for bringing the child to London so promptly and declared that they were all more hopeful that Josie would be much improved by Christmas.

"We are very much in your debt, Mr Carr. I know my wife will want me to thank you on her behalf. We expect her to improve considerably from now on and much of that will be owed to you," he said.

Josie did improve and regain some of her strength and, while Cassandra and Lizzie returned to Derbyshire with Mr and Mrs Darcy, Josie's parents remained in London, staying on at Portman Square, at Mr Darcy's insistence, to be close to their daughter. With her faithful Susan attending upon her and the presence of all those who loved her around her, Josie's spirits had clearly improved and hopes were high for her recovery.

Shortly before Christmas, Julian wrote to his parents, telling them how very hopeful they were. Thanking them for all they had done to help him and Josie, he proceeded to give them welcome news:

My dear Josie seems stronger and happier, more content than I have known her to be in many years. She felt able to come downstairs and help little Anthony decorate his Christmas tree. Our best reward came that night, when she joined us at dinner, seeming to enjoy both the food and the warmth of the love of her family. It was a very moving occasion for us all. You will not be surprised to hear that we are looking forward very much to enjoying Christmas together as a family again.

I am truly grateful for all that has been done to help her, by everyone, from yourselves, my dear parents, to Richard, Cassy, Lizzie, and Mr Carr; you have all been so wonderfully kind...

The letter was both welcome and timely.

In the wake of all this good news, Mr Carr sought a moment alone with Lizzie, arriving at their home with a hamper of Christmas fare from the farm. With both her parents away and her brother on an errand in Derby, it was left to Lizzie to thank him and offer him some refreshments in the parlour. The maid brought in tea and cake and Lizzie did the honours.

When they were seated, Mr Carr took the opportunity to remind her, as though such a reminder was necessary, of his words at the inn at Barnet, before asking if she had given them any thought. Lizzie had been preparing a proper little speech, knowing full well he would surely ask this very question at the first opportunity, but when he did, she became flustered and seemed to suffer a complete lapse of memory. After some moments of silence, which almost caused him to panic, she said, hastily, "Oh yes, yes I have, of course, Mr Carr."

In years to come, this quaint response would cause her to be greatly teased by Mr Carr and other members of the family, but, at that moment, Mr Carr was rather disconcerted by the matter-of-fact little phrase, which had become something of a habit with her. He asked again, gently, but determined to know her meaning, "My dear Lizzie, by that do you mean you have considered my proposal? And, may I conclude then, that having considered, you accept?"

Once again, embarrassed by a rush of unexpected pleasure, which left her temporarily tongue-tied, she hesitated before saying softly, "Yes, yes, Mr Carr, of course," and smiled as though she was surprised that he should have to ask.

At this, with a great explosion of joy, he gathered her into his arms and kissed her, before saying, "Lizzie, my darling, do you know how very happy you have made me with that funny little answer?" and this time, before she could even begin to respond, he said, "Why yes, Mr Carr, of course!" causing her to burst into laughter, breaking down the shyness that had trammelled up her speech, letting them enjoy to the full the delight of acknowledging openly their love for one another.

Lizzie had never known such happiness and had neither the inclination nor the sophistication to hide the extent of her pleasure from the man she loved, when he told her ardently and sincerely how deeply he loved her. Later, he promised to go away and compose a letter to her father, which he would present to him on Boxing Day, when he had been invited to join the family for dinner.

Dr Gardiner would want to speak with him, they supposed, and both agreed that it was best to keep their engagement a secret until then, out of courtesy to her parents. It would not be fair, Lizzie said, to have everyone else knowing and talking about it until her parents had given them their blessing. That they would, she had not a shadow of a doubt.

Mr Carr had some business in London, which needed urgent attention, he said, and assured her he would return very soon. A fond and reluctant leavetaking ensued, each promising the other what couples in such situations usually promise. "It is, after all, only for a very few days, my darling; I shall be back with you within three days," he promised and she agreed, although in her heart, she wished he would not go at all.

Neither anticipated a change in the weather, which delayed Mr Carr's return from London by several days, so that when he arrived to dine with the family on Boxing Day, the all-important letter had not, as yet, been written. Indeed, between dinner and coffee and the opening of gifts, there was hardly any time to explain and poor Lizzie wondered, at the end of the day, how much longer she could keep her precious secret.

Finally, on New Year's Eve, the deed was duly done. Every year, family and friends of the Darcys would gather at Pemberley on New Year's Eve. This year was no different, though the Tates and Julian's family were sadly missed. There was, however, the good news of Josie's recovery, for which they could all be grateful. Mr Carr, now regarded as a good neighbour and a friend of the family, had been invited, too, to the delight of Lizzie and the obvious pleasure of her brother Darcy, in whom his friend had already confided.

Calling at the Gardiners' place en route to Pemberley, Mr Carr had handed the vital letter, which he had taken all afternoon to compose, to Dr Gardiner, who, being rather busy at the time or perhaps distracted by other concerns, chose not to open it immediately. Instead, he placed it prominently upon his desk, proposing to open it on the morrow. Lizzie, visiting her father's study, had noticed it sitting unopened on his desk; which fact she conveyed to Mr Carr in a whispered remark, as they went in to supper at Pemberley.

The Pemberley supper parties were justly famous for the excellence of the food and wine and the generous hospitality of the hosts. This year, in spite of the somewhat dreary prognostications for the general state of business in the country, the estate and related enterprises had done well and the New Year's celebrations were proof of this. Never ostentatious, the Darcys had a well-earned reputation for sharing their prosperity with the community in which they lived.

On this day, Mr Darcy announced the extension of the Pemberley Parish School buildings, so they could accommodate older pupils from the area. In an arrangement with his friend and neighbour Sir Thomas Camden, land and funds were to be made available from both estates and the building named after Lady Mary Camden, who had died earlier that year.

The school was to be administered by Miss Jessica Courtney, daughter of the Darcys' dear friend and cousin Emily. Jessica, like her parents, had devoted much time to the education and care of the children of the district. Both Mr and Mrs Darcy held her in very high regard, upon which subject, Mr Darcy expanded in his speech.

While the speech held the attention of most of the party, Lizzie, who was seated to one side of the room, away from the general company, took the opportunity to ask Mr Carr an unrelated question.

"Why do you suppose Papa did not open your letter? Is it likely that he has correctly guessed what it contains?" to which he replied, "Now, if I were the father of a charming young daughter approaching her twentieth year and a gentleman handed me such a letter, I think I might have guessed what its contents might be and hastened to open it. But I cannot speak for your father, my dear Lizzie. Is it possible he thinks that you are still too young to be spoken for? In which case, he probably believes my letter pertains to matters of sewerage and sanitation in the tenants' cottages, of which he and I have spoken on another occasion."

He was teasing her, and Lizzie knew it.

Still adamant that it was neither of these things, she caught her brother Darcy's attention and called him over to join them, as the musicians were preparing to play the fanfare that always heralded the fireworks on the terrace.

"Let us see if my brother has a better notion," she said and together the three of them moved towards an alcove that afforded them an excellent view of the fireworks, while maintaining considerable privacy from the rest of the company.

Darcy Gardiner was of a mind to tease them both, since he was the only person in the room with the advantage of knowledge obtained from his friend as well as his sister. It placed him in a unique position.

Consequently, he entertained himself and the couple with a series of propositions that canvassed several improbable possibilities. "It could be any one of many reasons," he declared. "I understand a plague of mice has been troubling some of the farmers in the dales; several children have been bitten, it is a serious matter, and my father may well have thought the letter concerned a mouse problem at Rushmore.

"Or perhaps, he thinks the letter contains a request for a medical opinion and, as you well know, Lizzie, Papa treats such matters in confidence and probably will not open the letter until he can take it into the privacy of his rooms at the hospital."

This was all too much for Lizzie who put on a show of being exceedingly vexed with her brother and his friend, which immediately brought Mr Carr to tender an abject apology and reprimand Darcy for teasing her.

While all this harmless fun was going on and the rest of the party were moving to take tea or coffee, the three participants were unaware that they were being observed, quite closely, though not in any censorious fashion, by Mrs Darcy and her sister Mrs Bingley. While they could not hear what was being said, it was plain to Jane and Elizabeth that the three enjoyed a close and friendly relationship. Their obvious rapport and affectionate raillery was a clear sign to the two ladies, who had much experience in observing and picking out the true lovers from the flirts, that there was more to this group than met the unpracticed eye.

As they observed, with some amusement, it was plain all three shared some information, of which the rest of the company was, as yet, ignorant. Whatever Dr Gardiner and his wife may or may not have noticed about the situation, to Elizabeth and Jane, it was quite plain that Mr Carr was in love with Lizzie Gardiner and that she probably returned his affection. As for her brother, they were in no doubt at all that he was in the confidence of both parties.

Supper over, Cassandra joined her mother and aunt, hoping for some quiet conversation. To her surprise, she found herself being quizzed about her daughter.

"And when do you expect that your little Lizzie will be engaged?" asked her mother, to which Cassy's astonished response was, "My Lizzie engaged? Not very soon, I do not think, Mama. She is not yet twenty and does not appear to be in any hurry to be married."

Her Aunt Jane then asked if there was no particular gentleman in whom Lizzie had shown an interest.

Cassy shook her head. "No, Aunt Jane, not above any of the others. There have been one or two of Darcy's friends who seemed interested, but Lizzie would have none of it. Of course, there was a time, some years ago, when we were in London, and it looked as if Charles Bingley may have taken her fancy, but no one seriously believed it would come to anything. She was not quite fifteen! My Lizzie is very sensible, you know, Aunt; she will not give her heart easily to any man," she said, quite decisively.

Elizabeth, growing a little impatient with her daughter's apparent complacency, said rather sharply, "Not any man, certainly, but Mr Carr looks to be a very likely candidate. Cassy, my love, where have you been? Have you not noticed that Lizzie and Mr Carr are plainly in love?" she asked.

Cassandra was incredulous. "Mama! You cannot be serious; Lizzie and Mr Carr?"

"Indeed and I am absolutely serious, Cassy. Unless I am very much mistaken, Mr Carr seems to be quite serious, too. Your aunt and I have been observing them all evening, not that there is any lack of decorum on their part or any silliness, certainly not; but there is between them a certain closeness, almost an intimacy, that is unmistakable. My dear Cassy, I will wager anything you care to name that your daughter is either already secretly engaged to Mr Carr or very soon will be, and your Aunt Jane agrees with me."

Her sister nodded, smiling as she said, "If you do not trust our observation, I suggest you ask her brother Darcy about his friend's intentions. I am sure he knows more about it than all the rest of us put together."

Their words were lightly spoken, but Cassandra was both amazed and disconcerted by them. It was a possibility she had not contemplated since the earliest weeks of their acquaintance with their new friend and neighbour. Mr Carr had proved helpful, good neighbourly, and generous with his time, especially in the last few months. But she had long since ceased to regard him as a possible suitor for her daughter. He was much older than Lizzie. She had heard Darcy mention that his friend was thirty, and he was an American. Cassy knew few other Americans, but it was generally believed, especially in London society, that Americans, both men and women, were mostly in England to do business, acquire valuable properties and, if possible, spouses who were wealthy and titled. Young Lizzie was neither.

Cassy was confused. If her mother and aunt were right, then she must have been completely deceived—not deliberately, but as a consequence of her own inability to see what was right before her eyes. Determined, however, not to leap to conclusions, she decided to leave well alone, until they were back at home. She would speak to Richard first and acquaint him with the observations of her mother and aunt and, perhaps then, their son Darcy may be applied to for information on his friend's intentions, she thought. For the moment, she was not going to be stampeded into upsetting Lizzie or anyone else by asking awkward questions.

With her mother and aunt, she changed the subject, with characteristic equanimity, telling them of a letter she had received from her brother, which she had brought with her to share with them.

Cassandra knew well, it was one certain way of distracting her mother from any further speculation about Lizzie and Mr Carr.

Julian wrote hopefully:

I know, my dear Cassy, that you will be happy to hear that Josie is so much better now. When I proposed that she should come with me to Italy in the Spring, she agreed readily. I am convinced the warmer climate will improve her chances of recovery, even though I have to say to you, with a heavy heart, that the doctors have warned me not to expect too much. I am so grateful to have her back, nothing else matters.

My dear sister, I have to thank you and Richard for all you have done for Josie. Yet, I must now ask a further favour of you—that you have Anthony to stay with you, whilst I take Josie to Italy in the New Year. When Josie has recovered her strength and we return to England, I hope to ask Mama to let us stay a while at her farm in Sussex. I used to enjoy it immensely, when I was a boy, and I know the freshness of the country air will benefit Josie very much and help restore her to health.

I do not believe she wishes to return to the house in Cambridge.

I myself have had some reservations about continuing to work there...

So pleased had Cassandra been to receive this letter, she told her mother and aunt she had written immediately, to assure her brother that looking after Anthony would be a matter of no consequence. "He is not a difficult child and is good company for our James; they are almost like brothers, so I have written to say they should not trouble themselves at all on that score," she said.

Her mother and aunt were not surprised. Jane and Elizabeth knew that Cassy's selfless love of her brother and his family would have prevailed over any reservations she may have had on the matter. Elizabeth remarked upon Josie's extraordinary recovery, whilst Jane hoped that the miracle that had restored Josie to her family would also help in her recovery. Neither had fully comprehended either the virulence of her disease or the strange path it had hitherto taken. Dr Gardiner had not deemed it necessary or wise to trouble them with the details, with which he was only too familiar.

That night, returning home after the party at Pemberley, Lizzie Gardiner, unaware of the confusion that had invaded her mother's mind, went to bed with her head and heart filled with the exquisite happiness that comes only with the certainty of being deeply and devotedly loved.

It eclipsed all other concerns in her mind.

That Mr Carr loved her as fondly as she loved him, she was now assured. For some weeks, she had been aware that a new and exhilarating emotion was directing her life, but even she had not imagined it would make one person, whom she had known for not much longer than a year, more important to her immediate happiness than anyone else on earth. Yet, it was not with any trepidation, but with some wonderment and not a little delight, that she contemplated her present situation.

That her brother regarded the man she loved as a good friend and approved of their affection for one another increased her joy. On learning of their secret engagement from Mr Carr, Darcy had sought her out and embraced her. "My dear little sister, he is a fine man; I know you will be very happy together," he had said and, for Lizzie, there was but one more step to heaven: her parents' blessing. Her father would open Mr Carr's letter tomorrow morning, he would send for her, and Lizzie already knew exactly what she would say. This time, she promised herself, she would not be tongue-tied. She had practised it carefully and was word perfect.

However, as on many occasions in life, when plans are made only to be confounded, destiny decided otherwise.

Even as the party at Pemberley ended and the Gardiners returned home in good spirits, events were unfolding that were to inflict unimagined change upon their lives.

Sometime during that night, Josie suffered a relapse. By mid-morning on New Year's Day, while flakes of snow were falling in the quiet city, she passed into a feverish delirium and, despite the efforts of the best doctors her husband could summon, never regained consciousness. Shortly before nightfall, with Julian, her parents, and her faithful Susan beside her, she slipped away.

News of Josie's death came less than a fortnight after the family had celebrated the birth of Jonathan Charles, the first child of Anne-Marie and Colin Elliott. A letter from Jonathan Bingley had reached them shortly before Christmas with the news of the birth of his grandson. It had brought hope and happiness to end a year that had been fraught with problems.

When Julian's urgent message arrived, Mr Carr was with them, having arrived to see Dr Gardiner. He had been taking tea in the parlour with Cassandra and her daughters, when the express was brought in. On opening it, Cassy cried out and, having broken the news to her daughters, had rushed upstairs to her husband. Weeping copiously, Laura Ann followed her mother, leaving Lizzie in tears.

It was to Mr Carr she turned for consolation and it seemed quite natural and entirely right that he should take her in his arms and comfort her as she wept, unable to understand why, after all these weeks of hope, it had come to this. She had not known what her father had expected for some time; that a patient with tuberculosis would often rally strongly and seem to recover just before a fatal relapse.

Cassy, coming downstairs later and seeing them together, sensed the intimacy and tenderness between them and was reminded of her mother's words. Clearly she had, amidst all her other undertakings, missed something important that had been happening in her daughter's life. She determined that she would speak with her husband, at the earliest opportunity, but quite obviously, that was not today.

Cassy could not help wondering at the way a coincidence of joy and sorrow had often marked their lives. Recalling, with a deep sigh, the day of her engagement, forever bound up with the death of her beloved brother William, she wondered if life was always like this. Would Lizzie, like her mother, retain memories of Josie's death, linked to her own love? Was happiness too rich a draught to be drunk without some bitter trace of sorrow in the cup?

The funeral, which was held at Pemberley on a cold January afternoon, was a sad, difficult occasion. Mr and Mrs Darcy looked strained and wan. The news coming so soon after Julian's optimistic letters had them stunned and bewildered.

The Tates were desolated and neither was able to speak without weeping. Poor Becky Tate, who had at all times encouraged her daughter in her ambitions and hoped for great things from her marriage to the young heir to Pemberley, could not absorb the blow that had been dealt them, while her husband was left to wonder at the value of his material success and political influence. His favourite child was gone and his life, for all its wealth and power, was empty.

Not everyone knew the details of Josie's death.

The younger people in the area, who had known her as a girl, wept, confused, unable to comprehend the circumstances that had destroyed such a vibrant, young life. Few could believe that Josie Tate, their childhood playmate, was dead.

Not long afterwards, while Richard and Cassy were still trying to come to terms with the swift reversal of fortune that had taken them in so short a time from hope to despair, Julian, who had spent the last few weeks with his parents at Pemberley, arrived to see his sister and brother-in-law.

Cassandra was shocked by his appearance. He looked and sounded like a man resigned to his fate, already aware that it had little in the way of happiness to offer him. Refusing any refreshment, he thanked them for all they had done for Josie and revealed that he had decided to renounce his inheritance in favour of his son.

As Cassy gasped in disbelief, he explained, "Anthony will succeed as the heir to Pemberley directly from his grandfather. I have asked only for a modest income from the estate, which would enable me to continue my research work in Europe, where I will live for most of the year. I am well paid there and do not wish to draw upon the estate for anything more. Such resources as may accrue to me will flow on to my son and can be used for his upbringing and education, as well as the improvement of the estate.

"While I do not intend to sever my ties with Pemberley, I have no desire to live there permanently; there are too many deep scars and painful memories for me," he said, as Richard and Cassy listened, unable to say a word.

Julian went on, in a voice that suggested he had made up his mind a long time ago, "My work in bacteriology is now the centre of my life, and I shall devote most of my time to it. You will understand, Richard; it is an absorbing and important field, and I am committed to it."

He pleaded with them to understand and forgive him for what he had done. "I am well aware that I will be condemned by some, who are ignorant of my motives, for letting my family down, by not taking on the role and responsibilities of the future Master of Pemberley. But, I am convinced that it is not a role which I could carry out with distinction as my dear father has done these many years."

As his sister sought to protest at his words, denying that he would be so censured, he held up a hand, and continued, "Hear me out, Cassy, please; it is true, though it is kind of you to attempt to defend me. I need no such defence, for I know I am not the man to fill my father's place. I hope, however, that with his great example and advice, my son will do so with the same degree of dedication and success. I think you will agree, Cassy, that Pemberley and its people deserve the best master our family can give them."

Seeing the tears that had filled his sister's eyes, he went to her and embraced her. Richard, he was sure, would agree with him; in time, his practical wisdom would prevail and Cassy would be comforted, when she came to understand that he was right.

Julian had seen his attorney and, with his advice, drafted the necessary legal instruments renouncing his rights, together with a brief letter explaining his reasons for so doing; he handed copies of these documents to his sister.

Relinquishing all his rights to the estate in favour of his son, Anthony Fitzwilliam Darcy, whose care he entrusted to his sister, Mrs Cassandra Gardiner, Julian had written:

That my son, when he attains his majority, will live chiefly at Pemberley, where he will receive such training and further education as he may need to fulfill his future role as the Master of Pemberley, unencumbered by any obligations to myself.

Should he be required, by an untimely event, which I hope with all my heart does not occur, to take up his inheritance at an earlier age, I ask that he be guided in the task by my sister Cassandra and any other person whom she may appoint to assist her in this regard.

Until Anthony is considered ready to assume full responsibility for the estate, he will, in all matters concerning the estate, be advised by my sister Mrs Gardiner and my brother-in-law Dr Richard Gardiner, or any person they may appoint to advise him.

Placing the letter in his sister's hands, he said, "Cassy, I have already spoken to Mama and Papa. They understand my reasons. My father has been most generous with my allowance; he has granted my request, though he could not hide his disappointment. I know he will realise soon enough that it is for the best—for myself, for Anthony, and for Pemberley, which he loves so dearly.

Richard, I shall never forget how much I owe you both, and my dear little Lizzie, too," he said, turning to her as she sat a little apart, tearful and silent. "Josie was especially grateful for your kindness, Lizzie. She spoke of you often and wished you would be very happy. Thank you all, from the bottom of my heart; I wish I could have been as devoted to my duties as you have been to my family. God bless you."

And with that, he embraced them all and bade them farewell.

Two days later, having said his farewells to his parents and the many men and women he had known at Pemberley, Julian Darcy returned to France.

END OF PART TWO

Part Three

WHEN CASSANDRA WENT DOWNSTAIRS to her husband's study, it had been with the hope of finding him there alone. It being Sunday, she knew he would not go to the hospital, unless of course, there was some dreadful emergency; consequently, she had resolved to speak with him about their daughter Lizzie.

Everything that had happened since New Year's Eve, when she had returned home from Pemberley determined to broach the subject with him, had conspired to prevent her doing just that. Each time she had decided this was the moment, some unforeseen circumstance had arisen and embroiled them in a series of events that made any rational discussion of Lizzie's future impossible.

This time, however, she was quite single-minded about it. She knew Lizzie and Laura were gone with Anthony, James, and their new governess to church and were unlikely to return before midday. Her husband, having returned from his morning ride, had changed and gone down to breakfast, after which, he would, as always, read his papers in his study for an hour or so.

When she arrived at the door of the room, she heard voices within, Richard's and their son Darcy's. Vexed at being frustrated again, Cassy retreated upstairs, but only as far as the landing, from where she could hear the door open and shut as Darcy left the room. She was about to go downstairs when the door to the study opened again and Richard came out; he was coming upstairs himself.

Determined not to let this opportunity slip, she approached him, as he reached the top of the stairs. "Richard, I really must speak with you; there is something that has been on my mind this last fortnight, about which I need your advice. I should have spoken earlier, but with the sorrow and the shock we've suffered, it never seemed to be the right time."

Her husband had in his hand a letter. As she stopped speaking, he said, "You are quite right, my dear. I have had much the same problem; an important matter has come up, on which I must have your opinion, and for the very same reasons, it has been held in abeyance for some ten days or more. I know I should have responded earlier, but it is, as you have said, a matter of the appropriate time. Besides, I did have to make some related enquiries, which I have now completed, so perhaps we could resolve both questions at the one time."

Cassy was confused—she had no idea what problem he had been attempting to resolve, but before she could ask, he said, "Why do you not begin, my love? Tell me, what has been troubling you for a fortnight?"

"It's Lizzie," she began.

Her husband appeared astonished.

"Lizzie? Why, what has she done?"

Cassandra interrupted him. "There, you see, you did not know either. Here was I, berating myself for not noticing what was going on in my daughter's life…"

He stopped her and asked gently, "Noticing what, Cassy? Has Lizzie done something untoward? Has she displeased you in any way? If she has, it must have been unwittingly done, because that is certainly not like our Lizzie."

He sounded concerned and Cassy was rather put out by his questions.

"Well, I do not really know, Richard, that is the problem," she began, and he took her by the hand and sat her down, realising she was by now becoming unusually agitated.

Cassandra rarely became angry with him or her children. She was by nature calm and well tempered. Her husband was keen to discover what had caused this extraordinary state of disquiet. "My dear Cassy, hadn't you better start at the beginning and tell me what it is that's causing you such distress? I find it hard to believe that Lizzie can have done or said anything so bad as to upset you in this way."

When she did tell him, however, going back to New Year's Eve at Pemberley, of the remarks of her mother and Aunt Jane, as well as her own observations of the pair on the day the news came of Josie's death, her husband's initial expression of mild confusion deepened to one of bewilderment. When she had finished saying her piece, he was silent for a few moments, before taking up the letter he had brought upstairs and setting it down upon the table before her, with the comment, "I think, my dear, you had better read this letter. It may explain many of the things that have been troubling you."

She looked at the letter and, seeing it had been written more than a fortnight ago, said, "But Richard, this must have reached you weeks ago."

He nodded, "Yes dearest, a fortnight ago, to be precise. I do apologise; I should have told you of its contents earlier, but as you have said, there was always some circumstance in the way. It did not seem appropriate to be discussing it while we were in the midst of preparations for the funeral. But, it has to be answered, so please read it."

Cassandra picked up the letter and read it through quickly, then more slowly again, with care. It was from Mr Carr, written on New Year's Eve, informing Dr Gardiner of his happiness at having been accepted by his daughter Lizzie and asking for the blessing of her parents upon their engagement.

It set out also, in detail, his current circumstances, his business affairs, and income, and assured Dr and Mrs Gardiner that he not only loved their daughter dearly and hoped to make her happy, but that he had more than adequate means to do so, in a material sense as well.

As to his character and credentials, he referred them to two very reputable gentlemen in the city, one of whom was his attorney, a well-known lawyer of impeccable integrity, and to their own son Darcy, who had been his friend and companion for some years and knew him as well as any man in England, he said.

The letter was well written, though couched perhaps somewhat less formally than most, which Cassy put down to his being an American.

She handed it back to her husband, with a look of resignation on her face, and said, "It reads well," to which Richard replied with some enthusiasm, "It certainly does, my dear. I am impressed. It is a modest, courteous proposal, without presumption or self-praise and pleasantly devoid of sanctimonious hypocrisy."

Cassy could not help feeling some annoyance and frustration; her eldest daughter Lizzie, whom she had cherished with love and affection, to whom she had felt so close, had fallen in love and accepted a proposal of marriage from a man who had been a complete stranger to their family until a year or so ago. Yet Lizzie had never once sought to confide in her.

It would have been inconceivable, Cassy thought, that she would have acted in this way. She recalled, with some nostalgia, how she had entrusted her mother with her secret, confessing her love for Richard and borrowing her special jewels on the night of the Pemberley Ball, the night she had hoped he would propose.

She even remembered the excitement they had shared in the cold corridors of Pemberley House when, after all the guests had departed, she had gone to tell her mother that Richard would call on her father on the morrow. Cassy could not believe that things were so very different between herself and her daughter. What could possibly have gone wrong?

Not wishing to interrupt her reverie, Richard had moved away to the window. In the distance, he could see a group returning from church. Anthony and James were running on ahead, followed by their governess and Laura Ann. Much further back, two figures, whom he could just make out, came into view, Lizzie with Mr Carr, who had dismounted from his horse to walk with her. Even at this distance there was no doubting from their attitude and manner, his head inclined towards her, her arm through his, that they were much more than casual friends walking home from church.

His wife's voice broke in upon his thoughts. "What do you intend to say to him?" she asked.

Richard turned to look directly at her, seemingly puzzled by her question. "What should I say? I have made some enquiries through my attorney and it appears that all his claims here are perfectly true. He is well educated, well spoken, very well regarded in the city as a businessman, and has substantial means. Indeed, he has not included here the inheritance he can expect from his father in America, which, Darcy tells me, is probably in excess of what he already has in this country. It seems he has established himself in business, quite successfully.

"Darcy, who knows him well, speaks of him with affection and respect.

"Clearly, he is not seeking to marry our daughter for her money; he has more of it than any one of our five children can expect to have from me.

"So, from all accounts, Mr Carr would seem to be an eminently suitable person, to which, of course, one must add the not unimportant fact that they are in love and Lizzie has already accepted him," he replied.

Cassy frowned; she had not expected him to be so sanguine about the matter of his daughter's engagement. While she had no reason to disapprove of Mr Carr, she *had* expected her husband to have some reservations. Apparently he did not.

"I shall speak with her, of course, before I respond to his letter, but if they are already pledged to one another…" Cassy interrupted him. "But Richard, is it a suitable match for Lizzie? Have you considered that she is only nineteen? Can we be sure she knows her own mind? Besides, he is much older than her and he is an American, of whose family and background we know nothing, save what he has told us."

At that, he smiled. "Ah, what we do know, of course, is that his grandfather was a stable boy on the Fitzwilliams' estate in Ireland."

He paused and came around to where she was seated and, standing directly before her, asked gently, "Are you sure, my dear, that your anxiety about his background has not been brought on by that little discovery, one that Mr Carr cheerfully revealed to us himself?"

Cassandra was completely taken aback. Shocked by her husband's question and its implications of snobbery and worse, she was silent for a moment, unable to answer him and he continued.

"I might remind you, my dear, that when Mr Carr arrived in the district and expressed his interest in purchasing a property in the area, you were very keen for him to do so. You urged me to recommend him to Will Camden. You thought he would be an excellent neighbour. You did not question his connections then." His voice, though gentle, left her in no doubt of his opinion on the matter and she felt very uneasy.

Cassy looked at her husband and, realising how very well he knew her, said, "Richard, that was quite different. I do not deny it, indeed he is a very good neighbour; I can think of none better and he has been helpful and generous with his time when we needed help. I cannot fault his conduct in any of these matters. But to marry Lizzie? I need to be sure he is right for her. I have been so worried, especially after the disaster of Julian and Josie's marriage, which has been such a harrowing experience for all of us. I would feel I was not doing my duty if I did not pay close attention to it. He is a charming and amiable man and I fear that Lizzie, at nineteen, may not know her own mind," she looked at him, hoping he would understand her concerns. "You do not really believe that

I am the sort of woman who will condemn a man for his humble forebears, do you?" she pleaded.

Seeing her distress, Richard put his arms around her, reassuring her of his faith in her. "Of course not, my love, or you could not possibly have married the grandson of a man who began trading as a barrow boy!"

He laughed as she pulled away and looked at him, all astonishment at his words. Then, he nodded, and said, "Did your Mama not tell you? My father always told us the story to remind us that a man was to be judged not by his humble beginnings, but for himself and what he made of his life. So you see, it would not be fair or right to look down upon Mr Carr, because of his grandfather's occupation. Indeed, on my part, it would be gross hypocrisy."

As she listened, he went on to explain. "I did, however, have some concerns about his associates in the city; I am no admirer of the gentlemen of the stock exchange. But, I have, by my enquiries, satisfied myself that he is, as he appears to be, a decent, unpretentious fellow who makes an honest living through commerce; he has a few good friends and no obvious enemies."

Cassy looked at her husband and smiled for the first time in their conversation. "And you believe he is the right man for Lizzie?"

"I do and so does her brother. Darcy assures me Mr Michael Carr is a prince among men; he trusts him implicitly. But we shall wait to hear Lizzie's side of the tale before I write to him. If, as I think she will, she tells me she loves him and has made up her mind to marry him, I cannot see that we would do ourselves or Lizzie any good by objecting to her choice. She is a good sensible girl, Cassy, very much like her mother was, though not quite as beautiful. I doubt she will do something as stupid as marry the wrong man. She has your excellent example, after all."

This time, Cassy laughed and he could see she was more at ease.

"Was your grandfather really a barrow boy?" she asked, still a little doubtful, but Richard was adamant.

"Indeed he was, a small trader in the best sense of the word and by all accounts a very successful one. He did not remain a barrow boy forever; he moved up into trading from his own warehouse in Cheapside, where he built up the very profitable trade that my father, who had the benefit of a superior education, inherited. Of course he went further; while we continued to live in Cheapside, he purchased and developed the old Commercial Trading Company, engaged in import and export business with the Colonies. Subsequently, he went into partnership with your father and Colonel Fitzwilliam, and you know the rest. We, all the members of my family, owe a great deal to their enterprise and hard work and it all began with that young barrow boy."

He spoke lightly, but Cassy's arms tightened around him; he knew her well and would not let her take a wrong step, if he could help it. She was grateful and said so. "Thank you, Richard, thank you for telling me."

Hearing the children coming in, they went downstairs. The boys galloped up the stairs, followed by Miss Longhurst, their new governess, and Laura Ann. Lizzie was standing in the hall, her bonnet in her hand, when her father said, "Ah, Lizzie, my dear, would you come into my study? Your Mama and I would like a word," and Lizzie, a little surprised to see her parents waiting for her, set down her hymnbook and bonnet and followed them into the room.

She knew already from Mr Carr, whom they had met on the way home from church, that he had not, as yet, received a response to his letter, but he had very generously explained away the delay by pointing out that with the death of her Aunt Josie and the subsequent decision of her Uncle Julian to renounce his inheritance, her father must have had several important matters to deal with in the same fortnight.

"I would not be surprised if he has been far too busy to open my letter," he had said, urging her to be patient. "When circumstances return to normal, he will send for you and then I shall have my answer."

Lizzie had asked, "What do you suppose he will say?" and he had shrugged his shoulders. "He's your Papa, my dear Lizzie, you know him better than I do. What do *you* think he will say? Will he let you marry me?"

Lizzie had been surprised at the trepidation in his voice.

"Why should he not?" she demanded, and again, he had looked anxious and uncertain, as he replied, "I cannot say, my love; he may think, perhaps, that I am too old for you."

"You are not!" Lizzie protested, "Why, my Mama is almost ten years younger than Papa; nobody thought he was too old for her! I understand from my grandmothers that it was regarded as an excellent match by both families," she had said, adding defiantly, "Besides, as my Aunt Emma Wilson says, it is not those sorts of things that matter in the end, but what is in your mind and heart.

"She says, if you truly love and respect one another and want to do only those things that will make each other happy, that is what makes a good marriage. And my Aunt Emma should know, she was married twice; the first was miserable, but after his death, she is now so happily wed, you cannot imagine a better marriage."

"Your Aunt Emma sounds very wise," he said and added softly, "If that is the test, I think we shall have little difficulty passing it, do you not agree, Lizzie?"

"Indeed and I would marry you anyway, though I would be happiest if they gave us their blessing. I think Papa will, but I have no wish to hurt my dear Mama, so I do hope she will not be displeased either."

~∾~

Their conversation having ended when they reached the entrance to the drive, Mr Carr had taken leave of them and, mounting his horse, had ridden up the road in the direction of Rushmore Farm. While Miss Longhurst and Laura Ann had hurried up the drive behind the boys, Lizzie, her mind now fully occupied with the question of her father's response to Mr Carr's letter, had dawdled along behind them, lost in her own thoughts, until her father's voice broke into them. When she entered the study and saw the letter in his hand, Lizzie wished she knew more of what was in it.

Her mother was seated in her father's favourite chair by the fireplace, while her father sat beside Lizzie on the couch by the window.

Still holding the letter, he began, "Lizzie dear, I am sure you are aware that I have had this letter from Mr Carr," and when she nodded, he continued, "First, let me apologise to you and I will do likewise, when I see him, to Mr Carr as well, for the inordinate delay in responding to this letter, keeping both of you in suspense as it were. But, I know you will understand, what with all that has occurred since Christmas, do you not my dear?"

Lizzie nodded again and he went on. "Now, Mr Carr says in his letter to me that he has asked you to marry him and you have accepted him. Is this correct, Lizzie?"

She nodded once more and said, "Yes, Papa, I have. But that was before Christmas. Mr Carr was to write to you on Boxing Day, but he was late getting back from London and…"

Richard held up his hand. "You do not need to explain, my dear, I understand that sometimes these things are unavoidable; but Lizzie, my dear, did you not wish to speak with your Mama or with me, before you accepted him?" he asked.

Poor Lizzie thought this was beginning to sound ominous. She was silent for a minute or two, before saying quietly, but ever so firmly, "I am sorry, Papa, but I did not feel as though I needed to. It was not as though I was unsure; I do love him and I knew, when he asked me, there was no other man I wanted to marry, so I said 'Yes, of course'…"

At this, her father laughed lightly and Lizzie relaxed. He did not sound angry, she thought, and that was a good sign.

"And how long have you known with so much certainty that Mr Carr was the man you wanted to marry?" he asked.

Lizzie stopped to think a while. "I cannot exactly say, Papa. I think it has been coming along for a while now. But, if you were to press me, I would probably have to say that I knew, for certain, on the day in Meryton, when I was trying to get away from that horrible Mr Jones in the village, when he kept following me…and insisting on talking to me…and asking questions…I did not know what to do or whom to turn to, until I saw Mr Carr on the other side of the street…He was going into the saddlery and I was quite sure that if I could get across the street and find him, I would be safe. I knew he would protect me from Mr Jones and indeed he did! He was kind and considerate and I felt safe…I knew then that I could trust him with anything, including my life."

Her words tumbled out in a great rush and it was clear she was still distressed by the memory. Richard and Cassandra looked at one another, concerned and anxious and, in almost one voice, asked, "Lizzie, what's this about Mr Jones? Has Andrew Jones been here, in the village harassing you with his attentions?" and when she nodded, her face red with embarrassment, Cassy exclaimed, "Lizzie, my child, you have never mentioned this to me!" and her father asked, in a much more serious voice, "When did this happen, Lizzie?"

She related some of the detail of her ordeal and explained the manner in which Mr Carr had brought her home, discreetly avoiding the attention of Mr Jones and any other passersby in the village. They were impressed by his kindness and discretion, grateful he had been there to help her. But her mother was furious about Andrew Jones, whose part in the destruction of her brother's marriage and, consequently, the death of his wife, could never be forgiven.

"You ought to have told your father and me, Lizzie. While it was kind of Mr Carr to help you, your Papa and I were entitled to know, especially if you had been in any danger of further harassment by Mr Jones," she said, and then it was that Lizzie replied, "Yes, Mama, but I did not wish to trouble you; you were away at Pemberley most mornings, helping Grandfather with the business of the estate and then, there were all Uncle Julian's problems, too; I did not feel it was right to burden you with something more."

Cassy heard her words and shook her head, disbelieving. She could not accept that Lizzie had decided her mother was too busy to be troubled with her problems.

"Besides," Lizzie went on, "my brother knew of it. Mr Carr had told him and, while we were away in London, they tried to find Mr Jones and warn him to stay away from me, but he had moved to Derby. So you see, there was no longer any need to worry you with it."

As their conversation continued, it became amply clear to her parents that Lizzie's feelings were too deeply engaged, her esteem for Carr too great, for her to be dissuaded by anything they might say, even if they had wished to do so. She was quite determined to marry the man of her choice. Dr Gardiner, having given her his blessing, said he would write to Mr Carr immediately and have the letter delivered to Rushmore Farm by hand, together with an invitation to dinner, which her mother was happy to endorse. At which she flung her arms around her father's neck and kissed him, before embracing her mother.

They were now both in tears and Cassy said, holding her close, "My darling Lizzie, you must promise me that if you ever have any anxiety or fears, you will come to me. It matters not how busy I have been or who else has burdened me with their worries, I must know yours. Will you promise?" she pleaded, and Lizzie gave her word, realising that her mother had been hurt at being excluded from her confidence. She was sorry now that she had not spoken earlier.

That evening, Mr Carr arrived, looking cheerful and happy.

He was invited into Dr Gardiner's study, after which, the family dined together. Edward and Darcy were both present to congratulate their young sister, and Laura Ann was allowed to wait up to help celebrate her sister's engagement.

"Will I be your bridesmaid, Lizzie?" she asked and had to be hushed, because no one was discussing wedding plans so soon after Josie's funeral. Indeed, Dr Gardiner, in his conversation with Mr Carr, had made it clear that he did not expect Lizzie to be married until after her next birthday; it was a condition Mr Carr had no trouble accepting.

As usual, after dinner the company gathered in the drawing room, and the sisters were persuaded to play and sing. When Mr Carr rose and went to the instrument to join them, the family had to acknowledge that they made a very handsome couple indeed. When he asked her if she would sing "Les Petites Oiseaux," she smiled and said, "Yes, of course, Mr Carr," and it seemed his cup of joy was full.

Afterwards, the now-acknowledged lovers were left in peace to tell each other how very fortunate they were and all those other seemingly meaningless things that people say in such situations, while the rest of the family turned their attention to more mundane matters.

᠂ᢦᢆᢦ᠂

With Spring in the air, Darcy was soon wanting to return to London.

Hopes were high that, in the New Year, with Lord Russell leading the Whigs, the promised Parliamentary reforms would soon follow. Darcy's hero, Mr Gladstone, was going to play a prominent role in the new Parliament; Darcy was sure of it and wanted to be there, he said.

"I have had a letter from Colin Elliott. He says the Reformists are meeting before the new session of Parliament to plan tactics and he expects a most interesting period ahead. I cannot wait to hear the speeches."

Edward was rather more circumspect.

"I am not entirely sure that either Russell or Gladstone will get a Reform Bill through the Parliament; there are too may forces against it—some on their own side," he warned, but his brother's enthusiasm was not to be denied. While Edward was preparing for his marriage to Miss Angela Anderson, politics was still Darcy's chief preoccupation. He was leaving for London soon and would keep them informed of progress, he promised.

᠂ᢦᢆᢦ᠂

Later that night, when Lizzie had gone to bed, her mother came to her room. Cassy could not have failed to see the happiness that seemed to illuminate her daughter's face. Having but recently seen so much misery etched upon the faces of her brother and Josie, as well as the enormous burden of sorrow it had cast upon her parents, it was with genuine pleasure that she had watched Lizzie and Mr Carr together, hoping, indeed praying, that their joy would last, as her own had done.

Earlier in the evening Mr Carr, having received Richard's blessing, had thanked them both for their acceptance of him, promising he would do everything in his power to make their daughter happy. Still, there was a nagging feeling in Cassy's heart; she wanted to discover why her daughter had not spoken of her feelings, at all. Surely, she thought, it could not have been through lack of trust?

When Lizzie saw her mother enter her room, she sat up, pulling her bedclothes around her. Cassy sat on the bed beside her.

"No, don't you get up, my dear. I wanted only to say how pleased I am. I know you love your Mr Carr dearly, and it is quite plain that he loves you very much."

"And you are not displeased, Mama, that I did not ask your permission first?" she asked, almost pleading with her mother to understand. "You were always busy and my little problems seemed so trivial…I did not wish to bother you."

"Bother me? Why Lizzie, my darling, I am your mother and I want you to bother me with your problems, however small. Indeed, if I *was* a little concerned, it was because I felt you did not trust me."

Lizzie sat up and put her arms around her mother. "Not trust you? Mama, how could you ever think such a thing? Did you not know how much it meant to me, to have your blessing and Papa's?"

"And what would you have done if Papa and I said no?" Cassy asked, unfairly perhaps, forcing Lizzie to face the prospect squarely.

She did and, after a few moment's thought replied, but in the softest voice, "I still think I would have married him, Mama. I do love him very much, but it would have broken my heart to have displeased you."

With this frank admission, Lizzie's tears spilled out, and mother and daughter embraced, each more eager than the other to declare how well they loved one another and how very fortunate they both were. There would never be any question of lack of trust between them, they vowed, and Cassandra tucked her daughter in and made to leave the room.

Before she reached the door, however, Lizzie, now nestling comfortably under her quilt, asked in a deliberately casual voice, "Mama, if your Papa had said 'No, Cassy, you cannot have my permission to marry Richard Gardiner,' what would you have done?"

Cassy was almost at the door; she turned and smiled, knowing she had been neatly ambushed, and replied with characteristic candour. "Oh, you wicked little thing, to ask me such a question, when you well know the answer. I would have married him anyway."

Seeing her daughter smile, she continued, "You see, Lizzie, I knew that whatever happened, I would not lose my parents, we love each other too dearly; but if I had lost Richard, there would never have been such a man in my life again. I could not have been as happy with anyone else."

Lizzie smiled and said, softly, "Thank you, Mama, I knew you would understand exactly how I feel."

～✦～

As the early Spring sunshine poured in through the window and spilled over the table at which Cassandra Gardiner sat, writing her letters, her young nephew was in the garden with his cousins Lizzie and Laura, for whom the little boy was developing a deep affection.

He was already fond of Lizzie, since she had spent a good deal of time with him at their home in Cambridge and later, after Josie had gone to Mr Barrett. Cassy could not think of that dreadful time without a shudder, yet it was good to see that Laura Ann was taking an interest in the boy, too, for in a few months Lizzie would be too busy to spend her days playing with Anthony. The new governess, Miss Longhurst, would certainly help, Cassy thought; she came highly recommended by Caroline Fitzwilliam and seemed to have fitted in well.

Cassandra watched them, as they walked across the lawn and down towards the terraced garden, filled now with Spring blooms, her heart warmed towards all of them, yet she could not deny feeling some degree of trepidation at the task she had undertaken. When they moved out of sight, Cassy returned to her correspondence.

She had already attended to most of the formal letters of condolence and the many notes from friends, but a letter from her cousin Emma Wilson remained to be answered.

Emma had written after hearing from her brother Jonathan of Julian's decision to renounce his inheritance in favour of his son and leave the boy to the guardianship of his aunt.

Cassy had always enjoyed a special friendship with her cousin Emma and, when she had discovered what impossible anguish Emma had suffered during ten years of a harrowing marriage while she, Cassy, had enjoyed only the sweetest contentment in hers, the two young women had drawn even closer together. And now, Emma, widowed and happily married again, was someone to whom Cassy turned with confidence.

She read again her cousin's letter:

My dear, dear Cassy, she wrote,

> *With what a heavy heart must your poor brother have taken such a step?*
>
> *He must have known how deeply he would disappoint your parents and, as for yourself and Richard, the added responsibility for young Anthony must weigh upon your mind.*
>
> *James and I wish you to know, dear Cassy, that we will support you in any way possible and let me please ask you to call on us, if ever you need us, without hesitation. I gather from Jonathan's letter that there will be no problem with money, since the child will be well provided for from the estate, but it is surely in the expense of time, energy, and feelings, that such a responsibility is measured.*
>
> *Dear Cassy, if you should wish at any time for us to take Anthony and his nurse for a while, so you may be free to pursue your own life, we would be happy to have them, or should you and Richard wish to take a holiday in Kent, you must know, you will always be welcome at Standish Park.*
>
> *Remember, if there is anything at all we can do, you need only ask.*

The rest of Emma's letter was filled with news of her two boys, Charles and Colin, who were their mother's greatest joy, and her daughter Stephanie's forthcoming visit to Europe. Her husband James was busy with the new Parliament and she was well, and they both looked forward to a visit from Richard and Cassy.

Cassy, replying, thanked her cousin for the kindness and generosity for which Emma and James Wilson were renowned. It would be very pleasant, she thought, to spend some time in the haven of peace and tranquility that was

Standish Park. However, it was about another, more serious matter that Cassy was anxious to consult her cousin. After telling her the good news of Lizzie's engagement to Mr Carr, she came to the point of her letter:

Dearest Emma,

It is not easy for me to write this, but I have need of some counsel and I cannot think of any other person I would trust to keep this confidence. Ever since Julian left, my dear Mama has been living as if in a state of shock. I do not wish you to misunderstand me, it is not that she is at all ill or suffers overtly from depression, indeed, she seems to go about her normal life without any obvious hindrance, but there is no mistaking the intense sadness in her eyes.

Papa has suffered similarly, but with that heroic stoicism that is bred into men, he soldiers on. I know, from his remarks to me and to Richard, that he is bitterly disappointed in my brother, but he is better able to cope than poor Mama, to whom the loss of Julian to Pemberley is no less a blow than the death of William all those years ago.

She must wonder why it is that she, among all the women in our family, has been twice stricken in this way.

I wonder, dear cousin, if it would be too much to ask that you and James invite my parents to spend some weeks of the Summer with you at Standish Park?

I am aware that they plan to travel to the farm in Sussex in May; if it were possible for you to have them to stay later in the month, I feel sure both of them will benefit immensely from the change, as well as being with you and James.

I hope I do not presume too much upon your kindness, by asking this favour…

…and having concluded her letter, Cassy was about to ring for a servant to take it to the post, when she saw one of the smaller carriages from Pemberley, arriving at the entrance to the house. Going out into the hall, she was astonished to find her father standing there, alone.

"Papa! Why, it is so good to see you," she said as she embraced him and, holding onto his arm, steered him towards the morning room, where a good fire had been burning since breakfast, keeping the room comfortably warm. "I have just now finished a letter to Emma Wilson. She is keen to have us all at Standish Park this summer. But what brings you out, Papa?" she asked. His answer was not exactly specific to her question.

"Oh, it seemed such a pleasant Spring morning and, with your Mama busy introducing your cousin Jessica to the new Rector and his wife, I thought it would be a good time to call on you."

Cassy smiled as though she did not quite believe this tale, but said, "Well I am very glad you did. It is some time since you have been here."

Having seated him down, she wanted to ring for tea, or perhaps he would prefer some sherry, but her father would take neither. It was soon clear to her that he had something on his mind, which he wished to speak of and, to enable him to do so, Cassy closed the door and sat down beside him.

"What is it, Papa? While I am delighted to see you, I know there is more to this visit than a pleasant Spring morning, so why do you not tell me? Is there some problem? Is it Mama?" she asked, hoping by her directness to induce him to be frank, too.

Mr Darcy shook his head. "No, my dear Cassy, your Mama is not the problem; she never has been, not in all the years we have been married. Though, if I am to be honest with you, I must confess I have rarely seen her so deeply disappointed, so grievously hurt, as she has been by the actions of your brother and his late wife."

Cassy, took her father's hand; despite the warmth of the room, it was cold and she rubbed it between hers, as he used to do to her little hands when she was a child and they used to ride out together all over the Pemberley Estate. He smiled, remembering, too.

"Does Mama find it hard to forgive Josie?" Cassy asked quietly. "Does it rankle still that she left Julian for such a trifling reason and caused so much upheaval and sorrow?"

Mr Darcy sighed. "Cassy, my dear, I do not know that your Mama has ever forgiven Julian for not being more like William, for marrying Josie instead of Amy, and for preferring to be a scientist and live in Cambridge, rather than watching over Pemberley with me."

Cassy drew in her breath sharply, shocked by his words, as he went on. "And as for Josie, well, she made the mistake, in your Mama's eyes, of marrying Julian in the first place, when she had no real interest in Pemberley at all. Your Mama had set her heart upon Julian marrying Amy Fitzwilliam, you see. I told her the boy did not seem interested, but she kept hoping it would work out. She thinks that Amy would have helped keep Julian at Pemberley. Besides, in the future, she would have made an exemplary mistress of the estate, would she not? Like her mother, Caroline, she has all the talents and skills, as well as the resilience required for the role.

"As for Josie, poor child, she was a shock to your Mama. Restless, ambitious, impatient to go to London and be a writer, Elizabeth could not see her ever becoming the perfect Mistress of Pemberley.

"Josie was bored with country life; she loved meeting new people and writing about them. She wrote well, a good deal better than her mother, yet no one would publish her work. I did try to argue that it was possible she would come to see the place differently, as she grew older, but in the end, I suppose, the way things turned out, your Mama feels she was right all along." There was a deep sadness in his voice and Cassy bit her lip to hold back the tears that had filled her eyes as she listened.

It was not difficult to understand her mother's disillusionment and yet sympathise with the predicament of her father, who loved her dearly, yet appeared in this instance, unable to assuage his wife's sorrow.

"Do you wish me to speak with her again, Papa? I have before, but I can do so again, if it will help," she asked and his hand tightened around hers.

"If you would, my dear, I think it *will* help her to speak of it again; she fears her words will upset me. I have sometimes spoken up on Julian's behalf, trying to see his point of view, but I cannot seem to convince her."

Not wishing to appear critical of his wife, he explained, "Cassy, my dear, your Mama feels bitter at times and she does not wish me to see her so and will not say anything to me. It may do her some good if you could see her and let her speak her mind. Will you? I know it may be painful for you but…"

Cassy spoke up at once. "Of course, Papa, I shall go over tomorrow and stay to lunch and then perhaps afterwards, Mama and I could talk again…"

Then turning to him, she said, "Now will you take some refreshment? It is quite a long drive back to Pemberley."

And once again, he surprised her. "No, my dear, I am not returning to Pemberley just yet, I have an appointment with Sir Thomas Camden at Camden Park. Indeed, I do believe we are to lunch together, so I shall be all right."

Cassy was interested. Sir Thomas and her father were good friends as well as neighbours. Their properties adjoined one another and their families had been intimate for many years.

"Is this a special occasion?" she asked, half expecting a negative reply. The two men often met to discuss matters pertaining to local politics and their mutual interest. Both had an abiding interest in the prosperity of the area and the welfare of the people on their estates.

"Indeed it is," said her father, "a very special occasion. Sir Thomas has decided to sell Camden Park. This is not generally known and you must not speak of it to anyone for the moment, except Richard, of course; and here, I am letting you into a secret, Cassy, I am considering bidding for the property."

Cassy was astonished. Such a possibility had never entered her mind.

First the thought of Camden Park, where several generations of the Camden family had lived, being sold and then her father wanting to bid for the estate!

"Sir Thomas is selling Camden Park? But why?" she cried.

Her father replied that the departure of Will Camden's family to New South Wales and the death of his wife had left Sir Thomas very lonely.

"He has another, smaller property, in the South, one that used to belong to Lady Camden, near Mayfield, much closer to London and his daughter, who lives in Tunbridge Wells. I understand he intends to settle there. Which means Camden Park, which though it is only half the size of Pemberley is a jewel of a property, is available, and Camden has promised me the first option on it."

"Papa! Do you really think..." she had meant to ask if he really wanted to take on a new property at this time, but they heard the children returning and Mr Darcy put a finger to his lips to remind her of the need for discretion in the matter. Then as he rose and went out, he was surrounded by his grandchildren, with whom he was universally popular.

The boys insisted upon riding with him in his carriage to the top of the drive, where he would drop them off, and the indefatigable Miss Longhurst went with them, preparing to walk all the way back with her charges.

Lizzie and Laura, meanwhile, had a million things to do, they claimed, and rushed upstairs. There was certainly no more talk of Camden Park.

When her husband returned home, however, it was quite another matter. Cassandra could hardly wait until he was in their room to break the news of her father's visit and his intention to bid for Camden Park.

She was disconcerted to find that Richard did not appear as surprised as she had expected him to be, when she told him the news.

"Your father is very keen, no doubt, to prevent such a fine estate, one adjoining his own property, from falling into the hands of developers from London or Birmingham, who would probably subdivide it or enclose the commons or some such dreadful scheme, which would destroy the entire character of the district." he said. "Many of the landowners in the county have similar concerns."

These were the exact reasons her father would have given, had she had time to ask. Cassy was curious as to how her husband had them down pat.

"Have you known anything of this, Richard?" she asked, to which he replied truthfully and a little sheepishly that his father-in-law had discussed the matter with him on their last visit to Pemberley.

"Did he tell you then of his intention to bid for it?" she asked.

"Yes he did, but he also insisted I was not to speak of it to anyone. I was as surprised as you are today; I could not understand his desire to purchase a property like Camden Park, though it cannot be denied, Cassy, it is an excellent estate with the added attraction of Camden House, which is a most elegant residence indeed. Not as grand as Pemberley, but a very beautiful place, nevertheless."

Cassy laughed. "Oh indeed it is; who would wish to deny it? But what would my father do with it?" she asked. "Would he lease it perhaps? How else would he manage it, especially now with Julian gone? If he did so, what good would it do him? I cannot explain it. It is most strange."

Only then did Richard reveal what more he knew of her father's plans for Camden Park. Speaking as casually as he could, while concentrating on what appeared to be a torn fingernail, which he trimmed meticulously as he spoke, he said, "Cassy, my love, I believe your father hopes that sometime in the future, we will move to Camden Park and live at Camden House. He wishes to purchase it for us, as a future family home."

Cassandra was aghast. "Richard! Have you agreed to this scheme?" she demanded to know.

"No, not at all, there was no question of my agreement. He did not ask for it," he replied. "I am merely recounting your father's wishes. He knows we have taken on the responsibility of raising Anthony and you, my dear, are doing much more for Pemberley now than Julian has ever done. Your father values your work, indeed he has said so on many occasions, and I believe he wishes to do this for us, especially for you, Cassy. You must agree it is a most loving and generous gesture," he said, hoping she would understand her father's motives.

He was completely surprised by her response.

"Generous it may be, but I do not want it. I have no wish to move. I love my house and will not leave it for Camden House, however elegant it may be. Richard, we have built things together here, our children were born and grew up here, how could you consider leaving?" She was adamant.

Her husband, understanding her feelings, was conciliatory.

"Cassy dearest, no one is going to force us to leave this place; I love it, too, but you will admit, will you not, that we have outgrown it? Why, we have only one spare bedroom left; if both our sons are at home and we have more than one visitor to stay, we have not enough space to lodge them comfortably. Am I not right?"

When she said not a word, he went on, "And consider this, with Anthony staying permanently and a room needed for his nurse, we may have to put the two boys in together. While it may be fun when they are little, it may well lead to friction as they grow older and James may begin to resent his cousin's presence. Now Mr Darcy believes we need a bigger place in the future, and on that score, I agree with him. He wishes to purchase Camden Park for us," he explained.

"And do you agree with this plan of my father's? Do you not mind giving up what we have here, where we have been so happy? Would it not make you sad?" she demanded to know, the vexation reflected in her voice and eyes as she struggled to control her tears.

Richard knew he had to answer with great care.

"Indeed, my darling, I *would* be sad, of course I would miss this happy home of ours, but I think it would do no harm at all to look at Camden Park, that is, if your father's bid succeeds. We do not have to be rid of this place; Edward or Darcy could use it or even Laura Ann, when she is a grown-up young lady…"

But his wife was not to be diverted by such lighthearted arguments.

She was grieved that her father and Richard, the two men she loved most in her life, appeared to have conspired together against her in this venture. Doubtless, they could see advantages in the scheme, but Cassy was unconvinced that there was any benefit at all in it for her and her family.

~❧~

Meanwhile, Mr Carr and Lizzie Gardiner were busy making their own plans. There were a great many things to be done at Rushmore Farm, for which he sought her advice, and they were often driving up there to instruct workmen, and select colours and fabrics for the drapes and furniture for the rooms upstairs.

Mr Carr confessed that he liked simple, serviceable things, but urged Lizzie to use her excellent taste and artistic judgment to choose whatever she wished. Money, it seemed, was no object. He knew she, like the rest of her family, was neither extravagant nor ostentatious in her tastes and was, therefore, perfectly content to indulge her wishes.

As for Lizzie, it seemed she had never been happier. The prospect of her approaching marriage, to a man she loved and trusted, together with the excitement of setting up her own home, provided plenty of scope for delightful contemplation, as well as useful activity. Encouraged by her mother, she spent the times when she was alone making lists of all the things they needed to get done, which, when Mr Carr arrived, seemed to be quite forgotten, for he, it appeared, had thought of them already.

That, however, did not prevent them from setting out to discover what else may be required to complete the refurbishment of their future home. Mr Carr was determined that nothing should be wanting. Frequently, they were accompanied on these expeditions by Laura Ann, since Cassy was often busy at Pemberley or making her own preparations for the wedding, which was planned for the Autumn. Young Laura Ann loved the horses at the farm and a visit was always a treat, since it afforded her an opportunity to get another glimpse of the foals, who were growing up fast.

It was on one of these days, when they were driving home in Mr Carr's carriage, that Laura Ann saw Margaret Baines, who was obviously on her way home after work, and called out to her, "Margaret! Margaret!" leaning about as far out of the window as it was safe to be. Her loud calling not only attracted

Margaret's attention, causing her to look round at the carriage as it passed her, but it also startled a young man who was with her, because he appeared to dive off the road into the ferns and bracken beside it and disappeared from sight.

Undeterred, Laura called out again and waved vigorously; this time, Margaret waved back, belatedly but cheerfully. Laura kept her in view and waved again, just as they took the bend in the road, which hid her from their sight. Of the young man, however, there was no sign at all.

Neither Lizzie nor Laura gave the incident much thought. Lizzie's mind was so full of her wedding plans and how each day she spent with Mr Carr, she discovered even more reasons to love him, that she gave no thought at all to Margaret Baines. Laura Ann did mention seeing Margaret, when they were at tea, but her mother, still distracted by the business about Camden Park, paid little attention to it. No one said anything about the disappearing young man.

❧

Over the following weeks and months, several things changed that for many years had been taken for granted, affecting the lives of the Pemberley families, as well as those of all the people of England.

Since the death of Lord Palmerston, in October of the previous year, not three months after he had won an election, the Parliament had changed.

The Whigs and their allies the Liberals were now much more confident, with their new leaders Lord Russell and Mr Gladstone both committed to Parliamentary Reform. The Reformists had high hopes of finally achieving their goal, one which Palmerston had continually obstructed.

In the New Year, the recently elected Parliament was called together and those who gathered at Westminster to observe them were likewise excited by the prospect of change, long overdue. Others were less enthusiastic. As many columns were written and speeches made urging the retention of the status quo, as were devoted to the promotion of Reform. Britain's powerful elite were far from unanimous in their support of the democratic ideal of giving all men an equal vote.

Indeed, despite Lord Russell's efforts to bring in a moderate Reform Bill giving more, but certainly not all, men the vote, die-hard Conservatives allied with a clique of disgruntled Liberals (those whom Bright bitterly called "the denizens of the cave of Adullam") to frustrate Russell and the Reformists. Their action, seen as a ploy to exclude working-class men from any part in the election of their representatives, led to widespread dissatisfaction and the ultimate resignation of Lord Russell.

Darcy Gardiner wrote from London to his sister, expressing his frustration:

...everyone is outraged...there are political demonstrations everywhere, not just in London, but we hear also in Birmingham and many other parts of the country. The mood of the people is very sour and nasty indeed.

It is being said that the Queen herself urged Lord Russell not to resign, but he and Mr Gladstone are determined that they will not accept a further limitation of the franchise to working men and they have told the Queen so...

Lizzie read it out at breakfast and Laura innocently asked if their brother was intending to go into Parliament and was practising for it.

"I hope not," said Cassy, "for I cannot believe he will get much satisfaction from it, unless his hero Mr Gladstone is Prime Minister."

Lizzie pointed out that Darcy was bound to be very discouraged by the resignation of Lord Russell, and her father agreed.

"Darcy had great hopes for this government; it does seem a shame they have fallen through so soon," he said, finishing his breakfast.

Lord Derby, having formed a minority government, staggered on for a while, beset with a diplomatic dilemma in Europe (where Bismarck was setting out to establish German dominance on the continent) and financial crises at home. There was already news of the failure of a famous London financial house and the collapse of share prices on the stock exchange followed, creating panic in some quarters. Greedy investors who had believed the hyperbole of their agents were being left bemused and bankrupted.

Darcy wrote again, this time with an element of wicked glee:

Prices on the stock exchange have fallen sharply and the government seems powerless to do anything at all. Though I have not witnessed any myself, there are fellows in the club and at Westminster who claim that stockholders have been committing suicide, leaping out of windows and shooting themselves. There are not too many offering their condolences either!

While their brother's colourful phrases may have appeared to exaggerate the situation, their Aunt Caroline Fitzwilliam confirmed it. Returning from London, where she had been on business, Caroline arrived with bad news of many businessmen being ruined and fears of widespread unemployment to follow.

"Thankfully, Papa's business was predominantly in trade with the Colonies, which is still strong," she explained, when she came to tea with the Gardiners.

Richard agreed, adding that Mr Darcy and Mr Bingley had both acknowledged to him the considerable debt they owed to his father.

"They are very aware that their current prosperity is due in no small measure to their investment in Father's business. Had they depended solely upon their estates to produce the same high incomes they had enjoyed throughout the middle years of this century, they would have suffered the same fate as have many indolent members of the gentry," he said with a wry smile.

Caroline laughed as she told of several young "toffs" who'd been heard to complain that, "Papa no longer sends me an adequate allowance to let me keep a valet and a butler," and certain fashionable ladies who were getting their sewing women in to undo and make over last season's gowns! She certainly did not express much sympathy for either.

"I do believe Robert and Rose have escaped the worst of it by living in Paris for most of this year," she declared and Cassy, tactfully, did not ask her sister-in-law for more details.

Ever since their father's will had revealed his choice of Caroline to manage his business, relations with her brother Robert, and especially his wife Rose, had been rather cold.

In the midst of all this came extraordinary news from Westminster that Lord Derby and Mr Disraeli had decided that *they* were best placed to bring in a Reform Bill. Their ultimate betrayal of their own constituency, turning on its head decades of Conservative opposition to the cause of electoral reform, caused even more uproar, leaving the government of Lord Derby under attack from both sides of the house.

"Mayhem is guaranteed," wrote Darcy Gardiner, enjoying the discomfiture of his opponents.

There are Tories and their supporters who are talking of treason and calling for Mr Disraeli's head, while Gladstone and the Reformists are

wild, because the Tories are seeking to steal their bill and take the credit for
Reform. This is being seen as one of their schemes to seize the initiative.

My Uncle James Wilson is so incensed, he has returned to Kent in a
great rage, while Mr Elliott has sworn never to support any of Dizzy's
bills in future. Confusion is worse confounded.

❦

It was while all this was afoot that the families met at Netherfield Park to
celebrate the wedding of Jonathan Bingley's younger daughter Teresa to the
architect from London, Mr Frederick Fairfax. Despite the obvious happiness
of the young couple and their respective parents, the occasion was a sober one,
for no one could ignore the death of Josie, and the absence of Julian Darcy
served only to remind them of the tragedy the family had suffered only a few
months ago.

Following the wedding, Mr Darcy and Elizabeth, who had accepted an
invitation from James and Emma Wilson to spend a part of the Summer with
them, travelled on to Standish Park in Kent.

By the same happy set of arrangements, Mrs Gardiner, her daughter Emily
with her husband, James Courtney, and their youngest son, Jude, were afforded
the opportunity of spending the rest of Summer at Woodlands, Elizabeth's farm
in Sussex. A year after her husband's death, Mrs Gardiner remained in low
spirits, except when she had one or two of her grandchildren around her. The
precipitate departure of her youngest son Robert and his family for Paris had
taken away two of her grandchildren and she was grateful for the company of
Emily and her family.

Emily's husband, James Courtney, for many years now the Rector of the
parish of Kympton, was suffering from the effects of overwork, mostly the result
of an enthusiastic burst of evangelical activity with the poor Irish families in the
village. He had been ordered by his brother-in-law Dr Gardiner to rest. Which
was why Emily had welcomed her cousin Mrs Darcy's invitation to them, to
spend the last month of Summer at the farm.

Emily, who'd had her share of sorrow in life, was a great source of comfort
to her mother.

Her youngest daughter Jessica, who shared her mother's enthusiasm for
service to the community, had recently been appointed by Mr Darcy to take

over the running of the parish school at Pemberley. Well educated, a great reader, and a compassionate young woman, she had already moved to live at Pemberley like her mother before her.

Emily could not resist the comparison, yet she knew their circumstances were very different. Emily had been desolated by the death of her young husband at the time, whereas Jessica went to Pemberley untroubled by problems of that nature, her head and heart filled with plans and hopes for the future of her school. She was proud and happy to be entrusted with such a responsibility.

❧

Meanwhile, at Standish Park, Mr Darcy revealed to his hosts, who were not entirely ignorant of his plans, that he had successfully bid for the Camden Park Estate. Sir Thomas Camden had accepted his offer and he hoped the property would soon be his.

"I expect Sir Thomas will wish to have all the legal arrangements concluded before he moves to his property in Sussex," Mr Darcy said and, to his relief, unlike his own family, the Wilsons expressed no misgivings about the purchase, seeing it as a valuable addition to Mr Darcy's estate.

Even when he admitted that he had sold a couple of landholdings in Wales to finance the transaction, James Wilson appeared to applaud his decision as a sensible one. "The rapid expansion of the coal-mining industry is destroying the beauty of the area," he said, and Mr Darcy added, by way of explanation for his own actions, "Indeed, and any landholder who does not lease or sell is ultimately isolated, his land rapidly losing value, of no use for any other purpose. I thought it sensible to sell while prices were still favourable, especially to invest in such an excellent estate as Camden's. Our families go back several generations and he was happy to let us acquire the property. Besides, his price was a fair one."

Disclosing his plan to offer the place to Richard and Cassy, he said, "Their house is a pretty place, but it is far too small for them now; and Cassy ought be living within closer reach of Pemberley, since she carries out most of Julian's duties. She is also a great comfort to her mother and myself; we would enjoy having her close to us."

Neither James nor Emma appeared particularly surprised at his suggestion, although Emma knew, from a letter she had received from Cassy some weeks ago, that her cousin would not be easily persuaded to move from her present home, which held many happy memories for her and her family. However, she saw no reason to divulge this to the Darcys.

For the Darcys and the Wilsons, that Summer would pass easily. Both couples enjoyed good music, interesting conversation, and each other's company, a certain recipe for contentment. For James Wilson, Mr Darcy had great respect and it was clear the feeling was mutual, while Elizabeth loved her niece Emma no less than she loved her mother Jane, with whom she could not recall ever exchanging a hurtful word. Like many other visitors to the Wilsons' home, Elizabeth and Darcy enjoyed a remarkable feeling of well-being. The pleasing environment, together with Emma's serenity and warm, affectionate nature, had the effect of soothing her aunt's troubled feelings, and gradually, Elizabeth began to look and feel a good deal calmer, a fact not lost upon her husband.

Her improving humour and the return of her vivacious smile were welcome signs of her recovery from the slough of despond, into which she had slipped the previous Winter.

Back in Derbyshire, Lizzie and Mr Carr had been making a new acquaintance. In the village, they had met, quite by chance, a young man who had been buying fishing tackle and bait, in preparation, he told them, to spend the rest of Summer walking the dales, fishing the streams, and painting. He had with him a collection of what he modestly called "scribbles and daubs" and when Mr Carr and Lizzie, neither of whom could draw or paint with any degree of distinction, saw them, they were very impressed.

Mr Frank Wakeham, which is how he introduced himself, appeared to have a good eye and a genuine talent for capturing the unique quality and colours of the ancient landscape of peaks and dales. When Carr saw that Lizzie was taken with a particular watercolour rendering of the hills above Rushmore, he asked to purchase it and Wakeham was delighted. Taking out his artist's brush and palette, he signed it across the bottom right-hand corner and presented it to her, accepting a very modest sum in return. Mr Carr protested that the price was too low, surely, but the artist turned fisherman insisted it was all he wanted. Before they parted, Carr invited him to come up to the farm and paint the scenic views, if they should take his fancy. "We have the best view of the peaks for miles around," he said. "You are welcome to visit and paint it if you wish," for which generous invitation Wakeham thanked him, though he did not immediately accept the offer.

Mr Carr suggested that he should take the picture into Derby and have it framed. "It will give me an excuse to take you away to the farm, so you may decide exactly where you want it hung," he said and Lizzie blushed, but said with some firmness, "I shall have no difficulty with that; I know exactly where I want it."

They decided to keep their purchase of the painting a secret and reveal it to the family only after it was framed and hung in its appointed place, which was why Cassy and Richard heard nothing of the artist Mr Wakeham and his work.

Thereafter, both Lizzie and Mr Carr saw the young man from time to time.

Occasionally, they met him on the street in the village or saw him having a meal at the inn; but mostly, he was at a distance, working industriously in the valleys, sitting on a fallen tree trunk or on rocks by running water and, quite often, at the old quarry, which they passed on the road to Matlock, sketching some of the strangely shaped rock formations jutting out of the ground. On very few occasions, did they see him fishing, casting a line, or just waiting patiently for a bite. They knew no more of him but that he was an itinerant painter, with an interest in fishing. Certainly no one complained about him; it appeared he kept to himself and paid his bills.

Returning from the wedding of Teresa and Frederick Fairfax, where Mr Carr had been introduced to the rest of the family and Lizzie had received congratulations from her cousins and aunts on her engagement, the Gardiners had returned to the routines of their daily lives.

Except for some medical emergencies, like the birth of twins to two women in the village on successive afternoons, or an accident on the farm, life proceeded a while without incident or drama.

For Cassandra, however, in between making preparations for Lizzie's forthcoming wedding, there was the ever-present knowledge that her father, having successfully negotiated the purchase of Camden Park, would, on his return from Kent, invite her and her family to live there.

Loving him as she did, Cassy did not know how she would refuse him.

The problem consumed much of her time and, while she did not discuss it at all with her children, the news had got around and they all knew how she felt. While her parents remained in Kent with the Wilsons, she felt safe enough, but they would soon be returning home.

Richard knew also and was disturbed that she would not speak of it with him, mulling over it when she was alone and changing the subject when he mentioned it. It was as though, for the first time in their marriage, there was a problem they could not share and resolve together.

There was one other irritant disrupting her otherwise peaceful existence. Her father, aware of the innumerable tasks she was handling for him in the management of Pemberley, had suggested that they appoint a reliable and efficient assistant, who could handle the routine work on the estate.

Cassy had thought this was an excellent idea and Richard had agreed. However, more recently, a problem had emerged, of which Cassy had no warning at all. Having made some discreet enquiries, the manager, Mr Grantham, had discovered that the son of one of the Pemberley tenants intended to offer himself for the position. The same man had applied on a previous occasion for the position of steward at the Rushmore stud and had been turned down by Mr Carr on the advice of his manager.

John Archer was an assertive young man, well dressed and well spoken, but with a tendency to self-importance and very little familiarity with the people of the village. Recently returned from London, where he had worked for the younger son of a well-known, titled family for many years, he was back in Derbyshire. His master had left for Australia, where Archer had not wished to follow him, and he was looking for employment.

Unhappily, while his parents were respected and liked, John Archer knew few people and evoked their suspicions rather than their sympathy.

"My advice, ma'am, would be to appoint another man before John Archer can approach you. He is not the sort of man who would be able to handle our people with discretion and tact," Mr Grantham had advised, leaving Cassy in a quandary.

Her first instinct was to consult her father, who she knew would be returning to Pemberley at the end of Summer. In his absence, she sought out Mr Carr and discovered that Archer had been around to the farm as well, but had not been offered a position there either.

"I know very little of him, Mrs Gardiner, except he is not well liked in these parts," Mr Carr had said. "I was guided by the advice of Mr Grantham and my steward."

With no one to consult, Cassy decided she would not appoint anyone at all, until her father returned. It would mean that she would be kept very busy, but it was far better, she thought, that she should carry on alone, rather than appoint someone who might cause ill feelings among the staff and tenants.

The decision did put a considerable strain upon her. Twice in a single week, she had been called out to hear disputes that would normally have been settled by Mr Grantham alone. The first concerned the poaching of game on the estate, which she treated very leniently, and the other, a more serious matter of a squabble between two tenants over a piece of arable land. Neither were insoluble problems, but in both cases Mr Grantham had failed to conciliate between the parties, and they had demanded that the master or his daughter intervene.

"I am very sorry, ma'am, I did try my best; I did what the master usually does, I asked them to speak out openly, without fear of recriminations, but it seems they have no interest in speaking further to me. It is you they want, ma'am," said Grantham, apologising for his lack of success.

Cassy smiled, "Do you suppose, Mr Grantham, that they regard me as a naïve woman and think they can pull the wool over my eyes?" she asked and he was quick to deny this. "Indeed no, ma'am, most assuredly not. They are convinced that you, like the master, will be fair to them and hear their grievances."

"And you will not?" she was incredulous, "After all these years?"

"They know you have Mr Darcy's authority, ma'am. Besides, they hold you in high esteem and will accept, without quibbling, a determination from you."

Cassy wanted to believe him, in spite of herself. She was tired, it had been a long day, but she forced herself to go with him and meet the complaining tenants and the accused poacher. Cassy did as she was sure her father would have done. With the poacher, she discovered that the man had lost his job in Birmingham and returned home almost empty handed. His wife pleaded, "It was only to feed the children, ma'am, no more. He would not take game off the master's land to sell, I would never allow it. I'd sooner starve."

Her transparent honesty, no less than her desperate situation, affected Cassy deeply. "There's no need for that; you need not starve, when there is so much food to be had. But neither must your husband break the law," she said,

and promised the woman her husband would not be brought before the magistrate, on this occasion. "However, you must give me your word that, in the future, if you are in need of food and have none you can legally obtain, you will ask Mr Grantham here for permission to take some, or go up to the house and ask Mrs Grantham for help. You will never be turned away."

The woman was grateful and gave her word.

Turning to Mr Grantham, she said, "Mr Grantham, there is no need to report this matter; you may grant permission for them to take fish or game for food if they have none. My father would not want them to starve, but, neither must they steal or we shall have everyone doing it," she said, quite firmly, and seeing the tears in the woman's eyes, Cassy felt more shaken than she had expected to be.

She was glad she had acted as she had done. Her father would not have been pleased to see these poor people punished for what seemed such a trivial offence. There were too many harrowing tales of men out of work being transported for poaching to feed their families.

As for the warring tenants, the fact they had been settled in adjoining cottages and seemed to encroach upon each other's unfenced strips of land provided a clue to the problem. They were always in each other's way, their children and animals forever underfoot, a constant source of aggravation. The strip of land in contention was so small, it seemed hardly worth the trouble, but it was all they had and something had to be done to resolve the matter, or there would be no peace.

"Mr Grantham, is there no other piece of land upon which one of these men might work? I believe the solution is to keep them away from one another; if we could provide one with an allotment elsewhere, may it not help?" she asked.

When Grantham, having considered the matter, suggested a possible alternative strip of land nearby, Cassy decided she had the answer to their problem. To avoid setting one against the other, she visited both families and, having explained what was intended, said, "I think we have found a solution that will help you both. Mr Grantham will arrange to make it available to you, but I must have an end to this constant bickering; it is bad for your families and destroys the reputation of my father's estate. I want your word that it will stop." Both men, though not entirely satisfied, accepted her plan. It may not have provided a permanent resolution, but it would at least stop them quarrelling.

Thereafter Mr Grantham drove her home. He was very impressed with the manner in which she had handled the problems, which though slight, could have become an irritation for the master in the future. As they drove through the fading half-light of the evening, Cassy thought she saw a young woman, accompanied by a man, trudging along the path that wound down from the main road towards the woods.

She could not make out the man at all, but the girl was Margaret Baines.

Oh dear, she thought, that looks like Margaret Baines with some admirer from the village. I hope Grantham does not gossip about it, because if he does, everyone else will know and Margaret will be in trouble.

Wisely, she said nothing at all to Mr Grantham.

When she reached home, darkness had fallen and Dr Gardiner had already returned. Cassy, exhausted after her long day, was eager to bathe and change her clothes. Lizzie, meeting her on the stairs, stopped to tell her she looked very tired and Cassy remarked wearily that she probably smelled of the farmyard, too. It had been a long, hard day.

When she came downstairs later, to find that Mr Carr was not dining with them that night, Cassy decided that it was a good opportunity to relax and forget the day's labours. Sufficient unto the day…she thought as she lay on the chaise lounge with her feet up and urged her daughter to "play something tranquil and soft" before dinner was served.

Lizzie obliged and was astonished to see her mother doze off in the middle of it. It had never happened before.

When her husband came downstairs, he could see she was exceedingly tired and determined that he would speak with her about it. It was clear to him that Cassy was exhausting herself. She needed to take a rest from these daily chores. It seemed that, in Mr Darcy's absence, Cassy was shouldering all of the responsibility for running Pemberley.

What had happened, he wondered, to the scheme that his father-in-law had proposed? Where was the efficient new assistant? It was a matter about which he intended to speak quite firmly with his wife.

There was yet another matter, too, one that would interest Cassy and all the family, but Richard decided, probably wisely, that it could wait for another occasion.

When they went upstairs after dinner, he waited for his wife to come to bed. She had changed into her nightclothes and the fresh, scented linen was most welcoming.

As she got into bed beside him, he said, "Cassy, my dear, you really are over-working yourself; you are so tired, almost exhausted every evening. I think it is time you took a rest from some of these duties. While I know your Papa will be very grateful for all the work you have done, he will not be pleased, should it make you ill. Do you not agree, my love? Why, I don't believe I have ever…" he stopped short, realising when he had no response from her at all, that his well-intentioned lecture was falling on deaf ears.

His wife had snuggled down beside him and fallen fast asleep.

There was a hint of Autumn in the air when Cassy awoke and found her husband looking at her with great concern. She had overslept, but she was surprised that he had not ridden out as he did every morning.

"It cannot be the slight chill in the air, could it?" she teased, and he returned to sit beside her on the bed.

His expression was solemn. "No, it is something far more worrying; Cassy, I am concerned that you are doing far too much, you are thinner than I have seen you in years and last night, you fell asleep, even before your head touched the pillow. Dearest, this must stop; I cannot let you make yourself ill with overwork."

Cassy was genuinely surprised at his concern. She *had* been working long hours; going back and forth to Pemberley and coping with the preparations for Lizzie's wedding, which was but a few months away, had all taken their toll. But, she considered herself strong and resilient and tried to allay his fears.

"My dear husband, it is very kind and sweet of you to be concerned, but I assure you, I am not unwell and unlikely to be. I admit things have been hectic in this last week or two, but that is not usual. Once we move into Autumn and harvest time…"

He interrupted her. "Things will become even busier, will they not? Forgive me, my dear. I am not a farmer, but I do know that harvest time is one of the busiest times in the country. Where is this new man we were to employ, who would do all the routine tasks for you? Why is he not here?"

It was then she realised how little she had shared with him over the last few weeks. Richard, to whom she had always taken her problems, confident that his wisdom and common sense would help her resolve them, had not heard a word of the dilemma she faced with John Archer and her decision to delay the appointment of an assistant until her father returned. When the maid brought in her tea, she sat up and, as she drank it, slowly savouring the pleasure of the hot, sweet drink and the comfort of her warm bed, she told him everything.

It was not easy at first; Cassy had made decisions, which she had to explain, and there had been reasons for those decisions, of which Richard knew nothing. His logical mind probed, asking questions, to which sometimes she had no answer, except that she had relied upon her instincts. She felt exposed and uneasy, like a child who had been always praised for doing things well and had suddenly found she had, inexplicably, done something wrong.

Yet, Richard was the kindest, most reasonable of men. Sensitive to her feelings, aware of her unease, he took away her empty cup and, sitting close beside her, took her hands in his.

"And why have you not told me of these troublesome matters, Cassy? Did you not think I could help?" he asked, and she was quick to deny it.

"Oh no, that wasn't the reason; dear Richard, you have always helped me when I needed it, but I do know how hard you work at the hospital, how often you are called out to suffering people, who are in pain or dying.

"I had no wish to trouble you with trivial matters, tenants' problems, and men like John Archer…you ought not be bothered with them," she said trying to explain.

He responded with his usual concern for her. "Perhaps not with them, my dearest, but I do wish to know when something or someone vexatious provokes you. It matters not how trivial it may be; if it impinges upon your peace of mind and is likely to cause you aggravation, I *must* know. Because that is what our marriage is about, is it not?

"Whether I can help solve the problem or not is not the question; my concern is to share your burden and, if I can help in any way, then so be it. If not, we will attempt to find a solution or consult someone who can help. But, because I love you, Cassy, I *must* be allowed to try. You have to trust me with your troubles.

"Do you not agree? Is that not what we said to our daughter only a few days ago? Is it not one reason we have been so very happy together all these years?" His voice was warm and kind and there was little need for her to answer.

His words, gentle and persuasive, brought all her affection for him to the surface with expressions of gratitude and tenderness. She felt great relief, as she revealed, not just how much the petty grievances and vexatious problems she'd had to deal with had taken out of her, but the deep loneliness she had felt, being away from him and her children. Never before had it been so, and she promised him, then, that it would never be allowed to happen again. For her husband, who had endured the painful isolation from her without complaint for several weeks, it was all he had hoped for. Nothing mattered as much to Richard as the love they shared.

It was quite some time later that they decided it was time to go downstairs. The mid-morning sun was streaming into the breakfast room and, outside, they could see Laura Ann, James, and Anthony, with Miss Longhurst, reading in the shade of the oak, whose leaves were just turning to gold.

Breakfast was leisurely, continuing their present mood of fondness. "Are you not expected at the hospital today, Richard?" Cassy asked, as they took tea.

He shook his head and smiled. "No, not today, Henry Forrester is seeing my patients this morning. I had a presentiment that I may be needed at home."

Cassy laughed and poured out more tea. "To attend upon your recalcitrant wife?" she asked, her eyes sparkling.

"Indeed, and a more pleasant reason I cannot imagine, especially since she is recalcitrant no longer!" he replied, kissing her gently as he rose to go to the sideboard.

Returning to the table, he looked casually out of the window and saw Lizzie running towards the house. She looked dishevelled and very upset.

"Good God, what on earth can have happened? Lizzie looks very distressed," he said and, as they both went to the window, they saw Mr Grantham and Mr Carr striding up the drive behind her.

Cassy rushed out into the hall, just as Lizzie ran up the steps and almost collided with her mother. "Lizzie, darling, what is it? What has happened?" she asked, but Lizzie was cold and trembling. She could hardly speak, except to make dreadful sounds like someone who had seen a ghost. "Lizzie, speak to me please," begged her mother, but by that time Richard had gone out to meet Mr Carr and Grantham, who stood together at the bottom of the steps.

"He's dead, Mama; he's dead and it's horrible. Oh Mama!..." Lizzie found her voice and sobbed, hiding her face against her mother.

Cassy went rigid with terror.

"Who is dead, Lizzie? Tell me, child, who is it?" Her thoughts flew to all those of her family who were out of her sight or away from home: her father,

her two sons, Colonel Fitzwilliam, her brother…it was a moment of absolute paralysis, as she stood, holding her daughter, unable to discover who it was had died and caused Lizzie such distress.

Then Richard came in with the others. He saw and understood the unasked question in his wife's eyes and, wanting to reassure her, said quickly, "A body has been found on the floor of the quarry. A man…Mr Carr thinks it may be someone who has recently been in these parts, a certain Mr Jones…"

"Mr Jones? Not Andrew Jones the man who…?" before she could finish asking the question, her husband answered, "Yes, but a formal identification has still to be made. Mr Grantham has informed the police and I am afraid, my dear, I shall have to attend and provide a report."

The relief Cassy felt was so great, tears poured down her cheeks, as she held on to Lizzie and nodded when he asked if she could cope. Her maid Lucy appeared and they took Lizzie upstairs and settled her down in her room, before Richard embraced them both, assured them he would be back as soon as possible, and left with Mr Grantham.

Mr Carr, who had arrived to see Lizzie, had met Grantham at the entrance to the drive, where he had learned the grim news. It had been impossible to keep the story from Lizzie when she joined them.

Now, having been assured that Lizzie would soon be well, he decided to go into town himself and make some enquiries about Jones. What, he wondered, was Jones, if that was who it was and it seemed very likely from Grantham's description that indeed it was Jones, doing back in the village? All the information he had obtained had led him to believe that Andrew Jones had moved to Derby.

Lizzie, who was persuaded to rest in bed and tell her mother what she had heard, was at a loss to explain who had found the body and by what means Grantham had discovered that it was Jones. All she knew was what she had heard from Mr Grantham and Mr Carr, who had been discussing the terrible news as she went to join them at the entrance.

"I had no notion anything was wrong; I assumed Mr Grantham had come for you, Mama. I thought you were going with him to attend to matters at Pemberley. When I heard, I was so shocked, because we thought Mr Jones had moved to Derby," she explained. "Both Mr Carr and my brother Darcy said so, and yet it appears he was here all the time."

Cassy was baffled. "It is strange indeed that he should be here and why in that part of the country? No one, but people who have grown up in the farms and villages around Pemberley, would even know of the path that goes through the quarry. Some of the lads use it to save time coming across the Common, but how would Jones know of it? And, I wonder what brought him back?"

Cassy had only a vague recollection of Mr Jones, but Lizzie remembered him only too well. When her mother wondered aloud whether it could have been the same man she had seen walking with Margaret Baines, when returning last night from Pemberley, Lizzie sat up with a very startled expression, "Mama, did you say 'walking with Margaret Baines on the Matlock Road last night?'"

"Yes, I did. It was quite late last evening. Grantham was driving me home and we saw them, at least I am sure he saw them, too, but he said nothing. It was a young man; I could not see his face, of course, but I assumed he was young from his slim figure and the clothes he wore. They were very fashionable, good quality clothes. I assumed it was an admirer of Margaret's."

"His coat, Mama, was it long with a big collar, like so?" asked Lizzie demonstrating with her hands a wide collar of the type that some fashionable gentlemen in London favoured. Lizzie recalled that Jones had been wearing such a coat when he accosted her in the village.

Her mother replied, "I could not see how long it was, but yes, I did notice the big collar. Indeed, that struck me—I thought he looked something of a toff, and I wondered at Margaret keeping company with him. But I suppose I was just too tired to mention it last night."

Then Lizzie, recalling the evening when she and Laura had seen Margaret with a man, who had disappeared into the trees on their approach, uttered a cry and hid her face in her pillow. Her mother suddenly realised the import of her words and cried, "Oh my God, Lizzie, no, it cannot be. Margaret would not be so foolish, surely?"

There was not sufficient time to ponder the question, as a knock on the door heralded the appearance of Miss Longhurst, who brought the news that Margaret Baines had not arrived for work that morning.

"I am sorry, Mrs Gardiner, I had intended to draw your attention to it, but Dr Gardiner had told Lucy you were very tired and not to be disturbed, so I took the children out into the garden after breakfast and did not get another opportunity to tell you," she explained, then seeing Lizzie lying with her face hidden in her pillow, asked, "Is Miss Lizzie unwell? Is there anything I can do to help?" and Cassy said at once, "Indeed yes, Miss Longhurst, there is. Could you please ask Lucy to bring us up a pot of tea? Lizzie has been upset by some bad news; there's been a death in the village."

"A death! Oh dear," said Miss Longhurst. "Oh, dear me, that must be dreadful. Was it someone known to Miss Lizzie? A friend?" She was immediately solicitous and very curious.

Cassy shook her head. "Not a friend, no. It is not yet certain, but it looks like it may be a gentleman Lizzie met last year, at my brother's house in Cambridge. Dr Gardiner is gone to the scene with the police; we shall probably know by afternoon. Now, I do think Lizzie could do with that cup of tea, please, Miss Longhurst," Cassy prompted, and she was away in a trice, still shaking her head at the strange news.

No doubt she would pick up more details from the servants, thought Cassy. On these matters, they always knew so much more.

She was right. By afternoon, the entire staff seemed to know. The dead man was a Mr Andrew Jones of London and more recently from Derby, where he had purported to run a print shop, but no one could find anyone who'd worked there. Recently, too, he had been visiting the village, apparently staying with friends in Cromford, but drinking and occasionally sleeping overnight at the inn.

There was news, too, that in the last two weeks he had been seen in the woods, walking with Margaret Baines! She had been seen by the butcher's boy, who had told the cook and the scullery maid. Indeed, she had even been teased about it in the kitchen.

Later that afternoon, the butcher's boy called and more dreadful details were revealed. Jones's body, with its skull smashed and back broken, had been found by a farmhand, taking the shortcut through the quarry, who had fled in terror to Mr Grantham's house and told his story. Grantham had called the police who had sent him to request Dr Gardiner's attendance at the scene. The maid, Lucy, had it all and retailed it to her mistress and Lizzie.

By the time Richard returned home that evening, having attended the scene where the body had been found, a new nightmare had begun.

Margaret Baines had not merely failed to show up at the house for work that morning, she had not reached home last night. Her mother had arrived around midday, in search of her daughter.

"When she did not return home last night, Mrs Baines had assumed that she had been delayed here and decided, wisely, to stay overnight," Cassy explained to her husband, "Oh that it were true! However, there was no message from her today, her mother became concerned. No one has seen Margaret since she left here around four o'clock last afternoon. No one but myself, that is, for I am now quite certain it was Margaret I saw, walking with this man, on the Matlock Road, much later in the evening, when I was returning from Pemberley."

"Could you recognise the man she was with?" Richard asked, intrigued.

Cassy was unsure. "No, I did not at the time; I could not see his face. But when Lizzie described the coat he was wearing, Grantham had said the dead man was wearing a fine wool coat with a broad collar, I remembered it was exactly like the coat as the man wore who was walking with Margaret."

Her husband shook his head, his grave face and furrowed brow indicating that he was very concerned indeed, but he said nothing.

After they went upstairs, he revealed to his wife that the body had been identified by the innkeeper as that of Andrew Jones.

"He had stayed occasionally at the inn and, if the landlord is to be believed, was seeing a young woman quite regularly," he said, and when Cassy gasped, he added, "It may not be as bad as you fear, Cassy. The landlord did say they were walking out, but did not stay at the inn together at any time. He identified Jones, but knew nothing of the young woman, except that she had very striking auburn hair. So it does seem it was Margaret."

Cassy was so shocked, she could hardly speak. It grieved her that a girl like Margaret Baines, with so much promise and common sense, or so they had all thought, could have been deceived into an affair with a man like Jones.

"How could she, Richard? Did she not see that whatever he said, however many promises he may have made to her, they were probably all worthless? Did she not stop to think of the consequences for herself as well as her poor mother, who is worried sick and likely to be even more devastated, when the whole truth is out?"

Richard sighed and, when he spoke, his voice was low and even, as though he was keen not to wound her feelings.

"Do not judge the girl too harshly, my dear. Remember that only some months ago we were faced with the consequences of an intelligent, young woman of impeccable character and connections doing something very similar. Indeed, one might say that at least Margaret Baines had no husband and child to abandon. If she has been seduced by this man's charm and false promises, and of that we cannot yet be certain, she will not be the first young person to be so deceived. It is not easy for young women of very little means to resist the lure of such a proposition. They have not the knowledge and experience to help them see through the promises of a skilled liar, which Jones clearly was. Think, Cassy, if a woman of Josie's education and intelligence could be taken in by the false promises of Barrett and Jones, what chance has a girl like Margaret Baines?"

Cassy's tears fell, despite her efforts to control them.

Memories of Josie and Julian, and the appalling tragedy that had resulted from just such a deception, stung her deeply and Richard, understanding, held her and comforted her.

The truth, however, had to be faced and some action would need to be taken to find Margaret, if she was still alive.

"What has been done to recover her? Are they searching for her?" she asked, but Richard indicated that it was at the moment a police matter and, while her friends and family might look for her, it was now the chief responsibility of the police to carry out a search.

"But dearest, you know that they will be far more interested in finding Jones's murderer, than in recovering poor Margaret," she cried and he agreed, "Yes indeed, which is why Grantham proposes to make his own enquiries in the village and go to Cromford, if necessary, to discover more information. Pray God, they may yet find her alive."

Cassy felt some slight relief; she had great confidence in Grantham, yet nothing would be known for hours; it may even be days, she thought and, in her mind, began to form a plan, which she hoped might be put into action sooner.

It was useless to wait for the police, Cassy thought. 'Twere better to make an immediate start.

Tomorrow, she would send for Mr Grantham and Mr Carr and ask for their help. They were in a better position than she was to act. As for Richard, she would tell him, of course, once the plan was in place.

On the following day, Dr Gardiner left early for the hospital. Police matters, among other things, had kept him away on the previous day, but he had serious work on hand, which needed completion. A paper was being prepared to be presented to a distinguished gathering of medical men next month; he and his assistant Matthew Ward were working assiduously to complete the research and write up their results. Acceptance and publication would bring the hospital and the two men involved considerable recognition and, hopefully, more endowments for continuing their work.

Cassandra knew she had much of the day to herself. She despatched urgent notes to Mr Grantham and Mr Carr requesting their help. She had already decided upon a plan and was hoping they would agree to carry it out. By the time Grantham, who came in great haste, fearing the worst, and Mr Carr, who had intended to ride over to see Lizzie, had both arrived, Cassy had her plan clear in her own mind. It was simple, but it required the maintenance of strict secrecy; consequently, it could not involve her husband or any other person who held an official position.

Mr Carr, as an outsider, who had recently purchased a property, could help; his bona fides were unlikely to be questioned. As for Mr Grantham, as manager of the Pemberley Estate, where the missing girl and her family had lived, he was entitled, nay even duty bound, to do whatever he could to discover her whereabouts.

When she disclosed her plan to them, both Grantham and Mr Carr were willing to help, but warned that the prospect of success was remote.

Grantham was pessimistic, believing Jones had killed the girl.

Cassy disagreed. "I am convinced Margaret is alive," she said, "If she had died, too, her body would not have been far from where Jones's body was found. The fact that it has not been found gives me some hope," she said, describing how they were to question, discreetly, all the tenants, labourers, and servants on the properties under their control, to gather as much information as possible about Jones and Margaret.

It was a hope that was enhanced by the arrival of Mrs Baines, who revealed that someone had entered her cottage while she was out searching the village for Margaret and removed some items of clothing and food. This news brought even Mr Carr and Grantham to an acceptance that Cassy may well be proved right. She was overjoyed, convinced that the girl was now definitely alive.

"Not very much has been taken, but they are all personal and significant items; a travelling dress and coat which Lizzie used in London and gave to Margaret only a few weeks ago, some underclothes, a pair of shoes, and a hat. Now, it seems to me that Margaret is in hiding and means to get away from the area.

"We must find her before she does, because the moment she runs away, she becomes a suspect. The police will believe she killed Jones, as a result of a lover's quarrel, jealousy, self-defence perhaps, if he tried to molest her; who knows what motive they may attribute to a young servant whom they wish to accuse of killing a man from a wealthy London family. You can be sure, once they know she is alive, she will be hunted, found, and charged, and God knows how she will save herself then, for who will believe her?"

Grantham protested. "Margaret Baines is no murderess, ma'am," he said. "I have known her since she were a baby; she cannot have done such a thing."

"I know that, Mr Grantham, and so do you and all of us, but the police do not. To them, she will be just another suspect and, if convicting her will help solve their murder, they will not ask if she was capable of it. And if she runs away, she will look guilty and play right into their hands. Which is why we must find her before they do."

Cassy's passionate appeal moved both men sufficiently to let them assure her they would do their best.

"I shall talk first to my servants here and then to the staff at Pemberley, and Mr Carr, would you please do likewise at Rushmore? Do not forget the stud; the men may have seen something. Ask them also about John Archer. I am certain, though I cannot explain it or give you a logical reason for my feelings, that Archer is linked in some way to Mr Jones."

Grantham looked sceptical, but Mr Carr was of a mind to agree with her.

"You may well be right, Mrs Gardiner," he said. "I have been thinking, since his visit to the stud in my absence to enquire about the horses, that he could have been acting for Jones. I may not have mentioned this, but I am aware that someone has been trying to purchase a pair of my horses on a previous occasion; my recollection is vague, but I believe it was a man from Cromford. Now the innkeeper says Jones, who was also keen on a pair of horses, had been staying with friends in Cromford..."

Grantham interrupted, "And Archer was in Cromford last week; I saw him there myself," finally beginning to believe that the theory made sense.

"There you are!" said Cassy. "You *do* have something to be going on with. I have to rely on you to talk to the people in the town and the men who work on the farms; you have known them, Mr Grantham, for as long as I have been alive; they will trust you and tell you far more than they will tell the police. Tell them what we believe and ask for their help to save Margaret Baines. We must find her and discover the truth about Jones's death; it's her only chance."

Grantham agreed; he could see no other way to save the girl.

Mr Carr, by now completely convinced Cassandra was right, declared that in addition to talking to his servants, he would visit the innkeeper at Matlock, of whom he had made a firm friend. "I think I may be able to persuade him to tell me something more about Jones than he has revealed to the police. I shall certainly do my best."

Cassy saw them go with more hope in her heart than she'd had that morning. At least, something was being done to find Margaret Baines.

The arrival, later that day, of her son Darcy from London, albeit in such a state of weariness he could barely get up the stairs before falling into bed, fully clothed, was not entirely inopportune.

He, too, could be drafted into helping with their enquiries, she thought, for Darcy, unlike his elder brother Edward, was a gregarious young man and had many friends in the area. These were not drawn only from the gentry and professional classes either, for with his love of sport, being a keen cricketer and horseman, he mixed easily with the sons of tradesmen, mechanics, and farmers, who were sportsmen, too. This, his mother realised, could be very useful indeed.

Having slept for some hours, he bathed, changed, and came downstairs, still cursing the overcrowded train in which he had travelled to Derby, before making the rest of the journey in "a none-too-comfortable hired vehicle, drawn by ancient nags driven by a drunken driver!"

His colourful account of the journey won him some sympathy from his mother, but before long, while he was still savouring "the first cup of decent tea in weeks," she was keen to acquaint him with the details of what had occurred in the last forty-eight hours.

Shocked and outraged, he was eager to help and indeed was willing to set out at once, if necessary, to make enquiries among his many friends and acquaintances. Cassy had just persuaded him to wait until the morrow, hoping that he would drive her to Pemberley, so she could speak with the staff there first, when the sound of horses' hooves on the drive alerted them to the arrival of a visitor.

Darcy went out into the hall and, moments later, Cassy heard him welcoming Michael Carr. The two friends were enthusiastic in greeting one another and, as they entered the parlour, it was easy to see how close they were. However, when they had done and Mr Carr had accepted a cup of tea, he spoke with a gravity that presaged some serious news.

"Mrs Gardiner, forgive me for intruding upon you so unceremoniously, but I have bad news." Cassy braced herself. Please God, he was not going to tell them Margaret was dead, she prayed silently.

Darcy, sitting beside his mother, sensed her apprehension as she held his hand tightly while Mr Carr spoke, "When I got back to Rushmore Farm, I was informed that the police had been there in my absence and questioned some of my men and one or two of the tenants as well. I was rather perturbed that they had not sought my permission first, but let that pass. As I attempted to ascertain what they had been trying to discover, they returned. This time they did come up to the house, but only to inform me that they were going to arrest a young man, Josh Higgins, who works for my steward at the stud."

"Josh! That's preposterous!" cried Darcy, whose explosion of outrage interrupted Mr Carr only momentarily, as he continued, "Mrs Gardiner, as Darcy here will tell you, Josh is the most unlikely suspect you can possibly imagine. He is a decent lad, a little slow; one might even say simple, but good hearted and a prodigious worker. He loves the horses and, while he cannot learn a trade, he is not considered smart enough for it, he is amazingly good at his work."

Darcy was incredulous. "Surely they cannot believe he would murder someone?" But Mr Carr said the police suspected Josh of being involved. "They claim he was seen in the area; they have questioned him for an hour or more, though what he might have told them I cannot imagine, the boy is unlikely to know he is a suspect. They claim he killed Jones for his money, the man's wallet is said to be missing and the police say that Josh was in the village on the following morning trying to buy a pocket watch."

"Does anyone else at the farm believe this?" asked Cassy.

Carr shook his head. "No one; my steward says the lad could not kill anyone. He is squeamish about blood and will not even join the beaters on a shoot! But it does look as though the police are about to build a case against him," he said looking decidedly pessimistic.

Cassy's voice was sombre. "Oh my God, the poor lad, unless a witness to the murder can be found who says otherwise or Margaret Baines comes out of hiding and tells the truth, he will be charged…"

"And if he is found guilty…he will be hanged or at the very least transported to Australia," added Darcy, grimly.

"And that will surely kill his mother, poor woman," said Mr Carr. "She has been so proud of him since he started work at the stud."

Lizzie, who had come downstairs and heard most of the preceding conversation in stunned silence, said, "I'd like to visit his mother and sister, Mama. I know Josh, I know how absurd it is to have him accused of such a crime. They must be in despair."

She was eager to go, but both Mr Carr and Cassy advised against it.

"I understand your outrage, Lizzie, and it is very kind of you to want to comfort Mrs Higgins and her daughter," said Cassy, "but I do not honestly believe you would accomplish anything by visiting them at this stage."

"Why not, Mama? Surely there can be nothing wrong in wanting to help the family. Josh's sister Molly wishes to be a ladies' maid and I have promised to train her, when we are…" and she broke off in some embarrassment, looking at Mr Carr, "Well, can you not see what a blow this must be to her hopes, having her brother arrested for murder?" Her voice broke as she pleaded to be allowed to go.

Her mother looked most distressed, but Mr Carr intervened, gently and persuasively arguing that he would personally convey her message of sympathy and support to Mrs Higgins and her daughter.

"But, it would be best, my dear Lizzie, if you did not go yourself, for several good reasons, including the fact that your dislike of Mr Jones has been quite publicly demonstrated in the village," he said and gradually she came to accept that they were right. But, like her brother, she fulminated and raged against the injustice that had been done to young Josh Higgins. "Does this mean that if Margaret is found, she too will be arrested?" she asked, angrily.

"It is possible, my love," said Cassandra, "which is why it is imperative that we find her before the police do. She will at least have an opportunity to explain her actions and tell her side of the story."

Mr Carr agreed and, while he was unable to stay to dinner, he did promise to return on the morrow with more, if not better news.

Once he had left, Darcy declared he was of a mind to go to the police himself and speak up for Josh Higgins, protesting about his arrest.

But at that point, both Lizzie and her mother cautioned against such action. "It will do more harm than good, if we were to antagonise the police at this time," said Cassy.

His sister added, "It is more important to find Margaret, now we know she is probably alive. It is she, not you or I, who will be able to clear Josh of the accusation. If she can be persuaded to go before the magistrate and tell the truth, it may help Josh. I cannot believe that either of them is capable of murder, although it is possible that Mr Jones may have attempted to take advantage of Margaret, and she may have struck out at him to defend herself, not meaning to kill him. He may, as a result, have fallen and hit his head," she argued.

While this may have sounded quite plausible, Cassy had to point out that it was not consistent with the facts.

"Your Papa has examined the body, which is badly bruised from the fall; whatever it was that killed him, it seems like a great deal of force was used. His injuries were very severe," she explained.

Lizzie, horrified, hid her face in her hands.

She could still see Jones's face quite vividly, as he had importuned and pestered her, following her around in the village teasing her; she had wished then that she had had the strength to strike him and be rid of him. Lizzie could well understand such feelings as Margaret might have felt, but she kept her counsel and said nothing.

Seeing it was almost time to go upstairs and dress for dinner, Cassy said, "Your Papa will be home soon. I think his day may have been very busy and he is likely to be exceedingly tired, so I suggest we try not to speak of this terrible business at dinner. It is hardly the subject one wants to pursue at the table, especially with the servants present, and your father may welcome a change from such matters, having spent all of last afternoon with the police and the coroner."

So it was agreed between them, and Richard Gardiner, though he was somewhat surprised at the lack of questions on the subject, was also relieved. Matthew Ward and he had finally completed their work for their presentation and, though it had been exhausting and time consuming, it had also brought considerable satisfaction.

He was glad of the opportunity to enjoy the feeling of achievement and share some of it with his family. Their pride and pleasure in his success was always a source of great joy. Yet, he could not help wondering why the subject of Margaret Baines's disappearance had not been raised at all that evening. He could not believe it was from a lack of concern, the strain upon the faces of his wife and daughter was unmistakable; perhaps, he thought, Lizzie had been very upset and her mother may have wanted to spare her further distress.

Whatever the reason, the family spent a rather strange evening, when everyone knew what subject was uppermost in each other's minds, but no one was willing to raise the matter. It was as if they were all determined to suppress their concern for one reason or another.

Only when Lizzie sat down to the pianoforte after dinner and found she could not proceed beyond the first page, was it obvious that, whatever they may have hoped to do, not everyone was succeeding.

On the following morning, Mr Carr arrived soon after breakfast, having arranged to take Darcy with him to meet Mr Hand, the innkeeper at Matlock. A genial and talkative host, Hand was keen to welcome them when they arrived at the inn. He was cleaning out the floor of the parlour and said with a grimace, "I've lost my last two guests, sir, one of 'em left this morning on the coach for Derby, and the other's dead!"

He had taken quite a liking to the young artist turned fisherman who had spent several weeks in the district that Summer. "I was sorry to lose him, good quiet gentleman, with a love of painting and fishing, though I have to say, he were a better painter than a fisherman, sir; he never caught a fish worth speaking of," he said with a great laugh that echoed around the room.

Darcy had no idea of whom he was speaking and Mr Carr explained. "There's been a young artist working in the area these last few months; your sister and I have met him sketching and painting in the dales on many occasions. I have seen him fishing, too, down by the river, but I do not believe he was very successful."

"No, but I tell you he was a pretty observant fellow, sir," Mr Hand interrupted. "Kept to himself mostly, but he had an eye open for what went on around him," he added in a conspiratorial whisper, which, considering the place was quite empty, was really unnecessary.

Still, Mr Carr was interested in the rest of the innkeeper's story and so was Darcy.

He told a strange tale of a night when young Mr Wakeham had returned fairly late to the inn, "looking for all the world like he'd fallen asleep in a haystack," and seeming rather disturbed.

"It was most unusual, sir, as I said to my wife, he's usually a quiet type of gentleman, clean and sober, yet he looked as if he'd had a few rounds with the boys. He told me later he'd been up among the moors around the peaks, sketching; he showed me his pictures, they were the prettiest pictures you could imagine, he was very clever with his drawings.

"Anyhow, the lads in the bar were all agog about the body being found in the quarry, you know, Mr Jones...and they were taking bets, whether the girl or Josh Higgins would go down for it. Mr Wakeham, he didn't say anything at the time, but after dinner, which he always took in his room, he came downstairs, when I was cleaning out the bar and wiping down the tables, and said he wanted a word in private. Very troubled, he looked.

"He tells me he had heard the boys talking about the dead man that was found in the quarry; he didn't know him, he said, but he had seen him many times, in the woods and down by the stream with the girl, you know the one with the great head of flaming red hair." Seeing he had them absorbed, Hand continued dramatically, "One afternoon, he said he saw them together, when he was painting down in Dovedale and the man came up to him and tried to threaten him, claimed he was following them, but the girl stopped him, he said."

Mr Carr listened, intrigued, but Darcy was becoming impatient.

"Did he see them on the day of the murder?" he asked and, to his astonishment, for he had not anticipated the answer, the innkeeper opened his eyes wide and leaning over the bar, said in a dramatic whisper, "He did, sir, in the woods above the old quarry," and as Carr and Darcy leaned forward, he knew he had their interest and went on, "It was around five o'clock, he said, but he could not be sure, for he carries no watch, sir; he saw them and whereas most times, they were all loving, this time they were arguing. However, he was sure that it could not have been the girl who killed the man, he said."

Pausing for effect, Hand continued. "I asked him why he thought that, seeing as women could do the job just as well, if they had a mind to do it, but he was very sure, and here's the best bit, he says it could not have been young Josh Higgins either. Why? Because, on that day Mr Wakeham had been on the other side of the river, fishing with his usual lack of success, and Josh come along and helped him catch a fish, his first in weeks. He says he was so pleased, he gave the lad some money for his trouble."

Mr Carr looked at Darcy and though they said nothing, each had thought the same thing—that would account for the money Josh had, which the police thought he had stolen from the dead man.

"Did he say why he was dishevelled and disturbed when he got in?" asked Darcy, but unhappily the innkeeper had no answer.

Hand admitted that he had tried to persuade Wakeham to go to the police, but he had said they would never believe him.

"However, he was sure the truth would come out, because there was another man in the woods that day and he believes this man was watching out for the lovers," said Mr Hand and Mr Carr was puzzled. "Do you mean he was stalking them?" he asked.

"I do not know, sir. Mr Wakeham thought the man may have been a friend of Mr Jones and was probably keeping watch for him, in case someone came by."

"And how might we contact this Mr Wakeham, should we need to find him?" asked Darcy, keen to follow up the new information.

The innkeeper shook his head. "I wouldn't know, sir, he's from Hertfordshire, some little village over there I'd say. I cannot read much, but my wife once saw a letter that came for him, from Hertfordshire, let me ask her," he said and went within.

When he returned, he had in his hand a folded paper, like the cover paper of a letter with a part of the seal still stuck to its side. The direction, though written very ill, was still quite readable. It was addressed to Mr Francis Wickham, care of the innkeeper at the Matlock Arms.

"Wickham?" said Mr Carr. "This says he is Francis Wickham! He told us he was Frank Wakeham. Now I wonder why that is?"

"I do not know, sir, there's many folks change their names, probably hiding from his family, I'd say, sir. Or may be he's been in trouble with the law. Come to think of it, he did look very troubled when I suggested he tell his story to the police," said Mr Hand.

Darcy meanwhile had been gazing at the scrap of paper for a few minutes, before leaping up from his seat.

"Of course, Frank Wickham from Hertfordshire, that's who it is! Come on Carr, let's get back and tell my mother about this, she will know where we can find him."

Puzzled, Mr Carr followed him, having thanked Mr Hand for his help and taking the scrap of paper with him, not knowing what on earth Darcy was talking about. When they were back in the carriage and on the road, Darcy told him of the Wickham family; cousins, with whom they had little or no contact.

Carr was intrigued, "Why?"

"Because they are all either disreputable villains or dissolute libertines or both, and my grandparents will have nothing whatever to do with them, nor will my mother. I do know they used to live in Hertfordshire."

Mr Carr was amazed. "Have you never met any of them yourself?" he asked.

Darcy shook his head, laughing. "No, not officially. I did meet two of them in London, George and Philip, a very long time ago at the house of a mutual acquaintance; they were the most appalling scoundrels you could hope to meet. Don't tell Mama, please, she will be furious!"

"What about this fellow Frank, then? He seems a perfectly decent fellow as well as being a pretty good artist. Surely, he cannot be of the same family?" said Carr, quite bewildered, but Darcy was sure he was.

"The name rings a bell, there were three or four sons and I think one was called Frank; but never mind, Mama will know, and if we can track him down and get him to talk to the police, Josh Higgins may yet be saved. Unless, Wickham is on the run from the law, too," Darcy said and added, "I wonder who this other man was: was he a friend of Jones? Who could he be? Now he may well be a witness to whatever happened in the woods that evening."

Mr Carr could provide no credible answer. His lack of familiarity with the district and his inability to recall the names of some of the men he had met at the inn recently put him at a disadvantage. Darcy, on the other hand, was sure that the second man referred to by Wickham had to be someone from the area who knew the woods well and was familiar with people in the village.

As they reached the house, Cassy, seeing them arrive, came downstairs and met them in the hall with the news that her parents were back from Kent and they were all to go over to Pemberley on the following evening to acquaint her father with what had occurred in their absence.

"Papa is sure to give us some sound advice," she said.

To her great astonishment, her son interrupted her.

"Mama, we cannot wait until tomorrow evening. Some very important information has come to light and we must act quickly," he said and, between them, Mr Carr and Darcy related the gist of the innkeeper's tale, holding back until the end the identity of the artist, Mr Francis Wickham.

"Wickham! Oh my God, he must be Frank, Aunt Lydia's youngest son!" she cried and, thereafter, all was confusion, until Lizzie arrived and helped bring a modicum of order to the proceedings.

Darcy was determined that he and Mr Carr should leave for Hertfordshire forthwith and try to find Frank (or Francis) Wickham (or Wakeham) and persuade him to return and tell his story to the magistrate.

Cassy was not so sure; she was wary of letting her son become involved and exceedingly cautious of any contact with the Wickhams. Even though the wily Mr George Wickham, so detested by her parents for his duplicity, had died sometime ago, Cassy recalled that her Aunt Lydia was not the pleasantest person and she feared Mr Carr and Darcy would find themselves drawn into deeper water than they could cope with.

She pleaded with them to wait until tomorrow, but Darcy was determined, pointing out that "every hour that passes leaves less time to save Josh."

Mr Carr spoke up. "Mrs Gardiner, I understand the anxiety and disquiet you feel, but I give you my word, your son will not be allowed to put himself in any danger, I shall guard him with my life," at which they all laughed and Cassy reluctantly agreed, on condition that Darcy acted only with the consent of Mr Carr, and would not rush impetuously into any situation.

"I would not do that, Mama," he protested, but she knew him too well and would only be satisfied after he had given her his word to be ruled by his friend in all his dealings with the Wickhams.

"It grieves me to say this, Mr Carr, of a member of our family, but Mrs Wickham is not to be trusted; she is mercenary and every bit as guilty as her husband of guile and chicanery, so do be warned," she said, and was herself surprised at how much she had come to trust Mr Carr. His integrity and decency were, to her, beyond question.

Preparations were soon afoot for the departure of the two gentlemen to Hertfordshire.

"Will you take the train or go by road?" asked Lizzie, and her brother groaned, feigning agony even at the memory of his last train journey.

"Oh no, not the train again, I cannot bear it, not twice in one week. Even though the journey will be done in less than half the time, I shall be so sore; I will be of no use to anyone for a week. I am still suffering the consequences of my last journey, the seats, the crowds, and the smoke!"

"Did you not travel first class?" asked Mr Carr, who was quite accustomed to train travel in America.

"I did, but so did hundreds of other people; it seemed as though half of London was on the train, every man, woman, and child, each with its own load of luggage, including a parrot in a cage! No, Lizzie, I shall *not* take the train," he declared with so much passion that Mr Carr, still laughing at his friend's exaggerated account of the tribulations of train travel, suggested that they take his carriage. "It is comfortable and affords you some degree of privacy, but it will take twice as long," he warned, "so, we had better make a start immediately. We can go direct to the farm, where I shall pick up my things, and we can take the carriage and my men. That way, we should be on the road by one o'clock and have at least half a day's travelling done by tonight."

They wasted no more time. Darcy gathered together his things; Cassy found them Mrs Wickham's address outside of Meryton and wrote a note to Jonathan Bingley, requesting his help.

"I have written a note to your Uncle Jonathan Bingley, he is well known and respected in the area and will help you locate Frank Wickham, I am sure. But, be warned, Lydia Wickham is not an easy woman to deal with," she said, as she bade them farewell.

Even as she saw him go, Cassy was most uneasy about letting her son become so deeply involved in what was clearly a murder investigation. She would have preferred if it had been left in the hands of the police, but there was little she could do.

When her husband returned home that night, Cassy had to tell him of the new information that Darcy and Mr Carr had uncovered and explain that they had gone together to Hertfordshire to locate Mr Frank Wickham.

Richard was surprised; not having been privy to the enquiries that Mr Carr and Darcy were making, he had little knowledge of the developments in the case. Whilst he had some concerns about the disappearance of Margaret Baines, once it had been established that the girl was alive, though still missing, Richard had not taken any active interest in the matter, content to wait for the authorities or the girl's family to find her.

He listened carefully to what Cassy told him and asked, "And do you think, my dear, that this Frank Wickham or Wakeham, if he does turn out to be your Aunt Lydia's youngest son, will return and give his evidence to the police?"

Cassy had no answer. She knew very little of the Wickham family, save what her parents, principally her mother, had told her over the years.

"I cannot say, Richard, the family are not generally known for being upright and public spirited, but in this case, it does seem that Mr Wickham was concerned that Josh Higgins was under suspicion," she said.

"So concerned that he told the landlord at the inn, and no one else, before leaving the district," said her husband, somewhat sceptical. Richard had no knowledge at all of that branch of the family, except for the reports he had had of the Wickhams from his parents, from Mr and Mrs Darcy, and Julian, all of which had been uniformly bad.

No one, it appeared, had a good word for them, though he wondered about Frank having changed his name, to avoid recognition while staying in the area. Perhaps, he was ashamed of the reputation of his father and brothers and wished to put some distance between himself and his family.

He knew Cassy was keen for him to give her some encouragement and was reluctant to dash her hopes.

"It is possible that he is different from the rest of them. He may well be more thoughtful and less inconsiderate of others. But if that is the case, why did he pack up and leave? It does not sound like the act of a responsible man with a clear conscience, does it, my dear?"

Cassy could have wept. Frank Wickham was their last chance; if only, she thought, if only she had been on better terms with her Aunt Lydia. Then, she might have gone to Meryton with Darcy and tried to persuade Frank to return and tell his story. As it happened, she could only wait anxiously for news, some news, from her son and Mr Carr. And that may be days away.

※

Very early on the following morning, however, they had another surprise.

Lizzie crept quietly into her parents' room and, seeing her mother lying awake in bed, signalled to her to come out into the corridor.

Cassy eased herself out of bed without waking her husband, snatched up a shawl, and draping it around her shoulders, followed her daughter to her own bedroom. There, she found Lucy, her maid, and another young person, a girl not more than fourteen years old, sitting on the rug before the fire. She seemed nervous but not at all fearful.

"Mama, this is Annie, she has brought a note from Lucy's aunt, Mrs Thomas, who lives across the river, beyond Kympton, on the edge of the moors," said Lizzie. The girl handed Cassy a note, which had been sent to Lucy that morning.

The note, though written in an untutored hand, was quite clear and Cassy read it quickly, looking for the vital information she sought. Mrs Thomas wrote that Margaret Baines was with her; she had come to them two days ago, having hidden overnight in the woods. This note brought a message from her. She intended to leave the district very soon. If however, Miss Lizzie would meet her, she promised to tell her truthfully all that had happened. She begged them to believe that she had not murdered anyone and asked to be forgiven for her foolishness, by which Cassy took her to mean the clandestine affair with Mr Jones.

Looking up, with tears stinging her eyes, she said, "Oh poor, foolish Margaret, what a waste of a bright, young life," as she passed the note to her daughter. Lizzie was determined to go.

"May I go to her, Mama? Lucy can accompany me," she said eagerly, but Cassy was unsure; she did not want to let Lizzie go on her own. What if this was a trick to lure her daughter? An army of fears, real and imagined, assailed her and she decided there was no alternative, she would have to go herself. Urging Lizzie to stay in her room with the two girls, but prepare to leave at a moment's notice, she returned to her room. Her husband was still fast asleep. Leaving a note for him, which gave only the merest hint of the reason for their departure, Cassy dressed quickly and, collecting Lizzie and the girls, went downstairs; there, only a few of the servants were awake, preparing for the morning's work. Tea was made and they all partook of some, while Cassy sent for the small carriage, preferring it because it was closed and protected them not only from the cool morning air but from inquisitive eyes as well. Once they were across the river, Annie would show them the way.

Cassy's account of their journey and the meeting with Margaret Baines made exciting reading for her cousin Emma Wilson, when it was transcribed in a letter, written some days later; but no one would ever know the anxiety and apprehension that had accompanied her on her journey that morning. There were few people about and for that they were grateful. The road through the woods was far from easy and when they crossed the river, Cassy, who had never been in this area before, feared they were lost. Annie, however, was able, quite confidently, to instruct the driver and soon they were at the crossroads.

Turning towards the village of Rockford, which was little more than a handful of cottages, a forge, and a dairy lying in a scoop of land above the ancient ford, which had been augmented by a stone bridge a mere century ago, they had to stop, for what had been little more than a rutted dirt road now petered out into a footpath. Instructing the driver to wait, Cassy, with Lizzie and the two girls, alighted and walked up the path towards a cottage, half hidden by the trees that surrounded it. Annie led the way and they entered into a small, clean room, where they were met by a middle-aged woman, who, by her neat clothes and courteous manner, gave an appearance of polite respectability even in the face of hardship.

Her husband, Cassy had learned, was a labourer and had already left for work. He would not be back until dusk. The woman, Mrs Thomas, invited Mrs Gardiner and her daughter to be seated and went to fetch Margaret Baines.

Cassy was to write later:

Oh, Emma, if only you could have seen her. I could scarcely believe she was the same bright girl who had been in our home just a few days ago. Her face was drawn and thin and there was in her expression such a look of fear, almost of furtiveness, that one was immediately reminded of the young woman in a novel, on the run from the peelers. It was horrible. Poor Margaret, it was more than I could do to hold back my tears and Lizzie went to her at once and embraced her!

Margaret Baines had been persuaded by Mrs Thomas, who had taken pity on the girl, to tell her story to Mrs Gardiner.

It was not an easy tale to tell, nor was it painless for the listeners. She started and stopped often, until she was encouraged by Lizzie, who assured her that they wanted only to help her, and reassured by Cassandra, who said she firmly believed Margaret could not have been responsible for Jones's death. The final measure of persuasion came, however, when she heard that it was Josh Higgins who was now under suspicion and had been arrested for the crime.

"It was never Josh! No!" she cried, and there followed a recitation of the entire incident, her words flooding out in a rush.

Margaret confessed that she had been seeing Mr Jones, "not walking out with him, ma'am, but just walking home sometimes, when he would appear on the road that I took on my way home, or when I went into the village to get something for my mother. He would appear and walk with me to the end of the road, where it came out of the woods and then turn back, waiting to see me into the village."

Cassy wrote to Emma:

Quite clearly he had taken a fancy to the girl; he had been asking about her at the inn, noting her head of auburn hair, and, like the deceiver he was, started to accost her while pretending he was meeting her by chance, when he had clearly been waiting for her.

Margaret confessed she had liked him at first, and perhaps she had "flirted a little" with him, but protested that she meant no harm...and did not wish their association to go any further. She swore that she had no illusions that he wanted to marry her. "I knew he was a gentleman from a rich family. He told me his family owned a print shop in London and another in Derby; I was not expecting him to propose to me or anything. I knew he would not be interested in a girl like me..." she said, and Mrs Thomas butted in, "He'd be interested all right, in one thing only, of that you can be sure, and once he had that, you can be sure he'd be off."

But Margaret swore that no such thing had happened or even been attempted, even though he had brought her a gift once. She showed them what looked like a little locket on a chain. It was a tawdry trinket of little value—the sort of thing one could pick up in a gift shop in Derby.

She claimed, one day, a little more than a week ago, he had kissed her unexpectedly and she, confused and afraid, had run away from him.

"It was then I saw him, John Archer; he had been in the woods, I thought it was by chance, but it later came out he had been following us and he went after Mr Jones seeing what he'd done and had words with him," she said.

Cassy was astonished. "How well do you know Mr Archer, Margaret?" she asked at once.

"Quite well, when I was little, ma'am, but not since he's been away in London and come back. I haven't met him, hardly at all, but I have heard he has spoken of me to others. One of my cousins is a stable boy at Pemberley; he has heard talk among the men that John Archer was speaking of me, wanting to meet me, and such," the girl replied.

Cassy wondered what more was yet to be revealed. It would not surprise her if Archer had had designs on Margaret himself and was following the pair, through frustration and jealousy. She recalled that Mr Grantham had been very set against him being considered for the position at Pemberley, where, as an assistant to the manager of the estate, he would have had both access and influence. Could Grantham have known something of Archer's interest in Margaret and been unwilling to disclose it at the time? she wondered.

Cassy asked Margaret if Archer had ever propositioned her.

"Did her ever say anything to you? Apart from ordinary conversation, did he ask you to walk out with him or suggest he wished to marry you?"

Margaret blushed and appeared reluctant to answer, but said after a minute or two, "Not directly, ma'am, but he had asked about me, whether I was spoken for, but he never said such a thing to me."

It was beginning to look more and more like John Archer, rather than poor simple Josh Higgins, was the man the police should have been looking for.

But how was such a proposition to be proved?

Writing to Emma Wilson, Cassy explained how difficult the task had seemed.

Margaret Baines claimed that on the day after she had seen John Archer in the woods—that is, the day after Jones had kissed her and she had run away—she saw Andrew Jones again and, when she did, she told him that she would not accept his approaches to her.

"I told him I want no more of it, ma'am, no more of the kissing and cuddling and such, and I warned him we had been followed by John Archer, and I was scared of him talking in the village. I said my mother

would hear of it and I'd be in trouble and then most likely lose my job with you, ma'am," she said, and my dear Emma, you may call me naïve, but I do believe her.

There was no effort to hide any of her own silly mistakes; she broke down and sobbed as she told us that she had confided in one of the kitchen maids who had warned her to beware of London toffs, who deceive you and leave you with more trouble than they're worth. "I should have listened to her, ma'am," she said and, Emma, I really believe she was quite genuine and I am sure, so would you.

...Cassy wrote, unable to find it in her heart to condemn the girl.

In spite of her warnings and protestations, Margaret claimed, Jones only laughed and told her to ignore Archer and any other man who tried to approach her. He is supposed to have said, "Archer is only a servant, so are the rest. They're just jealous that you are walking out with me and not with them."

It is exactly the type of arrogance that one expected from Jones and his ilk.

Both Lizzie and her mother had heard the girl's story, with increasing feelings of depression. It was the kind of dishonesty for which dissolute young men were notorious and the consequences of their duplicitous behaviour were to be seen in the suffering of innumerable young women and girls, as well as their unfortunate, illegitimate offspring, who filled the poorhouses across the country.

Oh God, thought Cassandra, if she had only come to Lizzie or me. But, she had not, nor had she confided in her friend, the kitchen maid, who may have alerted the housekeeper earlier, when she went missing.

But, Margaret Baines did claim to have made a firm decision.

On the following day, she said, she had left work earlier than usual and met Jones in the woods, not by chance this time, but, she admitted, having arranged the meeting with him. She had made up her mind, she claimed, to tell him she could see him no more. She had concocted a story of being seen by one of the servants at the house and reported to her mistress, who had given her one last chance; she had to stop meeting him or she would lose her job.

They had been walking along the path that ran along the edge of the quarry, towards a small grove of trees, when she stopped and told him she would not come this way again, but would take the main road through the village, where she could not meet him, for fear of being seen. Jones had only laughed and accused her of wanting to tease him to increase his desire for her and, though she swore this was not true, he, as she tried to remove the chain from her neck to return it to him, had caught her unaware and pulled her towards him, kissing and fondling her roughly, frightening her so that she'd screamed as she struggled to get away.

Cassandra and Lizzie listened in astonishment as Margaret shuddered, recounting how afraid she had been. Clearly, she had enjoyed what had seemed a lighthearted flirtation with a handsome town toff, but his sudden change of mood had terrified her. She claimed that as she struggled and scratched at his hands, trying to break away, she heard what she could only describe as a roar, "like an animal when it is angry," behind them and, as she broke from him and ran, the roar continued and she'd heard the thump of bodies hitting the ground and thrashing around on the forest floor.

"I was so afraid, ma'am, I did not stop to look back; I knew it were probably Archer, he must have followed me and, when he saw what Mr Jones tried to do to me, I think he must have attacked him. I cannot say, because I did not see him, but it was a big man, from the noise he made running at him and shouting. I know it was not Josh!"

Margaret claimed she had run for her life and had not stopped until she was sure she was out of their reach. That night, she said, she hid in the woods, sheltering in one of the small caves until morning, when she had crept down to the village, hidden in the barn, with the cows and, when her mother left the house, she had gone in and gathered together a few clothes and some food, before returning to the woods.

There she had remained in hiding until nightfall, when she had gone down to Mrs Thomas's cottage.

"I took the travelling dress you gave me, Miss. I hoped you would not mind my wearing it to get away to town, maybe Birmingham or Manchester, to find work and a place to stay. It's a fine gown and I thought it would make me look a bit more ladylike, ma'am," she said and Cassandra shook her head, in dismay.

"Oh Margaret, why did you not come to us, to me or Miss Lizzie?" she asked, "Why did you not tell us when you felt this man Jones was pestering you and you wanted to be rid of his attentions? We would have helped you."

Margaret bit her lip; quite clearly she knew the extent of the trouble she was in as well as the quite grievous pain and anxiety she had caused to so many people. It did seem to Cassandra that she was genuinely sorry, but she was, as yet, determined to leave the district.

When Cassy told her that this would not now be possible, she looked alarmed and confused. At first, she'd had no idea that Jones was dead but, as Mrs Thomas and Lucy had discovered more of what had happened, she'd begun to panic. She knew enough about the ways of the police to realise that she would be under suspicion, as soon as the truth of her association with Jones was known. She had heard, too, of what it was like in the dreaded prison ships that took convicts to the Colonies and had no desire to wait around to be arrested and charged.

But, Cassandra made it quite clear that there was but one way and she would have to tell the truth or else, they could do nothing to help her.

Despite her own grief at having to put to the girl such an ultimatum, Cassy knew there was no other way.

"If you leave here alone, we are forced to tell the police that we have seen you; if we do not then all of us—myself, Miss Lizzie, and poor Mrs Thomas—will all be guilty of concealing evidence relating to a crime. That, Margaret, is a criminal offence, we cannot do it. When the police discover that you are on your way to Birmingham or Manchester, they will alert every branch of the constabulary on your route and you will soon be picked up and we shall not be able to do anything to save you."

Poor Margaret's cheeks were ashen and her hands as she gripped Lizzie's were icy as Cassy continued, "If, on the other hand, you stay and return with us and tell your story, truthfully to the magistrate, I doubt you will even be arrested. Or if you are, Dr Gardiner and I can vouch for you and have you bailed. After all, by your story, you have committed no crime; it is certainly foolish to walk out with a man you do not know very much about, but it is not an offence. There is no one who has come forward to accuse you of anything, you may have to give evidence if there is a trial, but that is all. So far, you are missing, but not a suspect. If you run away, you will immediately become a suspect and be hunted down.

"So, my dear Margaret, I strongly advise you to return home with us. We will send word to your mother that you are safe and she can come and see you, but it will be best if you stay with us."

The girl looked reluctant to do as they asked, but finally, after much argument from Cassandra, a stern warning from Mrs Thomas, and some tearful pleading by Lucy, she was persuaded to accept her mistress's advice and return with them to Matlock.

So long had they been that Richard, becoming concerned, had decided to set out in search of them. No one except the housekeeper knew even in which direction they had gone and, as the returning party reached the crossroads, Lizzie caught sight of her father, in his curricle, looking somewhat unsure as to which road he should take.

He looked rather bemused as she waved and called out to attract his attention and, when at last, she succeeded, the sheer relief upon his face was so obvious, Lizzie and her mother had to laugh.

"Poor Papa, he must have wondered what had become of us, we have been away for over two hours," said Lizzie and Cassy, though she said nothing, knew she would have a good deal of explaining to do, before her husband would understand the seriousness of the situation.

Many hours passed before the entire story had been told and Richard, still amazed at what his wife had undertaken, was proud, indeed, of her success.

As Cassy wrote to Emma:

I think the first thing I felt was a great sense of relief, because Margaret was not going to be tried for murder. However, there was the fact that she had been present and would have to give evidence at the inquest and probably at the trial, that is, of course, if there was going to be a trial. After all, no one, certainly not Margaret, had seen who killed Jones, if indeed he was killed.

If Darcy and Mr Carr return with Frank Wickham and his evidence helps clear Josh Higgins, there may not be a trial at all. Dear Emma, this may sound wicked, but if that were to be the outcome, I for one, will not be sorry.

I cannot help feeling some satisfaction that Jones, who caused so many people so much grief, has had his punishment at last. It must be remembered that it was his duplicitous promise, and that of his friend Mr Barrett, to publish Josie's poems that led to all that trouble between her and Julian.

Poor Margaret, even if she comes out of all this, she will not be unscathed. Her life here will never be the same. She may not have lost her virtue, but she has surely placed her reputation in jeopardy. In the village, she will be remembered as the foolish young woman who went walking in the woods with a London toff, who trifled with her and got killed for his trouble.

She is unlikely to get a responsible position in any household, despite the fact she is not guilty of anything more heinous than a foolish error of judgment and some very unwise behaviour. She is quite contrite now, but there may not be many people, other than ourselves, who will trust her anymore...

～❦～

For Mr Carr and Darcy Gardiner, there was good news when they arrived at Netherfield House in Hertfordshire, after almost a day and a half on the road. Jonathan Bingley welcomed the weary travellers and handed them a message that had arrived by electric telegraph that morning. The first sentence, which told them Margaret Baines was alive and willing to testify, brought welcome relief. However, the rest of the message, in which they were urged to hasten in their quest of Frank Wickham and persuade him to return with them to Derbyshire, in order to tell his story to the police, was to prove rather more daunting.

After they had been shown to their rooms, they bathed, dressed for dinner, and came downstairs to partake of drinks and refreshments in the saloon, where they were joined by Jonathan Bingley and his wife Anna, keen to discover the purpose of their hurried visit. Between them, Darcy and Mr Carr managed to explain the somewhat tangled web of circumstance, report, and rumour that had brought them to Hertfordshire.

As Mr and Mrs Bingley listened, with increasing astonishment and not a little alarm, Darcy explained that Frank Wickham might yet save poor Josh Higgins from the charge of murder if he could be persuaded to come forward. Yet, he had to confess, they had not a clue as to where he may be found, unless it were at his mother's house in Meryton.

"My dear uncle, we are totally in your hands; Mama hoped you might advise us on how best to locate Mr Wickham and persuade him that an innocent man's freedom, nay even his life, may depend on his willingness to testify.

It is a somewhat unusual role for a Wickham, I grant you, but unless he agrees, Josh Higgins will surely pay the price of his silence."

Jonathan Bingley could not resist smiling at the suggestion; he enjoyed the irony of the situation his nephew had described. "You are quite right about one thing, Darcy, there is not one family I know, less likely than the Wickhams, to produce a white knight; but, like you, I too have heard reports of young Frank Wickham that suggest he may be somewhat different to his idle, feckless brothers.

"I have had no contact with the family in many years, but I am aware through a mutual acquaintance that Frank Wickham lives apart from his mother in a cottage on the far side of the Longbourn Estate. Mr Bowles, who used to be my steward and recently moved to Longbourn, will be able to take you to him," Jonathan explained and added some cautionary advice.

"I must warn you, though, should his mother, Mrs Lydia Wickham, get wind of your presence in the area and the purpose of your visit, you may not find it easy to avoid her attentions," he said, and Darcy acknowledged his uncle's advice. "Indeed, sir, Mama has informed me that Mrs Wickham is not an easy person to deal with. I would greatly appreciate any advice on how she is to be approached."

Jonathan laughed. "With much caution, I would say, Darcy. Your mother is being very charitable in her description. Aunt Lydia has lost nothing of her guile and, since she is always full of complaints, an encounter with her can become quite wearisome. I suggest you take Mr Bowles with you; he occasionally takes her produce from Longbourn and Mrs Wickham is well disposed towards him."

Mr Carr intervened to say that time was of the essence and they would need to see Mr Wickham at the earliest opportunity.

"Every day's delay can mean less hope for Josh Higgins. At the time we left Derbyshire, the police were very sure he was their man," he said, hoping to impress upon their host the urgency of their cause.

Their conversation was interrupted by the arrival of Jonathan Bingley's eldest daughter Anne-Marie and her husband Mr Colin Elliott, who were to dine with them. Mr Elliott was the local Member of Parliament, a man much admired by young Darcy Gardiner. Together with his wife and their young son, he had moved earlier in the year to live at Longbourn, the property which had originally been the home of the Bennet family.

Through a series of fortuitous circumstances and one sad mischance, the sudden death of Mr Collins, heir to the estate by entail, Longbourn had ended up in the hands of Jonathan Bingley, who had gifted it to his daughter Anne-Marie on her recent marriage to Mr Elliott.

Mr Carr recalled meeting the remarkably handsome couple briefly at the wedding of her sister Teresa to Mr Frederick Fairfax, the architect. He noted also the remarkable resemblance between Anne-Marie and her cousin Lizzie Gardiner, who was soon to be his wife. In general appearance, he thought, they were so alike, one might have mistaken them for sisters, except that Mrs Elliott was older, more self-assured, and had an air of independence that he could not but admire in a woman.

Lizzie's attraction was the charming freshness and enthusiasm of youth, which she brought to all her activities and relationships; Carr had found it irresistible. As his thoughts returned to her, he felt suddenly alone amidst all these people who knew each other so intimately. He missed her terribly and wished he were back in Derbyshire, where she was but half an hour's ride away from his home.

He forced himself back to the present, wrenching his thoughts away from pleasanter prospects, to join in the conversation around the dinner table.

Mr Elliott had been applied to, by Darcy, for advice on their difficult undertaking. Having had some dealings with the intractable Mrs Wickham, on a previous occasion of similar difficulty, Mr Elliott agreed that it was certainly a daunting prospect, but he held out some hope. "At least with Mrs Wickham, one knows what one is dealing with," he said. "While she protests that she has some tender feelings, some sense of outrage about the way in which the world in general and some people, in particular, have treated her, and claims to have strong bonds of family loyalty and filial affection, all these may be immediately discounted, if sufficient money could be found to assuage her present discomfort."

Everyone chuckled and Anna Bingley even protested that the poor woman was surely not that bad. But Anne-Marie swiftly defended her husband's account of Lydia Wickham. "Unlike most ladies, she makes no pretence of having contempt for money; in fact, she has a great respect for it, which over-rides all other feelings," she said, to which Mr Colin Elliott added, "Indeed and she is quite open about it. When you approach her, Mr Gardiner, do so with your pocketbook well stocked with cash."

Like Jonathan Bingley, Elliott also recommended Mr Bowles.

"If anyone can help you find Frank Wickham or get information from his mother, Mr Bowles can," he said, promising to send him round to meet them on the morrow, so they could plan their campaign.

Later, after the ladies had withdrawn to the drawing room, where they were joined not long afterwards by the gentlemen, Anna Bingley and Anne-Marie entertained them with music and song. Though Mrs Bingley was undoubtedly the superior performer, having studied in Europe and acquired a high degree of proficiency and style, she was nevertheless well supported by Anne-Marie, who had recently, with the encouragement of her husband, started to take singing lessons.

As the mood of the company changed, softened by the music and the wine, the conversation moved to other matters. The ladies wanted Mr Carr to tell them how preparations were going for the wedding, to which, he was warned, they were all coming.

"Lizzie is Mr and Mrs Darcy's first granddaughter and you may be sure there will be a great party for her," said Anna, and Anne-Marie asked to be remembered to her young cousin. "Lizzie is a great favourite of ours; we are looking forward to seeing her as a bride," she explained.

Mr Carr tried to satisfy their curiosity to the best of his ability, but he knew very little of the wedding plans and could not give them much detail, except that Lizzie's sister Laura Ann was going to be her bridesmaid. He was, however, able to tell them a good deal more about the refurbishments he'd made at the farm and Lizzie's role in helping him make all the right choices for drapes and accessories.

"It's a fine, handsome old house and needed only the right touches to restore it to its former dignity. With Mrs Gardiner's excellent advice and Lizzie's good taste, I think we have done well," he said and Anna, who had a keen interest in these matters, said she looked forward, very much, to seeing it.

Darcy and Colin Elliott, meanwhile, recounted some harrowing accounts of the loss of the vote on the Reform Bill in Parliament and the consequent resignation of Lord Russell and his government. Neither could believe that a few intransigent Liberals had contributed to the downfall of their own government.

"Mr Gladstone must be furious!" said Darcy, and Mr Elliott confirmed that indeed he was. Jonathan introduced a somewhat more serious note, remarking upon the increasing number of violent demonstrations that had erupted around the country, especially in London and some of the larger towns, in the wake of the resignation of the government and the collapse of some large financial houses. Darcy had plenty to say on the subject, too.

Mr Carr, when the ladies went to attend to the tea and coffee, set out to get to know Mr Jonathan Bingley better. He knew from Lizzie and her mother that Jonathan was one of the most highly respected members of the family, ranking together with Richard Gardiner in the affections of Mr and Mrs Darcy.

His record of service to his party, the Parliament, and his local community was quite remarkable. He had twice been the recipient of significant civilian honours, yet, he was invariably modest, unassuming, and considerate of others. Knowing, as he did, Mr Bingley's achievements in politics and community leadership, Mr Carr was genuinely surprised by his total lack of self-congratulation or complacency, two attributes that had characterised most American politicians he had observed.

Their conversation was both amicable and interesting. Congratulating Mr Carr on the purchase of the farm and stud at Rushmore, Mr Bingley said, "I was happy to hear that you intended to live on the property and improve upon it. I know Mr Darcy is, too; it is the only way to protect the land and prevent its fragmentation by developers. They dispossess the village people and sell to absentee landlords, who have no interest whatsoever in the community."

Mr Carr agreed and revealed that he had also received a couple of offers for the stud. "There seemed to be several people interested, yet reluctant to come forward themselves," he said. "Approaches were almost always made through a third party."

Jonathan laughed heartily. "Ah yes, of course," he said, "because they want nothing to do with the land or the community that has worked it for generations. Their only interest is in the profit it will bring in when it is resold. You are wise, Mr Carr, not to become involved with these men. They are mainly from London or some large commercial city and have a keen eye for the money they can make from land. Some farmers are going through hard times and will sell to anyone who offers them a decent price. To these men, a property like the Camden Stud will be a veritable gold mine."

Mr Carr was adamant. "I certainly have no intention of selling, Mr Bingley.

I am very happy in the area and intend to settle there permanently. I have said so, many times, but they are very persistent."

Anna came over to join them, seeking to "interrupt their shoptalk," she said, and having offered Mr Carr more coffee, proceeded to ask after Cassandra Gardiner.

Mr Carr, whose love of Lizzie was equalled only by his admiration for her mother, told her as much as he knew of Cassandra's efforts to help manage her father's estate, Pemberley, while still coping with all the demands of her own family. "I have to say, Mrs Bingley, that I have never before encountered a lady who worked so hard and with such complete uncomplaining dedication," he said, and both Mr and Mrs Bingley agreed.

Jonathan declared that he had had a similar account from his mother, Mrs Jane Bingley, who was familiar with the situation at Pemberley.

"I understand that in Mr Darcy's absence, Cassy took over the management of Pemberley and did it so well, her father is now keen for her to continue."

"Indeed, sir, and while I know she would like to spend more time with her family at Matlock, she never complains. Miss Gardiner tells me that her mother believes it is her duty to support her father in the absence of her brother Julian."

"Cassy Darcy," said Jonathan Bingley, "is a most extraordinary woman and, one might say, a fortunate one. Her husband, Dr Gardiner, is not only an eminent physician, he has achieved what was thought to be quite impossible, convinced the hospital board to spend more money on research! He is also one of the finest men I have known."

Mr Carr was, by now, convinced that the family he was joining was not only a distinguished one, it was remarkable also for the concern and support its members showed for one another. But just then, as if to remind him that every family, however well regarded, had its black sheep, Darcy returned to remind him that they should have an early night, since they expected to rise early on the morrow and go forth with Mr Bowles in quest of the elusive Frank Wickham.

Mr Carr sighed. It had been an exceedingly pleasant evening and he was sorry it had to end. "Perhaps," he said to Mr and Mrs Bingley, thanking them for their gracious hospitality, "when all this is over, you will be my guests at Rushmore Farm?"

The invitation was accepted with enthusiasm.

The visitors, still weary from their long journey, retired early in preparation for what might prove to be an arduous day to follow. They did not expect to achieve their goal with ease and feared they may be hindered by the machinations of Mrs Wickham. Shortly afterwards, Anne-Marie and Mr Elliott took their leave.

Jonathan remarked to his wife that Anne-Marie was clearly a very happy woman. Anna, had no reason to disagree with her husband on this point. Her affection for Anne-Marie had led her to hope that she would one day be more happily wed than she had been to the dour and dull Dr Bradshaw. In marrying Colin Elliott, it was quite obvious that they had both found that happiness. There was certainly no mistaking the warmth of their affection for one another.

"I think you are right, dearest," she said and added, "From what I can make of Mr Carr, it would seem that young Lizzie Gardiner is soon to be similarly blessed."

Jonathan took his wife's hand and kissed it, recalling how much he owed to her love and understanding. She had been a tower of strength, his defence against despair, when he and his children had most needed affection and hope. "That, my love, is what we must all pray for," he said, as they went upstairs.

After breakfast on the morrow, Mr Bowles arrived to meet with Messrs Carr and Gardiner. Mr Elliott had already explained the purpose of their visit and Bowles was well prepared. Although he had served the family for many years, it was his practice not to become embroiled in the conflicts and squabbles that occasionally erupted even in the best-regulated families and disrupted the even tenor of their lives. He had maintained some contact with the Wickhams and, since the death of Mr George Wickham, Senior, he had, with the permission of his employers, taken over the occasional hamper of farm produce, a ham, fresh fruit, or game for Mrs Wickham and her daughter. It was clearly appreciated.

With her husband dead and her elder sons living almost permanently in London and far too selfish to offer her any assistance, Lydia Wickham was hard put to support her often self-indulgent lifestyle on her small annuity. Despite her best efforts, and no one could have tried harder, she had not as yet succeeded in persuading any wealthy gentleman to marry her daughter, whose strong resemblance to her mother must have proved less than advantageous.

Consequently, she was forever applying to her sisters Elizabeth and Jane for money to pay her bills and would even call upon Mrs Collins at Longbourn for a "loan," although there was very little chance of the money being repaid. She would run up debts with the local stores, and when she had no more money to pay them, she would close up the house and disappear for some weeks. On her return, she would write pathetic letters appealing to her sisters for help, warning that if they did not help her she would go to jail and disgrace them all!

She was, therefore, very glad of the gifts of produce that Mr Bowles and his wife Harriet brought her and would thank them as if they, rather than the Master and Mistress of Longbourn or Netherfield, were the source of the generous donations.

One advantage of this peculiar arrangement was now to become evident. Mr Bowles, complete with a basket containing poultry, fruit, and honey, was able to visit Mrs Wickham, confident of a cheerful welcome and an invitation to take tea in the parlour, while unbeknownst to his mother, Mr Carr and Darcy Gardiner were bending their efforts to persuade Frank Wickham to return with them to Derbyshire.

Writing to his mother a letter, which he despatched from Netherfield by express, Darcy gave his own version of the events of the day...

Dearest Mama,

I am writing in haste, so you must not mind my uncouth scrawl. I am concerned only to set your mind at rest at the earliest opportunity. This will go by express and should be in your hands well before we arrive home.

Before I proceed any further, let me say it, Frank Wickham is indeed the youngest son of Aunt Lydia Wickham and he has consented, albeit with some trepidation, to return to Derbyshire and tell his story to the coroner who, in all probability, will enquire into the death of Mr Jones.

Darcy was keen to give credit where it was due.

Our success is due, almost in its entirety, to the sound advice of my Uncle Jonathan Bingley and the absolutely splendid scheme devised by his man, Mr Bowles, who is the new manager of Longbourn.

Let me give you a brief sketch of events now, a more detailed account will follow upon our return. Frank Wickham seems a genuinely decent fellow. He lives alone in a cottage on the far boundary of the Longbourn Estate. For most of the Summer and Autumn, he travels around the country, sketching and painting, and having worked to complete the pictures, he takes them to London each Spring and sells them to dealers.

They are certainly not great art, but are pretty enough to appeal to some. He claims he makes sufficient for his needs, which are few, and he seems content.

He also teaches drawing and painting to private pupils, in their homes, when he can get the work. He would like to get more such work, I think, but appears to be disadvantaged by the reputation of his family, which precedes him everywhere. I do believe he would give almost anything to put as much distance as possible between himself and his older brothers George and Philip, whose disreputable behaviour seems to have adversely affected Frank's own prospects of obtaining any worthwhile position. Mr Bingley points out that this is not surprising; their appalling reputations have them barred from any respectable house in the district.

Frank Wickham, on the other hand, does strike one as having some principles, for when Mr Carr explained the plight of Josh Higgins, who was already in custody for a crime he could not have committed, Wickham agreed, albeit after some hesitation at the mention of police, to accompany us to Derbyshire. Should his story be believed, and there seems to be no reason why it should not, Josh should be completely exonerated and released.

Frank Wickham confirms everything that he is supposed to have told the innkeeper at Matlock as a true account of what took place. It was he gave Josh Higgins the money, which the police thought he had stolen from Jones.

Mr Carr, who played a most effective hand in persuading Wickham that he may well be responsible for the transportation if not the hanging of Josh Higgins, if he remained silent, believes that the police will have no option but to release Josh, which I am sure Papa and you will agree is an exceedingly good result.

Dear Mama, there is, however, one problem that may cause all of this to unravel.

Frank Wickham owes money, not a large sum, an amount of twelve pounds, to a man in Matlock, from whose shop he purchased materials and supplies during the Summer. He is the general merchant, Mr Brewer. When Wickham left in haste, he forgot to pay his outstanding bill. Now, he fears that Brewer may have gone to the police; if he has done so, it may well compromise Wickham and devalue his evidence. He does claim that he always intended to send the money and wishes to apologise for not having done so before leaving the area.

Mr Carr has undertaken to pay the bill for him, but since we are at least three or four days from reaching Matlock, he asks if you would send the money to Mr Brewer together with the note from Wickham, which I here enclose. Mr Carr wishes me to say he will reimburse you for the amount, in full.

If this matter can be cleared up before Frank sees the police and the coroner, there will be no reason for concern about his probity or the reliability of his story.

I know how eager you must be to have this matter settled and hope our efforts will help bring it to a satisfactory conclusion.

Both Mr Carr and I look forward to being back at home, for though my aunt and uncle have been most hospitable and kind, this vexing affair has hung over us and inhibited our enjoyment of an otherwise pleasant visit.

I have to say, Mama, that in spite of all the facts we have gathered, including Wickham's statement, we are no closer to discovering who killed Andrew Jones or with what motive. It has engaged our minds for many hours of each day, but to this moment, it remains a puzzle, the key to which has completely eluded us. Mr Carr sends his warmest regards to you all. My uncle and aunt send their love and have hopes of seeing you later in the year, when they will be visiting Pemberley.

Ever your loving son,
Darcy Gardiner.

In Derbyshire, where the early winds of Autumn had already begun to rustle through the woods, turning some leaves to gold and scattering others along the footpaths, roads, and gullies, Cassandra Gardiner and her daughter read the letter with interest. Each hoped to find in it some personal satisfaction. Both were keen to have the unhappy business of Margaret Baines and Mr Jones settled as discreetly and as expeditiously as possible. It was proving to be more than a distraction at a very busy period in their lives and, in Lizzie's case, had taken her beloved Mr Carr away, just when she wanted most to have him beside her.

However, while Cassy seemed reasonably satisfied with the contents of her son's letter, Lizzie clearly was not. She had read and re-read her brother's letter, looking for some small message, a sentence, a phrase even, from Mr Carr and found none, save for the general salutation. He had sent his "warmest regards to them all," including her with the rest; it could not have been duller, she thought. To say she was disappointed would be an understatement.

Since they had become engaged, Lizzie had not been parted from her Mr Carr for any appreciable length of time and this separation was beginning to take its toll upon her usually blithe spirit.

Lizzie had gathered from her brother's letter that it would probably be four days before they could expect them back and then, she wondered, how much longer would he be involved in the matter of Josh Higgins and Mr Wickham? She was aware that he took his responsibilities to the community seriously and surmised gloomily that it may well be several weeks before the coroner heard all the evidence, questioned the witnesses, and settled the matter. Yet, he had neither written to her nor sent her a message in her brother's letter. Young, vulnerable, and in love, she was hurt by his silence.

Lizzie was not to know that similar thoughts were absorbing the mind of the man whose absence was causing her grief. He, too, had scarcely been a few days away, before he began to crave the sight of her and long for her company. Yet, while he could sigh away his deprivation and complain to his friend, Lizzie was too shy to speak of her feelings to anyone.

Laura was too young to understand and her mother was, she judged, too busy with a dozen different tasks or too anxious about the dreadful business of Margaret Baines to be troubled by such trifling matters.

She, therefore, suffered alone, hoping the pain of her loneliness would end sooner, yet resigned to the fact that this was probably a forlorn hope.

For Lizzie Gardiner, who had led a relatively sheltered life, undisturbed by scandalous or shocking events, the year just gone had been a turbulent and disturbing one. At eighteen, when the highlights of her social life had been a cricket match, the harvest festival, a chamber concert, or the annual Pemberley Ball, she had viewed life with an innocent naïveté.

One year later, she had witnessed the gradual destruction of her cousin's marriage, the betrayal of trust and subsequent death of a young woman she had always regarded with affection. There followed the renunciation of his inheritance by her Uncle Julian Darcy, with all its attendant consequences for his family and her own.

Now, as if that were not sufficient, they were involved, through no fault of theirs, in the extraordinary escapade of Margaret Baines and Mr Jones, with another death and a possible murder enquiry to boot!

In this same period, Lizzie's own life had been changed by the arrival in the area of her brother's friend, Mr Michael Carr. The awakening of love in her youthful heart, the discovery that he loved her enough to want to marry her, and the admission that her life would be far less felicitous without him had changed her life profoundly.

In her diary, to which she confided her innermost thoughts, she wrote,

> *It all came upon me so gently, with none of the surprise and excitement one reads of in books, where young ladies and gentlemen declare that they have fallen in love instantly at the very first meeting, while bells peal in the background and flowers bloom at their feet! I knew none of this.*
>
> *Yet, now, so deeply am I in love, so ardently drawn to him, that if he were by some dreadful mischance (which God forbid) to be taken from me, I do not believe I would care to wake up upon the morrow.*

And on another page,

> *Ever since he has gone with my brother to Hertfordshire, I have missed him so terribly that I dare not speak of it, lest it is deemed unseemly to have such strong feelings, but I do so long for his return.*

Yet, despite this feeling of desolation, on the following morning, when her mother, after breakfast had been cleared away, asked if Lizzie would accompany her on a visit to her grandmother, Mrs Gardiner, she agreed without hesitation.

"Do put on your pretty new blue gown and bonnet, my love," said her mother. "Your Grandmama always enjoys seeing you dressed up, and since she does not get about much, this would be an opportunity for her to see you in it. It will cheer her up."

Lizzie could not help thinking it was such a pity that Mr Carr was away, because she had hoped to wear her new gown for his benefit.

Nevertheless, she went upstairs, dressed, put up her hair, wore her new bonnet, and came downstairs in less than half an hour. Cassandra was pleased. "There, you *do* look lovely, Lizzie. I am glad we got the blue muslin instead of the cream; it suits you well and that bonnet is very pretty indeed!" she said as they went out together.

They took the small carriage. It was not far to Oakleigh Manor, which lay in a pleasant valley, not far from the village of Lambton.

The day was warm and windless, with high white clouds sailing lazily across a sky so blue it hurt the eyes to look on it for long. Mother and daughter were both glad of the cover the carriage provided. Cassy had noticed that Lizzie had been rather quiet and had put it down to the strain of the unhappy business with Margaret Baines and Mr Jones. She was pleased they were driving out to Oakleigh today; it would provide a welcome distraction, she thought.

They were approaching the inn at Lambton, where the coaches from Derby and Birmingham stopped to drop off and pick up passengers. Despite the growing popularity of rail travel, many travellers still preferred the coach. As the inn came into view, they saw a figure on the road ahead. It was a tall man, and he was walking towards them at a fairly brisk pace, his overcoat flung over his shoulder. Clearly, he did not need it on such a warm day.

"Stop!" cried Lizzie to their driver, "Stop! Look, Mama, it's Mr Carr!" and even before the vehicle had been brought to a standstill, she was preparing to evacuate her seat, heedless of her mother's cries of caution.

As they drew near, the man, alerted by the sound of the carriage pulling up beside him, looked up at its occupants. Sure enough, it was Mr Carr and, as the door was opened, Lizzie leapt out of the vehicle and into his astonished arms. Cassandra could do no more than watch, as the pair embraced, their elation at this unexpected meeting clearly overwhelming any inhibitions they may have had.

While a little unsettled by their very public display of affection, Cassy, herself a woman with strong feelings and a passionate nature, understood how they might feel and was disinclined to attach blame to either.

She could not, however, avoid a sharp stab of guilt that she had neither detected nor sought to assuage her daughter's feelings, which were now so obvious to her and to anyone else who cared to observe them. She had not thought to ask and Lizzie had clearly suffered alone. Cassy blamed herself, as she saw her tears and then the mutual delight that suffused their faces as they were reunited, clearly reluctant to break apart.

When Mr Carr helped Lizzie back into the carriage, keeping hold of her hand, as he stood beside the vehicle, he explained that there had been a problem with horses at Derby. "I took the coach and travelled ahead, lest you should worry at the delay, Mrs Gardiner," he explained, "leaving Darcy and Wickham to follow. They will not be more than half a day's journey behind me."

Yet Cassy knew and she was sure Lizzie would know, too, that he had probably travelled ahead because he could no longer endure the separation. She could not fail to appreciate their delight in their chance reunion. It prompted a change of plan. Inviting Mr Carr to join them in the carriage, Cassy said, "We were going to Oakleigh Manor to visit Mrs Gardiner. I expect to spend the day with her, but if you choose, Lizzie and you may return to Matlock and send the carriage for me later."

The pleasure on both their faces was assurance enough that she had done the right thing.

If further proof was needed, it came with the warmth of her daughter's embrace as they parted at Oakleigh and her whispered, "Thank you, Mama." It was not only an act of understanding and love, but also an index to Cassy's trust in her daughter and Mr Carr. To Lizzie, it confirmed that hers was the best mother in the world. She would do nothing to outrage or breach her trust. For Mr Carr, however, Lizzie had another plan in mind.

The confidence she had gained from his warm and spontaneous greeting, and the subsequent pleasure she had from his compliments upon her appearance, allowed her some measure of liberality. She now used it to discover whether the man she loved could be contrite as well as loving.

With a degree of playfulness that disarmed him completely, she demanded to know why she had received no communication from him while he was away in Hertfordshire.

At first, somewhat disconcerted by the unexpected question, Mr Carr attempted to provide her with a reason, but found his path blocked, as Lizzie insisted, with a smile that belied her intention, that she could not see why, if her brother could write to her mother, he could not have done likewise and penned a note to her. As he struggled in vain for an acceptable answer, she wondered aloud. "Could it be," she mused, in a quiet but clearly reproving voice, "that his silence indicates that, having secured my affection and consent, he no longer thinks it necessary to accord me those gentle courtesies that were so much a part of our early acquaintance?"

At this quite outrageous suggestion, Mr Carr had to protest most strongly and, in words of increasing degrees of tenderness, he not only proclaimed his love for her, but told her how wretched he had been without her, how often he had told her brother so and wished he was back in Derbyshire with her.

When she asked, "But why then, did you not write to me?" he replied in anguished tones, "Because, my dearest Lizzie, I have not the talent to put down on paper all I feel for you and I was afraid if I had written of mere mundane matters that you would think my words inadequate."

"And you supposed I would prefer your silence?" she asked, determined to press him for an answer.

"I would. Rather silence than some well-worn string of phrases, signifying nothing. Had I loved you less, Lizzie, my darling, it would have been easier to write something sentimental and probably meaningless; but you are too dear to me to play at friends and lovers with you. I love you dearly, believe me, and I am truly sorry if I have hurt you by my failure to write. It was not in any way a reflection of my feelings, which have been uniformly wretched at being separated from you."

He looked and sounded so genuinely distressed, she had no doubt at all of his sincerity and she had to stop him and confess that she was teasing, adding cunningly, "It is, however, good to know that a gentleman is as capable of feeling remorse as he is of love."

As usual in such matters, the most pleasure lies in mutual appeasement, following each misunderstanding, and so it was with them.

By the time they had reached Matlock, both Lizzie and Mr Carr were convinced, beyond doubt, of each other's deep and abiding affection and had determined that it was quite impossible to tell which of them loved the other more. A happy condition, they agreed, which augured well for their future together.

That evening, Mr Carr joined the Gardiners for dinner. Dr Gardiner was given an account of the results of their journey to Hertfordshire.

Though they were all disappointed that Darcy and Frank Wickham had been delayed at Derby, Mr Carr was nevertheless very confident that the information they had obtained from Mr Wickham would greatly assist Josh Higgins.

"I expect he will be exonerated of the charge of murder and be released before the inquest, sir," he told Richard, with some confidence.

Dr Gardiner asked several pertinent questions, relating to the reliability of Wickham's statement, his willingness to testify, and even more importantly, his sincerity in agreeing to come forward.

"Are you quite certain he is genuine in his desire to help, or does he hope for some material gain by obliging you?" he asked, adding quickly, "Pray do not misunderstand me, Mr Carr, I ask only because the Wickhams do have an unenviable record of such behaviour and I would not want you to be taken in."

Mr Carr assured him that they had questioned Frank Wickham very thoroughly and were confident that his story was true in every particular.

"He is absolutely solid on the matter of meeting Josh on the other side of the river, while fishing that evening, and giving him some money. Darcy and I impressed upon him the need for truthfulness, not only in the interest of Josh Higgins, but in his own interest as well."

"Indeed," said Richard, "perjury is a serious offence. However, if you are both well satisfied, I daresay, it will all turn out well. Congratulations, Darcy and you have accomplished far more than I ever expected."

Lizzie, listening quietly to their conversation, was delighted with her father's approval for the man she loved.

After spending a while longer with Lizzie, Mr Carr left and Lizzie, looking much happier, went to her room.

Soon afterwards, the Gardiners went upstairs and, as they prepared for bed, Cassy told her husband of the encounter between Lizzie and Mr Carr on the road to Lambton. She confessed she had been astonished by the high degree of feeling in Lizzie's impetuous greeting.

"I blame myself," she confessed. "I should have realised she was lonely and missed him. I have been too busy, too concerned with other people's business to think of my own child. Poor little Lizzie."

Richard, who had observed how much more cheerful young Lizzie had been that evening and attributed it correctly to the return of the gentleman concerned, smiled and put a reassuring arm around his wife. He was well aware of the burden she had carried these past months.

"I have certainly not forgotten and I hope you have not either, my love, how one feels at such a time," he said, "I recall that we were parted for a much longer period, shortly after we were engaged, when Paul Antoine was dying and you stayed behind in Italy with your parents to support Emily, while I had to return to work at the hospital in Derby. I know how they must feel and I do think it is wise that their wedding is not delayed much longer than the end of Autumn. Do you not agree?"

Cassy did agree but was not easily reassured that she had no blame to bear in the matter. Frequently, as she hurried through the day, attending to work on her father's estate, she had stopped to consider practical domestic matters, but not once had she thought that Lizzie may have needed comfort. It was a serious omission and Cassy was filled with self-reproach.

In the very early hours of the morning, Darcy Gardiner and his companion, Frank Wickham, arrived in a state close to exhaustion. They were allowed to sleep late and breakfast well before Mr Carr, with an attorney-at-law in attendance, arrived to advise Mr Wickham and accompany him to the offices of the constabulary. There, they assumed the tedious processes of the law would begin.

Secure in the knowledge that the small but significant matter of his debt owed to Mr Brewer had already been paid, Frank Wickham was less uneasy and more ready to do his duty. Mr Carr and Darcy Gardiner made statements, attesting to the willingness of Mr Wickham to testify, and then Mr Wickham and the attorney went in. Some hours later, they emerged to inform those waiting that Mr Wickham's statement corroborated the story told by Josh Higgins in every detail and Higgins would be released into his parent's care, under orders not to leave the district until after the coroner's inquest.

Unhappily, that was not the end of the matter.

The police, having released their only suspect, now had no plausible evidence to present to the coroner, regarding the death of Mr Jones.

They had a dead body and little else. With only the girl, Margaret Baines, who was not a suspect at this stage, left to give evidence; there was some heightened suspense as to what would happen next. Would someone else be arrested?

Each morning brought more rumour and speculation and very little illumination or fact. If no one was responsible, what was to be the verdict? Not accidental death, surely? Clearly the man had either been pushed or had fallen in the course of a scuffle to the floor of the quarry, where his body had been smashed upon the rocks. His terrible injuries suggested it. But who was to blame? Some accused the girl, while others spoke of a mysterious stranger, seen in the woods, who had accosted and killed Jones. Speculation was rife. In the streets, at the inn, even it seemed, in the courthouse, there was talk. No one could agree.

Back at Matlock around the table that night, where Mr Carr and Mr Wickham had been invited to join the family at dinner, the conversation was, quite deliberately, of matters other than the death of Andrew Jones.

Richard and Cassy were eager for news about Jonathan and Anna Bingley, and Darcy was keen to tell of his conversations with Mr Colin Elliott, who was highly esteemed as a courageous Reformist, while Lizzie and Mr Carr were persuaded to provide the company with some gentle entertainment at the pianoforte. After weeks of anxiety and strain, the family enjoyed the simple pleasures the evening afforded them. The relief after days of uncertainty was palpable.

Watching them from the corner of the room, where he had sat seemingly lost in thought since dinner, Frank Wickham may well have been wishing for a similar life in a quiet domestic environment. It was the sort of normal, happy family life of which he had very little experience.

Suddenly, there was a loud knocking at the door. Thinking it had to be a medical emergency, for no one else would call at such an hour, Dr Gardiner rose, as the door of the drawing room opened to admit two officers of the local constabulary.

There was immediate silence, so quiet as if everyone had stopped breathing. Each person in the room had their own private explanation for this intrusion and none of them could have anticipated the news they brought. A man, a certain John Archer, said the senior officer, had given himself up. He had confessed to the accidental killing of Mr Andrew Jones.

There was general consternation around the room.

"Who," asked Darcy, "is John Archer and how is he involved in this?"

Dr Gardiner explained briefly and then asked the police officers, "Has he given you details of how this 'accidental killing' occurred?"

"He has, Dr Gardiner, but they cannot be revealed until they are either corroborated or contradicted by a witness."

"Corroborated by a witness? Does Archer say there was a witness to this accident?" Richard asked, somewhat bewildered by this statement.

"Not to the whole of it, sir, but there was another person involved, at least for some of the time, Archer says, who can confirm that he was there when the incident took place."

"And might one ask, who this person is? Not any one of us, I do not think?" Richard was increasingly concerned by the direction of this conversation.

"No sir, none of the persons in this room is in any way implicated," said the officer, looking round at the gathered company, "but, we are here, because we must have a statement from the witness. We know *she* is here, not in this room but perhaps in your staff quarters. The person concerned is Margaret Baines."

"Margaret?" said Lizzie, clearly shocked.

The officer nodded, "Yes, Miss Gardiner, only Margaret Baines can corroborate Archer's statement. Indeed, he has alleged it happened because he went to her aid, when she was attacked by Mr Jones, on the path above the quarry. He claims she called out for help and he responded to her appeal."

Lizzie rose and ran from the room and her mother followed her out, while Dr Gardiner sent for the housekeeper, who was requested to fetch Margaret Baines.

At this point, Mr Carr, Darcy, and Frank Wickham, feeling awkward and intrusive, strolled out onto the terrace, leaving Dr Gardiner and his wife to deal with the police and Margaret Baines.

Mrs Gardiner returned and sat beside her husband on the couch by the fire. Margaret Baines entered and was invited to seat herself on a low chair beside her mistress. The police officers sat stiffly before them and asked her questions, which she answered without hesitation. Previously, she had told the story of her brief association with Jones, but had made no direct mention of John Archer, unwilling to implicate him in any way.

Now, however, as they questioned her about the incident in the woods, she revealed more of what she had already told her mistress. She told them of the evenings she had walked home through the woods and the occasions on which Andrew Jones had walked with her. She told them how she had, on one occasion, noticed a man following them and had told Mr Jones of it, but he had been unconcerned, she said.

After she had discovered the man was John Archer, she had been afraid of being exposed by him and losing her job, she admitted. Relating the frightening experience of her final encounter with Jones, she revealed for the first time to the police the struggle she had heard taking place after she had broken away and fled from him.

It took very long, because Cassy insisted that the girl be given time to answer their questions in her own way. Finally, it was done.

The inquest, they said, would take place next week and Mrs Gardiner had to guarantee that Margaret Baines would attend, tell her story, and be prepared to be questioned by the coroner. Which Cassy, having glanced at her husband and seen him nod, agreed to do. Margaret would continue to stay with the Gardiners until her appearance before the coroner.

As soon as they were gone, Cassy, having cautioned Margaret to say not a word about her statement to the other servants, sent her directly to her room. Mr Carr had already taken his leave, taking Mr Wickham with him, and Darcy had long gone to bed, more confused than ever.

Cassy then went upstairs herself to reassure Lizzie and hoping to improve her own understanding by discussing the situation with her husband.

Richard was tired, too; it had been a long day, but he took time to explain to his wife what would be the most likely outcome.

"It is difficult to imagine a more extraordinary case than this one has turned out to be," he said, shaking his head. "For Archer to confess to the crime is a singularly brave thing to do. He is facing certain transportation or jail for the term of his natural life."

"Unless the coroner believes he did genuinely intervene to save Margaret from a dreadful fate at the hands of Mr Jones," said Cassy, who had not previously given much thought to Archer's fate.

"Of course, but is it likely? Jones was the son of a wealthy London family with important business and social connections. They will be well represented. Archer comes from a family of simple tenant farmers. He has had some education and has worked for one or two prominent families in London, but there is no comparison, is there? And not a great deal of hope for him, unless the coroner is a man of absolute integrity, who is not influenced by these matters."

His wife was not quite so pessimistic and believed that the coroner may well believe Archer's story, especially when heard in conjunction with Margaret's statement. "I do hope you are wrong, dearest. It seems so unfair," she said, hoping in her heart that Margaret's evidence would not be used to hang or transport a man, who had indeed acted to save a young woman from molestation, albeit somewhat precipitately and with terrible consequences for Mr Jones. Despite her reservations about Archer, Cassy could not believe he deserved such a fate.

~

The week following, Margaret Baines, modestly and soberly gowned, accompanied by her mother and the attorney, presented herself at the offices of the constabulary and thereafter attended the coroner's inquest.

There, John Archer told his story on oath, for all to hear.

He claimed he had loved Margaret Baines, though she knew nothing of his feelings; he had intended, he said, to apply to her mother first, for permission, before approaching the girl. But, he had loved her since the days when he, as a young man, had lived on the Pemberley Estate, before he had gone to work in London.

On his return he had hoped to find employment, marry her, and settle in the area, he said, speaking seriously and with such a degree of openness that he had to be believed. That was until he saw her with Mr Jones walking in the woods, he said. Asked if it had made him jealous and angry, he admitted to jealousy but denied anger, saying he knew little of Jones to make him angry at the time.

Later he had made enquiries about him from contacts in London and on learning "the man was a swindler and a notorious deceiver of young women all over town," Archer said, he had decided to follow the pair, chiefly "to ensure the girl got into no trouble" because he did not trust Jones.

He had followed them undetected for almost two weeks, during which time, he claimed "nothing untoward occurred," until the day he had seen Jones kiss the girl, when she had broken away and run from him.

It was the day Margaret Baines had first spotted him, he said, but he didn't think she had recognised him.

Asked if he was, by then, both angry and jealous, he admitted that he was.

Asked if he wanted to assault Jones, he denied that this was so.

"I was concerned for Margaret. I was glad she had got away. I was also happy to see that she did not welcome his advances," he said in reply. "I knew then she did not care for him and I was very glad of it. But I was sure he would not take no for an answer. His type never does."

Continuing, Archer told the coroner that, on the following day, he had stayed well hidden and managed to follow the pair, to the point where they had stopped on the path that ran along the lip of the quarry. He had remained at a distance, concealed by a dense thicket. There, as they stood, the girl had spoken in a low voice.

Archer said he could not hear her words, but then, he had seen Jones reach out for the girl, draw her towards him, attempting to fondle and molest her, whereupon, she had struggled and cried out for help. As he had rushed out towards them, she had broken free of Jones and escaped into the woods. Archer then claimed he had rushed at Jones "in a rage, like a madman" shouting at him, and Jones, taken by surprise, had struck out at him with his stick. Archer said he still carried the bruise upon his shoulder, a fact that was confirmed by the police.

Archer had carried no weapon, not even a stick, he said. In the ensuing mêlée, he had struck out with his fists and Jones had fallen to the floor and then, as he rose and lunged at Archer again, he had tripped and, losing his balance, fallen over, tumbling headlong down the face of the cliff into the quarry below.

Asked by the coroner if he had done anything to help the man or to verify if he was alive, Archer shrugged his shoulders and said it was a long way down and the light was almost gone. He had peered over the edge, but had neither seen nor heard anything, he declared.

"You heard no cry for help?" the coroner asked and Archer swore he had not. As he spoke, without emotion, Margaret Baines sat, her face red with embarrassment, her eyes downcast, blowing her nose from time to time on a large handkerchief provided by the attorney. Her striking auburn hair glowed in the light flooding in through a high window behind them, and each time Archer looked at her, he seemed to be gazing at her hair. Cassandra could not help wondering at his feelings for Margaret. Could he really be so obsessed with the girl, he would risk his freedom, even his life, by making such a plain confession of guilt?

There was a general feeling of unease in the room, a sense that Archer was already resigned to his fate. No one had suggested that the man was lying. The officers of the constabulary seemed content and most of the public appeared to sympathise with Archer. As for the man himself, he sat quiet and composed, as if nothing mattered.

After hearing all Archer had to say and questioning both Frank Wickham and Margaret Baines again, the coroner retired to consider the evidence, while everyone else went outside for a breath of fresh air.

The verdict, when it came, was a shock.

The coroner had concluded that there was no doubt Mr Jones had died as a result of the fall he had taken into the quarry. But, and here was the salient point, he said, "Archer had been trying to protect the virtue of an innocent, if rather foolhardy young woman, for whom he claims he had a genuine affection and honourable intentions. Had he not acted as he did, she may well have suffered a far worse fate at the hands of Mr Jones. Archer could not have been expected to remain unmoved. He had set upon the man, who had tried to molest the young woman and in so doing, Archer had accidentally caused the death of Mr Jones."

There was an audible sigh of relief in the room and Margaret Baines sobbed into her attorney's handkerchief.

Lizzie Gardiner had not been able to bring herself to attend the inquest. When Darcy and Mr Carr returned with her mother and Margaret, who was now at liberty to return to her home, Lizzie wept with relief. "At least Margaret will not have a death upon her conscience," she said, and it was clear to them that she did not mean the death of Mr Jones. "It would have been singularly unfair if a man who had tried to stop a helpless girl being molested was to lose his life or his liberty, because he had, by his action, accidentally caused the death of her attacker," and there was not a dissenting voice to be heard on the subject.

Cassy was immensely relieved, too.

While she had no liking for Archer, she was glad the matter had ended without the need for a trial, possibly followed by a hanging or transportation. Some of the tales that were told of the fate of men sent down for murder, sentenced to penal servitude at Godforsaken places like Port Arthur or Norfolk Island on the other side of the world, were too horrible to contemplate.

Cassy assumed that Margaret would now be free to live and work in the area as she chose.

"She will probably never want to see the man Archer again," she declared, as they retired to bed that night.

Her husband smiled and said, "Perhaps, but I cannot believe the girl was not flattered by his admission of a love lasting many years and such a public declaration of his intentions. Besides, just think, by his confession, he was declaring his willingness to give up his liberty or his life for her. Margaret must be touched, surely?"

"Oh, Richard, do you really believe that?" his wife protested, but Dr Gardiner was unwilling to be cynical, at least not until he had evidence to the contrary, he said, as he put out the light, pointing out gently that men had been willing to die for love, before today.

Cassy was not in any mood to be contrary; it had been a much more satisfactory day than many that had gone before and she had no wish to indulge in a pointless argument with her husband. Besides, she thought with a smile, he may even be right.

The police investigation into the death of Mr Jones had led, quite by chance, to the discovery of two other wanted men who had been apprehended at Cromford. They had been involved in setting up a string of fraudulent deals around the county, most of which led right back to Andrew Jones. Clearly he was the man they had been working for, and it was to their hideout, in an old manor house outside Cromford, that Jones used to retreat whenever the inn became too crowded for comfort or a stranger asked too many inconvenient questions.

News of their arrest brought general relief to the community and especially to the innkeeper, Mr Hand, whose suspicions had increased considerably in recent times.

Mr Carr, too, was glad to be rid of them; they'd been loitering around his property too often for his liking, yet he had been powerless to do very much about them. Their depredations had troubled many of the farmers and shopkeepers in the area, for they were suspected of thieving and worse. It may well be said that, knowing they were taken into custody and would soon be out of the county, the entire populace breathed a sigh of relief.

Indeed, it could be stated without fear of contradiction, and Mr Sharp the chief constable did say it: "The end of the investigation into the death of Mr Andrew Jones, and the activities of his henchmen, has resulted in an abatement in the criminal activities in the area and a marked mitigation of the strain that everyone in Matlock, who was in any way touched by it, has endured this last month," he declared. "Now, we can all get on with our lives in peace."

And many a voice said "Amen" to that.

For the Gardiners, this was indeed a blessing.

❧

Richard was preparing to go to London with Matthew Ward for the presentation of their research to a medical council meeting, while Cassandra and her mother needed to meet and make plans for Lizzie's wedding, which was closer now than ever. Mr Carr and his bride-to-be were especially pleased. They could concentrate upon one another again, as lovers are wont to do at such times. There was much that needed saying and doing and so little time.

Yet, it was surely Mr Frank Wickham who must have felt he had most to be thankful for. During the difficult days he had spent explaining his activities and present circumstances to Darcy Gardiner and Mr Carr, the latter had shown some interest in him, apart from his role in exonerating young Josh Higgins. Later, after the coroner's inquest was concluded and Wickham, who had been staying at Rushmore Farm, had been preparing to leave, Mr Carr had offered him the use of a small vacant cottage near Rushford, on his property. Frank Wickham, unable to believe his good fortune, had offered to pay some rent, but Mr Carr had a much better idea.

He had suggested that Wickham should, in lieu of rent, provide his services to the parish school, where he could teach the children to draw and paint.

"Unlike the children of wealthy parents, who can afford private lessons, these young people will never learn to draw or paint, because no one will teach them. If you are prepared to do it, you can have Rushford Cottage free of rent," he had said, and Frank Wickham had agreed with alacrity.

Even at his best, he was not an articulate young man; on this occasion, he was dumbfounded, barely managing to stutter his grateful thanks.

He was, he said, more grateful than he knew how to say, which fact was quite apparent to Mr Carr.

When he revealed to Lizzie the agreement he had made with Wickham, Mr Carr did so with some trepidation, knowing the acrimonious state of relations between the Darcy family and the Wickhams. He expected to have to argue and persuade and, to that end, was prepared with chapter and verse of the most logical arguments in favour of his plan.

He was, therefore, pleasantly surprised to discover that her response was quite the opposite.

In fact, Lizzie was delighted. "That is a splendid idea, I cannot imagine a better scheme, for not only will it give poor Frank Wickham a place to stay in a place where he can work in peace, as well as teach the children of the parish; it also gets him away from his impossible family. If he could only get out of the clutches of his insufferable mother and shake off the reputation of his disreputable brothers, he may be able to make his way in the world," she said, with the kind of illuminating maturity that often surprised him.

"Lizzie, my love, you sound exactly like your mother," he said, adding that in her case, it was a compliment of the very highest order, and Lizzie did not need to disguise her pleasure at his words.

An invitation to dine with Mr and Mrs Darcy, a fortnight later, took all the Gardiners and Mr Carr to Pemberley. There they found already arrived Jonathan Bingley, his wife Anna with their two young sons Nicholas and Simon, as well as Cassy's aunt Jane and her husband Mr Bingley, who was as amiable as ever, despite having been laid low with the influenza for a week. Their lovely daughters Sophia and Louisa were with their husbands, in London, he explained. Mr Bingley was exceedingly proud of his beautiful wife and daughters.

Cassandra was especially delighted to see Anna Bingley, for whom she had a great deal of affection and her husband, Jonathan, an intimate friend of both Richard and Cassy since childhood. They were to spend a fortnight at Pemberley and the two women looked forward to having more time together.

"I shall need your advice on our preparations for Lizzie's wedding in November, Anna," warned Cassy, and Anna Bingley responded with her usual generosity, offering her time and skill whenever she was needed.

The arrival of Colonel Fitzwilliam and Caroline, together with their son David and their niece Jessica Courtney, whose time was now mostly occupied with the parish school at Pemberley, completed the party.

Unhappily, Mrs Gardiner was not well enough to attend and Emily Courtney and her husband Reverend James Courtney were gone to Oxford, to visit their son William and stay with the Grantleys for a while.

To Mr Darcy and Elizabeth, their absence was a disappointment, for Emily was a very special friend.

Despite this, the occasion was a happy reunion of the families, as the first dinner party given at Pemberley since the death of Josie and the subsequent departure for France of Julian Darcy. There appeared, at first, to be no special purpose for the gathering, beyond an understandable desire on the part of the Darcys to re-establish their close relationships within the family, after what had been a period of some turmoil.

The talk at dinner was not all about domestic matters, however, with the financial problems and social unrest in the cities being the chief topics of interest. Fearsome rumours were abroad of the possible collapse of more investment houses and the descent into bankruptcy of many previously thriving businesses, bringing more unemployment and unrest around the nation. Colonel Fitzwilliam railed against the incompetence of the government, and Mr Bingley groaned about the greed of the bankers and stockbrokers. Mr Darcy, for the most part, appeared quite sanguine.

Pemberley had escaped the worst of the gloom, thanks to a good harvest and the investment made by Mr Darcy in Mr Gardiner's successful trading company. This enterprise was now, to all intents and purposes, managed by Caroline Fitzwilliam, with the help of her son David, who had been persuaded by the large parcel of shares left to him by his grandfather to finally abandon dreams of glory with the cavalry and turn his mind to the more practical business of commerce. It appeared from all reports that he, advised by his mother, was managing very well indeed.

Amidst all the congratulations, however, Caroline succeeded in introducing a note of caution, warning everyone to be less complacent.

"While the business is doing well, it will take very little, no more than rumours of a bank collapse, another mutiny in India, or an attack upon one of the British Colonies in Africa or the Far East, to cause a collapse in trade. Much of our trading success depends upon prosperity and peace in the nations with which we do business," she said, and as Cassandra listened in astonishment, she reminded them how the profits of several companies, who had put all their eggs in one basket, had disappeared when the Duchies of Schleswig-Holstein had been annexed by Bismarck.

Cassy had always admired Caroline's knowledge of the world of business and politics, and the obvious confidence with which she held the attention of the men at the table amazed her.

"Even the hint of such a problem is sufficient to create the kind of senseless panic that causes customers to close their order books and put their money back in their wallets," said David, while his proud father nodded sagely. Colonel Fitzwilliam was immensely pleased to see his son so keenly involved in the business. Years of anxiety for his mother, while David had pondered upon a military career, had finally ended. While neither Fitzwilliam nor his wife had tried to change their son's mind, their relief when he did had been immense.

It was at this point that Mr Darcy, who had been listening with interest, intervened to say that this was perhaps an appropriate time to give them all some good news.

He had decided, he said, in view of the prevailing uncertainty in the country and his own inability to travel more often to inspect them, to sell his properties in Wales and reinvest the proceeds in the Camden Park Estate, which had recently come up for private sale.

"And I have since made a gift of the property to my dear daughter Cassandra and her husband, Richard," he said.

Cassandra, who was sitting next to her father, looked across to her husband, who was safely ensconced beside her mother and she could not make out from his expression, whether he had known of this impending announcement or not. For her part, she was completely astonished, for while she had known of her father's intention to purchase the Camden Estate, and had prior warning that he would like them to live there; of his intention to gift the property to them, she had had no indication at all.

She looked up at her father, who had by now proposed a toast to her and her husband, thanking them sincerely for their help and comfort during what had been quite the worst year in a decade or two.

"I can say without the slightest fear of contradiction," he said, placing a hand on his daughter's shoulder, "that without the support of Cassy and Richard, my dear wife and I would have been hard put to survive the tribulations of this Summer past." Cassy touched his hand, as he continued, "And while this is in no way to be regarded as a reward for their efforts, for nothing will ever repay their kindness, affection, and sheer hard work, it certainly is a token of our love and gratitude."

Looking directly at Cassy, he added, gently, "I know my daughter is disinclined to move to live there at present; she has an understandable attachment to her own beautiful home, but I hope that one day in the future, while I am still here to see her, she will decide that Camden Park is a worthy home, of which I know she will make a charming mistress. Meanwhile, it is theirs to do with as they choose."

By this time, Cassandra could not hold back her tears and rose to embrace her father and thank him, to applause from around the table.

But, as she sat down, Mr Darcy continued.

He had more to reveal and his next announcement astonished them all, well, maybe all but one or two of them. Reminding his family that young Anthony was now the legal heir to Pemberley, he pointed to the obvious difficulties associated with a very young person inheriting an estate.

"Even if Anthony were to be fourteen or sixteen years old, should I live that long, he would need to have competent and trustworthy advisers to manage it for him. You are all aware that Cassy, as Anthony's legal guardian, has been given this onerous responsibility and we feel it is unfair that she should have to carry the burden unaided. While Mr Grantham handles the routine business of the estate very well, there are matters, which require greater family involvement, chiefly those relating to tenants' concerns and legal matters.

"There is also the investment in the Commercial Trading Company, which has to be handled with discretion and care. My wife and I have discussed these matters at length and I have decided to offer the position to a person, who will, I think, have Cassy's complete confidence and approval."

Turning at this point to look at Darcy Gardiner, he continued, "My young grandson Darcy has agreed to accept the position and will commence his training for the job, immediately."

"Darcy!" a chorus of voices echoed Lizzie's as they turned to the young man seated to the left of his grandfather and delighted applause broke out around the table.

Young Darcy stood up and took a bow, embraced his grandfather, his mother, his father and grandmother, and proceeded to do the same to all his relatives, probably because he had no idea what else to do. As everyone around her looked delighted, Cassandra struggled to contain her feelings.

This had come as a complete surprise; neither she nor Richard had guessed that her father would choose Darcy. Cassy was proud of her son. He had proved in the last few weeks that he was possessed of sound common sense as well as compassion; she prayed he would also have sufficient endurance to stay the course. The management of an estate as large and as complex as Pemberley was no sinecure.

Clearly, Mr Darcy had observed his grandson and spoken seriously with him before offering him the position. Cassy was certain it would not have been lightly done. Her father was too careful of the reputation of his estate to act upon a whim.

The ladies withdrew soon afterwards and, in the drawing room, where they partook of coffee, tea, and sweets, their talk was all about young Darcy Gardiner. He was, they all agreed, a fine young man, handsome like his parents, entirely agreeable in his manners, well educated, and sensible; they were convinced he would make an excellent job of managing Pemberley.

But his mother, ever vigilant, unwilling to have her children overburdened with superlatives and unrealistic expectations, was cautious. She urged her family to remember that Darcy had no experience in the management of an estate; he would need to learn everything, and there may be some difficult lessons along the way. Not too many of the others were as concerned.

In an age when many young men seemed to prefer to fritter away their time at gaming tables, theatres, and clubs of dubious repute, the Gardiners had been fortunate in both their sons. While Edward was such a model of professional practice and rectitude as to be almost dull, Darcy, in spite of the opportunities for lax living that London provided for a good-looking young man with an adequate allowance and pleasing ways, had retained an enviable reputation for honour and integrity. His parents had occasionally been concerned that he might not be working very hard at his studies, but never had they had any reason to question his conduct.

On returning home and retiring to their bedroom, Cassandra, though tired, was feeling elated. She could find no logical explanation for her mood, except that it had been one of those very special days when she felt that everyone she loved had been happy and content. Well, not everyone, she thought, recalling her unhappy brother, Julian, in France, alone, immersing himself in his research to blot out the anguish of his loss.

When her husband came to bed, she asked him if he had known of her father's offer to Darcy and whether he approved of it. He told her truthfully that he'd had no inkling of Mr Darcy's plans until they were announced at dinner.

"I was as surprised as the rest of the company, except Darcy and your Mama, of course, they knew all along," he said. "But now it is generally known, there seems to be genuine pleasure and goodwill among the family and I think it seems like a very sound scheme," and then, in a voice that was rather more serious than usual at this time of night, he continued, "I will admit, I have had some concerns, with which I have not wished to trouble you, Cassy, that Darcy was uncertain about his future. I know he is very keen on going into Parliament, but he is very young and may not get endorsement at this stage.

"Moreover, with the Tories in government, I cannot see him wanting to stand, at least until there is some chance of his beloved Mr Gladstone winning an election and becoming Prime Minister. That being the case, I have felt that for most of this year, our son has been somewhat at sea about his future. It is surely time he settled into an occupation."

Cassy confessed that, while she had not been too concerned, she also had noticed her son's interest in standing for Parliament waning in recent times. With the return of the Tories, something of the excitement had gone out of politics for young Darcy.

"In which case, do you believe that Papa's idea of having him manage Pemberley will be beneficial for him at this time?" she asked and Richard replied with undisguised enthusiasm, "Indeed, I do. I have no doubt that is how your father sees it, too. If Darcy does plan to enter Parliament, sometime in the future, he will do his chances of success no harm at all by serving out his time in waiting managing a property like Pemberley.

"It will teach him many skills, especially the ability to see both sides of an argument; he will appreciate the concerns of both landholders and tenant farmers. Better still, it will keep him in contact with the concerns and aspirations of ordinary people, instead of sitting around Westminster merely listening to fine speeches or frequenting bars and coffeehouses."

Clearly Richard was as pleased as her father had been with the situation. His wife had to agree that her husband's arguments were convincing and, though it had never occurred to her as the sort of work Darcy would want to do, she now saw all the good that could come of it.

When, some days later, she wrote to her cousin Emma, telling her the news, she expressed her pleasure in no uncertain terms...

Dearest Emma, I know you will be as happy as we are about this arrange-ment, though perhaps James will miss him at Westminster. He may not have as much time to spare as before, but I do know he is so devoted to Mr Gladstone and the Reform Movement, that it will not be possible to keep him away when the next election comes around.

Meanwhile, I must confess I am looking forward to seeing him at home for more of the time, though as my father has planned it, Darcy will be spending most of his time at Pemberley.

Tonight, however, having set that issue aside, there was yet another matter that needed resolution. Though it was very late, Cassandra decided that she was going to raise the subject. It had been on her mind for a while and she wanted her husband's advice.

"Richard, do you not think, dearest, that we ought, at the least, to visit the Camden Estate? If we do not, Papa may be hurt by our lack of interest in his generous gift," she said, in a complete change of mood that surprised him, following her strong opposition to Mr Darcy's plan.

"Mama has mentioned that they had been to dinner at Camden House, a week before the deal was done, and she thought the recent refurbishments made by Sir Thomas were of the very highest standard, he had clearly spared no expense. Mama said she thought it was a great pity, because he was not going to enjoy it for long, but then, Papa had said, he hoped *we* might do so, one day. Perhaps we should at least pay a visit?" she suggested.

Her husband had been about to extinguish the light, but on hearing her words, stopped and turned to look at her, with a smile.

"Cassy, my love, you must be blessed with second sight. Why, I was going to tell you tomorrow at breakfast; your father has already given me the keys to the house. He told me as we were leaving that he had arranged for the steward and the housekeeper to show us around the property. It being Sunday tomorrow, I thought we might drive over after church, just the two of us in the curricle, and have a guided tour of the estate. How would you like that?" he asked.

Cassandra was pleased beyond measure.

Since her father's announcement, she had begun to feel that she had been rather churlish and ungrateful, like a spoilt child refusing to play with a present because it did not suit her at the time. She was still unsure that she would ever want to move permanently to live at Camden House, but she did not wish to offend her parents, who were clearly overjoyed at being able to gift it to them.

And so it was settled; they were to go to Camden House tomorrow.

Sunday brought one of those Autumn mornings in England that inspire poets and painters to great creative heights. Mild and mellow in every respect, it was the right sort of day to be visiting Camden Park, where the sweetness of nature predominated without and was only enhanced by the art within. Though less than half the size of Pemberley or Chatsworth, the great estates which dominated this part of the county, the Camden Estate occupied one of the prettiest sites in Derbyshire. It lay in a fertile, alluring little dale, at the confluence of the Rivers Derwent and Wye at Rowsley, which then, together, formed the boundary between Camden Park and Pemberley, before flowing through several gorges and woodlands on their way to join the Trent near Derby.

Originally owned as one estate by the two Camden brothers, it had later been divided into the Rushmore Farm and Stud and the Camden Park Estate. While William Camden had taken on Rushmore Farm from his father and subsequently sold it to Mr Carr, Sir Thomas and his second wife had been childless and the unentailed estate was sold by private agreement to Mr Darcy, who was well aware that his long friendship with Sir Thomas had helped him obtain a most valuable property.

Aside from its worth as an asset, however, it had a singular charm, which could not fail to captivate anyone with an appreciation of such places. Cassandra Gardiner was no exception; she was enchanted.

The housekeeper, Mrs Wills, was a youngish woman, not much older than Cassy herself. She was the daughter of Mrs Bolton, who had held the position for thirty years. Together with the steward, she showed the new owners around every part of the property they wished to see. And of everything she saw, Cassy had to approve, for it was all so pleasing, so tastefully appointed and well cared for. Every aspect of Camden Park seemed intended to increase her pleasure. Not only did its grounds, with the vistas of mountains in the distance, and its delightful park and rose garden bring joy to her heart, the house itself was a treasure.

Nowhere as magnificent as Pemberley in scale, it was everywhere as pleasurable to the discerning eye, with windows affording superb views of the grounds and the surrounding countryside and each well-proportioned, handsome room, elegantly furnished with appropriate pieces and accessories. Nothing grated, everything was in harmony.

The housekeeper had informed them that the late Lady Camden had been both a painter and a pianist of some proficiency, with a great love of the fine arts, which fact was demonstrated, when on going upstairs, they were admitted to the music room. As Cassy entered the room, it took her breath away. Nowhere, not even at Pemberley, was there such an exquisite room, where the beauty of both nature and art had been so sweetly married.

High, wide windows provided a panoramic vision of the grounds, sweeping out over the park to the river and the hills in the distance. A most felicitous setting for the handsome Regency furniture, the fine collection of art works and the pièce de résistance—an elegant instrument—an Italian pianoforte, indeed, everything was as close to perfection as one could hope to see.

Cassy was overwhelmed. She was standing beside the piano, looking out across the lawn to the rose garden, when Mrs Wills excused herself, leaving them to enjoy the ambience of the room for a while. "Oh Richard, I love this room," she said softly, turning to her husband. "This house is more beautiful than I ever imagined it would be." Standing behind her, he asked, "Do you believe you could love it well enough to want to live here one day?"

She answered slowly and deliberately, "I have to confess, I am not as much against the idea as I was; much as I love our home, this is the most perfect place. How *did* Sir Thomas have the heart to part with it? However, I still feel somewhat daunted by the prospect of making it our home; it seems almost too grand for me."

Richard moved closer, so that only she would hear his words, and said, "Too grand for *Lady* Cassandra Gardiner?"

"What?" Cassy gasped and tried to turn to face her husband, but his arm was around her waist and he was holding her so close, she could not look up at his face. Looking out at the garden, she spoke in a whisper, "What did you say? Are you teasing me again? Please tell me, Richard, what did you mean?"

"I meant just what I said, no more, no less."

"And does that mean you have been offered a..."

He put his hand very lightly over her mouth. "Sssh, my darling, we do not want the whole village talking about it, before I receive the citation, do we?"

At last, he relaxed his hold and she succeeded in turning her head to look at him and, seeing his face and the smile that she knew so well, she believed he was serious. He had been offered a knighthood.

"And have you accepted?" she whispered.

"I have, just yesterday."

This time he could not stop her; as she turned around and kissed him, he held her in a close embrace, knowing how deeply happy she would be for him, having supported him in his work over many years. For Cassy, this was an undreamed-of honour; yet, one she knew her husband deserved in full measure.

Mrs Wills, returning just moments after they had drawn apart, invited them to return downstairs and take tea. As they followed her, they saw, from the window, Mr Darcy and his two grandsons, James and Anthony, alighting from a carriage that had drawn up at the entrance.

Cassy held tight to her husband's hand and asked, "Does Papa know?"

"I intend to give him the news tonight," Richard replied, and Cassy said, quietly but in a firm voice, "Well then, Sir Richard, it will be a night for good news, I think. I am sure Papa will be even happier to learn that I shall look forward very much to being the Mistress of Camden Park in the New Year."

One glance at her husband's face was sufficient to let her see how pleased he was.

As they descended the stairs, they saw Mr Darcy and the boys enter the hall. There never was a prouder grandfather.

"Ah," he said, catching sight of them on the stairs, "there you are, I *am* glad to find you still here; it saves me driving to Matlock. Cassy, your Mama has some good news about a particular piece of material you were seeking, was it French lace? I believe it has to do with Lizzie's wedding gown." And as Cassy nodded eagerly, he said, "Well, she would like you to come over today and see if it is what you want. And when you do, seeing you must eat somewhere, why do you not stay to dinner?"

It was agreed and, as they were going out to their respective vehicles, after taking tea in the comfortable and well-appointed parlour, Cassy and Richard thanked both the steward and the housekeeper.

Mr Darcy was eager to know their opinion of the property.

"Well, what do you think, Cassy? Do you like it? Is it not a gem of a house?" he asked.

"Oh indeed it is, Papa, it certainly is and so tastefully furnished, all those handsome accessories, those beautiful works of art, it is perfect," she replied, not even trying to hide the enthusiasm in her voice.

Her father seemed very pleased as he lifted young Anthony into their carriage. James had scrambled in already. They drove away, leaving Mr Darcy standing beside his carriage, smiling. Something in his daughter's voice and demeanour had told him she was enchanted by Camden House, as he had thought she would be. He thought it boded well for his plan.

That evening, they met again. This time it was just the four of them, for Jessica Courtney had gone to visit her grandmother, Mrs Gardiner. There could be no better opportunity and Elizabeth, who had been told by her husband of his meeting with them, waited only until the servants had left the room, to ask the inevitable question, "Well, what is your verdict on Camden House, Cassy?"

Both Richard and Cassy could not speak highly enough of its situation, the grounds, the handsome building with its elegantly furnished rooms; they had loved it, they said. Mr and Mrs Darcy listened with interest and then Darcy asked, "And what will you do with it? Do you propose to let it? You will need to advise Mrs Wills and Mr Adams, because if you intend to lease it, the tenants may not require the services of all the present staff."

Mr Darcy looked as though he was about to go on in the same vein, but Cassy stopped him in mid-sentence.

It was time, she had decided, to break the news. "We do not intend to lease Camden Park to anyone, Papa, it would be a travesty to do so. No, I think, after Lizzie's wedding is over, we will arrange to move to Camden House and I think we will let Mr Adams and Mrs Wills know soon enough that we hope very much that they will stay on."

And seeing the mixture of astonishment and sheer delight with which her parents greeted her words, Cassy said quietly, "And before you ask why I have changed my mind, apart from the undeniable appeal of the place, I think you should hear Richard's news."

Mr and Mrs Darcy turned to their son-in-law, still unsure of the reasons behind Cassy's change of heart. On the last occasion on which the matter had been mentioned, they had been left in no doubt; she was implacably opposed to leaving her present home for Camden Park. Her father remembered it well. Richard, who was pouring himself a glass of port, put down the decanter with studied care, seated himself on the sofa beside his wife, close enough to where Mr Darcy and Elizabeth sat, beside the fire, and in a quiet, measured voice told them the news. He had been asked if he would accept a knighthood, for services to medical research, and he had accepted, he told them; adding that his assistant, Dr Matthew Ward, would also be honoured by the Queen, for his work on the same project.

This information, he insisted, was totally confidential, until he received the letter containing the citation and he begged them not to speak of it to anyone, no matter how dear or close.

"What? May I not tell my sister Jane? After all Matthew Ward is her son-in-law," asked Elizabeth, who had few secrets from Mrs Bingley.

"No please, Mrs Darcy, it would be considered a grave breach of protocol, if it were to come out before the official announcement is made."

Having obtained the promise, Richard could permit them to congratulate him and drink a toast to his achievement. His satisfaction grew from the fact that, besides being honoured with a knighthood, his work would save the lives of thousands of patients all over Britain.

Cassy was so proud of him, she felt her heart could not cope with any more excitement and was therefore glad, when they reached home, to find that the rest of the household had gone to bed.

It seemed Richard was likewise pleased to have her to himself. It had been a very special evening and they wanted to savour its pleasure together. It was not lost upon either of them that the decisions to accept the knighthood and move to Camden House implied the acceptance of profound change in their lives. Tonight, however, there were no reservations and no regrets, only deep love and contentment.

Back at Pemberley, Mr Darcy and his wife could speak of nothing else that night. Sleep had fled, leaving them wide awake, as they talked of their son-in-law's success and their beloved daughter's position as Lady Cassandra Gardiner of Camden Park.

"How very felicitously it has all come together for them," Elizabeth remarked, as she put away her jewellery and prepared for bed, to which her husband added that it could not have come at a more opportune moment in their lives.

"It is entirely appropriate that they should move to a more spacious residence, now that Richard will be expected to maintain a greater public presence in the community," he said, pointing out that, "Titles and honours imply responsibility as well as distinction and, in Richard's case, the value of his work is such, he is certain to be in demand among scholars and practitioners alike."

Elizabeth agreed. She was equally pleased with the prospect of having her daughter close by and her grandchildren so easily accessible to her.

"Truly, I cannot, however hard I try, think of a more deserving couple. I do not say this because Cassy is our daughter..." she went on, but Mr Darcy, turning to her with a smile, said, "Oh come, Lizzie my dear, of course we are proud of Cassy and glad for her. Why should you not favour your daughter when she deserves it? Yet, I must confess that, like you, I can think of no two persons more deserving of good fortune and I am immensely pleased for them."

He sighed and, when she looked up anxiously, he shook his head.

"No, my dear, I am not unhappy tonight. It has been a singularly fine and satisfying day," he said, and his wife knew he was feeling happier than he had been all year.

※

As if these were insufficient good tidings, the post, on the morrow, brought more. Jessica Courtney, returning early from Lambton, found a letter waiting for her, which she read eagerly and, expressing great satisfaction with its contents, passed over to Elizabeth after breakfast.

It came from her mother, Mrs Emily Courtney, written from Oxford and read:

My dearest Jessie,

It is late and I am exceedingly weary after a very long day, but I cannot lie down to sleep without telling you all the news we have heard today.

There has been such good news, two lots of it at least, which I know you will want to hear at the earliest.

First, your dear cousin Amy is to have a child in the Spring. She and Frank Grantley are so happy, it is impossible for them to stop smiling.

We went to hear him take the evening service at the church yesterday and he could not keep from smiling, as if he had some special secret happiness, which of course he had, though none of the congregation would have known.

Amy says she feels well and I hope she continues so. She is very slight and not as strong as she should be, which concerns me a little. I believe she has already written to her Mama and Colonel Fitzwilliam, to give them the good news.

Second, and even more exciting for all of us, is the news that your brother William is invited to be one of the organists at the Cathedral during the Festival of the Twelve Days of Christmas.

All the others are famous men, with many years' experience, but the bishop was here this week and, having heard William play, has personally invited him to participate. It is a most significant honour, though William is, as usual, being very modest about it all. Everyone else, including Dr Grantley and his wife Georgiana, are convinced it is a great compliment, indeed.

I do hope we shall have the chance to see him play; I cannot, of course, be sure what your father will do, it being right in the middle of Christmas, but we shall see. I would give anything to be present.

Please, dear Jessie, tell your Aunt Elizabeth and Mr Darcy. It is due in no small measure to the generous assistance they provided to William when he was a student. Without their help, he could not have attained the level of proficiency nor the success he now has...

Mr Darcy and Elizabeth knew exactly what Emily meant.

William Courtney had shown, at an early age, signs of the same bright talent that had set their son William apart, talent which may well have taken him to the same heights of success, had he lived.

It was from the William Darcy Memorial Trust that funds had been made available for young William Courtney to pursue his musical studies and for that his parents were very grateful.

For Elizabeth and Darcy, however, it was not their gratitude that mattered, but the happiness that the fulfillment of William's dreams had brought to their family. For them, there would always be some pain associated with each of William's achievements, reminding them of their own terrible loss. Yet, never even for a single moment, did they begrudge William Courtney and his family the undiluted joy of his success.

The length of French lace Elizabeth had obtained was, indeed, precisely what Cassandra had sought for her daughter's wedding gown. No sooner had a design been decided upon, the dressmaker, who had made the gown for the daughter of the Duke of Devon, was summoned to Pemberley and the making of Lizzie's gown entrusted to her.

Elizabeth was determined her granddaughter was going to have the best.

Other preparations were afoot all around the estate, the staff pressed into service for this important occasion. Being the first of the Darcys' grandchildren to be wed, there was no question but that she was to be married in the Pemberley Parish Church and no trouble would be spared to ensure the success of the function.

※

As Autumn drew to a close, on a day that was at first overcast and caused her mother to say an extra prayer to the Almighty for fine weather, Lizzie Gardiner prepared to be married. Nothing, certainly not the threat of rain, could dull the promise of this day for Lizzie.

She knew in her heart that she was deeply loved; never had she known the kind of closeness to another person that she felt with her Mr Carr. Young and romantic, though with a good sprinkling of common sense, she shared her mother's capacity for strong feelings, deep dedication, and hard work, all traits that would enhance the quality of her marriage.

Thinking of what this marriage might bring her, apart from the bliss of being with the man she had grown to love so well, she was sensible of the fact that his knowledge and experience of the world would help her grow in maturity and understanding. She knew, because he had told her so, that she had brought sparkle and delight into his hitherto mundane life. Of their capacity to make each other happy, she was more certain than she had been of any other matter in her young life. As the day wore on and the mist that had swathed the hills behind Pemberley lifted, Lizzie knew it was going to be a day she would always treasure.

Though she could have asked for little more to add to her happiness, one thing had happened, which increased her joy immensely. On the previous morning, a note had arrived for her parents, from her Uncle Julian Darcy.

He wrote:

My dearest Cassy and Richard,
    I had hoped to see you somewhat earlier than today and so did not

deem it necessary to write that I was coming, but matters outside my control have delayed my arrival in England, to the extent that I shall only be in Derbyshire on the Friday night before the wedding. I am writing to reassure you and my dear niece that I shall be there to see her wed. Please tell little Lizzie that I could not have stayed away.

I shall see you all at Pemberley on Saturday morning. I cannot tell you how much I have looked forward to this happy day.

Yours etc.,

Julian Darcy.

No one in her family, except her husband, knew that Cassandra had taken the letter to her parents at Pemberley.

Their son was returning from France for Lizzie's wedding and though it appeared he had hoped to surprise them, there was no possibility of Cassy keeping such a piece of news from her mother and father.

When she saw their faces on reading the letter, she was convinced she had been right to come. The tears in Elizabeth's eyes and the pleasure upon her father's face were evidence enough for Cassy. She needed no approbation, happy indeed to have been the bearer of such good tidings.

As for young Lizzie, she was having her hair arranged, on the morning of her wedding day, with her maid still fussing over her, when there was a gentle knock on the door and her father came in with Julian.

Within seconds, uncle and niece had embraced, with no thought for his well-pressed coat or her fine French lace gown, both of which were in grave danger of being crumpled. Her maid cried out to her mistress to mind her gown and urged care with her hair.

Julian released her and stepped back to look at his niece. "Why Lizzie, you have turned into such a beauty!" he declared, as she turned around for him and showed off her gown. "I never noticed until today how lovely you were. I daresay it comes of having my nose buried in a book and my eyes squinting down a microscope, eh?" he remarked in the self-deprecating way that was so typical of him.

Lizzie coloured and laughed lightly to hide her blushes. "You look very well yourself, Uncle," she said, "and I must thank you with all my heart for coming today, all the way from France. When we had not heard, we feared we may not see you."

Julian shook his head and took her hand in his.

"After all you did for me, dear Lizzie, I could not have stayed away. I had to come, if only to show you how much I did appreciate those days you spent with us..." His voice trailed away sadly, but then, he smiled and leaning forward, kissed her gently on the cheek, and said softly, "You are indeed your mother's daughter, my dear; your Mr Carr is a very fortunate man."

As he left the room, Cassandra met him on the landing; the mother of the bride was busier than ever, unable to leave it all to the very efficient staff at Pemberley, as her father and her husband had advised her to do. As brother and sister embraced, this time Julian carefully avoided crushing the beautiful corsage she wore, and she said, "Julian, I am so happy you could come. I had hoped and prayed, but I was never certain."

Once again he reiterated his words to Lizzie, "How could I not come, Cassy? Not after all you and Richard and, above all, young Lizzie did for us. I had to come."

"Have you seen Anthony?" she asked, and when he said he had not, "You will be surprised at how much he has grown these last few months. I shall take you to see him, but you must go to Papa and Mama first."

"Will you go with me, Cassy? I fear my sudden appearance may upset Mama." He was plainly nervous and concerned.

But Cassy took his arm, reassuring him, "Have no fear on that score; I shall certainly go with you, but they are expecting you. Like you, I feared the surprise may have been too much for Mama and I did not wish her to weep on Lizzie's big day, so I brought your letter over to them; Julian, you should have seen their happiness."

As her husband waited for her at the top of the stairs, Cassy took her brother to her parents' apartments.

Richard knew how eagerly she had anticipated this moment. It had almost overshadowed the joy of Lizzie's wedding.

"Of course Lizzie's wedding is important, but I have no fears for her today; however, had Julian not arrived, as has happened on some occasions, his absence would have meant bitter disappointment for all of us, including Lizzie and especially for Papa and Mama," she had explained, reasonably. "Now he is here, it will serve to double the joy of her wedding day. Do you not agree, my love?"

And of course, he did.

Enhancing his happiness, as he watched her, was the memory of their own wedding day at Pemberley several years ago. Having had to wait, through force of circumstances, an inordinately long time for each other, their marriage had brought them such deep and abiding joy as neither had believed possible. So many years later, the sight of her could lift his spirits and make his heart race with love for her. They shared a very special intimacy.

When Cassy returned, having left Julian with their parents, she smiled as she approached; he held out his hand to her and drew her to his side as they waited for the bride.

No one present could have failed to perceive the happiness that welled up and spilled over the gathered family and their friends, as they entered the church, led by Mr and Mrs Darcy, with Julian and Cassy beside them.

William Courtney was there to play the organ and the choir of Pemberley children rose to sing, as Lizzie Gardiner arrived with her father at the church door.

As heads turned to see the bride, Cassandra could not bear to look, for fear that she would weep; yet she wished with all her heart that this wedding would be, as her own had been those many years ago, the beginning of a good marriage, conceived in love, nurtured with trust, and sustained with strength.

If little Lizzie's marriage could only be half as felicitous as her mother's had been all these years, Cassy knew her daughter would be a very happy woman indeed.

END OF PART THREE

An Epilogue...

THE WEDDING WAS OVER and, though there weren't many rose petals available this late in the year, there was no dearth of affection and goodwill for the couple who left Pemberley on their wedding journey.

It was generally thought that they were bound for the South coast. Some who claimed to know said Bournemouth and others whispered that it was Paris; however, unbeknownst to any but their closest confidantes, Mr Carr and his bride had planned to spend their wedding night, not at some hostelry en route to the South coast, but at Rushmore Farm.

The plan had come about simply and without fuss, when the couple had been walking in the woods around the farm. As they remembered her first visit to his home, when she had been enchanted by the woods and water meadows and had begged him never to fell the trees or drain the meadows, Mr Carr had asked with some trepidation, "Seeing how much we love this place, my dearest, how would it be if we were to spend the night of our wedding here, in our own home?"

Aware of her youth and gentle upbringing, he had expected some reluctance, a little shyness perhaps, and was concerned that she might think he was being too bold. To his delight, her response surprised him with its warmth and candour. After taking very little time to consider the implications of his suggestion, Lizzie had said quietly, "I must confess that I cannot think of any place I would like better to spend our wedding night," and added quickly, "It would surely be a much happier choice than some hotel, would it not?"

He could not agree more and they confirmed their compliance on this intimate matter with a kiss that expressed unreservedly the depth of their love. In the course of a year, their relationship had deepened from an amiable friendship to the realization that life apart from one another would be insupportable. Their wedding was only the beginning; they looked forward to their life together with hope of the deepest felicity.

And there, we need not trespass; for it is neither necessary nor seemly for prying eyes to follow them. Such tender expressions of love as they would surely indulge in are too intimate and personal to warrant intrusion; it would be considered so grave a breach of decorum and good manners, as to be very vulgar indeed.

Imagination, on the other hand, is free and unfettered; discreet and sensitive readers may use their own as they wish. Suffice it to say, there was no lack of ardent love between this happy pair, nor was there any reluctance to express it.

~

After the wedding, Cassandra and Richard Gardiner stayed over at Pemberley, as did Julian Darcy. There was no mistaking the satisfaction this brought Mr and Mrs Darcy, whose distress at losing their daughter-in-law had been exacerbated by their son's decision to renounce his inheritance and continue his work in France.

Their ability to understand Julian's anguish and assuage their own had been greatly assisted by their daughter's love, as well as the sensibility and support of their son-in-law, Dr Gardiner. On this, the happiest day the family had known in many months, to have them all together at Pemberley was a very particular pleasure and each of the members of the company gathered there knew it well.

For the first time since his wife's tragic involvement with Messrs Barrett and Jones, leading to her untimely death, Julian Darcy appeared to be at peace with himself. Clearly happy at being able to participate in the celebration of his niece's wedding, and with much satisfaction in his work in bacteriological research, he seemed less haunted by his past inadequacies.

He had, for some years, been secretive and uncommunicative, using the confidentiality of his work as an excuse for saying very little about his own plans to even the closest members of his family. This time, however, both Richard and Mr Darcy found Julian more than willing to talk at length about his research and even, on occasion, to disclose some of his hopes for the future.

"I have been invited by two of my French colleagues to travel with them to the French colonies in Africa and the Pacific, where there is much work yet to be done in the field of bacterial infections. Large numbers of children die of respiratory or intestinal diseases and research into their prevention could help save many lives. I believe the French government is prepared to fund our work in the colonies, and it would be an excellent opportunity for me to do what I can to help these unfortunate people," he explained.

His mother, hearing some of the conversation, appeared perturbed at the prospect of her son journeying in parts of the world where he was bound to be at greater risk than if he had remained in England or even in France. But with Cassy at her side to blunt the edge of her concerns, Elizabeth was wise enough to make no protest, content to wait until she could learn more from Mr Darcy or Julian himself.

She had been delighted to discover, earlier in the day, that he planned to remain at Pemberley a fortnight, during which time he hoped to spend time with his parents and his young son. "I think Richard and Cassy have done wonders for Anthony," he had said, and as they talked together, there was much to console his mother in his gentle and amiable manner. Elizabeth was pleased by his expressions of concern for her and his father. Perhaps, she thought, Julian has found a way to overcome his guilt through his work.

When she spoke of this to her husband later that night, Mr Darcy agreed, but added that it was even more probable that their son had finally discovered his true vocation.

"It is possible, my dear Lizzie, that Julian does not see the management of a family estate as his role in life. I do not mean by this to suggest that he belittles it or that he thinks it is an unworthy occupation, but Julian has always looked beyond Pemberley for his place in the world and, perhaps, he has found it, at last," said Mr Darcy.

"Like Richard, he is dedicated to the prevention of disease and the reduction of human suffering; the difference—and in this we and Cassy are particularly fortunate—is that Richard is concerned with the application of his research to hospitals and patients in England, whereas Julian looks further afield and, seeing much suffering elsewhere, feels he must go where he is needed."

"You speak almost in terms that would describe a missionary," said Elizabeth, her anxious eyes searching her husband's face for reassurance that her son would be safe.

But Mr Darcy could give her no such comfort. He knew only too well the risks that attend those who would travel to distant lands.

Tales told of men who had ventured to places like Africa and South America were legion and yet, knowing her fears, he said gently, "Indeed I do, my love, and how well you have understood my meaning. In time, Julian will be blessed with far greater contentment than any English landlord can hope to achieve. For while we may care for those who live and work upon our estates, we take few risks, other than those of a commercial nature, and none of us are called upon to imperil our lives in doing so. Men like Julian do just that, not for the money or the glory, but for the much greater satisfaction of easing the burden of human suffering. It is a noble enterprise, Lizzie, we must be proud of him and give him every encouragement."

Elizabeth was a little astonished at the passion with which her husband spoke, until he revealed that Julian had explained to him the extent of the misery that afflicted vast populations in the colonies, who had no access at all to any kind of medical treatment, relying for the most part on primitive remedies with often fatal consequences.

"So you see, my dear, Julian knows he must go," he said, and Elizabeth could not but agree, even though in her heart she was still fearful.

She could only hope and pray her son would be safe.

A similar conversation was taking place between Cassandra and her husband, as they prepared for bed, on a day filled with many delights. There was, however, but one difference. Cassy had already spoken with her brother and was well prepared for the news that he was about to undertake a research project in Equatorial Africa. Not only was she aware of his plans, she had encouraged him. Richard had been surprised; even though he knew her strong commitment to his own work, he had half expected her to express some reservations, particularly with regard to the boy Julian was leaving in her care; he had confessed that he'd had doubts himself.

He knew well that Cassy was already hard pressed with the duties she was committed to at Pemberley and, after Lizzie's wedding, doubtless Laura Ann, bereft of her older sister, would depend upon her mother to a far greater degree. Richard could not help but wonder at the wisdom of Julian's decision to leave for Africa, placing all the responsibility for his son upon Cassy.

But it seemed her belief in the value of her brother's work and his new sense of vocation had overwhelmed any reservations she may have had. "I can see how much it means to him, and while it would have been good for Anthony to have his father here, there will be much greater satisfaction for him, when he is grown up, to learn that his father is a man with an unselfish concern for humanity," she said, brushing her hair.

Richard understood but was a little surprised by her reasoning.

"Do you not mind, my love, that during all of the difficult years ahead, it will be you who must care for the boy, teach him, encourage and commend him, be an example to him and comfort him when he is distressed, whilst his father is half a world away?"

Cassandra smiled as she braided and tied her hair with a ribbon.

"Why should I mind, Richard? It may well be hard work, but we have brought up five of our own and Anthony is no different. Indeed, he is already proving to be a salutary influence on James, who might otherwise have been spoilt by too much attention. If, by my efforts, he can grow up as well as our children have, it will be reward enough. Besides," she added, with a definite twinkle in her eye and a note of laughter in her voice, "there will be the added joy of knowing, when my brother is honoured for his services to mankind, that I helped him attain that distinction, as in another instance somewhat closer to home!"

Her husband, in whose estimation Cassy could rise no higher, was certainly not about to deny her this satisfaction, even though he had his doubts about the selflessness of his young brother-in-law. There was no need to spoil what had been a particularly delightful day with argument.

Remaining discreetly silent on the matter, he waited for her to come to bed. When she did, it was to reaffirm the love that had been the bedrock of all they had achieved in their deeply happy marriage.

❧

On the morrow, Richard, Cassandra, and their younger children returned home to Matlock, there to begin the arduous task of moving their household to Camden Park in the New Year. It was in the midst of organising the vast array of tasks that this complex enterprise demanded that Cassy, sitting with Laura Ann in the nursery trying to decide which, of a plethora of items, they would take with them and which they would leave behind, was interrupted by her son James, who raced into the room.

"Mama, Mama," he called excitedly, "it's Margaret, Margaret is here!"

James was so excited he kept jumping up and down in front of his mother. She knew that both boys had been very fond of Margaret Baines, but since the girl had returned to her mother, following the end of the inquest into the death of Mr Jones, they'd had no word from her.

Cassy had been too busy to make enquiries and, having heard from one of the maids who had met Margaret in the village that she had seemed very well, it had been generally assumed that the girl had sought employment elsewhere. Cassy went to the window and, looking out, saw Margaret Baines playing with Anthony on the front lawn.

"Laura dear, do go down and take Margaret into the kitchen and ask Cook to give her some tea. She must have walked up from the village and is probably tired. When she has finished, you can bring her upstairs to me. I must get on with this work or I shall never have it done in time." Laura went, followed by James, and no more was heard for a while.

Some time later, there was a hesitant knock on the door and Margaret Baines came into the room. She looked fresher and healthier than she had been before and was neatly and demurely dressed as always. In her hand, she had a pot of lavender, which she placed on the windowsill.

"It's from my mother's garden, ma'am," she said and stood a little nervously by a table beside the window, while Cassy thanked her and continued to fold and put away items of linen and clothing to be sent to the church for distribution to the poor.

After a few minutes, during which time, Cassy asked after her health and that of her mother, it became quite plain that Margaret wished to speak of something particular. It was equally obvious that she was either fearful or embarrassed about it and was finding it very difficult to open the conversation on the subject.

Seeking, therefore, to ease the girl's discomfort, Cassandra asked, "I cannot believe you are here only to bring me that pot of lavender, Margaret, pretty though it is; so why do you not tell me what it is you have come for? Did you want your old job back?"

Before Cassy could begin to explain that since they were moving to Camden Park, they were not hiring any servants at this time, Margaret spoke, quickly and a little breathlessly, "Oh no, ma'am, that is not it at all, but I do have something to tell you, ma'am, and my mother says it is only right I should tell you myself."

Cassy looked up from her task and saw that the girl was pink with embarrassment; she could not think why. "Margaret, what is it? Surely, you cannot have got yourself into more trouble?"

For one dreadful moment, she feared the worst, yet Margaret did not appear at all guilty or concerned, except she had gone quite red in the face. "Oh no, ma'am," she cried again, "indeed, I have not, but I do have something to tell you."

"Well, so you keep saying; now come on, Margaret, do tell me, or I shall begin to wonder what on earth you have done."

This time, Margaret swallowed hard, as if steeling herself to come to the point. When she spoke, her voice was low but firm. "Yes ma'am, I am to marry Mr John Archer, ma'am."

"What? Mr Archer?" Cassy was astounded. "Margaret have you thought clearly about what you are doing? I thought you hated the man."

"Oh no, ma'am," said the girl for the third time, "I never hated him though I was afraid of him. I did not know how he felt about me, but during the last month, he has called on my mother and spoken with me and he has asked me to marry him, ma'am."

"And does he love you?" Cassy asked, knowing Margaret was young and, like most girls of her age, inclined to be something of a romantic.

"Oh yes, ma'am," she said, for a change, her eyes shining and her face wreathed in smiles, "he says he does, he has always loved me, like he told the coroner. Oh ma'am, no other man has looked at me as he does, with so much feeling, and no man has said out loud in front of everyone that he has loved me for years and years and wants to marry me."

"Do you trust him?" Cassy asked, determined to discover the source of this sudden attachment. Margaret was adamant. "I do, ma'am. No other man has put his life at risk to save me as he did; I must believe he loves me, as he says."

Cassandra did not know quite how to respond to this passionate recital.

Quite clearly, Mr Archer had converted Margaret's youthful fears into love, for it now appeared that she was convinced she would be both secure and happy with him.

As she listened, increasingly amazed, Margaret revealed that they intended to marry, soon after Christmas, and leave Derbyshire for Manchester, where Archer had obtained work. There, he apparently believed, he could avoid the stigma of his involvement, however unwittingly, in the death of Mr Jones.

Practical concerns were uppermost in Cassy's mind, when she asked, "And what will he do? Where will you live?"

Margaret's answer was precise. "Mr Archer has some savings, ma'am, and having worked for two gentlemen in London, he has good references, which have helped him secure a position in a gentleman's household, where he has obtained work for me, too, but only as a kitchen maid, at first," she explained.

It certainly seemed like sound common sense and Cassy wished the girl well, advising her to take great care in all her dealings with people.

She was a simple country girl and there were pitfalls aplenty for an impressionable young person in places like Manchester and the households of gentlemen, she warned. Having given her a gift of some linen and two pounds towards her wedding expenses, she urged her to write. "You must keep me informed of how you get on, Margaret; if you are sensible and work hard, I am sure you will not remain a kitchen maid for long. When you do return to Derbyshire, I hope you will come and visit. Of course, you know, we shall have moved to Camden Park by then."

Margaret's eyes filled with tears as she clasped the hands of her mistress, to whom she knew she owed so much, as she took her leave.

"Thank you for all you have done for me, ma'am, and Dr Gardiner and Miss Lizzie, too. I shall miss the children, ma'am, Master James and Master Anthony," she said sobbing and Cassy had to fight back her own tears.

She had never liked John Archer, there was something rather pretentious about him, which made it difficult to like him; yet she could not deny that she had been impressed by his honest admissions to the coroner and no one had doubted his sincerity, when he had confessed to his affection for Margaret, as demonstrated by his attempts to protect her from the advances of the appalling Mr Jones.

They were actions, which may well have earned him a death sentence or a very long stay in prison. Instead they had won him his freedom, and Margaret's gratitude and love.

Cassy was amused by the irony of it all. The man who had been a gentleman's servant had proved to be more of a gentleman, than the man who had claimed the title by birth, wealth, and social status. Perhaps, she thought, as she watched her leave, Margaret was doing the right thing after all. She needed a steadying influence, being still young and impulsive, perhaps John Archer would provide it.

Watching from the window, Cassy saw her say goodbye to the boys, their governess, and Laura Ann. The children were loathe to let her go, clinging to her hand and holding on to her skirt, as she walked with them. Cassy could not help feeling some regret that there had been no possibility of keeping the girl in her service. Now, she was to marry Archer, she would go wherever he went, she thought, sadly.

With a wry smile, she recalled her husband's words on the night after the coroner's inquest. Richard had believed Margaret would indeed be flattered by Archer's open declaration of love. He had been proved right and Cassy looked forward to telling him so.

There were however, other matters at hand and presently, she turned her attention to them. An invitation had arrived from Rebecca Tate, asking her to tea that afternoon. Mrs Tate was soon to join her husband in London, where he had spent most of the last month, prior to leaving for a tour of Europe in the Spring. She did not expect to return to Derbyshire until the following Autumn. Rebecca wrote:

> *Dearest Cassy, I have neither seen nor spoken with you for many months and I long to see you before I leave to join Mr Tate in London. If you will come to tea with me, I shall be so very happy."*

...and Cassy knew she had to go.

Becky Tate had been a friend since childhood and a most valuable ally in a number of causes, besides being Julian's mother-in-law. As girls, and later young women, pressing local councils and Members of Parliament on issues such as education for girls and hospitals for children, they had been as one, working successfully together to improve their community. They'd been a very happy, successful team, but since Josie's death and Julian's departure for France, they had seen little of one another.

The stresses and strains of the previous months had made casual social intercourse difficult, if not impossible.

Some time previously, Cassy had learned from her sister-in-law Emily Courtney, who was very close to Rebecca, that Mr Tate, heartsick with the loss of his favourite child, had immersed himself in his business affairs, leaving his wife to grieve alone. It was well known, Emily had said, that Becky Tate, once a gregarious and sociable woman, with a wide circle of friends and many interests, now hardly went out at all.

Cassy was understandably apprehensive, but steeled herself. She would go, she decided; she could not ignore Becky's appeal.

She need not have feared the encounter; Becky Tate had long wanted to see her friend again, especially since Lizzie's wedding, which she, being in mourning, had not attended.

She greeted Cassandra with genuine warmth. "I am so happy you could come, Cassy," she said, as if she had feared her invitation would not be accepted. So heartfelt was her welcome and so obvious her pleasure, Cassy was immediately glad she had come.

Their conversation was at first slow and confined to those subjects that were always easy to speak of, as they asked after each other's health or their plans for Christmas. Before long, however, it was clear to Cassy that Becky was eager to speak of other, more burdensome matters.

She had spent many agonizing months in contemplation since Josie's death and been riven with guilt and misery. The anguish of losing her only daughter in humiliating circumstances had isolated her from the rest of her family and friends. That she could find no excuse for Josie, nor anyone but her daughter and Mr Barrett to blame, only increased her distress.

Most of these tribulations, she had borne alone.

Her husband, whose indulgence of his beloved child had possibly contributed to Josie's stubborn determination to pursue her literary ambitions against all common sense, had turned almost totally to his work, spending less and less time at home, unwilling to share his own or his wife's grief. Only Emily Courtney, of all her friends, had continued to visit her and understood the extent of her anguish.

As poor Becky Tate poured out her unhappy tale, Cassy, having listened a while, moved to sit beside her on the sofa and put her arms around her friend to comfort her. It was as if she had opened the floodgates; the emotions raw and unchecked, rushed forth, swamping both women in a welter of sobs and words, which neither could stop nor comprehend.

Cassy held her, until she had done with weeping, helped dry her tears, and got her a cup of tea.

"There, you must feel a lot better now," she said. Mrs Tate nodded, gulping down her tea, and then, pressing Cassy's hand, she said, "Bless you, Cassy, it was kind of you to come."

Cassy stayed a while longer, during which time they talked of days past, recalling that they had all come out at the Pemberley Ball, in the Autumn of 1834. Emma Bingley, Cassy Darcy, and Becky Collins had all turned seventeen that year. They had been three vivacious young women and the Pemberley Ball had been given in their honour, by Mr Darcy.

"What a grand ball it was," said Becky. "I remember it as though it were yesterday. Mr Tate and I were not as yet engaged and I, hoping to please him, must have tried on half a dozen gowns before I settled on the one I wore. Your cousin Emma Bingley was by far the most beautiful girl present, but we all knew that young Dr Gardiner had eyes only for you, Cassy," she said, her voice softening with nostalgia, as she added, "What happy days they were, where have they all gone, Cassy?"

Cassy did not need reminding. Her memories of that Autumn were rather different to Becky's, but nonetheless clear.

Perhaps, Becky had forgotten, but it had been on the night of the Pemberley Ball that Richard had proposed; their engagement was announced on the following day, and later on that same fateful day, her young brother William had been killed, changing all their lives forever.

It was a day Cassy would never forget. However, there was no purpose to be served by reminding Becky of it now, she thought; it would only compound her sorrow.

Since that dreadful day, their lives had moved apart for some years, converged for a while when Julian married Josie, and now seemed about to diverge again.

Some time later, Cassy rose to leave, promising before she went that Anthony would come over to spend the day with his grandmother on the morrow. Mrs Tate's pleasure was obvious. Her young grandson was all that remained of Josie.

"Miss Longhurst will bring him to you and he may be excused from lessons, so you can give him his Christmas presents and he may do as he pleases all day long. I think he will enjoy that enormously and I know you will, too," Cassy said as they embraced.

Once again Becky Tate thanked her and expressed the hope that they would meet again soon.

"Emily and you are my only link with the family; I rely on you to write and give me all the news, Cassy, please," she pleaded, and Cassy had to say, "Of course I shall, Becky. You know that."

As Cassy drove away leaving her friend, a lonely figure at the entrance to an empty house, she wondered at the coldness with which fate dealt out a random hand, comprised of blessings and tribulations, with no thought for their consequences, leaving those who held the cards to play them as they saw fit and make what they could of their lives.

Becky Tate had been dealt a dreadful hand so far, thought Cassy, and it seemed so unfair.

Later that week, in a letter to her cousin Emma Wilson, Cassy wrote:

My dear Emma,

You will, I know, be delighted to learn that we have had letters from both Julian and Lizzie this week. They are both well.

Julian seems content to be working hard in Paris and is making preparations to travel to Africa, while Lizzie claims to be "blissfully happy," and her Mr Carr is likewise blessed, we are to understand.

I am very pleased about Julian, about whom we have all been concerned, but since his return for Lizzie's wedding, he seems a changed man. I know he still misses Josie, who would not? She was so full of spirit.

As for my Lizzie, I never would have thought she was the romantic type, yet, improbable as it might seem, here she is declaring that nothing any of us had said had prepared her for the delightful state of matrimony! Neither she nor her beloved Mr Carr can see anything but good in one another! Can one ask for more? I think not!

But my dear Emma, not everything is light and happiness. Having seen poor Becky Tate, whom I visited some days ago, I am filled with feelings of outrage at the unfairness of life. If Becky could have had one wish, it must have been to have her daughter Josie advantageously and happily married. With Julian as a son-in-law, it seemed she had all her wishes come true.

Yet now, Josie is dead and Becky is so alone, it is pitiful. Mr Tate appears to spend very little time with her. Her only consolation is that Anthony is with us and can visit her, or she him, whenever she is in Derbyshire. Dear Emily remains a close friend, of course.

Seeing her unhappy fate, I am so grateful for the happiness we have and yet afraid of what terrors the future may hold. But, as Papa has always said, "It is not the fear of the morrow, but the needs of today that must drive us..." and today, dear Emma, it is absolutely imperative that I complete my packing for our move to Camden Park.

I do look forward very much to your visit in the Spring, before which, of course, we hope also to see you in London at Richard's investiture.

Papa plans a small reception at Portman Place, afterwards. He is so very proud of his son-in-law. I know you and James will be there.

Your loving and devoted cousin,
Cassy Gardiner.

❧

With the return of Mr and Mrs Carr from their extended wedding journey in Ireland, their farm and its famous stud began to hum with activity in the Spring. It attracted the attention of those persons whose interest in horses often far outweighed their common sense, a state confirmed by their willingness to part with vast sums of money for an unproven animal that caught the eye.

It was at one of these yearling sales, on a warm Spring day, that Mr Darcy, seeking to purchase a colt for his grandson and heir, chanced upon a man who had been wandering around the paddock, pad and pencil in hand, sketching the horses. Anthony, who was hanging on his grandfather's arm, was interested and asked if he might have one of the drawings. The ladies, Elizabeth, Cassandra, and Lizzie, watching from the shade of a marquee where tea was being served, held their breath as Mr Darcy approached the itinerant artist. They could hear very little of what was said between the two men, chiefly on account of Anthony chipping in all through their conversation, but it all appeared perfectly amicable. Some money changed hands and Anthony had his drawing, which the artist signed with a flourish, before handing it to the boy. He then appeared to bow and thank Mr Darcy, as they parted.

Later, when they were all at lunch, Mr Darcy commented favourably on the man's work. "He's very deft and gets the spirit of the horse with a few bold strokes," he said, then turning to Mr Carr, asked, "Who is he? Does he live around here? I wonder, is he any good at landscapes? Would he do some sketches of the park and terrace at Pemberley for me, do you think?"

Once again, Elizabeth looked apprehensively across at Cassy, as they waited for Mr Carr to answer. What followed was a quite remarkable exchange.

"The artist," said Mr Carr, "is a Mr Frank Wickham," and despite Mr Darcy's initial look of surprise, he continued, without interruption. "You may recall, sir, he gave some vital evidence in the inquest into the death of the man Jones last year; evidence that helped exonerate an innocent young fellow, Josh Higgins, who looks after my horses."

As Mr Darcy nodded, remembering the incident well, Mr Carr continued, with an innocence based largely upon his ignorance of family history. "Wickham comes from Hertfordshire, but prefers to work in the Midlands and the Lake District. He has taken a cottage on my property for the Summer."

"I see," said Mr Darcy, quietly, and turning to Cassy, asked, "Cassy, is Mr Carr aware that Mr Wickham is your Aunt Lydia's son?"

Cassandra never hesitated, not even for a second. "Yes, Papa, and I believe he is also aware that we have had some problems with Mr Wickham's late father and two of his brothers in the past; but Frank is not like his brothers, Papa. He seems a decent sort of man and leads a very quiet life. Indeed, he has confessed to Darcy that he would like to get away from the rest of his family, which is why he chooses to work in this part of the country," she said, to which information, Lizzie adeptly added her own contribution.

"He has also begun teaching the children at the parish school to draw and paint, in return for the use of the cottage. Mr Carr made an agreement with him and the children at the school are delighted; they have never had such an opportunity before."

Whether it was the fact that Mr Carr had never been privy to the bitter feud between Mr Darcy and his *bête noire* the late George Wickham and therefore spoke without fear or favour, or whether Mr Darcy had decided that forty years was long enough to dull even his righteous wrath, they would never know. Having listened to their explanations, he nodded and shrugged his shoulders, reflecting no doubt upon those other Wickhams, before saying to Mr Carr, "Well, he certainly has a talent and is entitled to make a living. Perhaps, Mr Carr, you would be so good as to ask him to call on me one day next week. He should bring along some of his work; if I am satisfied, I should like to commission a series of sketches of some parts of the grounds and aspects of Pemberley House. We could discuss terms and he could start work as soon as possible."

The relief around the table was palpable.

As young Darcy Gardiner told it afterwards, "It was as though we had all been expecting Grandfather to explode in a fit of rage at the thought of a Wickham in the neighbourhood. But to everyone's amazement, once Mama and Lizzie had explained it all, my grandfather just nodded and looked as if he had never heard of the dreadful George Wickham in his life. He is even ready to commission Frank to do some sketches of the park at Pemberley!"

His brother Edward, who was rarely troubled by such matters, especially now he was a contented, married man, said in a laconic voice, "Perhaps Grandfather has grown weary of the whole thing and would rather forget it. It *was* a long time ago."

Cassy responded immediately. "Your grandfather has certainly not forgotten George Wickham's monstrous conduct, but I think he knows in his heart that it is uncharitable to visit the sins of the guilty upon the innocent.

"Frank Wickham is not responsible for his parents and is entitled to be treated as an individual, not just as the son of Mr Wickham and Aunt Lydia. I believe Papa has decided to do just that. He has no feud with Frank Wickham, who has done none of us any harm; it would be unjust to punish him for his father's misdeeds and we all know that Papa is never unjust to anyone."

Cassy's loyal defence of her father silenced both her sons. Her husband, who had listened without comment, finished his tea, rose, and kissed his wife, before preparing to leave the room.

"I think your mother has had the last word on this matter. I could not agree with her more," he said, and walked with Cassy to the entrance, where the carriage waited to convey him to Derby.

Some days later, Frank Wickham arrived at Pemberley with a folio of his drawings. Cassandra had been invited to assist her father in appraising his work and negotiating his fee; to her great delight, the matter was quite amicably and swiftly settled. Mr Darcy seemed well satisfied with the work presented to him and, for Mr Wickham, the singular honour of working at Pemberley far outweighed the monetary value of his commission. He made it quite clear that he felt very honoured to be asked to do the work. Neither man mentioned the connection between their families.

Over the next few weeks, Frank Wickham worked on his assignment with great zeal, and a series of sketches of the house, the terrace, and features of the park were duly produced. Though not in the same class as the masters of the art, Wickham demonstrated an eye for line and perspective and simplicity of execution that his patron clearly appreciated. Having had the first two or three sketches approved, he was left to complete his commission, which he did to the complete satisfaction of Mr Darcy, his wife and daughter.

Writing to her friend Charlotte Collins, Elizabeth expressed amazement at the ease with which her husband had accepted Mr Frank Wickham:

Irritated and angry as I have often been, with complete justification, at the behaviour of my sister Lydia and her late husband, I have to say, dear Charlotte, I am pleased to see Mr Darcy move to make peace with Frank, their youngest son. Indeed, I can find nothing of either Lydia or Wickham in this young man, who is both talented and modest, a rare combination these days, as I am sure you will agree.

It is partly Cassy's doing, of course, and Mr Carr's. For it was they who made their first meeting possible and what followed thereafter. I know you will not speak of this matter to any one else, Charlotte, for if it were to become generally known and spoken of in Meryton, I have no doubt at all that Lydia will feel it is her right to arrive at Pemberley herself, to view her son's work.

While my dear husband is most appreciative of Frank Wickham's work and speaks well of him, I have no illusions that he will be as charitable towards his mother. I trust you are still well, my dear Charlotte, and look forward to seeing you when we visit Jonathan and Anna in the Summer.

Yours etc...

Elizabeth Darcy.

Postscript...

SPRING HAD BROUGHT SOME significant changes, though many things stayed the same.

The Gardiners, now Sir Richard and Lady Cassandra, with their younger children and young Anthony Darcy, had moved, without mishap or undue fuss, to Camden House, which was soon to become one of the most admired properties in the county. For Cassy, much pleasure was to be derived not only from the elegance of her new home, but from its close proximity to Pemberley and her parents as well as her daughter's home at Rushmore Farm. The distinction bestowed upon her husband by the Queen was but one more element in the sum total of her happiness.

Visiting her parents at Pemberley, Cassandra went upstairs to the library, where she found her father supervising the hanging of the series of sketches, which had been appropriately framed.

After spending some time admiring them and proffering advice on how they might be hung, Cassandra approached her father, to ask, gently, if it were not fitting that the artist be invited to dine at Pemberley.

"I know how you feel about the family, Papa, I understand that the prospect of Aunt Lydia at Pemberley is abhorrent to you and Mama; but, would it not be possible to ask Frank, so he knows that we do not hold his parents' misdemeanours against him?" she pleaded, and her father laughed and put an arm around her.

"My dear Cassy, so you are concerned that Mr Wickham may feel slighted? Well, we cannot have that, can we? Talk to your Mama and, if she agrees, you can send out the invitations. I cannot have you worried about the fellow's tender feelings. Besides," he added almost as an afterthought, "he has done some good work and, like any artist, is entitled to see it in its proper place, is he not?"

Cassy smiled and embraced her father; she had been very confident of his magnanimity.

"Indeed he is, Papa. I knew you would not be unfair to him. Thank you. It is but a small matter for us to ask him to dine at Pemberley, but to a man in Frank Wickham's occupation, where so much depends upon recognition and patronage, a generous gesture of appreciation is far more valuable than a fee," she said, and Mr Darcy could not help being moved by the fervour of her voice.

"Sage words, Cassy. I know I can count on you to remind me of my obligations, if ever your mother should forget. Whatever shall I do without your wise head, my dear?"

Cassy laughed. "Why should you, Papa? I am even closer at hand, now we are neighbours," she said and went to find her mother, whose astonishment at this turn of events rendered her almost speechless.

Never had Elizabeth expected to see the day when Mr Darcy would voluntarily and gladly invite one of "Wickham's boys" to dine at Pemberley. Again she was convinced, as she had written to Charlotte, that it must have been all Cassy's doing.

"I shall never understand how you persuaded your father to do this, Cassy," she declared, as they went together to find Mrs Grantham and make arrangements for the occasion.

❧

Frank Wickham came to dinner at Pemberley and, though he never did become a close friend of the Darcys, his work for them enhanced his reputation. He continued to occupy the cottage at Rushford and to teach at the parish school. Moreover, his friendship with Darcy Gardiner, whose charm opened many doors for him, also gained him entry to Camden House, where he was invited to dine with the Gardiners.

He had the highest regard for Sir Richard and Lady Cassandra, to whose compassion and generosity he owed much of his present good fortune. A modest man of moderate habits, he never overstepped the bounds of propriety, nor did he presume upon his acquaintance with the family. He was well aware of the need for discretion and, despite the untiring efforts of his mother to discover where he spent his Summers, he kept his secret very well.

As for Cassandra, with her son Darcy taking over most of her duties at Pemberley and young Lizzie drawn more deeply into her husband's work at Rushmore Farm, she was free to enjoy the pleasures of her own family. As the wife of Sir Richard Gardiner, one of the country's most respected physicians, she now had several public duties to perform, and these she did with a grace and elegance that greatly enhanced her husband's reputation and standing in the community.

As the guardian of the young heir to the Pemberley estate, Cassy had her hands full ensuring that young Anthony was being trained to take on his appointed role one day, which she hoped with all her heart was in the distant future. Her parents, with whom she met often and whose love strengthened her every resolve, were prouder of their daughter than they would admit to anyone but each other.

Cassy's life was busier and happier than it had ever been. Yet in spite of the many demands upon her, she still found time for those she loved and neither her husband nor their children ever felt any diminution of her care and affection.

Love and respect, deeply felt, given, and received, brought enhanced satisfaction in every aspect of her life, and she contemplated the future with an enviable degree of equanimity and contentment.

A list of the main characters in *Mr Darcy's Daughter:*

Cassandra Gardiner (née Darcy)—daughter of Fitzwilliam and Elizabeth
Darcy of Pemberley

Dr Richard Gardiner—husband of Cassandra, son of Mr and Mrs Edward
Gardiner (Mr Gardiner, deceased)

Edward Gardiner and Darcy Gardiner—elder sons of Richard and Cassy

Lizzie Gardiner and Laura Ann Gardiner—daughters of Richard and Cassy

James Gardiner—youngest son of Richard and Cassy

Mr Michael Carr—a friend of Darcy Gardiner and a newcomer to Derbyshire

Julian Darcy—son of Fitzwilliam and Elizabeth Darcy of Pemberley

Josie Darcy (née Tate)—wife of Julian, daughter of Anthony and Rebecca Tate
of Matlock

Rebecca Tate—Josie Darcy's mother, daughter of Charlotte Collins

Anthony Fitzwilliam Darcy—young son of Julian and Josie

Emma Wilson (née Bingley)—daughter of Charles and Jane Bingley, cousin of
Cassandra and Julian

James Wilson, MP—Emma's husband

Jonathan Bingley—brother of Emma Wilson, son of Charles and Jane Bingley

Anna Bingley—Jonathan's wife

Colin Elliott, MP, and Anne-Marie Elliott—son-in-law and daughter of
    Jonathan Bingley

Emily Courtney (née Gardiner)—sister of Richard Gardiner, daughter of Mr
    and Mrs Edward Gardiner

James Courtney—husband of Emily, Rector at Kympton Parish

William Courtney—son of James and Emily

Jessica Courtney—youngest daughter of James and Emily

Caroline Fitzwilliam (née Gardiner)—sister of Richard Gardiner, wife of Col.
    Fitzwilliam (Mr Darcy's cousin)

Frank Wickham—youngest son of George Wickham and Lydia Bennet

And from the pages of *Pride and Prejudice*:

Fitzwilliam and Elizabeth Darcy of Pemberley

Charles and Jane Bingley of Ashford Park

Mrs Gardiner—widow of Mr Edward Gardiner, aunt of Elizabeth and Jane,
    mother of Richard, Robert, Caroline, and Emily

Colonel Fitzwilliam—Mr Darcy's cousin, husband of Caroline Gardiner

Charlotte Collins—Elizabeth's close friend, widow of the late Mr Collins

Lydia Wickham—sister of Elizabeth and Jane

Acknowledgements

THE AUTHOR WISHES TO thank all her readers, especially those who have written to express their interest and pleasure in her work, and Ms Averil Rose and Mrs Jenny Scott of England for their kind encouragement and help.

Special thanks to Ms Claudia Taylor for her valuable research and assistance with proofreading the text, Ben and Robert for technical assistance, and Ms Natalie Collins for organising the first printing and production of this book by Snap Printing in Sydney, Australia.

Thanks also to Mr David Gilson of Swindon, UK, for including the Pemberley series of novels in his collection of Jane Austen and related works, to be lodged in the library at King's College, Cambridge.

To Ms Beverly Wong of Alberta, Canada, many thanks for her expertise, which has taken the Pemberley series to readers all over the world, via the Internet, at the website www.geocities.com/shadesofpemberley.

And, of course, heartfelt gratitude to Miss Jane Austen, for her inspiration and example, as well as some of the happiest times of this author's life.

December 2000

The Pemberley Chronicles

For readers who wish to discover how it all began, we offer an excerpt from Book One, *The Pemberley Chronicles*.

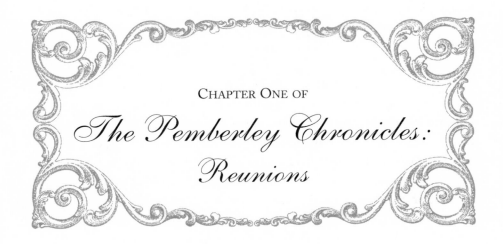

CHAPTER ONE OF

The Pemberley Chronicles: Reunions

SINCE HER MARRIAGE TO Mr Darcy some seven weeks ago, Elizabeth had wanted for nothing to complete her happiness, unless it was a chance to see her sister Jane again. Which is why her excitement increased markedly as they drove into London and around mid-morning found themselves approaching Mr Bingley's house in Grosvenor Street. Her husband could not conceal his amusement, as she cried out, "There they are!" like a little girl on her first visit to the city. As the carriage pulled up, she could barely wait to be helped out, before she flung herself into the welcoming arms of her sister.

Charles Bingley, who had been waiting beside Jane, smiled broadly as he exchanged greetings with Darcy, now his brother-in-law. They waited for the sisters to break from their warm and tearful embrace, the men's expressions of indulgent affection mixed with a degree of helplessness. It was Mr Bingley who intervened as the servants unloaded the travellers' trunks onto the footpath. Putting a solicitous arm around his wife and her sister, he said, "Shall we go indoors and let the luggage be taken upstairs?" He led them indoors, while Darcy followed, carrying Elizabeth's silk shawl, which had slipped off her shoulders as the sisters embraced.

They passed from the open hall into the comfort of a warm, pleasant room, where a fire crackled in the grate and a sideboard with an ample array of food and drink welcomed the travellers. While the gentlemen helped themselves to sherry and warmed themselves in front of the fire, Jane and Lizzie escaped upstairs, ostensibly so that Lizzie could divest herself of her travelling clothes and boots.

There was nothing the sisters wanted more than the privacy of a bedroom, where they hugged and kissed again as the words tumbled out, with neither able to wait for the other to finish a sentence. There was mutual acknowledgement that they had missed each other, they were both blissfully happy, they had the best husbands in the world, and they wished everyone could be as blessed as they were. The only matter upon which they could not agree was the question of which of them was the happier.

There was so much to tell, but it had to wait awhile; Jane promised they would have the afternoon to themselves as Bingley had planned to take Darcy out to his club to meet mutual friends.

Coming downstairs, they found Georgiana Darcy and Mrs Annesley come to call; they were staying in town at Mr Darcy's elegant townhouse in Portman Square and had been invited over by Jane to meet the returning couple. Georgiana, whose love for her brother was matched only by her devotion to her sister-in-law, whom she regarded as the sister she had always longed for, greeted Elizabeth with warmth and affection. Jane, looking on, wished she too could feel the same confidence of gaining the affection and approval of her in-laws, Caroline Bingley and Mrs Hurst. She felt not a little sadness as she saw the obvious satisfaction that Darcy felt as Lizzie and Georgiana embraced and talked together for all the world like loving sisters.

But, being Jane, she soon shook herself free of any trace of melancholy, as her husband came to her side and whispered, "I've arranged to take Georgiana and Mrs Annesley back to Portman Square, after which Darcy and I will go on to Brooks for an hour or two—that should give you and Lizzie plenty of time together. How would you like that, my love?" Jane replied that she would like it very much indeed and added her heartfelt thanks to her husband, whose sensitivity was a source of constant pleasure. As she said later to Lizzie, "I can hardly believe that he is so good and kind a man and yet preferred me above all others, knowing he could quite easily have had any of a dozen young ladies of greater substance and standing than myself." To which, Lizzie's reply was a reproachful reminder to her sister not to let her natural modesty trap her into undervaluing herself.

"For there is no one I know with a nature as good or a disposition as sweet as yours. Believe me, Jane, Mr Bingley is well aware of it and is considered, by his friends, to be a singularly fortunate man."

Earlier, they had partaken of a light luncheon of fresh rolls, sliced ham, cheese, and fruit, with tea, hot chocolate, or wine, as desired, before Georgiana and her companion left with the two gentlemen, who promised to be back in time for dinner. As the servants cleared away the remains of the repast, the two sisters returned upstairs to the comfort of Jane's boudoir to spend the rest of the afternoon in the kind of happy exchange of news and views that only two loving friends—both newly wed and blissfully happy—could hope to enjoy. Unhappily, the news from Longbourn was not good. Mrs Bennet, whose health was never the best, had not been well, having suffered from exhaustion after giving away two of her daughters at once. Their father, in his last letter to Jane, had asked that Lizzie be permitted to complete her travels undisturbed by this news.

"You know how it is, poor Mama will insist on having everyone over for Christmas; but this year, Lizzie, your kind invitation to us and Uncle and Aunt Gardiner to spend Christmas at Pemberley has relieved Mama of the strain. Because she cannot undertake the journey to Derbyshire, Papa has decided that he will remain with her at Longbourn, while Mary and Kitty will travel North with Aunt Gardiner," Jane explained. At this piece of bad news, Lizzie cried out, for she had been hoping so much to have her father at Pemberley, because she wanted him to see how happy she really was, especially in view of the doubts he had expressed at the time of Mr Darcy's proposal of marriage.

Jane offered some comfort, "Lizzie, Mr Bingley and I have talked about this. We knew how disappointed you would be if Papa could not be with you, so we have a plan. How would it be if Mr Bingley and I returned home at the New Year and had Mama to stay at Netherfield, so Papa could come to you for a few weeks?"

"Has he agreed to this?" asked her sister, somewhat surprised.

"Not yet, but we think he will, if Mr Darcy will ask him, tomorrow," said Jane. "Tomorrow?" Lizzie was astonished and more so when Jane replied, "He is to be at Aunt Gardiner's where, you will remember, we are all asked to dine tomorrow."

Elizabeth's pleasure at the news that she would see her father sooner than expected was much enhanced by the realisation that her sister Jane had gained in marriage a totally new confidence. If there was one criticism that could have been made against Jane, for all her sweetness of nature and strength of character, it was a diffidence—a reluctance to make judgements. To Elizabeth, it seemed as if this tiny flaw, if one could call it that, had disappeared since her marriage to Mr Bingley. However, she said nothing, not wanting to embarrass her sister. Besides there was so much to talk of their new lives, their husbands, their travels and so much love and happiness, that they quite forgot the time, until a maid ran upstairs to tell them the gentlemen were back.

Lizzie wished to bathe before dressing for dinner, and the luxury of a hot bath scented with lavender oils, prepared for her by Jane's maid, reminded her that this was London and not the inns of Gloucestershire or Wales, which, despite their charm, had been less than modern in their toilet facilities.

When they joined the gentlemen downstairs, they found there, to their surprise, Colonel Fitzwilliam, who had not been heard from since their weddings, when he had carried out his duties as Darcy's groomsman with aplomb.

Having greeted both sisters with affection and expressed satisfaction at finding them looking so well, he let Bingley explain his presence. "We found him at the club, where he has been staying all week," said Bingley, which led Jane to protest that he should have come to them.

"You could have stayed here, we have many empty rooms."

"I did not wish to intrude," Fitzwilliam said apologetically, "and I had no idea when Darcy and Elizabeth were expected."

"Well, you are here now, and you must stay," said Bingley firmly, as if that was the end of the matter, "until your ship is to sail." Amid cries of astonishment from the ladies of "What ship?" and "Where is he sailing to?" Fitzwilliam explained that he'd been at a loose end after the end of the war with France, and when he was offered a berth on a ship going to the new colonies of Ceylon and India, he had accepted. "That's the other side of the world!" said Jane, but Fitzwilliam assured her it was opening up fast and many people were going out there.

"I wanted a change of scene," he added by way of explanation.

It was an explanation Jane did not fully accept. Later that night, she reminded her sister that it was Charlotte's opinion that Fitzwilliam had been very partial to her, when they had been at Rosings last year, before Mr Darcy entered the picture. Elizabeth laughed and brushed it aside as a rumour, mainly a product of young Maria Lucas' romantic imagination. Fitzwilliam had left promising to return the following day to go with them to the Gardiners, to whom also he wished to say his farewells.

As they went to bed that night, Darcy and Elizabeth both agreed on the remarkable change in Jane since her marriage. It was a change Darcy welcomed for her sake and that of his friend, Bingley. "She will make him a stronger and better wife, and that will make him a stronger and better man," he said, adding more gently, "it was an aspect of your beautiful sister I used to worry about, my love, because I knew how important it was for Bingley." Ever ready to tease her husband, Elizabeth asked if he'd had any doubts about her own strength, to which Darcy replied firmly, "None at all, because, my dearest, you never left me in any doubt right from the start. Indeed, it was what I first admired in you, apart from your beautiful eyes, of course."

So pleased was his wife with this response that she stopped teasing and relaxed into the gentleness that she knew he loved. Darcy had never doubted his own feelings; Lizzie wanted him to have no doubt at all of hers. On such openheartedness was their marriage founded that concealment or archness was unthinkable.

The following day, plans were made to visit the shops on the other side of town, since the ladies wished to see the shoemakers and milliners. While breakfast was being cleared away, a carriage drew up, and, to the huge delight of their nieces, Mr and Mrs Gardiner were announced. The visitors, though unexpected, were warmly welcomed, especially by Mr Darcy. Elizabeth noted with great satisfaction the obvious pleasure with which he greeted them, and the sincerity of his welcome left no doubt in her mind of his regard and affection for them.

Mr Darcy's instant response of open friendliness and respect for her aunt and uncle, when they first met at Pemberley last Summer, had been the turning point in her own appreciation of his character. Their relationship had grown slowly and with increasing confidence upon this foundation. It had grown in strength, and each time they had met with the Gardiners, whose estimation of Darcy was of the highest order, Elizabeth found her opinion endorsed by them. That Darcy, whose family had, by his own admission to her, encouraged an inordinate level of pride in class and status, could have developed such a strong relationship with Mr and Mrs Gardiner, was remarkable in itself. That his behaviour to them was not merely correct in every particular of courtesy and etiquette, but was genuine in the friendship and affection he showed them at every turn, was proof enough for her that her husband was a man of estimable qualities. That she could be so much in love with a man she had almost loathed a year ago was well nigh miraculous!

Elizabeth knew she could have married him in spite of his low opinion of the stupidity of her sister Lydia or the silliness of her mother, but never could she have formed an alliance with anyone who did not share her love and regard for her favourite aunt and uncle. Their mutual respect was now something she took completely for granted. It was an essential part of their love for each other.

It was agreed that the ladies would drive to the shops in Mr Gardiner's carriage, while the gentlemen would stay behind to discuss matters of business. Soon, capes, shawls, and bonnets were fetched, and they set out determined that they would not be seduced into buying French fashions, which seemed to be in vogue! In the carriage together, Lizzie and Jane were keen to discover what business it was that their husbands were discussing. Mrs Gardiner was able to enlighten them, just a little. "I do not know the detail of it, my dears, but I believe your husbands have been clever enough to realise the great opportunities for trade with the new colonies and have expressed a wish to invest in your uncle's business. I think a partnership has been suggested."

"A partnership!" Both sisters were intrigued. They were well aware of the Bingleys' links with trade—it was the source of their fortune—but Darcy?

Elizabeth felt sure he would tell her all about it, when there was more to tell. Having satisfied some of their curiosity, Mrs Gardiner protested she was far more interested to hear how her favourite nieces were enjoying being married. The girls had no difficulty convincing their aunt of their current state of bliss; she could see for herself. "And what about Christmas?" she asked, to which Lizzie replied, "That's been settled—you are all to come to Pemberley at Christmas."

And so they went out to the shops in excellent humour and spent an hour or more in the pleasantest way. Lizzie bought some new boots—her own were worn with travelling, she declared, and Mrs Gardiner insisted on buying her nieces two pairs of French gloves in the most modish colours of the season. Mrs Gardiner was delighted to find Jane and Lizzie so happy. She was young enough to understand the intoxicating effects of love and marriage on two lovely young women, recently wedded to two of the most eligible young men one could hope to meet.

When they returned to Grosvenor Street, they parted almost at once, since the Gardiners had to hurry back to await Mr Bennet, who was arriving by coach around midday. Driving back to Gracechurch Street, Mr Gardiner was as anxious as his wife had been to hear the news about his nieces. "And how are Mrs Darcy and Mrs Bingley, my dear? Such grand names!" he said in jest, almost mimicking his sister, Mrs Bennet.

Mrs Gardiner was delighted to tell him of their happiness, "I am so pleased, Edward, I could not be more so if they were my own daughters. Indeed, I should be well pleased if Caroline and Emily were half as fortunate as Jane and Lizzie."

It was a verdict she was to repeat to her brother-in-law, Mr Bennet, over lunch, appreciating his keenness to hear news of his daughters. Her husband added, "And having spent quite some time with Mr Darcy recently, what with one thing and another, I can safely endorse those sentiments, Brother. There would not be two young men more deserving of your wonderful daughters than Mr Darcy and his excellent friend, Mr Bingley."

Mr Bennet waited impatiently for the evening, when he would see his beloved Jane and Lizzie again. His memories of their wedding day were a blur of activity, smiles, and the unending chattering of his wife. He had missed his daughters terribly and longed to know they were happy. When the party from Grosvenor Street arrived, Mr Bennet noted that Jane and Lizzie looked extremely well.

The young Misses Gardiner—Caroline and Emily, given special permission to dine late with their cousins—admired the exquisite jewels, gifts from their husbands, and fine gowns they wore and begged Lizzie to tell them all about the wonderful places she had visited.

After dinner, there came the usual request for music. Lizzie obliged with a song and invited Caroline and Emily to join her in a pretty ballad, which they had all learned last Summer. It was a great success, and an encore was immediately demanded. Fitzwilliam, who had a fine tenor voice, was pressed into service next; he delighted everyone by singing a pretty little duet with young Miss Caroline Gardiner, whose sweet, clear voice harmonised perfectly with his.

Mr and Mrs Gardiner looked so proud that Jane, sitting with her aunt, thought she would surely weep with joy, but she merely gripped her niece's hand very tightly and applauded enthusiastically when it was over. Colonel Fitzwilliam bowed deeply and kissed Miss Gardiner's little hand in a very gallant gesture, at which Bingley jumped to his feet and applauded again.

Mr Bennet did not need to ask if his daughters were happy. He could see, from the glow on Jane's face and the sparkle in Lizzie's eyes, that they had no regrets about the men they had chosen to wed. Watching his sons-in-law as they stood engaged in animated discussion, he turned to Lizzie, who had just brought him his coffee, "I have to say, Lizzie, that Mr Darcy appears to be much more cheerful and relaxed. Marriage has done him a deal of good, and it must be all your own good work, eh?" "Whatever do you mean, Papa?" asked Lizzie, pretending to be quite unable to understand his drift.

"Why, Lizzie, I have never seen Mr Darcy smile so much and look so pleased. I do believe I even heard him tell a joke—or perhaps that was Bingley?"

"Well, I did assure you he was perfectly amiable, did I not?"

"You did, my dear…" he began, but at that moment, Mr Darcy approached, and Lizzie went to him, leaving her father smiling, quite certain his daughter's happiness was not in question. Was it Chance or Destiny, or was Mrs Bennet right after all? Poor Mr Bennet would never know the answer. Later, when the guests were gone, and he sat with his brother-in-law before a dying fire in the drawing room, he returned to the topic.

"They are fortunate to have married two such fine young men—but then, Jane and Lizzie deserve the best," he observed. Mr Gardiner was quick to agree, adding that while Mr Bingley was a most charming and amiable young fellow, it was Lizzie's Mr Darcy, whose nobility of character, generosity, and devotion to his wife had endeared him to them, who was their favourite.

"Mrs Gardiner and I are agreed that, had your Lizzie been our daughter, there is no other man above Mr Darcy to whom we would have preferred to entrust her happiness." This was high praise, indeed, and Mr Bennet was content. He could return to Longbourn and face Mrs Bennet's unending chatter about all the servants, carriages, and fine clothes they would have, knowing that both his daughters were cherished and happy.

The following day, as Mr Bennet waited for his coach, Darcy called very early in the morning. He'd come to invite his father-in-law to spend a few weeks with them at Pemberley, in January, since sadly he was unable to join the family at Christmas, due to Mrs Bennet's state of health. "If you would advise me, Sir, of dates and times, I shall send my carriage to meet the coach at Lambton," said Darcy, adding that they were all looking forward to his first visit to Pemberley. His graciousness, generosity, and good humour completely won over Mr Bennet, in whose estimation Mr Darcy had been rising very rapidly. He accepted the invitation gladly adding that he was looking forward very much to using the excellent library of which he had heard so much. Darcy looked very pleased, and they parted, each man having increased his respect for the other, both looking forward to their next meeting.

Darcy returned to Grosvenor Street and found Lizzie in their bedroom, looking out on the deserted street below. She had risen late and assumed he had gone out riding with Bingley. When he told her of his visit to her father, she turned to him in tears, "My dear husband, I told him you were a good and amiable man, but I did not say you were perfect!" at which he coloured deeply and fumbled for words, saying it was of no consequence... simply a part of his love for her. Elizabeth was in a teasing mood, "You should have let me see, rather earlier in our acquaintance, how kind and generous you really are; it might have saved us both a great deal of heartache," she complained.

Darcy, touched by the warmth of her love so sweetly expressed, was serious as he held her close. "How could I, Lizzie? How could I lay claim to qualities and values I barely recognised, until you, my dearest, made me acknowledge my own inadequacy." She tried to hush him then, unwilling to rake up the memories of her reproof and his agonising over it, but Darcy was determined to acknowledge it. "No, my dear Lizzie, it is all your doing. If I have done some good things, if I have been less selfish and arrogant, it is because of you, because I loved you and sought your love in return." His voice was very low with the unaccustomed weight of emotion, and Lizzie, knowing the strength of his feelings, let him speak, responding only with a loving kiss.

Later, Georgiana came over and stayed to lunch. They made plans; Georgiana and her companion would travel to Pemberley on Tuesday, with instructions for Mrs Reynolds to prepare for the arrival of Mr and Mrs Darcy with the Bingleys, a week later. They would be staying on in town only until Fitzwilliam sailed. Mrs Reynolds was also to arrange for the accommodation of the other guests at Christmas; Lizzie noted that the list did not include the

Hursts or Caroline Bingley. Jane had already reassured her that the Bingley sisters and boring Mr Hurst were invited to Rosings, by Lady Catherine de Bourgh! "Ah well," Lizzie remarked, "They're sure to get on exceedingly well. No doubt much time will be spent expressing their indignation at my daring to defy Her Ladyship's orders and marry her nephew!" The other guests were the Gardiners and their children, Kitty and Mary Bennet, and Dr Grantley, who would be arriving on Christmas Eve. Darcy explained that his sister always had her own party on Christmas Eve for the children of the Pemberley Estate. Jane thought it was a wonderful idea to have a party for the children of the estate, and Georgiana said that it had been her brother's idea, when she, as a little girl, had been unhappy that the children of their tenants and servants had no party of their own at Christmas.

"He started it, and it was such a success, we've had it every year." Lizzie thought how well it fitted with Mrs Reynolds' picture of a caring Master, whose tenants and servants rewarded him with singular loyalty.

Looking across at Darcy, she felt proud to be his wife, proud of the innate decency and goodness that was now so clear to her. She felt ashamed of the prejudice that had been allowed to cloud her judgement, when they had met, but just as quickly she put aside her guilt, blaming Wickham for poisoning her mind with lies. She looked again at her husband; this time their eyes met, and they smiled.

The Bingleys intended to stay on at Netherfield Park only until Spring, when the lease ran out. Charles had already sought Darcy's advice on purchasing a suitable estate, not far from Pemberley, unless as he said, "You want Jane and Lizzie to be forever pining for each other." Darcy agreed that this would not do at all and promised to make inquiries about suitable properties in the area. The prospect made Jane and Lizzie very happy indeed. Elizabeth realised that Mr. Bingley seemed to thrive on the bright lights and social whirl of London and her sister Jane, to whom this was an exciting new world, appeared to match his enthusiasm. Darcy, on the other hand, loathed the social obligations and artificial rituals of the London Season, and Elizabeth had no taste for them either. They couldn't wait to get away to Pemberley, but there were contracts to be signed and Fitzwilliam to be farewelled, so they remained in London, moving into Darcy's townhouse at Portman Square.

They spent many hours in Galleries and Museums, attended a soirée and a chamber concert, and when they dined at home alone, indulged in that favourite pastime of loving couples—congratulating themselves on their excellent judgement in marrying each other!

The following Sunday, their last in London, with the Bingleys visiting friends in Windsor, Darcy and Lizzie took advantage of some rare Winter sunshine and drove down to Richmond. This beautiful spot on the Thames, which had become quite fashionable with the London set, afforded them the privacy they craved.

They talked of Jane and Bingley—for they had both noticed how Jane seemed much less diffident about showing her feelings. Recalling Jane's concealment of her affection for Mr Bingley and the inordinate length of time taken by Charles to declare his love for her, Elizabeth rejoiced that they appeared so much in love, with so very little concern as to who knew it. Darcy said he thought they had both matured a good deal in the last year. Elizabeth agreed but wondered aloud whether everyone was as cautious in such situations; but, even as she spoke, before she could finish her sentence, she saw her husband's wry smile, stopped, and started to laugh. "Oh dear!" she said, as Darcy smiled and shook his head, "Neither of us were particularly cautious, I'm afraid."

They recalled that first occasion at Hunsford, when Darcy had declared himself in the strangest way, rushing headlong, throwing caution and sensibility to the winds, and Elizabeth had responded with a degree of sharpness of which she had never dreamed herself capable. She begged him not to remind her of the hurt and harm she had done, with her reproaches, but Darcy disagreed, claiming that her frankness and honesty had been just what he had needed to jolt him out of his smugness and complacency. "It forced me to look at myself to confront the fact that I had no right to claim the status of a gentleman unless I behaved like one to all those I met and mingled with. No, Lizzie, had you not spoken and taught me the lesson I had to learn, we might never have found out that we cared for each other." Lizzie's cheeks burned as he went on, "Look at us now, could we ever have been this happy if we had not been honest with one another?"

"You are probably right in that, dearest, but are we in danger of becoming a tiny bit smug and complacent ourselves?" She was teasing him, but he replied seriously, "Never Lizzie, whilst ever you set such high standards for us both." Lizzie smiled. "I must agree we are very happy and comfortable together. I had feared we might be too reserved with each other, but it has not been so," she said.

"That is because you, my love, with your open, honest manner, would defy anyone to be reserved," he said, smiling as he added, "it was the quality I found most engaging and hardest to resist."

This time, Elizabeth could not help but tease him. With her eyes sparkling, she quipped, "Especially when you were so determined to do just that!" Darcy would not permit her to continue, not even in jest, protesting that he had proved his love and would do so again, if necessary. At this point, Lizzie decided she would tease him no more; there was never any doubt at all of his love for her. "Could we go home?" she asked, softly, and sensing her changed mood, Darcy rose immediately and helped her into the carriage.

There was something very special between them. Theirs was no "unequal marriage" of the sort her father had warned against: a marriage in which one partner found it hard to respect the other, the kind of union that, they acknowledged without ever saying a word, existed between her parents. This type of marriage Lizzie had dreaded all her life. She and Jane had frequently vowed to remain unwed, rather than submit to that ultimate indignity. With Darcy, Elizabeth already knew she had a marriage after her own heart; she could unreservedly say that the love they shared was stronger for the esteem they had for each other.

They drove back into town, wrapped in a warm, affectionate silence, and went directly to Darcy's townhouse in Portman Square. "We're home," he said, helping Lizzie out. They embraced as she alighted into his arms and went upstairs, leaving their coats and scarves in the hall.

That evening, they dined with Fitzwilliam and the Bingleys. He was sailing on the morrow for Ceylon and India, where he was to work with the East India Company for at least three years. He confessed to being suddenly sad to leave, knowing it would be a long time before he would see England and all his friends again. He had dined the previous evening with the Gardiners, and all these farewells were taking their toll upon his spirits.

Elizabeth had sensed the sadness that seemed to overlay his earlier enthusiasm and said so to her sister. Jane was convinced that it had more to do with losing Lizzie than leaving England. Their husbands, on the other hand, much more interested in the business opportunities than in Fitzwilliam's state of mind, did not remark upon it at all.

Two days later, they were on the road themselves, deciding to make the journey North before the weather worsened. When it was decided to break journey in Oxford, Elizabeth was delighted. It would give Jane a chance to meet Dr Grantley. Jane, who had heard so much about him from her sister, was in complete agreement with her after they met and dined with him that night. His distinguished appearance, cultured conversation, and remarkable reputation quite overawed her, until his unassuming manner and friendliness drew her out.

When they retired after a most pleasant and stimulating evening, Jane expressed her surprise that he was unmarried. Lizzie laughed and warned her against matchmaking—which had been the bane of their lives at home. Jane protested that she had no intention of doing so but added, "Lizzie, he is such a charming and educated gentleman, that I find it impossible to believe, that had he wished to marry, he could not have found a suitable partner. Surely, he does not intend to remain a bachelor?" Lizzie laughed and begged her to remember that Dr Grantley was but a few years older than Mr Darcy, so there was hope for him yet!

And so, on to Pemberley...

About the Author

A lifelong fan of Jane Austen, Rebecca Ann Collins first read *Pride and Prejudice* at the tender age of twelve. She fell in love with the characters and since then has devoted years of research and study to the life and works of her favourite author. As a teacher of literature and a librarian, she has gathered a wealth of information about Miss Austen and the period in which she lived and wrote, which became the basis of her books about the Pemberley families. The popularity of the Pemberley novels with Jane Austen fans has been her reward.

With a love of reading, music, art, and gardening, Ms Collins claims she is very comfortable in the period about which she writes, and feels great empathy with the characters she portrays. While she enjoys the convenience of modern life, she finds much to admire in the values and worldview of Jane Austen.